Accl[aim for]
The Shadow Saga

"A politico-religious thriller reminiscent of the novels of David Morrell. A delightful read and a noteworthy debut by a writer who cares passionately about the stuff of horror. Harrowing, humorous, overflowing with characters and plot contortions, abundantly entertaining . . . a portent of great things to come from Christopher Golden."

—Douglas E. Winter, *Cemetery Dance*

"One of the best horror novels of the year. Filled with tension, breathtaking action, dire plots and a convincing depiction of worlds existing unseen within our own. One of the most promising debuts in some time."

—*Science Fiction Chronicle*

"You can damn near chase me a mile these days with a vampire novel. Then, along comes Christopher Golden. His work is fast and furious, funny and original, and I can't wait until his next book."

—Joe R. Lansdale,
three-time Bram Stoker Award winner

"Christopher Golden has painted a canvas, full of action, sweep and dark mythology; a novel that unfolds like a vampiric Kabuki theater. Golden is smart and savvy; a writer with a bright future."

—Rex Miller,
author of *Slob* and *Chaingang*

"Just when you thought nothing new could be done with the vampire mythos, a fresh new talent comes along and shows us otherwise. Christopher Golden has quite a career ahead of him!"

— Ray Garton, author of *Live Girls* and *Dark Channel*

"If your vampiric diet has been dominated by Rice, then this book should excite the most jaded palette. A heady chili con carne composed of heretical theology, magick, violent fantasy, and shape-shifting horror. It builds to a climax that leaves the reader gasping for breath."

— Philip Nutman, author of *Wet Work*

"A promising debut. In his world of vampires and dark magic, Golden presents us with a complex canvas to rival Brian Lumley."

— Craig Shaw Gardner, author of *The Changeling War*

"An intriguing adult mystery, not for the faint of heart."
—*Murder Under Cover, Inc.*

"Passionate . . . Excellent . . . Golden has written one of the best . . . a deep probe into the inner-workings of the church and a surprise explanation for vampires. [A] brilliant vampire novel in a blizzard of bloody tooth bites this year."

— *LitNews* (published on Compuserve)
and *Dark Channel*

"Golden stands many time-honored concepts about vampirism on their heads."

— *The Overlook Connection*

"Golden has created a new myth. A real treat for those who are tired of ideas that are as old as yesterday's blood . . . worthy of the praise it has already received, and more."

— *Eclipse Magazine*

"A fast-paced action thriller that will hold the reader's attention from the first page to the last."

— *The Talisman*

"Golden combines quiet, dark, subtle mood with Super-Giant monster action. Sort of M.R. James meets Godzilla!"

— Mike Mignola, creator of *Hellboy*

Of Masques and Martyrs

CHRISTOPHER GOLDEN

ACE BOOKS, NEW YORK

This book is an Ace original edition,
and has never been previously published.

OF MASQUES AND MARTYRS

An Ace Book / published by arrangement with
the author

PRINTING HISTORY
Ace edition / December 1998

The Penguin Putnam Inc. World Wide Web site address is
http://www.penguinputnam.com

ISBN: 0-441-00584-5

ACE®
Ace Books are published by The Berkley Publishing Group,
a division of Penguin Putnam Inc.,
375 Hudson Street, New York, New York 10014.
ACE and the "A" design are trademarks
belonging to Penguin Putnam, Inc.

PRINTED IN THE UNITED STATES OF AMERICA

10 9 8 7 6 5 4 3

With love and respect, this one is for José R. Nieto,
whose talent is matched only by his nobility.

Acknowledgments

Thank you so very much to everyone who really pushed for a third book in this series. Especially Madeleine and Roni. Thanks to Ginjer Buchanan, who found the orphan a new home, and to my agent, Lori Perkins, who never gave up on it.

I'm indebted, as always, to my regular support crew, particularly Tom Sniegoski, Nancy Holder, Bob Tomko, Jeff Mariotte & Maryelizabeth Hart, and Stefan Nathanson.

Finally, to my sons, Nicholas and Daniel, and to my extraordinary wife, Connie, who has been a part of all this since day one, and who has always believed. I couldn't possibly do it without you, sweetheart.

Of Masques and Martyrs

Prologue

AS THE FIRST HINTS OF DUSK BEGAN TO TAINT
the wispy blue spring sky above Washington Square Park,
the music abruptly stopped.

A handsome young black man with a shaved head and
stubbly goatee glanced nervously at the pink-edged clouds
and packed his saxophone away in its case. He looked almost ashamed and didn't meet the eyes of the muttering
tourists and strolling locals who commented on the speed
of his departure. He just went.

"Too bad," said a dark-haired teenaged girl, whose ragged clothes and sickly pale face might have given the impression that she was a homeless person, if not for the
three-hundred-dollar sunglasses she wore.

"I was hoping he'd play that blues riff again," she
added.

The large, blond, well-muscled man on the bench beside

her offered no response but a slight nod. He too wore sunglasses, but of the cheap plastic variety. Blue jeans and white sneakers and a sweatshirt with "Sorbonne" embroidered across the front completed his ensemble.

An oddly matched pair, even to a casual observer. Not family, surely. And unlikely as lovers for a number of reasons, not the least of which was their apparent age difference. Otherwise, the two were determinedly unremarkable.

They sat and watched as the exodus continued. Dusk was coming on full speed. It had been unseasonably chilly that last week of April, and the night seemed heartened by the memory of winter, creeping quickly over the city as though full-blown spring weren't a week away. Though growing longer, the days were still too short by far, all things considered. And the long nights were very sparsely populated. Only the foolhardy, the romantic, and the desperate tended to stay on the streets after sunset.

It simply wasn't safe.

Parents left first, strapping infants into strollers and lofting toddlers to shoulders and whisking their families away home. Which was never very far. Even those brave or foolish enough to stay out after dark didn't stray too far from home.

Then the sky began to grow dark. The first star appeared. And the park's crowd thinned more rapidly. Soon, only half a dozen skateboard kids still roamed the tree-lined park—kids whose parents worked nights, or were on crack, or just didn't give a fuck—feeding each other false courage, baying to the moon, laughing at the night. Maybe they didn't care what happened to them. Maybe they just didn't believe it could happen. Human nature, that was. It isn't real unless you can see it with your own eyes, touch it with your own hands, smell it, taste it, hear it.

They'd been out there night after night after night, for months on end, those forgotten, daredevil children. Nothing bad had ever happened to them. Around them, most certainly. To people they knew, of course. There wasn't anyone left in Manhattan who didn't know someone who'd been taken by the night.

By the shadows.

With the coming of the night, the city began to quiet down. People were still out, but traveling in packs; in cars or on the subway. Bass beats still thumped the air outside the front doors of dance clubs, but the one-night stand had gone the way of the drive-in theater and the record player. Rarer than rare. Lunch dates were the thing now. House parties were big too. Adult sleepovers.

Still, the city was far quieter after dark than it had been a year, even a few months, earlier. On the bench where they still sat—bearing witness to the terror that had transformed daily life in New York, and so many other places across the world—the silent man and the attractive brunette girl sat and waited and listened to the way the city had changed.

The trees whispered with a warm breeze, a tease that tomorrow spring might finally triumph over the stubborn winter. In the distance, a police siren began to scream in horror. Just the first of many, like every other night. The clack-clack of skateboard wheels, of jumping and spinning and falling; the laughter of American youth—smart enough to know better but too jaded to care.

"Tonight, you think?" the young woman asked. "It's been nearly two weeks watching these punks. I'd hate to move on. If we find some other bait, I'm sure that'll be the night they come for our skate-boys."

The silent blond man seemed to ponder her words. He looked at her, ice blue eyes narrowing a moment, remembering how young and arrogant she'd seemed when they'd first met, not very long after she'd been murdered on a dirty back alley in Atlanta, Georgia. She'd been sixteen when she died. She seemed so much older than that now, but looked exactly the same.

He smiled half-heartedly, and turned to watch the skateboarders again.

"Let's hope," he said, but his voice was only in her head. He hadn't spoken aloud. Couldn't, in fact. Rolf Sechs was mute.

So they sat in silence, Rolf and Erika, as they'd done for too many nights, and they watched. On this night, they didn't have long to wait. Less than an hour after full dark, the clack-clack of skateboards came to a clattering halt.

"Jesus! What the fuck is . . ." one of the boys shouted. Angry words laced with testosterone.

Sad counterpoint to the shrill screams that followed.

"Yes!" Erika rasped.

Together, she and Rolf melted away from the bench, bones snapping, skin stretching, shrinking, changing. A pair of filthy pigeons, too stupid to fly south for the winter, winged up into the night sky and across Washington Square Park. The birds came to roost atop the landmark arch in the middle of the park.

From there, they watched the slaughter.

Blood jetted skyward, spattering the cobblestones as five young lives were extinguished in an almost balletic act of carnage. The skateboarders never stood a chance. Ever silent, Rolf watched, with Erika at his side, as a trio of barbaric vampires feasted. For perhaps the first time, he relished his muteness. If he'd been able to speak, he would never have been able to control the urge to cry out in horror at the savagery of his own race.

For they were of his race. Semantics had separated them, and loyalties as well. He and Erika were shadows, members of Octavian's coven, and dedicated to peaceful coexistence with humanity. These others belonged to Hannibal's brutal clan, whose goal was the enslavement of a human race they perceived as nothing more than cattle. They eschewed the less volatile name of shadow, embracing instead the title of myth, of terrible legend—vampire.

Shadow and vampire, one and the same, and yet now forever at war. And by their very nature, the vampires were destined to triumph. For shadows did not recruit, did not steal life and thus violently draft new souls into the war. New shadows were created by individual choice. While the ranks of the vampire swelled, the number of shadows rose ever so slowly.

But the shadows counted many humans among their ranks. They were even allowed to become members of the coven, these living, breathing souls. And it was to that alliance that Octavian's faithful now looked for some spark of hope.

Most of them.

But Rolf was different. Rolf Sechs had many reasons to want the vampire lord Hannibal dead, not the least of which was the murder of his one-time lover, a human soldier named Elissa Thomas. He also knew Hannibal better than the rest of Octavian's coven did. Better, perhaps, than anyone but the immortal madman himself.

In the brief time when humanity and shadows had lived in peace, Hannibal and Rolf had worked together to police the vampires of the world. But Hannibal had not been in the game for any benevolent purpose. Rather, he had been there to find followers, to uncover those immortals whose personal philosophies might be aligned with his own.

He was shopping for warriors. And he found them. And when the time came that the world, human and otherwise, needed him most, Hannibal betrayed them all.

Hannibal's crimes were an endless litany of horror and betrayal, and his perversion spread more each day. Major cities across the face of the globe cowered in fear of the dark. No matter what skirmishes they won, what nests they destroyed, the shadows could not seem even to slow the spread of Hannibal's reign of chaos.

Rolf was tired of it. Of fighting to hold ground rather than take it. Of fighting the slaves and not the master. He longed to hold Hannibal's head in his powerful hands and crush it, to feel the vampire's skull shatter, and blood leak through his fingers.

He had abandoned Octavian's coven because he couldn't

wait any longer. The only way to stop Hannibal's campaign of terror, in Rolf's mind, was to destroy the elder vampire himself. Thus had begun the descent into hell, the investigation which had led him here, to New York City.

Erika had come along without being asked. He knew she loved him, but he kept her at a distance. She had been there, had witnessed the horrors Hannibal was capable of. She wanted him dead as well. But it wasn't the same thing. And he could not offer her much of a life together until this one thing was done.

So he watched. Together, they watched. They listened to the sounds of murder and saw the gore spread playfully around the park and the corpses of strong, young American boys defiled in ways Rolf—who was centuries old when Hitler came to power and still shivered in horror at the predations of the Nazis—had never imagined. Together they watched.

And did nothing.

When the vampires had drunk their fill, had painted themselves in blood and shit and danced a grotesque jig in the viscera of their victims, the savages laughed together like drunken college boys and shoved one another around in play. One by one, they transformed into huge, filthy bats, and flew into the northern sky. Confined as they were by Hannibal's loyalty to traditional myths, the vampires could choose from a limited array of changes.

The shadows, on the other hand, could be anything their minds might imagine. Anything. From city birds, Rolf and Erika transformed once more, to become birds of prey. Two large hawks took flight from atop the arch in Washington Square Park and set off after the trio of blood-matted bats flying north.

Inside the lead hawk, the mind of Rolf Sechs burned with hatred, sang with a lusty bloodsong that the peaceful shadows rarely allowed themselves. The time had come. He felt it within him as surely as he felt the thirst upon him. Hannibal would die beneath his powerful hands, flashing talons, razor fangs. Rolf would show the arrogant elder the true face of the vampire.

At her lover's side, Erika Hunter flew in silence. Though he could not speak aloud, Rolf had become quite talkative in the year they'd spent together as a couple. Telepathy was only possible among shadows of the same bloodline. Fortunately, they shared an ancestor, and she was able to hear his kind voice in her mind, and was often required to communicate for him.

Yet, over the days they had spent waiting for Hannibal's followers to appear, so that they might follow the bastard creatures home to their master, Rolf had communicated with her less and less frequently. And when he did speak in her mind, she could feel the tension, the obsession, the darkness welling up within him.

Erika wanted Hannibal dead. Without question, the coven led by Peter Octavian *needed* Hannibal dead. But she wondered, as they flew, hawk eyes focused on fleeing bat wings, if Rolf realized how suicidal this mission really was.

They were going to die. If Erika had to bet, it would not be in their favor. Shadows, vampires. Whatever they called themselves and each other, they were very hard to kill. Through some combination of humanity, divinity, and demonic influence Erika had never completely understood, the race of shadows had achieved a kind of cellular consciousness and control. They were shapeshifters, really, and could become anything.

Or, at least, that was the potential. But long centuries earlier, the Roman church had handicapped the shadows by implanting certain psychic controls. Myths. The sun burns. The cross terrifies. Silver poisons. Running water. Native soil.

Bullshit. But psychically altered to believe in such things, the shadows' cellular consciousness would react. A psychosomatic reaction of the most destructive and fundamen-

tal kind. It made them easier to kill. At least until the
Venice Jihad six years ago, which revealed the truth, uncovered the conspiracy. The world's shadows had begun to
shake off the church's brainwashing, but individual success
had varied. Some were still susceptible to the old flaws.
And Hannibal's insistence that his followers pay heed to
ancient tradition, to hunt only by night, to limit their transformations to creatures of darkness . . . made it more difficult for them to liberate themselves from the myths, thus
making them more vulnerable.

So, Erika thought with amusement, the shadows had that
going for them. Not much, considering the vastly greater
number of the vampires, of Hannibal's coven. But something was always better than nothing.

Not that it would help.

A siren wailed in the distance. Televisions blared from
within apartments locked up tight. Cab drivers ferried home
unfortunate souls who'd had to work late; the taxis' wind-
shields were festooned with garlic and crucifixes, in hopes
that they would have some kind of effect. Erika wondered
how much such kamikaze cabbies could charge for a ride
home through the murderous night.

She felt the muscles in her hawk's wings ripple as she
and Rolf soared between and above the buildings of the
Bronx. Erika allowed the city to distract her, to turn her
thoughts away from the coming confrontation. But when
the Bronx disappeared behind them, and they began to enter
the more suburban area of Westchester County, she realized
that they must be getting close. It wouldn't be logical for
Hannibal to be much farther away from Manhattan.

Her thoughts turned again to losing. To dying.

There were all kinds of tricks they could use to try to
infiltrate Hannibal's headquarters, wherever it was. But to
kill him, and then escape with their lives? Erika just didn't
believe it was possible. So be it, then, she thought. If tonight was the night, she would die by Rolf's side, with the
blood of her family's greatest enemy on her lips.

The Tappan Zee Bridge appeared on the horizon, and for a moment Erika thought the vampires might be heading for Tarrytown, or Sleepy Hollow, which she thought might have suited Hannibal's taste for the perverse. Less than a decade earlier, before running away to become a capricious and clever little goth girl on the streets of Atlanta, Erika had lived in Tarrytown. She wondered if her too-straight parents still lived there, still mourned her; and suddenly she was revolted by the thought that Hannibal might have tainted the peaceful little town.

But no, the vampires flew on. What had once been an automobile manufacturing plant passed by below, and now Erika was insanely curious. This would have made an ideal headquarters.

Where then? What better place could he have? . . .

Then she saw it, in the distance, stark and cold against the trees, with the railroad tracks running alongside. A mountain of ugly gray stone and glittering silver wire, hard and silent. The Hudson River flowed past to the west, complement and counterpoint, showing the mountain what it could never have, could never be.

Up the river. The phrase came unbidden to Erika's mind. In gangster movies it meant being sent to prison. This prison.

Sing-Sing.

Of course, she thought, letting Rolf see into her mind, hear her words.

The vampire bats dipped on the night air, gliding down toward the prison walls. Rolf swooped low to follow, but Erika held back a moment.

What's the plan, Rolf? she asked. *How do you want to go in?*

She sensed his confusion, and realized that, so driven was he by his obsession, he had nearly forgotten she was there at all. It hurt. Erika knew that, fond of her as Rolf may be, he'd never really loved her. There had never been room in his heart for her, not with all the hatred there.

We're in this together, damn you, she thought, and directed her mind at him.

I know, he finally replied. *I'm sorry. Part of me wants to just fly right in and wait for Hannibal to come to us.*

Erika flew into the branches of a massive oak tree across the street from the prison, and Rolf circled to join her there a moment later.

He might not come to us at all, she reasoned. *They might just kill us.*

He'll come, Rolf argued. *But we'll exercise a little caution. We'll wait until morning to go in. Then all we'll have to do is slaughter his human servants—*

It isn't that simple, Erika thought.

Yes, Rolf replied. *Yes it is.*

At dawn they dropped from the oak tree and landed next to one another on the paved sidewalk of a nice suburban town called Ossining, New York. A nice prison town. They were themselves again, Rolf Sechs and Erika Hunter. Lovers. Shadows. Briefly, they embraced, then turned to walk toward the prison hand in hand, as if they were tourists.

At the front gates of the prison, four men stood guard. It should have seemed odd to the townspeople, having four men in front of an empty prison. Erika figured over time they'd grown so used to seeing armed personnel there that it never occurred to anyone to question it. And Hannibal's coven didn't kill the people of Ossining. Or even nearby. That was a tenet of the old covens: you don't hunt at home.

Erika's long, tattered jacket flapped behind her in the breeze off the Hudson. Rolf's broad shoulders were straight as he marched determinedly toward the gate, toward the guards. Somewhere far away, a child screamed with pleasure, already awake with the risen sun.

Every muscle tensed, Erika brought her hands up inside her jacket, reaching for the twin nine-millimeter semiauto pistols that Will Cody had given her as a gift for her birthday several months earlier. She felt the hardness of the pistol butts beneath her touch. Her lip curled in disdain as the guards suddenly noticed her and Rolf approaching. They snapped to attention, whispering between themselves like amateurs.

Traitors to their own race; Erika hated them.

No. Rolf's stern voice entered her mind, and he tapped her on the shoulder.

Erika looked at him and saw his eyes flicker toward her chest, hands . . . toward her guns.

Damn Cody and his fondness for Hong Kong action movies, Rolf thought to her. *You go for the guns when you need them not for recreation.*

Erika took her hands away from inside her coat and shot a hard look at Rolf. *Who the hell are you, my father?* she thought.

But Rolf wasn't looking at her; he was smiling and waving at the guards. *No,* he mentally replied, *just a guy who wants to live through the next five minutes. Kill them quietly.*

"Sorry, folks, they stopped giving tours about two months ago," a guard with a natural orange buzzcut announced.

Next to him, a goateed, bald musclehead raised his weapon in alarm.

"What the hell are you doing here this early in the morning?" Baldy asked.

"You want fucking quietly . . ." Erika growled.

It was all one motion, a split second of death. Her arms flashed forward, fingers digging into Baldy's face, his eyes pulping under the pressure of her grip. Erika pulled him forward, and even as she twisted his head, shattering his spine at the neck, she used his weight for leverage and kicked out at a slender black man who'd only just begun to move. Her foot crushed his ribcage to powder and slammed him against the prison wall. When he fell to the ground, he left behind bits of hair and bone and blood at the spot where his head had struck.

That quiet enough for you? she thought as she turned to Rolf.

Perfect, Rolf replied, even as he gently lowered the twisted corpse of the orange-haired jarhead to the pavement. The other guard, an uncharacteristically chubby Asian, lay there already, face and nose ruptured, probably killed by bone shrapnel exploding into his brain.

Quiet.

Without exchanging a word, Erika and Rolf each knelt by one of their victims and drank of their cooling blood. No use passing up a free meal, Erika thought. But that thought she kept to herself. The thirst was a frequent topic of conversation among Peter Octavian's coven—and their greatest curse, the ultimate obstacle standing between what they were and what they so desired to be.

They pushed through the gates together, tensed in preparation for the appearance of more guards. More human slaves to Hannibal's slavering clan. A fine line separated these human collaborators from those who worked with Peter, who volunteered their aid and often their blood. Both breeds of human were clearly fascinated by the immortal shadows, but some thrived on fear and horror, others on hope and kindness.

Where are they all? I don't like this at all, Rolf thought.

Too late for that now, Erika replied. "We're in the lion's den."

Rolf reached behind his back to withdraw his own weapon, which had been hidden beneath his sweatshirt at the base of his spine. A gun, similar to Erika's weapons, and loaded with silverpoint bullets, just as hers were.

Erika smiled at him.

"So now it's okay?" she asked with sarcasm and withdrew her weapons from their armpit holsters.

Rolf nodded grimly, not the response she'd hoped for. But she should have known better. They were close now. It was time. The moment they'd been waiting a year for. The silver bullets would not kill Hannibal; but they had discussed it, and Rolf seemed to think it might at least steal Hannibal's focus, trapping him in his corporeal form for a few vital seconds. If that failed, and they could at least get him out under the sun, they might be able to disturb his concentration enough to kill him.

But that might take a while. And there were sure to be dozens of other vampires with him. There was no way. . . .

No. Erika pushed the thought away. It was time to act. To hell with the consequences.

"Where do you think—" she began.

The cells, Rolf replied. *He'd enjoy that.*

Even without having to search offices, cafeterias, laundry, and other areas, their search took time. Despite the obvious size of the prison, Erika was astonished at the vastness of the cell blocks. Nearly half an hour after they'd entered the prison, their footsteps echoing through the cement and steel of cell block seven, they came upon their first sleeping vampire.

I don't like it, Erika thought, staring down at the still form of an androgynous undead killer, blood still on its lips.

I know, Rolf replied. *No way would they all sleep tight in here with only four amateur tough guys at the gate. But . . . there's no way he could have known we were coming. How could he know?*

The vampire on the floor opened its eyes, mouth stretching into a grotesque smile.

"Shit!" Erika snapped.

"Hap-py Birthday!" the vampire cried and leaped to its feet to caper wildly from one side of the cell block to the other, not even trying to attack them.

"I love that cartoon!" it shouted in a voice that gave no greater definition to its possible gender. "Don't you remember *Frosty the Snowman*?"

Shut him up, Rolf thought.

Erika was already moving, and she grunted in pain as

her fingers elongated and sharpened into silver points. Slow poison for her, but she wouldn't need them very long. And Hannibal's coven would never break the rules and shift into anything silver.

"I like Rudolph, actually," she whispered.

Blood spurted from the vampire's mouth as she speared its heart with her silver-tipped fingers. She glanced around at the dark cells as the dead creature slid to the ground.

"I don't get it," she said softly. "He didn't even fight back."

Then, from the darkness at the end of the row of cells, a familiar, mocking voice drifted with insinuation.

"She, actually," Hannibal said. "Never been quite right since her transformation. Putting her in your way was considered merciful."

Rolf growled a mutilated sound that might have been his attempt at saying the name of their despised adversary.

"Hannibal," Erika sneered.

"Kill the mute," Hannibal commanded, scowling.

Vampires rose from the shadows in the cells and drifted as mist from the ceiling. It was a swarm, moving on Erika and Rolf too quickly for even the inhuman eye to follow.

"Fuck!" Erika roared as she dove on her belly on the concrete, nine-millimeter twin sidearms erupting in a shower of silver, even as Rolf began firing his own weapon.

She was thrilled to be greeted by shrieks of pain and horror. One nearby vamp girl actually burst into flame, and Erika smiled to herself. *Ignorant bitch,* she thought, but not too dismissively. Ignorance was a weapon they could use.

"We're compromised," she shouted back to Rolf. "Let's get out of here!"

She'd already begun to withdraw, firing in front and behind her simultaneously, keeping the vampires off and backing up through the hole her silver barrage was opening. When Erika ran out of ammunition, she tossed one of the guns and shifted her left hand into a huge bear claw. Partial transformations required concentration. They were going to

lose. They were going to die. The smart thing to do would
be just to mist on out of there, retreat, and live to fight
another day.

"Rolf!" she shouted. "Did you hear me—"

Erika was interrupted by a roar. She whipped her eyes
left and saw, to her horror, that Rolf was charging ahead
through an ocean of vampiric flesh, tearing undead warriors
from his path with a ferocity that split skulls and ripped
limbs from their sockets. At the end of the corridor, Hannibal stood unmoved by his enemy's determination, laughing softly as his eyes burned in the darkness.

He wasn't going to make it. There were too many of
them, and already they were beginning to drag him down.

Claws raked her back and ass, and Erika screamed in
pain. Without even really glancing back, she fired two silver bullets into the face of her attacker.

Rolf, no! she shouted into his head.

He didn't even flinch. Didn't turn. It was a kind of insanity now, she sensed. Her only choice was to stand by
him, or save herself.

It was Erika's turn to roar, as she moved in after Rolf,
firing her remaining nine-millimeter into the crowd.

A sharp pinprick of pain in her neck. Erika slapped a
hand to the spot, almost expecting to crush a bee or wasp
beneath her fingers. What she found there instead was a
dart.

"What the . . ." she asked, and then the vampires
swarmed over her, dragging her down.

As she fell beneath them, she saw a pair of darts fired
into Rolf's back. She turned to see the wielder of the dart
gun. A white-haired vampire, his hair whiter even than
Hannibal's; he'd allowed himself to remain old despite his
shapeshifting abilities. She recognized him.

"Yano?" she asked weakly.

"Sorry, Erika," Sebastiano replied grimly. "You
shouldn't have come."

Overwhelmed, with no hope of helping Rolf or herself,

Erika realized her only hope was escape. She concentrated on turning her body to mist, a form the other vampires couldn't hope to attack or even follow for very long.

Nothing happened.

Nothing.

Erika concentrated again on changing. Into anything. Still, nothing happened. She was frozen in her original human body, unable to shift into any other form. No way, then, to escape. No way, even, to . . . to *heal.*

"Oh my God," she said softly.

Somehow, Hannibal had found a way to *change* them. Erika didn't know if it was science or magic, but it hardly mattered. He'd made them vulnerable. Killable.

Rolf wailed in fury and surged up against the dozen vampire bodies that held him down. Several more jumped on the pile to hold him down. He was an elder shadow, with strength considered prodigious even among his kind. He stared up into the burning eyes of his enemy, unable to shout his hatred for the bastard to the metal rafters of the prison, and now somehow unable to change, to shift.

He didn't care. He'd killed with his bare hands for centuries, and he'd kill Hannibal the same way. If he could just . . . get . . . up.

"Pitiful sight, really," Hannibal chuckled. "But don't worry, you won't have to suffer this indignity very long."

Rolf could hear Erika screaming from behind him and hoped that she, at least, would be able to escape. He felt the grip of his gun wrested from his hand. Stared up as Hannibal aimed at his forehead. Impossible as it was, Rolf thought he could see the glint of silver inside the barrel.

No changing. No healing. However Hannibal had done it, Rolf knew that Peter and the others would be unsuspecting. Another major advantage the vampires would have over the shadow coven. They had to figure out how it was done. Someone had to warn them.

As Erika shouted in fury, Hannibal emptied the clip of silver bullets into Rolf's face.

---------------- ✳ ----------------

1

You better come on in my kitchen, baby,
it's goin' to be rainin' outdoors.

—ROBERT JOHNSON,
"Come On in My Kitchen"

AT THE CENTER OF NEW ORLEANS'S FRENCH
Quarter, Bourbon Street was all flash; garish face paint obscuring the true identity of the most fascinating city in America. At least, that was the way Nikki Wydra felt about the Big Easy. She'd only been there five days, but already she was in love with the place. New Orleans, to her, was like a seductively dangerous man, whose charisma would never allow casual observers to witness his true nature.

Boy, she'd known a lot of men like that.

Sang about them, too.

That was her job. Nikki had often been told that she sang the blues just a little too well for a twenty-two-year-old white girl from Philadelphia. Hell, there'd been times people had gotten pissed off at her just for singing: as if she didn't have any right to sing the blues because of her age, or her sex, or her race. The idea appalled her. It was music, and it belonged to anyone who would listen. Music meant everything to her. Nobody was ever going to take that away.

Not even the vampires.

The world was getting a bit frightening, no question. Los Angeles, New York, Atlanta . . . it was just crazy to hang out after dark in those cities. But she'd heard good things about New Orleans. Dangerous, sure. But somehow, the Crescent City had avoided the atmosphere of terror that had begun to descend on many other major urban centers.

Nikki knew it was only a matter of time before that changed as well. The vampire presence seemed to spread week to week. She shivered as she wondered how long it would be before the entire human race stayed in after dark. But for now, New Orleans was home. She'd adopted it the moment she'd stepped out of the cab in front of A Creole House, the bed-and-breakfast she'd been in all week. And she was cocky enough to think that maybe the city had adopted her as well.

Cocky, yes, but not stupid. With its growing reputation as something of a haven from the vampires, New Orleans was already becoming the place to run to when you just couldn't take it anymore. Like Atlanta at the turn of the millenium, New Orleans was growing so crowded with newcomers that rents were skyrocketing and jobs at a premium. It would have been foolish for her to move there without a source of income.

That in mind, Nikki had sent a tape of the two videos she'd done, and some other audio demos, to the manager of Old Antoine's, and made sure she had a gig before buying a planet ticket. She'd worried, at first, about the club's proximity to Bourbon Street, that it might be difficult to draw a crowd away from the bars and strip clubs there. But Bourbon Street turned out to be no competition. The tourist mecca was nothing more than flashing lights, bare-assed junkie runaways who gave stripping a bad name, karaoke, expensive drinks and their corresponding drunks, and mediocre music.

Not that she didn't love the rest of the French Quarter. It was the most enticing place she had ever seen.

At a quarter past eight, that Wednesday night—the night it all changed for her—Nikki strolled down Rue St. Peter swinging her guitar case, and just took it all in. Laughing couples walked hand in hand, couples of every imaginable combination. On balconies above, vines twirled inside wrought iron until she had to wonder if they were all that held the metal to the buildings.

On the corner of Rue Decatur, in the recessed doorway of a stately home, two ancient black men sat together, unspeaking, faces so wrinkled their eyes were invisible in the folds. Half a block away, a brass band in rumpled uniforms played a rousing chorus of ''When the Saints Go Marching In.'' And, Nikki was certain, it wasn't just because of the football team. On Bourbon Street, maybe, but here, just blocks away, it was another world. Another Quarter. Another New Orleans.

The smell of devastatingly spicy jambalaya wafted through the open saloon doors of a restaurant whose name was barely legible on a faded sign. But it didn't need a name, not with food that smelled that good. She'd eaten inside the little establishment three times since she'd been here, and each night, it seemed, the meals improved. How anyone could make something that tasted as good as the gumbo they served was beyond her ability to imagine.

Half a block from Old Antoine's she could clearly hear Swamp Thing, the New Orleans funk–infused jazz trio that served as the bar's house band, ripping through a completely insane version of Bob Marley's ''Could You Be Loved.'' It was beautiful, entrancing.

Nikki had never been so happy.

Southern Comfort burned sweetly in her throat and belly. Nikki swayed, her hands caressing the strings of her guitar as she growled her way through Robert Johnson's immortal ''Come On in My Kitchen.'' It was the fourth song in her set, after she'd run through Clarence Carter's ''Sweet Feelin','' Billie Holiday's ''Lover Man,'' and Bonnie Raitt's

mournfully sexy "I Can't Make You Love Me." Shafts of
smoky blue light punched through the darkness and she
turned her face to their brilliance as if to the sun.

She lived for those lights. For the cloud of smoke that
clogged her lungs. For the silence of the audience while
she poured her heart out to them, and the roar of approval
when she was through. Her sets moved from bluesy pop
standards like Bob Seger's "Main Street" to the absolute
core of the blues. It was stripped-down, soul-baring music
she'd come to love as a child, trying desperately to fall
asleep as her mother sat and drank herself into a stupor
listening to Blind Willie McTell and Elmore James and Big
Mama Thornton and T-Bone Walker. So many songs. So
much pain.

Until the day she died, Nikki's mother, Etta, had still
listened to music on vinyl. With a record player. The memory was bittersweet, like nearly all her thoughts of her
mother were.

She put the sadness into her voice, into the song, and
gave it to the audience as a kind of offering. Maybe they'd
all feel a little better when she was done. At least that's
how she'd always thought of it.

When she was through, she barely allowed the audience
a moment to applaud before launching into Bonnie Raitt's
version of "Love Me Like a Man." It always made her
feel sexy to sing such a raw, inviting song. She let her eyes
drift over the shadowed faces of the audience, where they
sat around tables and tipped back Lone Stars and Dixies
and glasses of whiskey. Suddenly the men stopped drinking.

They always stopped drinking during this song. Their
eyes riveted on Nikki, on the way her body moved against
her guitar. She invited it, moved with it. That's what the
song was all about. She slapped the front of the guitar in
time with her picking and strumming, and she smiled with
mischief toward the faces in the dark.

"I need someone to love me, I know you can," she sang

throatily. "Believe me when I tell you, you can love me like a man."

Her eyes continued to trawl across the audience. Then stopped, frozen on one face. A handsome, chiseled, intense face, belonging to a man who'd come to see her four nights running. He had short, raggedly cut hair and a goatee, and when her gaze stopped on him, he held it with his own. His mouth blossomed into a lopsided grin, and Nikki felt the whiskey-warmth in her belly spread further through her.

The words to the song almost eluded her, but she caught herself and went on, unable to look away from the dark-haired man leaning against the bar. There was an intimacy to their exchange now, and she began to blush with the sexuality of the song.

What's wrong with you? she chided herself, and shook it off. She looked away, continued the song. Remembered the man. His easy smile, the confidence in his bearing. Not a freak, certainly. Charming as a stalker. But that didn't mean he was one. Just a fan, then. A really, truly, good-looking fan.

When her gaze swept past him again, it was Nikki's turn to smile. She ran through the rest of her first set feeling a kind of tingly excitement she wasn't at all used to. Unexpected as this feeling was, she knew it was also unwarranted. There was no reason for her to expect the guy at the bar to be anyone she'd want to get to know.

But when she laid her guitar down and stepped offstage, Nikki waded through the smoke and the applause, brushing past chairs on a direct path for the man at the bar whose darling grin and smiling eyes drew her on.

She was perhaps twenty feet away from him when a broad stone wall of a man blocked her way, a leer stretching his lips and a Dixie in either hand. He held one of the beers out to her, stepped in closer, and she felt suddenly, oddly, cold.

"I like the way you sing," he said suggestively, his southern drawl more pronounced than that of the locals.

"Like you're lonely and wet and can't help yourself."

Nikki felt her stomach churn. Her upper lip curled back in an involuntary sneer.

"You're a fucking poet," she shot at him, and stepped to one side, intending to go around.

She heard the dropped beer bottle shatter on the floor in the same instant that the big, cruel-eyed man wrapped her right bicep in a crushing grip. Nikki cried out, less in pain than in fear that he would break her arm just by holding on to her.

"Hey, asshole!" somebody shouted from a nearby table. "Why don't you leave the lady alone?"

A tall black man appeared next to her and reached out for the steel fingers that had trapped her there in the middle of the club. The big man who held her wasn't about to let go. His other hand shot out in a flash. He grabbed the tall man by the throat, gave a jerk, and her would-be savior's neck snapped with a gunshot crack.

"Oh my God!" Nikki screamed.

The killer leaned in close to her, pulling her to him in an almost intimate embrace. He spoke softly, snarling, but she felt no breath on her face.

"That's your fault, bitch," he whispered. "You killed that fella, sure as I'm standin' here. And I was only tryin' to be nice. Now, *you* gonna be nice or do I have to start gettin' mean?"

He smiled, waiting for an answer, and she could see his fangs. Nikki whimpered, unable to scream, barely able to breathe. Even as she cringed away from him, she was ashamed of her fear. This was a tyrant, like so many other men she'd known, an animal whose basic instinct was to inflict pain on others to feed its own delusions of power.

She was terrified. There was no getting around that. Perhaps she was about to die. In the few seconds that he waited for her response, her emotions were in turmoil. But she knew this: he might take her life, but she would never surrender her dignity again. She wouldn't give him that.

"Last chance, darlin'," he drawled.

Nikki Wydra balled her left hand into a fist and swung it as hard as she could into the big vampire's face. Felt it give way beneath her knuckles. Smiled as she saw the blood squirt from his now broken nose.

"Fuck you," she growled.

With a roar, the vampire yanked her hair, pulling some of it free of her scalp. He drew her head back, bared his fangs with a hiss, and shot his mouth toward her throat. Tears burned at the corners of her eyes, but she knew she would be dead before they fell.

"You want to see mean?" a soft, commanding voice asked.

She heard the vampire grunt in surprise and pain, and forced her eyes open. A hand was twined in the huge monster's hair, his own head yanked back, throat exposed.

It was him. The man from the bar, the man with the lopsided grin who'd come to see her night after night. The vampire towered over him, was double his size, but the handsome, goateed man easily held him down, biceps bulging but not straining with the effort. How? she thought. How could he . . .

Then she knew.

"This isn't the way things are done in New Orleans," the man from the bar said quietly, sternly, as if he were reasoning with a small child. "If you'd wanted to live like this, to behave like an animal, you should have stayed with Hannibal's clan."

The huge vampire slapped the man's hand away and rounded on him. Nikki backpedaled, unable to look away but frantic to escape further attack.

"What makes you think I'm not still part of that clan?" the huge vampire sneered. "You think I'm gonna take orders from a pussy like you, man won't even take what's his by right?"

The man's eyes widened at the vampire's words.

"Oh," he said amiably. "A spy, eh? Did it ever occur

to you to wonder why I've been hanging around Old Antoine's for the past few nights?''

Now it was the vampire's turn to register surprise. Nikki didn't understand what kept him from attacking the man. They were so close, he could have reached out and killed him just as he'd done to the other man who'd tried to help her. And the way he moved, nervously, from side to side. It was almost as if he were afraid.

But that was ridiculous.

"No? I didn't think so. I begin to doubt Hannibal's vaunted wisdom. Only a fool would send an idiot like you to do a job that requires some brains," the man snarled.

The huge vampire began to change then. Fur sprouted all over his body, and his face elongated into a snout full of gnashing, flashing death. Hands lengthened into claws and Nikki got her first good glimpse of what a werewolf looked like.

"You're dead," the wolf growled, in words barely decipherable.

The man actually chuckled. "Ah, little cub," he said. "If you had any idea how many times I've heard those words, even you would have to laugh at how stupid they make you sound."

That did it. Despite his obvious trepidation, the wolf could take no more. The huge, howling vampire launched himself at Nikki's savior and admirer, claws extended, reaching, ready to rend and tear.

Green light spilled from the man's eyes and sprouted from his right hand. He moved so fast that if Nikki had even blinked, she might have missed it. The green glow blazed around his fingers and the man stepped forward, into the wolf's charge. His hand slammed into the huge monster's chest, shattering bones and ripping flesh.

"This is how we deal with spies," the man said.

As he withdrew his hand, the dark-haired man stepped aside. The vampire, already changing back to his human appearance, crashed into an abandoned table and tumbled to the floor on his back. There was a steaming hole in his chest where his heart had once beat.

Now it burned. In the hand of the man who had saved her, who had looked at her so enchantingly from across the room, was the black heart of the vampire. It burned green and bright for a moment, and then its ashes scattered to the ground. Nikki stared at them as they fell like snowflakes to the sticky floorboards.

"Are you all right?" he asked, his voice filled with warmth and concern.

Nikki jumped, startled to find him there, next to her. Then she relaxed. She should have been terrified. He wasn't human either, that much was clear. Vampire. Sorceror. Whatever he was, whatever insane things existed in this new world since the Venice Jihad six years ago, she ought to have run screaming from them. From him. But she didn't feel afraid. She felt . . . safe. That was the only way to describe it. He had saved her life. And there was a kindness and wisdom that came through his every glance, his every word.

"Thank you," she said, her voice cracking.

"You sing beautifully, Nikki," he observed by way of response, and smiled again, white teeth splitting his tightly trimmed goatee. "My name is Peter."

"Peter," she repeated, tasting the flavor of his name on her lips.

He reached out to her, his fingers lightly brushing against her hand. She ought to have pulled away. But she simply didn't want to. Then, at the back of the club, metal stage doors clanged shut, the scraping clamor echoing through the room.

"Octavian!" a woman roared from the dimly lit front entrance.

There were five of them, all together. At least, five that she could see. A pair of lanky, slinking males approached from the stage door. At the front door, a long-haired Latino man and two women moved further into the club. The one who had spoken walked in front, apparently leading them. She was young and petite, a slight Asian girl who radiated a power that belied her size.

"Nobody move, and maybe you'll survive to be dinner another night," she sneered, her beautifully sculpted face split by a sickening grin.

"Hello, Tsumi," Peter said coldly. "I haven't seen you since Hong Kong. What was it, 1854? Or was it '55?"

The girl named Tsumi smiled. "I'm glad you remember," she said.

The five vampires continued to move in, obviously intending to encircle the other, to trap Peter between them. As they passed the bar, Sidney, the bartender, took a step or two away from them. The long-haired Latino grunted as his right hand extended into a horrible wooden pitchfork of a claw. As he passed the bar, he whipped his arm out and sliced cleanly through the bartender's throat. The vampire didn't even look at the man as blood sprayed across the bar. Nikki felt sick as Sidney crashed into a rack of liquor bottles, hands flapping wildly, trying to staunch the flow of blood from his throat.

Nobody else in the club moved. Not at all. Some whimpered. Some actually cried. Ash grew long on the ends of burning cigarettes. But nobody moved.

"When they come for me, run for the door," Peter whispered in Nikki's ear.

"Ah, is she with you, then?" Tsumi asked.

"Not at all," Peter replied. "She's just a wonderful singer. Though I see you're still the jealous type. Does Hannibal know you have a personal vendetta against me, or does he think you actually believe in his politics?"

"Politics?" Tsumi snapped. "You are a fool, Peter. This is about survival. Survival of the fittest."

Then she softened. "Once upon a time, when I loved you, you would have known that. You were the greatest warrior I have ever known. But that was a long time ago, wasn't it? What's become of you?"

"I was a warrior, Tsumi. Never a predator," Peter replied.

He began to move his hands in odd circles at his waist, fingers contorting, and Nikki could see that his lips moved as he whispered so softly she could not hear.

"And now you're a coward," Tsumi said curtly. She looked at the other four vampires who had arrived with her, and who had remained silent during their exchange. "Kill him," she said.

"Go!" Peter shouted at Nikki, even as the four vampires leaped toward him from all directions.

She ran. Her legs pistoned beneath, fueled by terror. Nikki was a woman of formidable character, but she was only a woman. These creatures, even Peter, whom she'd found so attractive, they weren't even human. Murderers. Predators. Monsters.

Behind her, someone screamed and, despite her horror at what he was, she silently prayed it wasn't Peter. She glanced ahead, the way to the door clear. There was another scream, and then the fear that had paralyzed the people in the club edged up a notch . . . and the spell was shattered. As one, they rose and began to crowd toward the front door.

"Out of the way, bitch," a salt-and-pepper-haired little man barked as he shoved her aside.

Nikki was jostled and shoved, but the tide of fear carried her along toward the door, and she gave in to it.

"Fire!" a woman shouted, and pointed over toward the bar.

Nikki turned to look, and there it was. Crackling hungrily behind the bar, was a small but quickly spreading fire. Her mind flashed with a picture of Sidney smashing into a rack of liquor bottles. A detail that hadn't seemed important before now rushed into focus. Sidney had been smoking.

The cries grew and the press toward the door surged more urgently forward. Someone pushed her from behind, and Nikki began to fall. She reached for the leather jacket

of the man in front of her, but he shook her loose as he
jockeyed for position at the exit. She fell.

When the first foot slammed down on her right arm,
Nikki screamed in pain and frenzied panic, praying that her
arm wasn't broken.

Then suddenly there was space around her, and a strong
hand grabbed her around the waist and hoisted her up. The
crowd had somehow spread out, moving away from her,
and she was relieved to be away from their crushing weight.

She was spun violently around, and a hand laced in her
hair and pulled. Pain shot through her already torn and
bleeding scalp. Nikki stared into the black eyes of the vampire girl, Tsumi. She saw the hate there, wanted to whine,
to plead, to tell Tsumi that she was nobody special, that
she wasn't worth killing. But she couldn't say even that,
for Tsumi gripped her by the throat and, despite her short
stature, held Nikki by the neck and hair several inches
above the floor.

"Octavian, not another move," Tsumi ordered.

The vampire girl moved slightly, and finally Nikki could
see the center of the club, empty now of humanity. Only
monsters there. Fire licked across the bar and leaped up to
begin consuming the ceiling above it. It was spreading fast.
The long-haired Latino and a lanky, bearded white male
stood just behind Peter, ready to attack again, but the other
two were dead. The third male vampire was impaled on his
back on a steel microphone stand. He was drenched with
something—beer, Nikki guessed—and he twitched and
sparked with electricity running through him. The female's
body lay inches from the flames.

Octavian held her head, dangling from its hair, in his
right hand.

"You brought nothing but amateurs with you, Tsumi,"
Peter said, eyes not even glancing at Nikki. "I'm a little
disappointed, to be honest. You come into my town, risk
running into my people—you know we've outdistanced
your own clans in the development of our abilities—and

you bring pups. Children, really. You're a fool, Tsumi, and a savage bitch at that. And you wonder why I left you there, in Hong Kong.''

Peter took a step toward the spot near the entryway where Tsumi held Nikki. Barely able to draw breath, Nikki jumped in alarm. What was he doing? she thought. He was a vampire, certainly. Some kind of monster. But he'd seemed different. He cared about human lives, that much was obvious. He wouldn't just throw her life away.

He couldn't.

''Another step and I'll rip her head off,'' Tsumi snarled. ''Surrender now, allow yourself to be captured, and perhaps Hannibal will kill you quickly.''

''Tsumi,'' Peter said, as if to a petulant child. ''Hannibal couldn't kill me any more than you could. And if you want a head . . .''

He threw the female vampire's head gently onto the floor, where it slid and skittered and finally rolled to a stop just a few feet from where Nikki still sucked air greedily into her raw and constricted throat.

''Bastard,'' Tsumi sneered. ''Now I will kill her.''

''Suit yourself,'' Peter replied. ''But if it helps at all, I surrender.''

Immediately, Nikki felt Tsumi begin to relax. Then, the next instant, a sudden whistling began behind her, like the sound inside a conch shell but so much louder. Despite the fire, she was suddenly cold. Colder, perhaps, than she had ever been. Coldest of all, though, were Tsumi's fingers on her throat.

Shivering and numb, teeth chattering, Nikki looked at Tsumi's face. Cheeks blue and white, splotched with red, the vampire girl was frozen in place. Nikki struggled to escape her icy grip, and Tsumi's claws dug into her throat.

Octavian spun toward the lanky, bearded vampire and his hands came up quickly, sending out a wave of green light. As though he'd been struck by a bulldozer, the vampire was swept back by the green light and, so quickly he could not even think to change his form, he was crushed to a pulp against the club's far wall and fell in a gory mess into the leaping flames.

"*Hijo de . . .*" the Latino began. Then he stood tall, chin up, and stared Peter in the eyes. "Sorcerer. You're nothing without your magick, sir. And when Hannibal is through with you, you will be nothing indeed."

Tsumi's frozen thumb snapped off and Nikki crumpled to the floor, bleeding from the head and throat, cradling her injured arm as she shivered from frostbite and began to slide into shock. Still, she watched, waiting for Peter to kill the long-haired vampire with whatever incredible magick he had at his control.

Instead, Octavian drew himself up as haughtily as the Latino had done.

"Nothing, boy?" Peter said, his disgust obvious. "I was born Nicephorus Dragases, the bastard child of the last emperor of Byzantium. I gave my soul to kill the Turks who tore my empire down. I drank the blood of armies. I brought to their knees the churchmen who would have herded us like cattle, and, for my trouble, I spent one thousand years in Hell."

He paused here, and watched the weight of his words sink in. Nikki saw the fear beginning to show on the previously pompous Latino's face. The club was empty but for the three of them now, and silent but for the crackling of the spreading fire. Nikki knew she should get up and run. Escape. From the dead men trying to kill one another, and from the blaze eating the club that had become her livelihood.

But she couldn't move. Somewhere in the back of her head a little voice told her she was in shock. She barely heard it.

"I'm not a braggart, boy, and I'm not a murderer," Peter said, softer now. "I just want you to know what you face, so you'll feel less the coward if you decide to make a run for it."

"You'll . . . just let me leave?" the Latino asked, incredulous.

"I didn't say that," Peter replied. "But I promise you this. I won't use any magick to kill you. And I won't use silver, which your kind still abhor. And I won't use fire, or any other form Hannibal has forbidden you to take on. Just shadow to shadow, fang and claw. Does that make you happy? Is that fair, do you think, you little brat?"

In the haze of shock, losing blood fast, Nikki's vision began to blur. Or perhaps it was smoke inhalation from the fire, or blood dripping into her eyes from her scalp. It didn't matter, for what she saw before her now was a nightmare scene out of Hell itself. Two men bursting the seams of humanity, monsters erupting from their flesh, wolf-things that were so much more than animals.

They rushed at one another, claws flashing and jaws gnashing. Blood flew and howls pierced the air. Mind smothering, Nikki watched as Peter tore the other vampire to shreds. It took seconds. In the end, he lifted the long-haired Latino, now unable to hold on to his wolf-shape, and hurled him into the raging fire.

Blackness swept over Nikki, and she slid sideways, sprawling on the floor. She began to cough and couldn't stop. The smoke had filled her lungs. She smiled a bit, happy that she was too numb to feel the pain in her injured arm, or her torn and bleeding throat.

In a final flash of consciousness, she saw Peter above her, leaning over, genuine warmth and concern on his features. His hands were burning green, and she felt the warmth of that green fire as it swept over her. She didn't hurt so much anymore.

Kind eyes, that's what she thought. As her eyes closed and she fell away into nothing, she thought, insanely, that she could hear him singing "The Sky Is Crying," an old Elmore James song that had always made her mother pour herself another drink.

She might have felt his arms around her.

Then nothing.

2

> *My head is full of voices,*
> *and my house is full of lies.*
> *This is home.*
>
> —SHERYL CROW,
> "Home"

ON A FORGOTTEN DIRT PATH, OFF A DUSTY narrow road that led across the plains from a little-used highway, Will Cody and Allison Vigeant sat on the hood of their battered red Jeep Grand Cherokee. They leaned against the windshield, sipping powerful Jamaican Blue Mountain coffee poured from a thermos, and watched the dawn approach in silence. Will drank with his left hand, so he could hold Allison's hand in his right.

They were just outside North Platte, Nebraska, a place Will had called home for forty-four years and where his life had left quite an impression. There were streets and schools named after him, among many other things. His old homestead, Scout's Rest Ranch, was still there, a tourist attraction now. The people who took care of his celebrity, or the memory of it, were trying desperately to convince America and the world that the vampire who'd been calling himself Will Cody was nothing but a charlatan.

In his heart, Will hoped they would succeed. The last

thing he would ever want would be for the actions of Hannibal and his followers to forever taint the glory of what Will had built while alive. But then, "alive" had been a long time ago. Perhaps it wasn't as important as all that.

But if it wasn't important, why was he doing this? Why had he dragged poor Allison across North America on a tour of all the places that had meant something to him while he was alive?

They'd started on Prince Edward Island, where he'd stood over the graves of Codys and Feehans, and met a bearded man with kind eyes who'd come to do the same thing. Will had given his name as Frederick Cody there, and he and the man had established that they were cousins or, at least, that their ancestors were. It was a part of his family history that Will had never explored, and he lamented now that he couldn't go meet all those people, cousins from far and wide.

After that moment he had determined it was best to be the pride of these people, not their shame.

From Prince Edward Island they'd gone to Lookout Mountain in Colorado, where his bones were supposed to be buried. And Cedar Mountain, which looked down on a Wyoming town named after him. The two towns had fought over his remains, and Will was glad they'd never dug him up. It would have caused his family too much heartache to know that his body wasn't where they thought it was.

Still, he took some small amusement from the knowledge that neither of the places which had sparred over his supposed corpse ended up being his resting place. He didn't know where he wanted to be buried now. There'd been so much life since his death. But he suspected that, in the end, he'd like to be laid to rest somewhere around North Platte. Or even better, on Prince Edward Island, which he and Allison had felt was a little bit of paradise. Somewhere quiet, in any case.

In the end.

When was that going to be? He'd thought about it a lot,

of late. His life had been filled with such joy that he'd jumped at the chance to prolong it, no matter the cost. But the life of a shadow was filled with violence and grief, and Will honestly didn't know how much longer he could go on with it. If it weren't for Allison . . .

He squeezed her hand in his and looked over at her hazel eyes, at the tiny crinkles around them that told him she was growing older, at the blond hair she had adopted as a small attempt at disguise. Will had offered her the "Gift." Immortality. She had turned him down, a response he hadn't really understood at the time. Now he wouldn't dream of offering it again. He envied her, in a way. In fact, he'd allowed himself to grow a little older as well. For her, and because he didn't want to be recognized as they traveled. He looked nearly fifty now, but still trim and fit, with neatly trimmed hair and beard.

He'd been truly old when Karl Von Reinman had made him a vampire, but his shapeshifting abilities had combined with his vanity to regress him. His love for Allison had changed all that. They would age together now. Will liked the idea of growing old with her. The subject of her actually dying, however, was one he refused even to consider. That day would be the death of him as well, without question.

"So," the petite woman said, her voice husky with the morning, "you feel like Buffalo Bill today? Now that you're home?"

Will looked at her and offered a weak smile. He glanced up at the sky; it was changing colors magnificently as the sun came over the horizon, stretched across the plains toward them.

"I never felt like Buffalo Bill," he said quietly. "Not here, or anywhere else. Jim Hickok never called me anything but Will, nor did Louisa."

Allison was staring at him.

"Hey," she said, bringing his fingers up to brush them against her own cheek. He looked at her, smiled again, and breathed deeply of the Nebraska air.

"If I'd known you were going to get all sad on me, I never would have agreed to come out here with you," she said. "I know that was just a name for you, like an actor on a stage, but it's still a part of your life."

"Not anymore it's not," he said without rancor. "Buffalo Bill never really existed, but this place was where Will Cody lived. There were moments out here, in this little town, with so many people who loved me and so many of nature's gifts to man, moments that were so close to perfect that if one more little girl with a ribbon in her hair had smiled at me, or one more young man had told me his little boy wanted to be a great scout . . . well, God would've had to bring me home to heaven right then, because nobody deserves to be that happy on Earth."

When he looked at her again, Allison was biting her lip and her smile was gone, replaced by a frown of sadness and sympathy. She pulled him to her with one hand, and, in unison, they held their coffee cups out to either side to keep them from spilling.

Her chin on his shoulder, she whispered to him, "Every time I think I understand you, you surprise me a little more. Crass as can be one minute, the soul of eloquence the next. They don't make men like you anymore, Colonel. They truly don't."

Will smiled to himself. "I love you, Allison," he said.

They kissed then, and when she returned his profession of love, her words were muffled by the joining of their lips. When they looked up again, the sun had almost cleared the horizon, and the temperature had risen several degrees.

As Will sipped his coffee again, Allison said, "This is harder for you than you expected, isn't it? We can go anytime you want, you know."

"Yes, much harder," he answered. "And we'll go soon. Let's just sit a spell, while I try to decide whether I really want to go see the ranch, or even go into North Platte."

A few minutes later, Will poured Allison the last of the

coffee. He'd already decided to drive the Jeep into town, at least to try to get a decent breakfast.

"It's beautiful out here," she said. "Really it is. I understand why you loved it so much when . . . before."

"There are so many memories out here for me. So much I can't remember, too," he replied. "Fort McPherson used to be not far from here. It was a different world when I first saw it, when I was stationed there. A different world entirely. No cars, no planes, no television. No fax machines or cell phones or nukes. For better *and* for worse, it was a much simpler life. Just people, trying to get by day to day, with only one another for company.

"The first time I set foot here was in May of 1869. I was guide then to the Fifth Cavalry, and we were on the trail of Tall Bull, a vicious Indian warrior—but no more so than the rest of us. I wasn't fool enough to want the Indians dead because they were Indians, or because they didn't pray to God. The finest, most generous, most trustworthy friends I ever had were of Indian blood, and I employed as many as I could, hoping to keep them from wallowing in the sorrow of their lost tribes. But back when I was a scout . . . well, they were the enemy then, and that was all that mattered.

"Still, it was a fine time, when the Fifth rolled into Fort McPherson. I fell in love with it straightaway. My friend Lew had a saloon in town. Bartender there was Texas Jack Omohundro, who'd trailed three thousand head of Longhorn up from El Paso. I think a lot of that McMurtry fella's writing is influenced by Texas Jack's exploits as a young man."

Will laughed then, and smiled widely and warmly for the first time.

"We went to the circus that first stay, too. Dan Costello's Circus, I recall. Stole a lot of ideas from Dan when I started the Wild West Show. But, then, hell, I stole from them all."

• • •

Allison looked at Will and sipped the last of her coffee.
She was worried about him. As hard as she tried to keep
her concern from showing, she couldn't help it. He loved
her, she knew that, and because of it she didn't expect him
to do anything rash. But the events of the past few years
had taken a horrible toll on him.

When he was still human, Allison knew, Will had been
adored by millions around the world. Controversial though
his reputation might have been, his charisma was never at
issue. After his first death, when he became one of the
shadows, he lived in secret even as his celebrity continued
to grow. Reluctantly, he joined Karl Von Reinman's coven
and tried to hunt only the worst of humanity. Eventually,
he couldn't do even that, instead taking blood only from
willing donors.

After the Venice Jihad, when the world learned that the
shadows were real, Cody reveled in his second round of
fame and adoration. He tried to re-create at least a part of
his great celebrity. Then Hannibal had declared a savage
war on humanity, and on any of the immortals who op-
posed him.

For the first time in his life, the world turned against
Will Cody. He was reviled instead of applauded. It had
been that way for more than a year now, and Allison had
come to believe firmly that it was killing him, destroying
her lover as surely as some horrid disease.

Hannibal's betrayal had not only changed the world, but
it had changed them all individually as well. Allison had
abandoned her life as a broadcast journalist to disappear
into the shadow of America. The world knew her lover was
a vampire, of course. So Hannibal had destroyed her life
as well. Living in fear changed her priorities, that was for
certain.

Her generation had never known what war really meant.
But Allison knew now. War was living, squeezing life from
every second.

Will had become more serious, more intense, over the

past year. That had been the whole purpose of this trip, to relax, to forget Hannibal, at least for a little while. They'd reasoned that in places like North Platte and Cedar Mountain, there wouldn't be any shadows, nor any vampires. Except Will.

It had helped some. But not enough. Allison still felt as though her presence was the only thing that could make Will happy. That was a lot of responsibility for a woman in any relationship, but living on the run, in the middle of a guerilla war, it was even harder. The hardest part was not becoming just as dependent on him as he was on her. It might already be too late, she thought. Nothing mattered to her the way Will did. Allison didn't know what she would do without him.

Then there was Peter. She didn't know if it was his new familiarity with sorcery, or the unfathomable time he had spent away from anyone who cared for him, but Octavian had set himself at a distance from everyone. He still had a certain nobility and charm, but his warmth seemed to have disappeared. Except with George Marcopoulos, the aged human doctor who had been Peter's friend through it all.

"You ready?" Will asked, his fingers lightly running through her hair. She wore it cut fashionably shorter now, at shoulder length.

"So we get breakfast after all?" she asked with a smile.

"I suppose you deserve it," Will replied archly.

"Suppose?" Allison cried, feigning insult. "You wound me, sir."

Will leaned in and kissed her then. For a long moment after, he rested his forehead against hers. Then he sighed and withdrew, eyes closed a moment and with a tiny smirk on his face. Allison began to reach behind his head to pull him close for another kiss, but Will waggled a finger in front of her eyes.

"Now, now, young lady," he said sternly. "Let's not start that again, or we'll be out here all morning."

Allison laughed, summoned up her strength, and with

one mighty shove pushed Will off the hood of the Jeep. With the speed that was a trademark of his kind, he could easily have turned and landed on his feet. Instead he offered her a look of mock hurt and despair and plummeted to the hard-packed dirt road with a grunt.

"Come on, old man," Allison said as she slid off the hood. "I'm getting hungry."

As she opened the passenger door, she saw Will pop up just beyond the Jeep, chuckling to himself. Sweet relief washed over her. For once, he was relaxed. He'd forgotten his troubles, just for a moment.

Inside the Jeep, the cellular phone trilled. Allison frowned and looked down at it. When she looked back up at Will, the smile had vanished from his face. At the third ring, he started for the driver's door.

"Peter knows this is supposed to be a vacation, right?" Allison asked, forcing levity into her voice.

Will shot her a glance that she read all too easily. Peter Octavian was the only person with their cell phone number. He knew how important this trip was to both of them. If he was calling now, it could only be bad news.

He reached for the phone and flipped it open; Allison watched his eyes as he said, "Cody." After a few seconds, Will winced and began to grimace, and Allison began to gnaw her lip and rock a bit, almost unconsciously, as she wondered what had prompted the call.

"We're on our way now," Will said, and slapped the cell phone shut before dropping it on the console between the front seats.

He hung his head, and Allison just waited. Finally, Cody looked up at her.

"Rolf and Erika were in New York trying to track Hannibal. They were supposed to check in last night but nobody's heard from them," Will explained.

Allison let that sink in for a moment. Will seemed so angry, so anxious, she wanted to assuage his fears. Erika they didn't know all that well, but Rolf was a blood-brother to both Will and Peter—they shared the same vampiric father—and meant a great deal to both of them. To the entire coven, actually.

"Well, he's alive, anyway," she said. "If the worst had happened, you and Peter would both have felt his passing."

Will wouldn't look her in the eye.

"What?" she asked. "You didn't feel anything, did you?"

He shook his head, and when he looked up, there were tiny tears of blood on Will Cody's face.

"No," he replied. "But I reached out for him just now—Peter's already tried—just to check and make certain he's all right. See if he needed help. And there's nothing there, Alli. Nothing."

"How . . . how can that be?" she asked, horrified.

"I don't know," he growled, and slapped his right palm on the side of the Jeep. "I can't even guess what it means, because my only guess is that he's dead and somehow we couldn't hear him. But I'll tell you this much, I'm going to find out."

"*We're* going to find out," she said. "I'm going to New York with you."

Will nodded slightly, then looked up at her.

"Get in."

Nikki swam, disoriented, through unconsciousness. Just above the surface, she could hear garbled, fluid voices. She swam toward them as if toward the sunlight streaming down through the waves. When her eyes flickered open in the dimly lit room, her mouth felt parched and she couldn't focus her vision.

". . . drugged . . ." she managed to say.

She was startled when the face of a white-haired old man burst into her line of sight. Nikki blinked several times, then realized the old man was speaking to her. His voice seemed familiar, though she didn't recognize him, and she wondered how long she'd been unconscious.

"Ah, you're finally awake. You'll feel better in a moment," he promised. "Your arm will heal nicely, by the way. It wasn't even a full break."

The old man went on like that for a bit. It took her clouded mind a moment to realize he was a doctor.

"How . . . how long have I been out?" she asked, voice hoarse from disuse.

"Just since last night," the doctor said. "Perhaps twelve hours or so, but that was partially because of the medication. You're going to be just fine, Miss Wydra. Really."

She nodded slightly. Then, belatedly, Nikki noticed how odd her surroundings were. She lay in a king-size cherrywood sleigh bed, in a room with little decoration—yet enough to show that it was unlike any hospital room she'd ever seen.

"Is this—" she began, then had to clear her dry throat. "Is this a hospital?"

The doctor smiled. If he was a doctor. He shook his head slowly.

"No, miss," he said kindly. "Peter was concerned about your safety at a hospital. That's why he brought you here to the convent."

Convent? Nikki was about to ask for clarification, but she didn't get the chance.

"That's enough, George," a low, commanding voice said from the doorway.

Nikki turned to see the man—Peter?—who had saved her life the night before. He stood at the threshold of the room, his hair and goatee well groomed, his smile white and wide. Handsome and intelligent and soft-spoken and kind in a way that so few men were. Those were all her impressions of him from the night before, from the minutes before the . . . attack, and from the chaos itself.

She didn't smile back, though. Instead, Nikki shivered and turned away, pulling herself up into a fetal position. Her heart raced the way it had when she was a little girl afraid of the dark. The sun shone warmly through the window of the bedroom. She wondered if it was his bedroom, and closed her eyes against the light.

"Miss Wydra?" the old doctor said, and she fought the urge to block her ears.

Peter was an illusion of a good and decent man. A mirage. Reality was as deadly and unforgiving as the desert. Reality was, he was a dead man. A monster. A vampire, who preyed on human beings to survive long after nature and God had decided his time was up.

"It's all right, George," she heard him—it—say. "Nikki's got a lot to deal with right now."

Then he was gone. She didn't turn to watch him go, but she knew he had gone just the same. For an instant, she regretted having been so cold to him, after he'd done nothing but enjoy her music—and then save her life. But he wasn't even . . . human.

"Miss Wydra?" the doctor ventured.

A chilling thought struck her, made her breath catch in her throat. But she had to know.

"Are you—Are you like him?" she asked, still not turning to face him.

The doctor chuckled softly.

"No, dear," he said. "There's really nobody like Peter. But I do know what you mean. And no, I'm just an old man, a mortal man. I'm not a shadow."

"A vampire, you mean," she corrected, her voice heavy with indictment.

When she heard the old man's heavy sigh, she did finally turn around. He looked worn, and tired, and far more decrepit than her initial impression had implied.

"I understand," he said, and she stared at him quizzically.

"I'm sorry?"

"I understand," he repeated. "How you feel. How you all feel. But I've known Peter Octavian since you were in grade school, young lady. He isn't a vampire."

She stared even harder at that.

"None of them are," he added.

"What in God's name are you talking about?" she asked, angry now.

"You'd be surprised," he said, and finally a small smile returned to the old man's face. "You can learn more later, if you're so inclined, but what it comes down to is this: there is no such thing as a vampire. Not the way you think of them. But these people, these undead, shapeshifters, whatever you want to call them . . . they are the root of all the legends.

"And they're at war with one another.

"It's a civil war, you understand," the old man went on. "Ever since Salzburg, when the United Nations and part of the Shadow Justice System fought together, and against one another, it's been a war. The lunatic in the White House isn't helping matters any, either.

"You see, the world is changing because, for far too many centuries, the shadows lived the myth. And when the myth was exposed, some of them didn't want to change. Some of them—sadly, most of them—liked the old ways. Liked the power of terror and the taste of death. Hannibal leads them, now, and his 'family' is spreading across the globe. The cities where people fear the dark, his power has done this.

"But New Orleans is different, you understand. For this city is where Peter Octavian makes his home. Octavian's coven is vastly different. I am human. I don't want immortality; perhaps I don't have the courage for it. But I am a member. There are a lot of humans in the coven, people who want to work with Peter's shadows, to aid them."

It was all too much for Nikki; she shook her head, shivered, turned away. On the nightstand was a small pitcher of water and a glass. Slowly she sat up and swung her legs over the edge of the bed. Nikki gritted her teeth against the pain in her belly and arm, but she tried not to let her pain show.

After she'd had half a glass of water, she spoke again.

Without turning, she asked, "Why? Why would you want to help them? Even if they aren't like the others, they are still vampires. I'm sorry, but they are. And they drink blood, don't they?"

"It's more complicated than that," George said, obviously beginning to lose his patience. "But you should rest. Maybe later we can talk about it more. Suffice it to say that Peter's coven is the only thing standing in the way of Hannibal eventually turning the entire human race into slaves or, even worse, cattle.

"I know it's a lot to handle all at once, but he's a good man, Miss Wydra. If he weren't, do you think you'd still be alive? Maybe you ought to think about that a bit," the old doctor said.

"I'm Nikki," she said quickly, before he could leave. It was almost an apology, offering him her first name. Almost, but not quite.

"I'm Dr. Marcopoulos," the old man replied. "But please, call me George."

"Will you come back, George?" she asked, feeling very lost.

"Of course. I'll just let you sleep a bit more, and then we can talk again. You have a lot of deciding to do. Old Antoine's is gone, I'm afraid. And Tsumi, the woman who attacked you, is still out there in the city somewhere. If she thinks you mean something to Peter, she'll be looking for you."

"Wonderful," Nikki sneered, and the sarcasm somehow made her feel better. "But I don't understand why she would think I meant anything to your friend."

George smiled warmly, and for a moment it was almost as though he were the grandfather who'd died when she was too young to remember.

"Ah, but you fail to see the obvious," he said. "Peter has shut out pretty much everyone since the traumatic experiences he had in Salzburg and in—and before that battle.

Everyone with the exception of myself, for which I am grateful.

"But somehow, you do mean something to him. Your music does, at least. That's why he kept going back to the club. He hoped to meet you last night, though I'm sure the horror of the circumstances weren't what he had in mind," the old man said.

Nikki remembered the way Peter had looked at her, when she'd thought he was just another man. Remembered his smiling eyes, and the easy intelligence with which he carried himself. Remembered, with an embarassed flush, that she'd walked offstage and been about to approach him at the bar, when all hell broke loose. But she couldn't help also remembering the killing and the fire and the screaming. And that he wasn't just another man. Wasn't a man at all, despite everything George had said.

"Is this his room?" she asked.

The doctor looked at her oddly, cocking his head slightly.

"Yes," he replied. "Yes, it is."

Nikki glanced around the room. A large cherry wardrobe stood against the far wall. On a small table in front of the window was an array of flowers that looked several days old. Not for her, then. Just because he liked them? The walls were bare but for two large paintings. One was an apparently unremarkable seascape, the kind of thing she had seen bedraggled fishermen working on in beach parking lots her whole life.

The other was an extraordinary portrait of a woman grieving over the body of a child, a domed cathedral in the distance. The eyes reminded her of something by El Greco, a painter who could give more life to a face on canvas than anyone else ever had. But, of course, this one couldn't be . . .

"It was a gift," George said admiringly, and Nikki turned to him again. "It's one of my favorites as well."

"A gift?" she asked.

"Certainly," the old man replied. "The Greek still paints,

you know. Well, I'm sure you didn't know, actually. But he does.''

"Oh, my God," Nikki said and put a hand to her forehead. "I don't know how much more of this I can take."

"You should rest now, anyway," George said and went to the door. "I'm not being a very responsible doctor, am I? Try to sleep, and I'll be back in a few hours."

Nikki glanced around the room again. At the paintings. At the bed. Finally, at the flowers.

"George," she said, just as he was about to turn away.

"Yes, Nikki?"

"It was . . . very kind of Peter," she said. "To bring me here. To let me stay here."

The doctor beamed with pleasure and relief.

"I'll tell him you said so," he replied, and then he was gone.

And Nikki was alone in a house full of monsters. Monsters who loved art and flowers and music, who were gentle and kind, and who killed without hesitation when necessary.

Nikki tried to go back to sleep, but she couldn't push the image of Peter's eyes from her mind. His eyes, and the eyes of the grieving mother in the extraordinary painting on the wall. And she realized, just as she finally drifted off, that despite the smile and the joy she saw in his eyes, there was a horrible sorrow there as well. Like the mother in the painting, he had seen too much.

She dreamed of him. And in her dream, she comforted him.

3

I had a dream last night. . . .
The whole world was standing still,
and the moon was turning red.

—THE NEVILLE BROTHERS,
"Fire and Brimstone"

IN HIS DREAM, THE YEAR IS 1199 AND KURO-
maku is a samurai in the service of the shogun Yoritomo.
But the dream does not progress along the same path as
reality. That was the year the shogun died, and the year
Kuromaku gave up his blood to the shadows, became a
vampire, to take vengeance upon Yoritomo's killers: the
shogun's own sons.

In his dream, Kuromaku is killing Yoritomo himself.
Stealing through the darkness into his home and tearing
the black-robed man's throat out with his teeth and drink-
ing down the life-blood of the most powerful man in Japan.
When he wakes, Kuromaku will know that the false dream
reflects eight-hundred-year-old guilt for not protecting the
shogun. In truth, after the shogun's murder, he went rogue,
became a ronin, and an immortal as well. He savaged the
shogun's duplicitous sons and turned the shogunate over
to Yoritomo's father-in-law.

In his dream, he is in Japan. In reality, he has not re-

turned to his native land since leaving eight centuries earlier. As a ronin, he wandered the nations of the world, serving no one master but fighting and killing in honorable wars, and for righteous causes, down through the years.

Without preamble, the dream changes. This is closer to memory. Not a nightmare, but a fond remembrance of his subconscious mind.

It is January 1820, and Kuromaku finds himself marching on Madrid with the revolutionary forces of Colonel Rafael Riego. The colonel is familiar with the shadow race and has more than a dozen shadow warriors serving alongside his men. The Spanish king, Ferdinand, has abandoned the constitution. Riego's troops force Ferdinand to yield; they keep him in their control, almost a prisoner, for more than three years.

Side by side with Kuromaku in this triumphant strike against tyranny is the finest warrior he has ever seen. Octavian is his name, and he is fierce and swift, with flashing sword and regal bearing. A finer, more loyal friend and ally Kuromaku has never known. Together, they bathe in the blood of the oppressors, the moon turning red above them with the spray. Cannon fire fills the air, pounds their ears. When the battle is over, Octavian makes a gift of his sword to Kuromaku, to honor their friendship and his respect for Kuromaku's skills as a warrior.

Once again, the dream shifts. No memory now, but a warning. The moon is still red and full, and a cacophonous roar fills the air. But it is not cannon fire. Kuromaku stands next to Octavian, and the dead flow in waves against one another, and blood runs in the gutters. They are allies yet again, but their enemies are shadows like themselves, long of fang and swift of claw. Strangely, Octavian again wields the sword he had given as a gift of honor so long ago. In this nightmare Kuromaku sees bright colors and hears music merging with screams of terror and agony.

He knows this place. He has been here once before. Long

ago. But it looks different now, despite the war and the blood. It is an older city now.

Kuromaku and Octavian stand back to back, and the ronin turns to his old friend, and in the dream . . . in the dream, he sees the oddest thing. Octavian has been slashed in the side, just beneath the ribs. Under his clothing, Octavian bleeds.

And bleeds.

And does not heal.

And in his dream, Kuromaku begins to fear that Octavian is going to die. . . .

Kuromaku's eyes snapped open. He stared into the darkness of his sleeping chamber, the only sunless room in his little villa in the south of France.

"*Kami,*" he whispered, but the gods didn't answer.

They never had.

Kuromaku rose quickly and dressed in the dark. He phoned the pilot in his employ and asked the woman to have his plane standing ready at the small airfield nearby in twenty minutes. Then he packed a small traveling case and laid out his weapons on the bed.

To his own array of blades, he knew he must add another.

Kuromaku went to the eastern wall of his chamber. From its place of honor there, he drew down the sword of the greatest warrior he had ever known.

For what he had experienced was no dream, but a prescient vision. He had had such night visions perhaps a dozen times in his long life, and invariably they had been true. If the images from his nightmare were in fact a glimpse of things to come, it seemed Peter Octavian would have need of his sword once more.

Perhaps more than he ever had.

The lamp was an antique, its shade a globe of blown glass with a painted rose pattern. Its light was insufficient for the room, and so it cast a reddish-pink tint across the bedchamber of the vampire lord Hannibal. His long white hair seemed washed in the color, reflecting it back as did his pale flesh.

But the blood staining his bedsheets looked black in that light. Black as his soul, he might have boasted. Hannibal had neither the time nor the inclination to boast, however. Nor did he believe he had a soul.

A Strauss concerto flowed from the CD player. He was not without culture, after all. But the volume was not up terribly high. Hannibal wanted to hear every scream and whimper of his victims. It was the only thing that could arouse him anymore.

With the music lilting softly in the pink light, Hannibal extended his right hand once again. The claw of his index finger elongated even further, its tip a razor needle. Once more, he drew it across the deeply tanned, gently curving belly of the woman who lay on his bed, wrists and ankles trussed with thin wire that cut her flesh each time she moved.

She shrieked in pain, and Hannibal slapped her left cheek openhanded. The crack was quite satisfying to him, and her flesh split just over the cheekbone. He bent and licked the blood from her face and she whimpered all the more.

They were deep within the bowels of Sing-Sing prison, where the sun's rays could not reach them. Hannibal liked the way the woman's cries echoed through the steel and cement labyrinth. It was why he'd chosen to set up his own quarters so far from the less primitive rooms once inhabited by the warden and his staff. Hmm, yes. He liked the screams.

"In case you're wondering, my dear," he whispered to her, "I am going to make love to you."

Her eyes went wide, then squeezed shut, tears springing forth as she bit her lip to keep from screaming again. They rolled down her face and mingled with the blood where her skin had split.

"Please . . ." she rasped, hoarse from where he'd choked her, just to watch her face turn blue. "Please don't—"

"Oh, not to worry," Hannibal interrupted. "You won't feel it. I won't find you at all attractive, not sexy in the least, until you're very, very dead."

She screamed again, and Hannibal threw his head back and laughed loud and long. He was having himself a wonderful time. He glanced over at the corner of the cold, damp cement room, and saw that his other captive was struggling against his bonds, despite the fact that the wire had already cut his wrists to the bone. This one had a gag, only because Hannibal didn't want to hear his whining pleas. Only the agony interested him.

"Oh," he said. "I'd almost forgotten you were there."

He didn't know the man's name, either. But he did know what was important. Hannibal's eyes flashed as he smiled at the man.

"Your sister does seem to be enjoying herself, doesn't she?" he asked.

The man nearly cut off a foot trying to get at him after that. He flopped on the cold floor in his own blood.

"Well done," Hannibal said. "Good show, young man."

A short time later, when the woman was dead but still warm, and her brother had passed out from loss of blood, Hannibal grew bored. A knock at the door made him look up from the woman's corpse.

"Come," he ordered.

Two of his lieutenants entered the room. Behind them, a third vampire dragged a prisoner behind him.

"Ah, the girl," Hannibal said appreciatively. "I'd almost forgotten we were to speak this afternoon. Erika, isn't it?"

Erika was thrown to the floor, hands tied behind her back, and her face slapped concrete. When she looked up at him, sneering, her lip was bleeding.

"Fuck you," she said grimly.

"I think not," Hannibal replied. "On the other hand . . ."

He launched a swift kick at her gut, catching her just below the left breast, and she tumbled backward to the floor once more. Erika heaved and coughed, and a moment later, after sitting up again, spit blood out on the concrete.

Hannibal crouched down in front of her and grabbed the front of her shirt. Hauled her forward so that their eyes met, only inches apart.

"You'd better learn some fucking respect," he snarled. "Or you'll be just as dead as my old friend Rolf."

She winced at that, and Hannibal smiled.

"Oh, yes, he's quite dead," Hannibal said, and enjoyed the sound of his voice in the echoing chamber. "Dead as the silly human bitch on my bed."

Erika glanced over at his bed, and her eyes widened at the sight of all the blood. Her heart began to beat a bit faster. Hannibal realized that, though she'd done her best to hide it, the smell of the blood alone must have had her salivating. The sight of it would only add to her hunger.

"How long has it been since you ate?" he asked her. "Two days? Three?"

"Five," she replied and looked at him evenly. "Five days. And she volunteered."

"Got to love the volunteers," Hannibal said happily. "But you don't have to leave them alive. It just doesn't taste the same if you're not killing them."

He strolled over to where the dead woman's brother lay slumped on the floor, grabbed the man by his hair, and dragged him back to drop him just in front of Erika.

"Free her hands," he ordered. Instantly, one of his lieutenants stepped forward to cut her bonds.

Erika flexed her hands, stared down at them. After a moment, she looked up at Hannibal, brow furrowed with suspicion and doubt. Hannibal reveled in her emotions, her fear and her pain. The girl had been the protégée and more than likely the lover, of the deluded Rolf Sechs. Rolf, who might have been Hannibal's right hand but instead joined with that self-righteous bastard Octavian.

She deserved to suffer. But there was a way Hannibal might have even greater satisfaction, a way he might spit on Octavian, humiliate him and show, for all the undead to see, who was rightful lord of all their kind.

As Hannibal watched, Erika stared at the wounded, unconscious man. His chest rose and fell with each rasping breath. The man was still bleeding profusely from his hands and wrists, where the wire had cut to the bone. He was naked and stank of fear and sweat. But the blood scent overpowered any other smell.

Erika glared at Hannibal again, and he smiled. He could almost feel her hunger, and her growing hatred for him.

"What are you waiting for?" he asked. "He's already lost a lot of blood. He's going to die. Why waste what little is left in him? You're just going to let it soak into the concrete?"

Her lips curled back and her fangs were visible, but did not lengthen. Nor did she change in any other way. Of course not. She couldn't. Not after Hannibal had injected her with the serum. But that didn't mean she wasn't going to try yet again to change. It was pitiful, in a way, and Hannibal chuckled at the sight. The vampire girl's nostrils flared and she began to breathe heavily, as if she were in the throes of passion.

"You hate me," Hannibal observed. "I want you to hate me. And fear me. I'm sure you'd like more than anything to alter your form, to become something horrible right now—perhaps even some silver-clawed thing, eh? Since you *shadows* seem so fond of that disgusting, poisonous metal.

"But you can't, girl. You can't change."

Still, though, Hannibal had to give her credit. She kept trying until a bloody tear slipped from the corner of her right eye. Erika kept her head down after that. Hannibal assumed it was more so she wouldn't have to look at the bleeding man in front of her than in order to ignore Hannibal himself.

"Can you smell the heat from his heart?" Hannibal asked. "Can you taste the copper tang on the tip of your tongue, feel its thickness slide down your throat?"

"Stop it!" she screamed finally.

"Ah, perhaps you can, then," Hannibal said gleefully.

"Why can't I change?" the girl asked.

That was what he'd been waiting for. She was so defiant, but she needed so much from him. Not only blood. Not merely her freedom. But information. She needed to know what had happened to Rolf, why and how he had died. And Hannibal planned to tell her all of it, in good time. For the worst thing he could do to Octavian, and the way in which he might truly soil the memory of Rolf Sechs, would be to make this girl a member of his own family. To take her for his own, to make her a real vampire, instead of this pale shadow of her true nature.

"To understand what is preventing your change," Hannibal began, pedantically, "you must understand one important thing: despite the demonic and divine origins of our vampirism, it is still essentially a scientific process. Somehow, we have a molecular consciousness."

She stared at him, as did the three lieutenants who were in the room with them. They had never had these things explained to them, either, and Hannibal chose to keep them in the dark. Knowledge is power.

"Get out," he said sharply. "All three of you. I will call to you when she is to be removed."

The silent vampire warriors glanced at one another, but none of them was foolish enough to question his will. When they had gone, Hannibal turned to address Erika again. She had inched herself, perhaps even unconsciously, ever so slightly closer to the man quietly bleeding to death on the cement floor.

"As I say . . . somehow," he began, emphasizing the word. "But the end result is that we can shapeshift because not only can we transform our cells on a molecular level, but the cells themselves have a memory of their structure. From woman to wolf or mist, and back to being a woman.

"But in order to do that, a message must be communicated from the brain to the body, and passed from cell to cell through synaptic messages. The serum I've developed inhibits the chemical transference of those messages. You can't *change* anymore, Erika. You can't communicate with your bloodkin. You're going to grow old, now. Eventually, you'll probably die the true death. You still need the blood, you still have the strength. But you won't heal anymore, either."

The girl stared at him, horrified, and he couldn't help but laugh.

"Come now, my little one," he said. "It isn't as bad as all that."

"You're everything I swore I'd never be," Erika whispered, under her breath. Of course, Hannibal heard.

"Let's put that to the test, shall we?" he asked. "You see, there is an antidote. There is a way to give you back the power that makes you a vampire. But if you want it, you will have to pledge your fealty to me, and to this coven."

She opened her mouth to reply, to rail at his suggestion, to berate and condemn him. But she closed her mouth again without uttering a word. That's when Hannibal knew he had her.

Erika quivered with anticipation and, Hannibal thought, self-loathing, as she crept forward on her hands and knees. She dipped her mouth to the throat of the still-unconscious man bleeding on the concrete floor. Her hands and knees were stained by his pooling blood. Tears of blood ran down from her cheeks and mingled with the man's own blood as Erika ripped his throat out and drank deeply, her feeding punctuated by heaving sobs of profound remorse.

Aroused by her despair, Hannibal looked down and was pleased to find himself hard. Remembering a promise made just a while before, he glanced back at the cooling corpse of the woman on his bed. His breath came faster as he returned to his victim and took her as his lover.

His triumph was so sweet.

The interior courtyard of the Ursuline convent—where the coven of shadows who followed Peter Octavian made their home—was awash in the colors and scents of flowers and fresh earth. Despite the threat they lived with each day, Peter and the others had made it their business to bring beauty to their home. It had rained a bit during the day, but now at dusk, as darkness fell, the sky splashed vivid shades of red on the horizon. As if the heavens were a garden all their own. And perhaps they were, Peter thought.

He strolled a path that wound through the garden. Sweet floral aromas rode the breeze that brushed across his short, ragged-cut hair. Peter had a great deal on his mind. He was torn, within and without, drawn in so many directions. His instincts were splintered and thus inaccurate. He had never felt so desperately nostalgic in his centuries of existence. Peter was certain that at another time in his life, he would have seen the circumstances of his friends, his coven, with more clarity. Would have known immediately what actions to take.

Peter Octavian was a man, and a monster. Dead and yet somehow not. Shadows were both demonic and divine. Peter, himself, had lived as a warrior, and now wanted only peace. If he would allow himself to be overwhelmed by the aggression he felt toward Hannibal, it might drive him to do something unthinkable. To take lives, to forcibly create new shadows to combat the vampires of Hannibal's clan.

He wanted to do it.

He really did.

And so he refused to even think about it. Instead, Peter hid those urges away in his mind somewhere, hoping they would stay there. They were the thoughts of the warrior prince he'd once been, not the man he'd become in time.

Peter could be brutal when it was necessary, when he was forced to it. But, not for the first, he wondered if that moment would arrive too late.

Hannibal's numbers were growing.

There was more to it, however. He was torn not only by his past and present, his dual nature, and the dangers his people faced. He was torn by magick.

For a millennium, at least in the way time is reckoned in such places, Peter had lived in Hell itself. During that time, he had learned a great deal about magick, a great deal of sorcery better forgotten. It made him powerful, there was no question about that. But what else had it done to him?

Ages ago, and for centuries thereafter, the church had called his kind "Defiant Ones." Eventually, Peter had learned the origin of the name. Vatican sorcerors had been able to call to heel a great many demons from other dimensions, from Hell or elsewhere. But the shadows could not be controlled by their magick, because each shadow had a human soul.

Now those same demons, and so many other magickal forces, were Peter's to command if he so desired. The magick repulsed him and fascinated him simultaneously. The more he used it, the more he wanted to experiment. Yet each time, he felt a little bit less the warrior he'd once been, and even less the man he'd tried to become.

Still, he had spent time cultivating the spells and enchantments that had nothing to do with demons. Peter had long since had his fill of other dimensions and their denizens.

Somehow, he was determined to master the magick at his disposal and retain the respect for humanity that drove him on. And he would do it. He had to.

A short time later, Peter stopped at a green-painted wrought-iron bench at the center of the winding path and sat. He ran a hand across his goateed chin and scratched his head. When he leaned back, finally, to simply appreciate the garden, he found to his great surprise that there was a smile on his face. For many days, only Nikki Wydra's music and raspy voice had been able to give him that gift.

A pair of enormous lilac bushes grew wild just across the path from the bench. The wind shifted suddenly, and the breeze blew the smell of lilacs in a wave across him. Peter inhaled deeply. It was a beautiful smell, but after a moment the breeze subsided, and it was gone.

Peter was restless. He knew that, despite all else that had happened, including Tsumi's coming to New Orleans, there was one major reason for his anxiety. Rolf.

Despite the fact that Cody was on his way to New York—might, in fact, have arrived there already—to investigate Rolf's disappearance, Peter's heart was heavy, filled with a terrible foreboding that he could not shake. If it weren't for Tsumi's sudden arrival in New Orleans with more of Hannibal's followers in tow, he would have gone off to New York himself.

For a moment he watched the last light as it drained from the sky, the tint of dusk long since disappeared. Then, in the same idle fashion in which he'd scratched his head and run his fingers across the stubbly texture of his beard, Peter began to do magick. The garden itself seemed to take notice, its rustling subsiding as the wind began to pass around the bench where Peter sat. Nature did not appreciate the intrusion of sorcery, which was, by definition, unnatural.

In his right hand, where it lay palm up on his thigh, a green flame began to burn. It flickered up, blazing higher. Peter turned his hand, cupping it, lifting his index finger and swirling the arcane light. It grew and spread, and soon a torrent, a seeming whirlpool of magick shimmered above his hand as if it were some sort of verdant halo. Idle no longer, Peter focused his mind on Tsumi, on their time together, and their brief but visceral struggle the night before.

And he saw her. As if in a mirror, he watched Tsumi's reflection in the scrying pool he'd created out of air and light. She lay atop a stone slab, inside a crypt of some sort.

As Peter watched, she began to stir. He tried to concentrate, to pull from the image, from her mind, her precise location.

The image of Tsumi in the scrying pool changed suddenly. The green glow shimmered, and Tsumi tensed. In a rage, she spun and glared into the shadows of her chamber. Somehow she had sensed him, but assumed that the threat to her was close at hand.

Then he lost her. The scrying pool darkened and began to fade. Peter sighed. He'd try again, and keep trying until Tsumi was found. If they were to defend themselves against Hannibal's inevitable attack on their New Orleans stronghold, Peter would have to know more about the vampire lord's current activities, and the number of undead in his clan.

In his open palm, the scrying pool shattered like a mirror, shards turned to flame, and green fire blazed once more, even more vibrant now that night had truly come. Then it was gone, with only the scent of sulphur left to mark its passing.

"Quite a show," a voice spoke from the garden path.

Peter glanced around to find Joe Boudreau standing several yards away. For a long time, especially after Salzburg, Joe didn't smile at all. Now he nearly always wore a grin on his face. Why not? He was in love, after all.

"How's Kevin?" Peter asked.

"He's great," Joe replied. "Thanks. But I didn't come to discuss my love life."

Peter nodded and beckoned Joe to come nearer. Even those who had once been close to him tended to keep their distance now. He had changed. He was aware of it, of course, but there was little he could do about it. It was impossible to unlearn magick.

It also seemed to him that, despite his happiness, Joe was reluctant to discuss his relationship with Kevin. Like many shadows, after the death of his human self Joe had found less of a gender distinction when choosing a mate. When one had forever to live, such things seemed almost childish.

Nonetheless, Joe still had enough of the prejudices of his first life to make him uncomfortable with the idea that others might disapprove.

Peter didn't push. Besides, they did have more important things to discuss.

"No sign of her?" he asked.

"Not at all," Joe confirmed. "Kevin and I took half a dozen shadows out into the city, mainly hitting clubs and bars. If she's still here, she's keeping a low profile."

"She's still here," Peter said.

Joe looked at him expectantly, and Peter brought his right hand up to massage his temple. He'd begun to get a headache, and couldn't recall the last time he'd had one.

"Do you ever wish Charlemagne had stayed?" Peter asked him.

"All the time," Joe answered. "But not because I think he would have made a better leader. Peter, I've known you since before Venice, when you had given up on the shadow race completely. You made the hard decisions before the rest even had to think about them. You went through Hell, quite literally, and came out the other side with wisdom and power . . . and, yeah, maybe a little bit of craziness.

"Before I met you, I'd been a quitter my whole life. But you taught me to fight. You taught me that there's always something worth fighting for. Sure, Charlemagne could lead, but he's still not completely whole after more than a year. And Cody would do a fine job as well. Maybe even Rolf. But none of them has seen what you've seen. Or knows what you know.

"So just stop worrying and accept it, buddy. You're all we've got," Joe said, the passion in his voice dwindling into amusement.

Peter shook his head, smiling. "Thanks," he said. "I think."

"So what now?" Joe asked as he brushed his brown hair away from his eyes. Eyes which had once needed glasses, but no more.

"Now we do what I've wanted to avoid," Peter replied. "First, we go on patrol. The last thing I wanted was to have to police this city, but if we want to keep it safe for ourselves, we don't have much choice. Second . . ."

Peter rubbed his temple again.

"Second," he continued, "we begin active recruitment of all volunteers and human members of the coven. Explain the threat, and specifically ask them to accept the Gift."

Joe stared at him, eyes narrowed.

"It goes against everything we've ever discussed," Joe said quietly.

"Yes," Peter agreed. "Yes, it does. But don't think it makes us like Hannibal, because it doesn't. We offer a choice. In this case, we're in trouble, and we're asking for help. That's all."

Joe nodded but said nothing further. He stood, looking at Peter a moment longer, then turned to walk back up the path. It was then that both shadows noticed that a third person had entered the garden. It was George.

"I'll give you your answer before you ask," the old doctor said. "My answer is still no, thank you."

"I wasn't going to ask you again," Peter explained. "You've made your feelings clear to me many times."

"I'm glad," George replied. "The older I get, the greater the temptation. But, no."

Peter nodded. He watched as Joe left, quietly greeting George on the way out of the garden. The old man, his closest surviving friend, approached slowly. His age had begun to wear on him far more in the past few months than ever before. When he reached the bench, George sat without preamble.

"I don't like being old, Peter," he grumbled.

"Then why—"

"There are so many things that the young do not understand," George continued. "The older I get, the clearer things become to me. Pain is a lesson. Age is an entire study in loss. I understand life a bit more with each day that passes."

Peter looked away a moment. The subject of his friend's inevitable death, however tangentially they might touch upon it, never failed to disturb him.

"And what if you don't live long enough to understand it completely?" Peter asked.

"Well of course I won't," George said, his surprise genuine. "I won't really understand it until I'm gone. But I suspect that you . . . I'm sorry, but I'm not sure your kind could ever possibly understand it. That's why it frightens me so."

Peter laughed. "Did you come out here to cheer me up?" he asked incredulously.

"Apparently not," George said, allowing a smile to creep across his wrinkled features.

"Actually, I came out to tell you that Nikki is up and around, and I think you ought to see her. She has a lot of questions, and unless we're to turn her out of the convent—which might be very dangerous for her—I think you'd better be the one to answer those questions," he explained.

Peter nodded slowly, then winced and reached up to his temple yet again.

"Peter?" George asked. "What is it?"

"Nothing, really," Peter replied. "Probably just stress. That's the answer for everything these days, isn't it? I'm just not feeling very well."

"Not feeling—How long have you felt ill?" George asked, his concern obvious.

Peter understood. Shadows, vampires, whatever you wanted to call them, didn't get sick. Well, silver poisoning might make a shadow slightly ill, but not really sick. Other than that, their control over their cellular structure prevented illness.

But something was wrong with him, and Peter had no idea what it might be. All he knew was that his entire body felt strange, and achy, as if there were changes taking place without his knowledge. Which was impossible, of course. That control was what made them what they were.

"It's passing now," Peter lied. "I'm sure I'll be fine."

George frowned and watched him closely, but Peter ignored his friend's scrutiny. If the feeling intensified, then Peter would work with George to investigate its origins. But right now, the threat of internecine war amongst the shadows was imminent. And Rolf's disappearance made that threat seem all the closer.

"Let me know if it returns," George said grumpily.

Peter agreed. George didn't believe him, that much was obvious. But they'd been friends for many years, and George didn't push.

In a shared, silent moment, they sat back and looked at the sky, at the gardens, and the high stone walls of the Ursuline convent's interior courtyard. It was the oldest building in the entire Mississippi Valley, though beautifully restored. There hadn't been nuns there for one hundred and seventy-seven years, but it had served many other purposes over the years. When the American Catholic bishops had abandoned what remained of the Roman church six years earlier, the building had been seized by the state as a historical monument. It had cost Peter more than fifty million dollars to purchase it, but between Charlemagne and Kuromaku, he had raised the money without difficulty.

He made them an offer they couldn't refuse, and his shell corporation had even promised to keep the convent's appearance up, as befit a historic building. In a way, it was a deal for the Louisiana legislature. They no longer had to finance the care of the structure, but tourists could still gawk as they walked by. Few cared much for its religious value after the way the church had fallen apart.

Peter inhaled the scent of lilacs again.

"Have you considered the irony of this place as our chosen headquarters?" he asked George.

"It occurred to me the first day," George admitted. "But I was reluctant to point it out because it's only a perceived irony. Actually, I find it quite appropriate in a way."

Peter looked sidelong at him.

"You're an extraordinary man, Dr. Marcopoulos."

"I might say the same of you, Mr. Octavian," George said.

"You might?" Peter asked archly.

"I might," George teased, smiling wickedly.

Peter's thoughts went back to the woman, Nikki. He stood, ran a hand through his close-cropped hair, and offered George his hand to help the old man stand.

"I think I'll sit for a while. It's very peaceful out here."

"All right. I'm going to see if I can't find our Miss Wydra," Peter announced.

"It's about time you noticed another woman," George noted.

"She sings beautifully," Peter observed.

"So you've said. Quite a few times."

"Well, she does."

---------------- * ----------------

4

The secrets of eternity—
We've found the lock and turned the key.

—DON HENLEY,
"Building the Perfect Beast"

AS THE PLANE CIRCLED ABOVE JFK INTERNA-
tional Airport, will cody scratched his beard and stared
down at the lights of New York and felt a terrible dread
begin to overwhelm him. Unless Rolf checked in, there was
just no way they were going to find him in a city the size
of New York without telepathic contact. If he was even still
in New York.

If he was even still alive.

Will had his doubts about that.

"It'll be all right," Allison said, clutching his hand as
the plane descended. She didn't like to fly. "You'll see,"
she promised. "It really will."

He didn't answer at first. But when she held his hand
tighter and shook it a bit to get his attention, Will finally
turned to face her, brow furrowed with worry.

"No," he said softly. "No, honey, I'm sorry but I don't
think it will. Until Rolf disappeared, I was pretty successful
in ignoring it, dancing around the truth. Now it's hard not

to see what's coming. We may live through it, but with their numbers so much greater than ours, I just don't see how we can even hope it will turn out all right.''

Will expected a snappy riposte. Some kind of tart rejoinder that would put him in his place, tell him he was simply being a pessimist, offer him some kind of faith that their love and determination would be enough to get them through.

Allison said nothing.

They stayed that way, in silence, until the plane had landed.

JFK was quieter than usual. But of course it was. It was after dark, and so few people were willing to fly into or out of New York after nightfall that airlines had actually eliminated most of those flights. On the other hand, Will thought, hotels near the airport were probably doing great business.

He and Allison had only carry-on bags, so they didn't have to bother with waiting at baggage claim. After the initial wait to get off their plane, they moved quickly through the airport, following the signs for ground transportation. They'd rented a Toyota from Avis, despite the fact that Will didn't have much of an idea how to even begin searching for Rolf. Never mind where he was going to park in Manhattan.

It occurred to him, then, that there was probably a lot more parking in New York these days. And a lot of empty apartments. People were moving out in a rapid exodus, according to the media reports. And nobody was moving in. One poll suggested that in another year's time, Manhattan would be a ghost town.

Will didn't believe for even a moment that it was going to take that long. Hannibal wouldn't wait a year. Of the ten or twelve cities around the world that his clan was feeding on, New York was clearly suffering the greatest number of attacks. It made a kind of sense, though. Up until recently, the city had had the highest concentration of human beings in America.

His boots clicked on the terminal floor, echoed along the corridor. Up ahead, Will could see the Avis sign burning red. There were only two people behind the counter. The night shift probably stayed through until morning, Will realized. It would be safer than going out at night, though not much.

In addition to the two Avis employees, there was an elderly couple at the counter. They were angry that neither of the employees was willing to take them out to the parking lot to show them *exactly* where their rental car was parked.

"Lady," one of the employees snapped, "you can stand here and shriek at me all night if you want. No way in hell am I going out there. My advice is, take a long nap right here. When the sun comes up, I'll carry you out to your car on my back if you like. But until then, forget about it."

Will let out a breath and shook his head slowly.

"I knew it was bad . . ." he began.

"But you never realized how bad," Allison finished for him. "Me either."

"Will?" a voice said from up ahead.

He scanned the Avis waiting area. For the first time he noticed a petite brunette woman, a girl really, sitting in the shadows near the restroom doors. Will blinked, but it only took him a moment to realize who it was.

"Erika?" he asked, incredulously.

"Oh, thank God," Allison sighed, and Will shared her sentiments.

Together, they rushed forward. Will threw his arms around Erika, and the vampire girl returned his embrace. She was smiling broadly, her relief just as plain as his own.

"I don't understand," Will said. "I'm thrilled to see you—we didn't even have any idea where to begin to look. But how did you know to meet us here?"

The smile disappeared from Erika's face; she fell into a

dark, grim expression, her eyes downcast. Will backed up a step, surprised by the sudden change.

"Well, you had to come, didn't you?" Erika said, something like grief in her tone. "When Rolf dropped off your radar, we knew you'd be coming. It was easy enough to hack the airline computers and search for Allison's name and your many pseudonyms."

Will still stared at Erika. He was tense now. There was a danger here, and he didn't quite understand the feeling. Erika was one of them, but it was almost as if this wasn't Erika at all.

Allison didn't see it.

"Well, I for one am just happy you figured it out," she was saying. "I don't want to spend any more time here than necessary. It's like New York is one big game reserve for Hannibal's vampires."

While Allison spoke, Erika paid no attention to her. The vampire girl's eyes were on Cody. When he was alive, truly alive, he'd trusted everyone. It had led to a less than glorious death. He'd passed on after losing everything he had because of his great debts and bad business deals. He'd been too nice a guy, too trusting, too willing to help.

Death had taught him.

"Where's Rolf, Erika?" he asked, taking another step back.

For the first time, Allison noticed the tension that had descended among them. She glanced up at Will, saw something in his eyes, and took a step away from Erika herself.

"Will?" she asked. "What is—"

"Rolf?" Erika interrupted. "Well fuck, Will, I figured you already knew. He's dead."

"Jesus!" Allison said, bringing a hand to her mouth. "How?"

Will just watched Erika. Her face was calm, almost amused. But there was a pain in her eyes. He didn't understand the dichotomy.

"Very dead, actually," Erika continued. "Two silver

bullets in the head, execution style. Hannibal has a fondness for Martin Scorsese movies, apparently. Wants to track Scorsese down and turn him, I think.''

Erika's eyes twitched left, toward the Avis counter across the hall. That decided it for Will. He spun, grabbed Allison, and got her moving away from Erika instantly. He gave her a shove, propelling her along the corridor so that she nearly fell, blond hair tumbling over her face. But she didn't fall, and that was the key.

''Run!'' he roared.

Allison had been through enough with him not to argue. She ran.

In the torn jeans she'd had on the night before and a Tulane University sweatshirt she'd borrowed from Peter's closet, Nikki Wydra stood and stared out the bedroom window. She hugged herself tightly, partly because it was a bit chilly in the convent, and partly because she was scared.

Not terrified, though she might well have been. But scared and excited and anxious all at once. She looked at the lights of New Orleans in the distance and realized that the safety it had once represented to her was an illusion. Not completely, of course. But if George was telling the truth, and she had no reason to think he was lying, that meant that nobody was safe.

A civil war between vampires. Oh, my God, she thought, what that could mean. The horror of such a thing was almost unthinkable. But the world had survived the unthinkable before.

Nikki thought about Reggie, who'd hired her to work at Old Antoine's to begin with. And Pepper, her best friend from high school. She'd had a fight with Pepper two years ago and had spoken with her only once since then. She thought about her father, Craig, who'd taken early retirement and moved to La Jolla, California, to relax and ''watch the waves come in and the girls go by,'' he'd said.

As terrifying as the evening news had become, for them

and most of the other people Nikki cared about it was no more real, no more a threat to their own existence than a war in some third world country.

They had no idea. Just from the little George Marcopoulos had told her, Nikki had a sense that unless something changed dramatically, this horrible civil war and its aftermath were going to be just the beginning to a much darker world.

That was the irony. She was in the enemy camp. The convent was filled with vampires, shadows, whatever they called themselves. And yet, she felt profoundly that she was safer here than almost anywhere else in the world. Certainly safer than out on the streets of New Orleans tonight. The previous night's events had already shown that the more savage tribe of vampires was beginning to cross over into what she presumed was Peter Octavian's territory.

As she thought of his name, she hugged herself again and glanced around his bedroom. One wan light was all she had to keep the darkness at bay, but even in the dim illumination it cast, the room felt comfortable. Its decoration was Spartan, but warm.

Human.

That was what had taken her off guard at first, and again when she'd woken just before dark. It was the bedroom of a man with good taste and simple needs. But a man, without question. It was not the lair of some blood-ravenous monster, stalking the night. On the bedside table were several items she hadn't noticed before: an antique silver hairbrush, a small photograph of an attractive blond woman, and a hardcover book, *The Life of Sir Arthur Conan Doyle.*

A man.

Behind her, someone began to sing.

"Come on, into my kitchen . . ."

Nikki turned, startled, and stumbled slightly against the window. Fortunately, it didn't break. Peter Octavian stood in the doorway, leaning against the frame, his eyes closed as he sang softly. Badly.

"It's going to be raining outdoors," he finished.

Nikki stared.

Peter opened his eyes and his mouth stretched into the same lopsided grin that had attracted her at the club. He really was a handsome man. His hair and goatee were cropped close and gave him a look that was both rugged and somehow neat. He was tall and thin, but still muscular. For the first time, she noticed his eyes. They were a stunning green, a deep, almost artificial color that she'd never seen before. They couldn't be real, she thought. Maybe contacts . . . or maybe just whatever Octavian wanted them to be.

"You're still afraid," he said matter-of-factly, and the grin went away.

She wanted it back.

"No," she said quickly, snapping out of the defensive stance she had unconsciously taken, straightening up, trying to loosen up and failing miserably.

"Yes," she admitted. "Yes, I'm afraid."

"You'd have to be a fool or a little crazy not to be," Peter said gravely. "But I promise you, Nikki, as long as you're here with us, you'll be safe."

She stared at him still, unable to respond. Nikki wanted to take offense at his so intimate use of her name. But that would be foolish. It was the dawn of the twenty-first century. Nobody called each other Mr. and Mrs. anymore. Nobody under fifty. But coming from him, it sounded so . . . personal. Nikki realized she liked it.

"May I come in?" he asked.

"Oh," she said nervously, "I mean, of course you can. It's your room, isn't it?"

Nikki let her auburn hair fall across her eyes, hiding behind her long mane a moment. It was a habit of hers. But she'd spent enough time hiding as a girl, and had vowed years ago to stop. She tilted her head back, letting the hair fall to her shoulders and meeting Peter's gaze with all the strength she could muster.

He stepped into the room, and she had a moment to think about that old myth, the one about vampires having to be invited into a home. But that was foolish. This was Peter's own room.

"I . . . borrowed your sweatshirt," she said, at a loss for anything else.

"It looks nice on you," he said.

She wanted to snicker, to think of it as the kind of bullshit line guys just couldn't help but spout. But coming from Peter, it seemed different. He meant it. How he could think the baggy sweatshirt did anything for her appearance was beyond her, but maybe when you lived forever, your standards changed.

Nikki actually laughed, then caught herself, brought a hand to her mouth.

"I'm sorry," she said, smiled again, then shook her head as if she could shake it away.

"Not at all," Peter said. "I'm glad you can laugh. Sometimes it isn't easy. Laughter is a gift."

He came further into the room, and this time Nikki didn't feel the urge to withdraw. Peter sat down in a black wooden chair, where George had been sitting earlier. He leaned back, comfortably, as if he spent a lot of time in that chair.

Nikki sat on the edge of the bed, both feet on the ground. She'd never been so aware of the distance separating her from another person. It was like being in the room with a nuclear bomb, she thought. Not that it was going to explode, but that it had the potential to destroy her in an instant. Still, such feelings were at war inside her with other, more curious thoughts and emotions.

Peter's presence made her feel safe. His easy smile and natural confidence were winning, attractive.

"I'm told you have some questions I should answer," he said. "George seems concerned that you might run off and get into trouble. Unfortunate as it may be, and I'm sorry because it's mostly my fault, Tsumi will probably be watching for you."

"Run off?" Nikki repeated. She glanced out the window at the lights of New Orleans again. Thought of Tsumi and the other vampires from the club. "Not much chance of that," she said. "I don't know what I'm going to do, where I'm going to go, but I'm starting to think the farther from a major city I can get, the better chance I have of staying alive."

Peter leaned forward now, fingers stroking his goatee as he looked at her intensely. It made her uncomfortable, but in a way, she liked it also.

"You're wise to want to leave," Peter told her. "But I want you to know that you're welcome to stay here as long as you like. We're a family here. We call it a coven, but that's only to illustrate the ties that bind us. You'll be protected as long as you're here."

"I'm kind of used to protecting myself," Nikki said, surprising herself with the tiny sting of angry pride in her voice.

Peter smiled. "Of course. I can see that. But the world is changing, and I thought you should know what we're about here."

"What are you about?" she asked.

"Living," he replied simply. "Surviving. Trying to live with what we are, trying to stop the vampires from killing us, or from spreading any further. We've done a poor job of that, I'm afraid."

"Vampires," she said, chewing her lip slightly. "I understand, and I think I can even accept, that your people here aren't like the rest. But I guess what I don't understand is why."

Peter smiled again.

"I'm not sure you'll believe me," he said.

"I think I've got a pretty open mind," she said, gesturing to indicate the room around them, the convent itself, and the indisputable truth of its residents. "Try me."

So he told her. About the first vampire, a claim that challenged her childhood faith, but made a great deal of sense.

About a war with the Catholic church that lasted nearly two thousand years. About the Venice Jihad, and how for a time even the most savage of shadows were forced to behave with the spotlight of the world's media shining down on them. And about Hannibal, and his quest to return to the past. To the terror and the dark mythology of another age.

"And no matter how badly the U.N. and the president want to destroy us all, they can hardly be expected to track and kill a race of beings who can be literally anything," he said.

Nikki only stared at him.

"What about you?" she asked. "Tell me more about yourself."

"My father was the last emperor of Byzantium," Peter said proudly. "Though he never acknowledged having sired me. The night before Constantinople fell to the Turks, I met a man, a shadow, who offered me a way to have vengeance upon the enemy. They wouldn't be able to kill me, he promised. But I could kill hundreds, thousands of them.

"How could I say no?"

Peter held his hands up, a small, sad smile on his face, as if part of him regretted that decision of long ago.

"History was never my best subject. What year was that?" Nikki asked. When the answer came, she wasn't prepared for it.

"1453."

"Fourteen . . ." She put a hand to her forehead and let her hair fall in front of her eyes again. "I don't think I can handle this after all."

"Actually," Peter said, "I think you're doing remarkably well. I suppose when a person's life is in danger, it becomes a lot easier to accept the incredible."

"I'd like to know more," Nikki said, surprised at her curiosity—and at her own candor. "About you. About all of you, but about your own personal history as well."

"Anything you like," Peter replied. "But it's past nine

o'clock, and you really haven't eaten anything since last night. Why don't we have dinner first? I know a little place just off Jackson Square with the greatest jambalaya in town, and they do these Creole boiled potatoes that are amazing.''

Nikki blinked several times. "Are you . . . ?" she began, but let the question go unfinished. "Never mind," she said. "Just, uh, give me a few minutes, okay?"

"When you're ready, I'll be in the foyer," he replied.

Peter had already turned to go, flashing her a smile, when Nikki called his name.

"Hmm?"

"Why are you being so nice to me?" she asked. "I mean, you saved my life, but that doesn't make you responsible for me. There are a lot of people in this city who could use your help. So why . . . I guess, why me?"

Peter cocked his head slightly to one side. He stood with one hand on the door frame, about to leave. After a moment, he raised his eyebrows and looked over at her.

"I love your voice," he said softly. "The way you sing, the way you talk. You have a kind of weary wisdom, a warmth and humor that somebody your age has no right to. It's extremely . . . provocative. I hope you don't mind my saying so."

Nikki didn't reply.

Peter shrugged a bit, his smile twisting further, a bit of irony there.

"You asked," he said. Then he turned and left.

In the rush of confusion that filled her in his absence, Nikki was surprised to find herself blushing.

"We're not going about this the right way," Joe said suddenly.

He stood just outside the Café du Monde at the edge of Jackson Square. Kevin was there, and he reached out to rest his right hand on Joe's shoulder then, trying to alleviate his lover's frustration, or at least to share it. Joe offered a weak smile, but shook his head at the same time. He was at a loss.

They had searched all day, with a much larger group. After dark, they'd split up into teams of four, trying to scout the major tourist spots. It was only logical that Tsumi and any other of Hannibal's clan who had arrived in New Orleans would hunt in the most highly populated areas.

"No, we're using logic," Stefan said. "It made sense that they'd hide out in the warehouse district during the day, and it makes sense to search for them in the Quarter now."

Rachel shook her head. "No, I don't think so," she said.

Stefan glared at her. He didn't like her at all, Joe knew that. She'd been a volunteer until a few weeks ago. She was the youngest shadow in the coven, and there were times when she did appear a bit too gung ho even for Joe. But she was smart, and fast, and reliable in a fight. Had been, even when she was still human. They needed more like Rachel, and Joe wasn't about to let her overconfidence make him forget that.

"Go ahead, Rachel," Joe prompted. "What do you think we're missing?"

"Well," she said, obviously enjoying the attention, "warehouses and the basements of abandoned buildings make a certain amount of sense. Even clubs, which are closed during the day, I can understand. But when you really think about it, with this obsession Hannibal has with the old myths, with the trappings of the legendary vampire, there's one place we haven't discussed. I suppose because it wouldn't have occurred to any of *us.*"

They looked at one another. Joe frowned, not understanding right away. Rachel smiled, waiting for them to get it, and for once Joe agreed with Stefan. Her cockiness was a bit annoying.

It was Kevin who got her point first.

"Of course!" he snapped, scowling instead of pleased.

"We should have thought of it today. It won't help us much now until morning."

"What?" Stefan asked grumpily.

"Why, cemeteries, of course!" Kevin replied excitedly. "They're laying around in coffins or crypts or some silly bullshit like that!"

At first, Joe wanted to shake his head, to say that was only one possibility. But the more he thought about it, the more he examined internally what he knew of Hannibal's philosophy, the more sense it made.

"All right, then, smart girl," he said, smiling at Rachel. "Which cemetery?"

"Well, where would you want to be if you were hunting?" she asked.

"Close to the action," Stefan replied.

"St. Louis number one," Joe said aloud.

It had to be. Rachel was correct. Tsumi and her crew would want to be as near as possible to the highest concentration of humans. That would be the French Quarter, of course. And St. Louis Cemetery number one was at the far outer edge of the Quarter, on Basin Street.

"Let's go," Joe said. "Maybe some of them are still there."

"Right," Kevin agreed. "Or they might bring a 'date' back there for a quick bite."

Joe frowned and looked over at Kevin. He was relieved to see that, despite the play on words, his lover was merely being sarcastic, not actually finding humor in their situation. Their relationship was young enough that they were still finding out new things about each other every day. Yet with Kevin, he hadn't been disappointed yet. It kind of scared him.

The four shadows were silent as they descended upon St. Louis Cemetery number one. They moved across the street in a dark wave, blending with the night, and each kept his or her own counsel. In the event that there were still members of Hannibal's clan at the cemetery, they didn't want the vampires to have any warning of their arrival.

Like all the local burial grounds, the corpses in St. Louis number one weren't actually buried. Instead, the cemetery itself was like a miniature stone city, with row after row of granite and marble crypts, inside of which coffins would be laid on the ground or stacked on top of one another, depending upon how large the family had been.

Hundreds of crypts. And a long stone wall, with sealed "doors," six high and an infinite number of corpses wide, where those who could not afford crypts would lay shoulder to shoulder until the apocalypse, or until the stone crumbled away untended. Whichever came first.

Somewhere, not far from the entrance if the guidebooks were to be believed, was the grave of Marie Laveau, the legendary voodoo queen of New Orleans. Having seen more than his share of real magick, Joe had a healthy wait-and-see attitude toward voodoo. But so far, the coven had had no contact with voodoo or its practitioners, and certainly not with the supposedly immortal queen of them all.

With Rachel and Kevin on his left and Stefan on his right, Joe stepped deeper into the cemetery. There was a long aisle in front of them that ran off deep into the darkness. It was the path obviously most traveled by tour guides and their charges during the day. It didn't make sense that Tsumi and the others would have broken into a crypt where their vandalism could so easily be discovered.

"Kevin," Joe whispered, breaking their silence.

The other three shadows gathered around him. Joe glanced around nervously, and had a strange flash of his childhood, when he and his friends would run in a neighborhood cemetery at night. Even though they knew that ghosts and ghouls and vampires didn't really exist—and what an irony there—they couldn't help but be a bit frightened anyway.

In a way, Joe realized, children's fears were far more practical than their parents' weary confidence that such things were merely fantasy. But then, the whole world had learned that lesson six years ago. The terrors of childhood would never again be so easily brushed aside.

Joe glanced around the cemetery again, but he sensed nothing, saw nothing, and he could tell that the others felt the same way.

"We'll split up," he whispered. "Rachel and I will take to the air. Stefan, you and Kev walk through. Try to determine which section of the cemetery is least traveled."

Each of the others nodded in assent. Joe glanced at Rachel.

"Pigeons?" she asked.

"Right," Joe agreed. "Nice and inconspicuous."

With Rachel at his side, Joe began to change. His body warped and twisted painfully and, somehow, its mass disappeared into the air around them and he became a fat, dirty pigeon. Together, they took flight, soaring up and over the cemetery.

From above, Joe saw Stefan and Kevin begin to run soundlessly through the darkness, scouting the cemetery. It wasn't long before Joe determined that the northwest corner of the cemetery seemed to be in the greatest disrepair, and therefore was probably the least visited. Other than their two fellow shadows, neither he nor Rachel saw anything moving on the ground.

After less than two minutes in the air, Joe banked to one side and flew toward that crumbling northwest corner of St. Louis number one. He changed before he even reached the ground, dropping the last several yards as a man. His boots thumped softly on the dead earth. Behind him, he heard Rachel groan a bit as she changed. She wasn't used to the pain. Not yet.

Sure enough, less than twenty feet from where they landed, a crypt had been vandalized. Its door was unsealed, the top edge shattered, and was leaning against the interior of the doorway. A cursory examination might overlook it as just another example of deterioration, but this was definitely something more purposeful.

"Here," he whispered to Rachel and moved toward the crypt.

"Shouldn't we wait for the others?" she hissed from behind him.

Joe shook his head. More than likely, Tsumi and the other vampires were hunting out in the city proper. Their best bet, the way he saw it, was to confirm that this was their lair, and then simply wait them out. After they'd all gone inside, and the sun had come out, that would be the time to take them. Hannibal's warriors were legion but the superstitions he encouraged made them, generally speaking, easier prey. Particularly during the day.

Yes, Joe thought, it would be best if they watched, and waited, until morning. Their advantage would be substantial then, even over greater numbers. But first, he had to make completely certain this was indeed their hiding place.

Silent as the tombs that surrounded him, Joe moved up to the dark entrance to the vandalized vault. Where the door leaned against the inside of the frame, there was a gap through which he could see nothing but darkness. He edged closer, reached a hand out to run his fingers over the shattered upper edge of the door. He would have to move it aside to get a better look inside. But he knew he would need to do it quietly.

Behind him Rachel tapped a foot impatiently.

"Relax," he whispered. "We'll be out of here in a—"

The granite door fell back into the tomb and shattered across the top of a metal casket inside. For a moment, Joe was so stunned he simply stood, blinking, with his mouth open. He hadn't disturbed the door enough for it to have fallen in.

There was another sound behind him. A wet, dripping sound.

As he began to turn, something flashed in front of his eyes. Pain ratcheted from his chest all through his body.

Something horribly jagged and painful tore into his back, severing his spine, and Joe crumpled to the ground.

He tried to will himself to change to mist, or flame, or something with wings. He had to escape. He had to . . .

Joe Boudreau saw the long silver dagger protruding from his heart, and his eyes widened. From the darkened crypt stepped a heartbreakingly beautiful Asian woman who could only have been Tsumi, the vampire Peter had sent them to hunt for.

But it was they who were hunted.

Tsumi glanced at him, tsked, and looked past him. Joe did his best, as darkness swept over him, to crane his head around to see what she was looking at.

A huge, naked man, with long blond hair and beard like a Viking, stood on the damp cemetery ground covered in blood. At his feet, in a spray of hair, was Rachel's head. Behind him her body lay on its side, and Joe thought he could see a large, dark hole in her chest.

The naked Viking was eating her heart.

"The new ones are always the tastiest," the Viking grunted, blood and pulpy muscle on his chin and teeth.

Joe wanted to weep for Rachel, but could think only of himself. And of Kevin; of the incredible softness of his black skin. Kevin and Stefan were still out there in the cemetery. What was to become of them? He had to help them. Pushing the darkness away, he focused his mind, ignored the pain, and felt the change begin to come over him.

Fire. That's what he would be. Burning flame that would scorch them all, razing them from the Earth.

Then Tsumi took a second silver knife and castrated him. Joe screamed, and in the raging red haze of pain, he saw a swarm of vampires appear from the darkness around the tombs. They descended on him, fangs and silver blades flashing.

---- ✳ ----

5

*In a sky full of people, only some want to fly.
Isn't that crazy?*

—Seal,
"Crazy"

CODY AND ERIKA FACED EACH OTHER IN A standoff that was quicker than a heartbeat. He'd given Allison a shove and sent her running in the opposite direction.

Erika was one of them, part of Peter's coven, and had been Rolf's lover for nearly a year. But Will wasn't taking any chances with the life of the only person who really meant anything to him.

His own voice, when he'd shouted for Allison to run, still echoed in the corridor. He could hear the soles of her shoes slapping tile. Erika's smile grew even wider and her eyes flicked again to Cody's right, to the Avis car rental counter he knew was just behind him. There'd been an elderly couple there a moment ago, and a pair of customer service agents behind the counter.

He didn't turn, though.

He didn't want to take his eyes off Erika.

Until he heard the rasping voice snarl, "Go after her!"

Then he had to look. The two employees, a man and a

woman, had died silently; their necks hung at odd angles where they lay across the counter. The elderly couple were elderly no longer. The female had shifted her form, become a perfect-complexioned, tall black woman. The other, the one who'd spoken, was a huge, bald man whose narrowed eyes spoke of murder, and meant it.

He stood his ground while the black woman set off after Allison. Will moved to intercept her and was brought up short as fingers like metal spikes dug into his shoulder and spun him around.

"No," Erika said, unsmiling.

"Hannibal wants you, Cody," said the bald vampire.

"I reckon Hannibal can fuck himself," Will snarled.

Behind him, Allison screamed. Will winced, ignored Erika's talons where they tore into his shoulder, and forced her to move with him as he turned around. The tall, black vampire woman had Allison.

By the hair, pulled back taut and tearing, her eyes screaming for help in a way she was too strong and proud to allow her throat to do. Her throat was exposed, skin stretched and ripe. The vampire woman was licking Allison's throat, her long pink tongue unnaturally distended as it ran along the neck to the jawbone and up to the ear. She bared her fangs and scraped them along Allison's earlobe, drawing blood. Allison squeezed her eyes closed, and a solitary tear appeared.

The vampire kept her eyes on Will's during this entire process. Even when she twisted Allison's body to lick her tongue across his lover's lips, the vampire woman stared at Cody, taunting, defying him to do something. To take some kind of action.

Will turned away. He stared back at Erika now, his heart grown cold as he watched her eyes, tried to decipher what it was he saw there. After a moment, he realized it didn't matter. Maybe she was in conflict over what was happening, maybe she wasn't, but he was certainly not going to expect any help from her. He stared at her hand where it still gripped his shoulder, and she released him. Perhaps she realized that she couldn't have held him long against his will. Perhaps she simply knew that she had him.

They had him.

"Don't hurt her," he said grimly.

"Beautiful," the bald vampire said off to his right, his voice echoing along the tile corridor. "He's begging now. Amazing what sex will do to a man. Even a dead man."

But Erika stared right into Will's eyes and she knew the bald vamp had it figured wrong.

"That wasn't a plea, it was a warning," she said. "Colonel Cody here was telling us what's what, weren't you, Will?"

"That's right, you traitorous bitch," Will said evenly. "Now, what do you want?"

"Vlad told you already," the black woman snarled behind him, and he heard Erika whimper. This time, Cody didn't turn to see how Allison was. He didn't want to know. It would only make what was to come more difficult. "Hannibal wants to see you," the black girl continued. "Just come with us, and your little human twat here won't get herself hurt. Though, she is pretty tasty."

He ignored that.

"Vlad?" Will asked and smiled. He turned to the bald vampire. "That's your name?"

Then he started to laugh. Long and hard. Erika raised her eyebrows, and Will heard a gasp behind him. From the Avis counter, Vlad roared and took three stalking steps toward Will. His face became distended, jaw becoming snout; his ears began to point as hair sprouted all over his body.

"Don't push me, cowboy," Vlad growled.

"Vlad," Erika warned. "Hannibal gave specific instructions."

"Yes, Vlad," Will teased, his mind moving away from the comfortable midwestern twang of his youth to a harder, more cynical language he knew all too well.

"You don't want to piss off your master, Vlad. What the

hell kind of name is that, anyway? Is Hannibal just taking every vampire wannabe in America, or only the ones with stage names?''

"Will, stop it!" Erika shouted at him. "You want to save Allison's life, you come with us now!"

But she was too late. Vlad was going to snap any second. Will was certain of it—and it was just what he wanted. If he stayed and fought, Allison was dead for certain. And if he gave himself up, they would have gotten what they needed from her and, there again, she was certain to be killed. There was only one way to give her a respite, to buy some time for Allison—and for himself. Because without her, he might as well be dead.

"Come with you?" Will asked. "Okay, but surely *Vlad* must have some neo-gothic teenybopper rave thing to go to? Somewhere people will be impressed by him?"

The huge vampire had transformed himself into a true wolf-man, a savage, slavering thing walking on its hind legs. His eyes burned red, and they grew even wider as Cody said this last.

Vlad lunged for him. Allison screamed.

"No, Vlad, wait!" Erika shouted and started forward to stop the huge werewolf from disobeying Hannibal's orders.

Too late.

Vlad was fast, Will had to give him that. But it was like an eight-year-old dealing with a toddler. Vlad still hadn't mastered the abilities that vampirism gave him. That was the handicap shared by most of Hannibal's followers. But not Erika. She was the one he had to watch.

As Vlad came for him, Cody burst into flame. The werewolf staggered through fire and cinder, its fur catching ablaze. Even as he passed, Will was coalescing again, becoming himself. Now he faced Vlad's staggering form from behind. With all his strength, he thrust a fist forward. Midstrike, it transformed into a stout, thick oak branch, carved to a point on the end. He drove it through Vlad's back and into his heart.

The wolf fell hard.

For a moment, Cody thought about going for Allison, trying to save her. He glanced to one side and saw that the tall, black woman still held her tight, only now her fingers were long yellow claws.

"Back off or she's dead!" the vampire woman screamed.

"No!" Erika shouted. "Not until he's with us!"

Will knew then. Erika had almost given him permission to do what he needed to do next. But it was the most difficult thing he'd ever had to do in his life.

On the tile floor, blood pooling beneath him, Vlad was already starting to stir. Will was displeased to note that the big vamp was built of sterner stuff than he'd imagined. Not much time.

"Will . . ." Erika said tentatively and reached out for him where he stood staring down at Vlad.

She didn't see it coming at all. But she was a traitor, and should have known better. Before Erika could react, before she could even conceive of what was going to happen, Will reached out and grabbed Erika's hand. He spun her around and ratcheted her arm painfully up behind her. She opened her mouth to speak.

With a roar and a burst of strength, Will Cody shoved Erika forward and ripped her right arm out of its socket. Her words turned to screams. Blood sprayed Will's face and the tile floor. Erika staggered forward and slammed into Vlad where he was trying to rise from the floor.

"Freeze right there or I do her, you crazy fucking bastard!" the black woman screamed in a panic.

Will knew he couldn't reach her before she killed Allison. There was only one thing he could do.

"I'll be back for you," he said, staring into Allison's terrified eyes, in a moment that would haunt him for the rest of his life. "I swear I will."

He turned and ran at the glass wall that separated corridor from parking lot. Will didn't bother shapeshifting. He crashed through the glass in an explosion of jagged shards. Then his feet were slamming pavement.

Fifteen steps, and he turned to mist. Floated up to the next parking level. When he re-formed, he didn't even look like Will Cody anymore. Will was gone.

Disappeared.

"My God, this is hot!" Nikki said, fanning her open mouth.

She speared a slice of cucumber smeared with French dressing from her salad and popped it into her mouth. It lay on her tongue, soothing.

"I thought you liked jambalaya," Peter said, a small grin on his face.

"I do," she said, mumbling past the cucumber as she chewed it, trying to swallow it quickly so that she could speak freely. "This is delicious, but it's hotter than I've had it anywhere else."

"I'm glad you like it," Peter replied.

Nikki glanced up at him a moment as if he were a madman, then she started to laugh. Several people turned to look at her, and she grew self-conscious. It was the kind of restaurant a tourist would never dare enter. Dark and aging like its staff, and yet, also like them, so much the soul of New Orleans. This was a place where the locals ate.

A moment after they'd glanced over at her, several people at one table locked eyes on Peter's face, then turned quickly away.

"They're afraid of you," she whispered.

"A little," Peter admitted, and she thought she detected a bit of sadness in his voice. "But they respect us as well. Those of the locals who realize that we're here at all understand what's going on. Many of them have offered to help. I think when more of Hannibal's followers join Tsumi here in New Orleans, even more people will come to help us. Humans are a fearful race, but almost always willing to fight for what is theirs, and for the ones they love.''

"Tsumi," Nikki said thoughtfully, letting her hair fall in front of her face to hide her fear. "Aren't you afraid she'll see you out tonight, attack you again?"

Peter nodded slowly. "I'm more afraid of what she might do to you, because she saw that I protected you. Or what she might do to any other innocent tonight. And the night after that. For myself, she can't really hurt me. I've been a shadow far longer than she, and I have other . . . abilities that she doesn't share.''

Nikki understood. She had seen Peter work some kind of horrible sorcery when he saved her life. But there seemed to be something in his tone which asked her not to pursue that subject.

"I take it she's an old girlfriend or something?" she asked.

"Or something," Peter replied. "We had different philosophies. It didn't work out. I actually got along far better with her brother when I met him for the first time. I haven't seen him in decades, but he's one of very few other shadows I've ever really trusted."

"What about Cody?" Nikki asked. "I've heard several people mention him. You and he are pretty good friends, right? What's he like?"

Peter chuckled. "Another time. You've had enough insane information to process today, I think."

"I'll be the judge of that, Mr. Octavian," Nikki said, eyebrows raised, flirting.

Flirting.

"Oh, Jesus," she said, and let her hair fall across her face again as she reached up to cover her eyes.

"What is it?" Peter asked.

But what could she say? For a moment there, she'd forgotten. She was fascinated by him, by all of it. She'd been flirting, had forgotten that he wasn't what he appeared to be.

"I'm sorry," she said after a moment. "I mean, I knew

there were vampires. I came to grips with that years ago. It became a part of everyday life for everybody . . . every human being on Earth. I talked to this drummer I used to jam with, an old guy, and he said it was kind of like living during the Cold War, when they thought the Russians were going to attack with nukes at any second. Knowing vampires were out there was a lot like that, he told me.

"But knowing it and living it are two different things. I mean, they tried to . . . tried to kill me last night. You have to understand how weird this all is to me."

"Believe me, I do," Peter said gently. "People deal with it a lot of different ways. Violence, humor, denial . . . terror, of course. It's okay."

"You don't get it," Nikki argued. "For a second, it almost felt like this was, you know, an actual date."

Peter had been leaning forward, a warm smile on his face. Now he sat back, blinking, and glanced away. His smile changed, became ironic, self-deprecating.

"It isn't?" he asked, and made a silly face. "How foolish of me."

Nikki laughed uncomfortably.

"Listen, if you want to go, I'll—"

"No," she said quickly. "No, I'm sorry. Eat your dinner and I'll tell you my boring life story."

Peter relaxed and dug into his jambalaya, and Nikki spent all of ten minutes regaling him with tales of home and Mom and the blues.

"Not much of a life, especially in light of all you've experienced, but it's mine," she said when she was done.

"It sounds like a wonderful life," Peter told her. "I envy you, in a way. And I have sympathy, as well. If we're not able to stop Hannibal, these may seem like the good old days to you."

"Isn't that a fucking optimistic thought," Nikki said, laughing in disbelief at Peter's morbid sentiment. "I guess you're just going to have to make sure that doesn't happen."

Peter blinked.

"I guess you're right," he said simply.

They ate in a more comfortable silence for nearly a full minute. Nikki watched him eat, glanced away when he looked at her, tried to push the confused thoughts from her head. Tried to make sense of the danger, the horror, the attraction. Her old life was over, she knew that much. It had ended the moment Tsumi and her friends came into Old Antoine's the night before.

She made a decision then. She would stay at the convent, or go wherever else Peter's coven went. At least until Hannibal was destroyed and the world was safe again. The idea of being alone in the world, with predators in every shadow, did not appeal to her at all. No, she would stick with Peter. And she wasn't at all certain that fear for her own safety was the only motivation for her decision.

"Can I ask you a question?" she said, breaking the silence.

"Anything," Peter replied.

"Who's the blond on your bedside table?"

Peter raised his eyebrows.

"Now that sounds like a date question to me," he said.

"Does it bother you?" Nikki asked.

"Far from it," Peter replied. "Her name was Meaghan Gallagher. She was a lot of things, to a lot of people. To me . . . well, she was the last woman I took out for a nice, quiet dinner."

Nikki smiled, looked away. "I don't quite know how to respond to that," she admitted.

"You're not expected to," Peter said.

Then he grunted, low and surprised, and reached up to his forehead. The frown on his face spoke of pain and anger. Annoyance, most of all. In that moment, Nikki saw another part of Peter Octavian. His warm kindness was no mask, but it was hardly all he was made of. He'd been a warrior all his life, after all. Fought and killed and died and rose again to kill some more.

He was no saint.

Nikki found the danger in Peter Octavian startlingly attractive.

Peter grunted again and bent over slightly in his chair, massaging his temples with both hands.

"Peter, are you okay?" she asked.

"I'll be all right," he said grimly. "I've been getting these headaches. This one's the worst."

"Maybe we'd better go back," she suggested.

Peter nodded. He took a sip of water and signaled the waiter to bring the bill, paid in cash, and stumbled to his feet. Nikki found herself holding his arm and partially guiding him on their walk back toward the convent.

Drunken revelers burst from a bar on Rue Dumaine, and Nikki started in fear and stared at their faces, terrified she'd find a beautiful Japanese vampire woman among them.

With Peter almost staggering in pain, Nikki realized that she didn't feel safe at all. If he wasn't able to protect her, then being with him made her even more of a target. Part of her wanted badly to leave him to his own devices, to run and hide and forget all about the people, both living and dead, in the old Ursuline convent just a few blocks away.

But she stayed at his side, and walked him the rest of the way home. She owed him that much at least.

And, after all, she had nowhere else to go.

The entire French Quarter, and then some, separated St. Louis Cemetery number one from the old Ursuline convent where Peter Octavian's coven made their home. It had never seemed a long distance before. But as Kevin struggled against Stefan's powerful grip, the screams of his lover echoing across the cemetery toward them, it might as well have been the other side of the world.

"Kevin!" Stefan snapped. "We've got to go!"

"No!" Kevin roared, breaking free of Stefan's grasp.

Stefan reached for him again and clamped a crushing

hand down on Kevin's shoulder. Kevin spun and reached for him, his hand changing without any conscious thought, and tore deep, bloody furrows across Stefan's pale face. The other shadow snarled and clutched at the fresh wounds, but stopped. His face changed from pain and shock to fury. Stefan grabbed Kevin by the front of his shirt, hauled him up short.

"I know you loved him," Stefan said. "But there's nothing to be done for him now, not unless you want to throw your life away! You want to fight for him, you want vengeance? Fine! But it can't be right now! We've got to get back home, get reinforcements, tell the rest what's happening here! Don't be an asshole!"

Kevin snarled, his fangs elongating as he shoved Stefan away. He was going to retaliate, to strike out with a fury usually reserved for bigots. How could Stefan speak to him like this, he thought, while the laughter of the vampires and Joe's screaming could still be heard across the cemetery. Kevin's lover was in agony, and there was nothing . . .

Nothing.

The screaming had stopped.

No laughing either. Not a sound. Just the wind among the gray stone crypts. For the first time Kevin felt the warmth of the tears that streaked his cheeks, rich scarlet blood on ebony flesh.

"They're coming," Stefan said curtly.

For a moment all Kevin could do was watch in fascination as the wounds he'd slashed in Stefan's face closed by themselves, healing instantaneously.

Then he wiped the bloody tears from his face, glanced quickly around at the matrix of tombs that surrounded them, and something turned inside him. Turned cold. And dark. He drew himself up to his full height, a full four inches taller than Stefan.

"I'm sorry," Kevin said, without feeling.

Stefan nodded.

As if that were their cue, two slavering vampires cried

out from atop a nearby sepulchre, and then leaped down a
yard away from Stefan and Kevin. He knew they had to
leave, had to get word back to the others—Stefan had been
right about that, without question—but Kevin reveled in
the attack. Even as Stefan traded savage blows with the
other, Kevin turned toward the vampire closest to him.

The primal thing shrieked as it scrambled at him. These
two were no match for them, nothing more than watchdogs,
he suspected, like dobermans in the car dealership lot. But
they might buy the others time.

Kevin blazed into fire, and the vampire passed right
through him without slowing. When it turned, its hair was
ablaze. It didn't even bother trying to smother the flames.
It simply came for him again. Kevin sidestepped, over-
confident, and the thing raked his belly open with barely a
whisper, so sharp were its claws.

Enraged, he held his viscera in, forcing the wounds to
heal, even as the thing came at him again. His left hand
burst into flame. With it, he grabbed the savage vampire's
face and shot forward, feet barely touching the ground. He
slammed the vampire's skull into a marble crypt that had
an angel mounted on its roof, and heard a satisfying crack.
Skull or marble, he didn't know. Perhaps both.

His right hand transformed into a massive silver spike,
and Kevin punched it through the vampire's chest and
heart. He realized he was screaming, but what exactly he
was screaming he couldn't be certain. Blood flowed down
his cheeks once more, tears of rage and grief. He pounded
the silver spike that was his right hand into the vampire's
body over and over, heart and spine and groin and throat.
It writhed, still alive, until he spiked it through the skull,
let his right hand return to normal, wrapped his fingers
around the vampire's brain, and burned it to ashes.

As he backed away, the angel atop the crypt, unsettled
by the violence, slid another millimeter and then tumbled
down to shatter what remained of the vampire's corpse.

He heard applause. Turned to see that the vampires' plan

had worked. An attractive Asian female stood with a dozen or so others behind her. The woman must be Tsumi, he realized.

"Sima," Tsumi said to the huge warrior. "Kill them for me."

"Sorry, bitch," Stefan said, stepping up behind Kevin. "We're not staying."

Then Stefan grunted in pain, and Kevin spun to see a huge axe in the other shadow's skull. A huge, naked male, blond and bearded, with a ragged scar down his face, stood over Stefan and pulled the axe from his brain. It would take a few seconds before Stefan could recover, and by then he'd have been beheaded.

Kevin doubted more than a handful of vampires had the will to survive a beheading. Stefan wasn't one of them. He couldn't save Stefan, but Kevin knew his friend had been right. Kevin had a duty to the coven. Hate boiling up inside him like bile, he turned and threw off two vampires who had rushed at him, then spat his words at the Asian woman who commanded them.

"I'll be back for you, you little bitch," Kevin snarled.

Instantly, he transformed himself into a falcon. Part of him railed at his planned retreat, demanded he stay, for honor's sake. Bullshit. He would honor his love for Joe, and his fidelity to the coven, by doing what was right, what he should have done minutes ago.

Kevin pumped his wings, speeding over the lights of New Orleans. Over the French Quarter and toward the Mississippi River. Tsumi and the other vampires gave chase instantly, of course, but they were bound by their loyalty to Hannibal. They could only take certain forms, and of those forms, only bats could fly.

And there was no way even the largest bat could keep up with a falcon. It was just that kind of handicap which gave Kevin even a glimmer of hope for the future. But they'd have to take the battle to Hannibal soon, or it would be too late.

Kevin had never been vicious. Never been a warrior.

Now he'd been made one. And that bitch Tsumi, and Hannibal himself, would regret it.

Inside the chapel of the convent, which was bare but for the crucified Christ that still hung on the wall, George Marcopoulos stepped up onto the altar. He sat in a high-backed, hard wooden chair and faced the row of fifteen pews. George surveyed the seven faces that looked up at him in expectation. Black and white and Asian and Latin. Men and women.

All human, like him.

But unlike George, they were all young. He felt very, very old. Ironic, he thought. Yes, those gathered to listen to him speak were youthful, not one of them had yet reached forty years of age, but a great many of the other beings in the convent were far, far older than George. Older than George would ever grow to be.

In the way his eyes wouldn't quite focus anymore, in the way his hands shook ever so slightly, in the bone-deep ache that never really went away, in the late nights when sleep seemed as distant as his memories of youth—in all those things, George Marcopoulos felt death approaching. And despite the fact that immortality was offered to him nearly every day, he did not struggle or balk at the approach of death.

In death, he had every faith, he would see his Valerie again. He had seen with his own eyes proof of God's existence. Heaven waited, in some form or another, he believed. To George, the approach of death was as satisfying as sitting in a rocker on the front porch of his old vacation house in Maine, watching the sun drain away over the lake after a long day. His work was done. Soon, he would rest.

But not yet. Peter needed him, this one last time. And he would hold death itself at bay in order to stand with Peter in a time of need. This one last time.

"Thank you all for coming," George began. "I have

recently come from a meeting with Peter and have a great deal of disturbing news. I hope you will spread it to those of us who could not make it. We, the humans of this coven, are about to be faced with an extraordinarily difficult decision.''

He waited, scanning their faces. George knew, better than anyone, the fear and temptation that was about to confront them.

''The rest of the world remains ignorant of the real threat Hannibal and his vampire clans pose to our way of life. In their hatred of our kind, the leaders of the world have made cooperation impossible. You few, and those of your friends and family and acquaintances you have informed, are the only people on the face of this Earth who truly understand what we face.

''I feel sick at the very thought of it, but I have to tell you now that Peter doesn't think we can win,'' George said bluntly.

His words had the desired effect.

Horror.

''George, what de hell are you talkin' 'bout?'' demanded a broad-shouldered Cajun man George believed was named Dennis, or Denny.

''Yes, George, how can you even say that?'' asked Janine, a beautiful mulatto woman descended from the quadroons of New Orleans.

The controversy raged a moment. George did not interfere. He waited a full minute, then held up his hand, asking for silence without raising his voice. Conflict was not what he wanted, but he knew they needed time to vent their fears and anger.

''Let me finish, please,'' George said, and all seven faces turned toward him again.

''You're all, as always, perfectly welcome to leave at any time. You have joined us for your own reasons, and by your own will. No one will blame you if you decide to leave now,'' he promised.

"But human civilization is in jeopardy. Peter doesn't think we can win, that's true. At least, not without help," he said.

George glanced around the room, waiting for his words to sink in. For the understanding to begin. After a few moments, he noticed Janine drop her head to her hands and draw in a loud breath of realization.

"Mon Dieu," she whispered.

"Indeed," George replied, and she looked up at him, eyes wide.

"Peter has asked that all of you, and all of the other human members of the coven, and anyone else you know sympathetic to our fight, gravely consider the possibility of taking the Gift," he explained.

"Of dying, you mean?" Denny said, doubtful.

"Of living forever," corrected a thin Vietnamese man behind him.

"It's a horrible decision," George added. "Whatever your choice, you will always wonder if it was the right one. And nobody will be forced to pass into the life of shadows against their will."

"I don' want to be a vampire," Denny said tentatively.

"Neither do I," Janine said, "but I want to choose my own destiny. And having Hannibal decide whether I may live as a vampire or die as a human appeals to me even less."

"I will leave you to your decisions," George said, using the armrests of the chair to rise with a crackling of his old bones. "It would be best if you could decide within the next few hours. The final struggle could begin at any time."

At any time, George thought. *The end can come at any time.*

6

I'll tell you why baby's crying.
'Cause she's dying. Aren't we all?

—HARRY CHAPIN,
"Taxi"

THE MAN BEHIND THE WHEEL OF THE TAXI
stank of sweat and whiskey. He never looked in the rearview mirror, never spoke, just kept his eyes on Pontchar-
train Expressway as it unfolded in front of the vehicle and
was swallowed beneath it.

In the back of the taxi, Kuromaku sat in silence. His body
hummed with nervous energy, and he urged the car on with
his every thought. The dream, or vision, still lingered with
him. Of him fighting by Peter's side, and of Peter bleeding,
perhaps dying. In the dream, they had been in this city, the
city of New Orleans. But where, exactly, he was uncertain.

Kuromaku had amassed considerable wealth over the
centuries. He traded in antiquities, when he conducted any
business at all. It had been a simple thing to have his own
pilot fly him from Bordeaux to New Orleans. Even better,
it had been dark already, and as they were flying west, it
was still night when they landed. Six years ago, Kuromaku
had learned about the Venice Jihad the same way the rest

of the world had—from CNN. It was there that he first saw video of shadows, of his own kind, standing in the sunlight and surviving.

Two full years passed before he had the courage to try it himself. Though he now came and went as he pleased, Kuromaku was still far more comfortable sleeping during the day and conducting the rest of his life at night. However, in the past year, with the world on a vampire hunt, that had become more difficult. He'd had to take extra efforts to hide his true nature, far more than he had ever done.

So he had been pleased to arrive in the Crescent City just after three o'clock. The airport was quiet in the early morning hours. As he was a dealer in antiquities, the weapons posed only a small problem getting through American customs. But even those few minutes had seemed precious to him. For Kuromaku had no idea where to begin searching for Peter Octavian. None at all.

"There she is," the driver mumbled, almost incoherently.

Kuromaku glanced through the windshield, and the lights of downtown New Orleans and the French Quarter lifted his spirits a bit. Even at nearly four in the morning, the city was still alive. He'd been here decades earlier at a particular Mardi Gras when the world's shadows had migrated to the Big Easy along with human volunteers who'd known what they were and given up their blood, and often their lives, freely.

The Venice Jihad had changed all of that. The church had nearly been destroyed forever, and the shadows themselves freed from two thousand years of psychological conditioning. Free to live. But free to kill as well, without much fear of reprisal. Peter's great effort may have unintentionally begun a process that would destroy the human race.

In the silence of the early morning, the taxi turned slowly down Decatur Street. A short time later the driver turned left, and soon Kuromaku saw the facade of the Omni Royal

Orleans hotel just ahead. He couldn't very well search the streets at dawn. And if he needed a place to stay, why not the best hotel in the French Quarter?

Kuromaku smiled to himself. He'd softened a bit in the twentieth century. He knew that. He'd cut his long hair short and begun to favor business suits; though he told himself they were the costume of the twenty-first-century warrior, they never felt quite right. He'd grown tired of battle, and more and more fond of pretty things, exotic foods, and outrageous lovers. New Orleans was the city for him, then, he thought.

Suddenly he became angry with himself. He was thinking like a fool, soft and content. He'd come here for war, and the warrior he'd once been anticipated it with something akin to lust. He would slough off the softness of his wealth like dead flesh.

Kuromaku was taken aback to realize he was staring into the rearview mirror at the driver's eyes.

"Sir?" the man asked, obviously afraid he was responsible for Kuromaku's sudden change in demeanor.

Kuromaku might have said something to reassure him. He did not. The man was a boorish skunk, who risked his own life and the lives of any human passengers by drinking while on duty. To hell with him.

The taxi stopped in front of the Omni, and Kuromaku opened the door. The driver also got out and went round to the back of the vehicle to pop the trunk and remove his passenger's bags.

"New Orleans is quite a city," the driver said. "I hope you enjoy it, sir."

Bucking for a tip, Kuromaku thought. But then another thought entered his mind.

"You are from this city, then?" he asked.

"No, sir, but I've driven a cab here for goin' on twenty years," the man replied. "It's home to me now."

Kuromaku smiled at him, and the cabbie seemed to brighten a bit.

"Tell me, sir," the vampire warrior said, "do you believe in vampires?"

The driver looked taken aback. He actually moved back a step, tilted his head, and studied Kuromaku more closely.

"Well, I'd have to, I guess," the man said. "Kind of a part of life these days, aren't they? I wouldn't want to live in New York or Atlanta, I'll tell you that. And L.A., I don't know there's any real people left out there. 'Course, that town was always full of bloodsuckers."

The driver chuckled at his own humor. He handed Kuromaku's bags to the bellman, then beamed with pleasure as the vampire gave him his fare with a spectacular tip.

"So, there aren't any in New Orleans?" Kuromaku asked, smiling.

"Well, sure we got our share," the man said. "But we don't have many attacks, if that's what you're concerned about."

"No," Kuromaku said. "That was not my concern at all. In fact, since you know this city so well, I had hoped you might be able to tell me where one might go if one wished to . . . meet a vampire."

Immediately the taxi driver's face underwent a drastic change. His upper lip curled and his nostrils flared. His eyes narrowed, and he snorted derisively as he pocketed his money.

"One of those, huh?" the driver said, and it was more comment than question. "More of you freaks every damn day in this town."

The driver opened the taxi's door and slid his stinking mass of flesh onto the fake leather seat. He snorted and spat on the pavement before slamming the door.

"You haven't answered my question," Kuromaku said menacingly and stepped to the open window of the taxi. "I wouldn't want to get the impression that people in New Orleans were ill-mannered brutes."

"No," the driver said, sneering. "No, that would suck, wouldn't it? Listen, you want to find blood freaks and vamp wannabes, check out the Harvest Moon on the corner of Toulouse and Burgundy. 'Course, they don't open 'til after dark.''

"Thank you," Kuromaku said politely. "You have been very helpful."

As the driver pulled away, Kuromaku could hear him mumbling. "Hope you get bit, freak," the driver said under his breath.

"Not for a long time, my aromatic friend," Kuromaku said to himself.

He smiled and smoothed the lapels of his suit, then turned to the waiting bellhop and indicated that the man should lead the way. Soon he was safely ensconced in his hotel room, and he settled down to sleep as much of the day away as his anxiety would allow.

When Allison regained consciousness, the first thing she was aware of was pain. In her forehead and behind her eyes, a kind of headache that doesn't come naturally. She let her eyes flutter open, then squeezed them shut against the pain. What little she'd seen told her she was alone, in darkness. It was impossible to know if it was day or night.

All she knew was that pain in her head. She tried to sit up, felt the cold concrete beneath her, a small sticky patch under her fingers. Once more, she opened her eyes and pain lanced through her skull. Allison reached up to search her forehead and scalp for injury, and found what she was looking for. She hissed as her fingers grazed a ragged patch of torn skin two inches above her left eye, where the pressure of a contusion added to the pain of the wound.

Blood on the cold floor, and it was hers.

She breathed deeply several times, desperately trying to orient herself, to move beyond the pain. She was almost certain she had a concussion, at the least. Finally she felt a bit more clearheaded. Once more, she peered into the darkness.

Allison knew she was a captive, but she was shocked to

find herself in an actual prison cell. Gray walls and bars. Dim light somewhere down the corridor beyond the bars. And silence.

She felt the urge to call out, to see if there was anyone who might help her. Then she groaned, because a smile would have pained her. How foolish of her, she thought, and chalked it up to head trauma. Erika was working with Hannibal, that much was obvious. She didn't know for how long, or how willingly, but enough so that the little goth girl who had once been their ally was willing to attack Cody and abduct her. Erika and Vlad, the hugely muscled, bald vampire who'd been with her at the airport, had thrown Allison into the cell with such force that her head had struck the wall, then the floor, and had knocked her unconscious.

She might have broken her neck and died at that moment. That she hadn't was sheer luck. Those were not the actions of a friend, nor even an ally. No, calling out for help would only be humiliating.

Sitting on the concrete, the cold seeping through the seat of her jeans, Allison cradled her head in her hands and thought of Will. She was a woman of strength and independence, but she was also not an idiot. She needed him now, more than ever. There was no question in her mind that his retreat at the airport had been the only way to save her life. The fact that she was breathing at all was surely due to her value as bait.

So, how to stay alive until Cody could come and break her out? That was the billion-dollar question, no doubt about it.

"Comfy?"

Allison started, and her skull was spiked with pain again. She stared through the bars into the dimly lit corridor. Vlad stood there, his huge mass etching a dark silhouette across the front of the cell. He leered at her. Behind him were two other vampires, neither of whom she had seen before. One, however, was a curiosity. He was old. His hair was white and his face sagged with age. When she searched his eyes, he wouldn't meet her gaze.

"You smell nice," Vlad said and smiled, showing off his fangs quite self-consciously. "The blood, I mean. Sweet, maybe a bit tangy, nice bouquet."

He inhaled deeply and, despite herself, Allison shivered.

"Want to play, little girl?" he sneered. "I know you've got a thing for vampires. Does Cody bite you when you fuck?"

Allison swallowed.

"Tell you what, you dickless poseur," she said, hating the way her voice, unused for hours, cracked when she spoke, "why don't you just come in here and rip my throat out? Rape me, I dare you."

Vlad's eyes went wide. Allison smiled. Hannibal wanted her alive, at least for the moment, and his lackey wasn't about to defy the master.

"Fucking coward," she sneered. "Run along now, Vlad. Come back when you've grown a set of balls."

The bald vampire's jaw dropped, mouth gaping open, as he stared at her in horror. Then his eyes darkened to a profound crimson, and his face pushed out into a wet snout. Fur spurted from his flesh and the growl that erupted from his throat almost made Allison lose control of her too-full bladder.

She'd gone too far.

The old, white-haired vampire grabbed Vlad around the throat with one huge, meaty hand and drove him across the corridor, pinning him with a clang to the bars of the opposite cell.

"Don't be an idiot," the old vamp said softly. "He'd kill you."

"But Yano," Vlad whimpered, already returning to his human form, "she . . . she . . ."

"Oh, shut up, you pussy."

Both vampires looked left, down the corridor. Allison didn't have to look; she recognized the voice.

Erika.

"Yano just saved your life, Vlad," the little brunette told him. "Allison would have been fortunate to have you kill her. Time spent with Hannibal will be infinitely worse."

Vlad began to smile. He strolled over to Erika, kissed her on the forehead, and then glanced over at Allison.

"Maybe he'll give you to me as table scraps," Vlad said. "But I'll get a taste of you, one way or another."

When he'd gone, Erika approached Allison's cell. Yano stood behind her a moment, but she motioned for him to leave as well and, with a guarded look, he did so. After she seemed satisfied they were alone, Erika returned her attention to Allison.

"Nasty head wound, there, Alli," she said.

"Fuck you," Allison said bluntly, but Erika didn't even flinch.

"You know why you're here?" Erika asked her.

"I'm not stupid," Allison said. "Maybe I should ask you why *you're* here."

"I want to live," Erika replied. "The whole New Orleans coven is going to be destroyed. Another couple days, at most, and they'll all be dead. If somebody doesn't fuck it up for Hannibal."

Allison tilted her head to one side, and received a painful reminder of her wound. She stared at Erika.

"What are you saying?" she asked.

Erika smiled. "I hope you live long enough to find out," she said.

Somebody hissed farther down in the corridor, and Erika glanced up worriedly, then quickly turned to mist and drifted back into the darkened cells behind her. Ventilation ducts would allow her to go anywhere she liked. For the first time, Allison wished that she were one of the shadows. She wouldn't be stuck in this hellhole.

The harsh clack of boot heels echoed down the corridor to her cell. Allison stared out into the hall, waiting for this latest in her parade of visitors. But she knew who it was.

The only person Erika would have run away from.

"Hello, Hannibal," she said, and tried to force herself not to cringe.

Like the vampire Erika had called Yano, Hannibal's long hair was white. But unlike Yano, Hannibal did not look old. In fact, he was every inch the vampire lord he had made of himself. Tall and slender, with eyes a compelling, frosted blue, and a mane of flowing white hair, Hannibal looked, quite simply, cruel.

For just a moment, the world went away. Allison flashed back to the first time she'd met Hannibal. A party, at his house in Venice, for shadows and volunteers—humans who offered themselves up by choice. She had been a reporter then, working undercover to investigate a vast network of disappearances and what she thought was a murderous cult. She'd been knocked unconscious. And when she woke . . . God, those sounds . . . Hannibal had been defiling the wounds of another woman's corpse, fucking her in the abdomen, only a few feet from where Allison lay.

"Allison," Hannibal said, and his smile widened.

She recoiled as if he'd slapped her, then raged against her lack of self-control. Not that it wasn't understandable. After all, she'd seen the depths of Hannibal's depravity. She knew what she faced.

"He'll kill you, you know," she said as matter-of-factly as she was able.

"Yes, I know," Hannibal replied. "If he can. So really, it doesn't matter what I do to you, as long as you're whole enough to lure him here."

He misted, then, and passed through the bars in an instant, re-forming inside, only a few feet from Allison. Against her will, she found herself scrambling backward to get away from him. She remembered thinking just moments before about how strong a woman she was.

But courage only went so far.

"Please," she said, "just leave me alone."

"Oh," Hannibal replied, smiling, "I really don't think so."

It was his smugness that did it. Allison, steeling herself against his inevitable reprisal, turned on Hannibal. Her hatred and fear boiled over together, pouring out of her in waves. Bile rose in her throat, and she spat it, hot and thick, in Hannibal's face.

"Do your worst, you bastard," she said quietly. "Every time you hurt me, every tear and every scream, I'll think about what's going to happen to you when Cody finally catches up to you."

"Please do shut up now," he replied.

Hannibal wiped the back of his hand across his face, then licked her phlegmy spit off his hand. As if it were the same motion, he backhanded her. Allison's cheekbone cracked and her nose broke, blood spurting from her left nostril. She flew across the cell and slammed her right shoulder against the cement wall. She could hear something else crack on impact, and the pain screamed up into her whole body. When she landed on the cement, she was close to passing out again.

"No," Hannibal said wearily. "Not for a while yet."

He tore her from the ground by her blood-spattered blond hair, scalp ripping from the speed and power. That woke her up. Allison screamed, and the tears she'd known would come finally arrived.

"Don't feel as though you can't beg," Hannibal teased. "It won't make a damn bit of difference one way or the other."

His right hand closed on her good shoulder, and with his left, he broke her arm.

Again, she began to pass out. But then the horror brought her back around. The pain and humiliation as Hannibal literally tore her clothes from her body. In seconds Allison lay naked and bleeding, cracked and broken on the cement floor. She couldn't feel the cold of the concrete anymore.

Hannibal leaned over her and covered her mouth and

nostrils with his right hand. Allison's eyes bulged in panic. She couldn't breathe, and for a moment, the pain was set aside. Death was imminent. Black spots appeared before her eyes, and she began to calm down. Death had its attractions. Already, the pain was fading.

The hand went away. Allison sucked air greedily into her lungs. The pain was unimportant in that instant. She wanted to live, no matter what.

"You're a tough one," Hannibal said appreciatively. "That's nice. I want you to be able to appreciate this."

Then he began to scar her.

In the year since the catastrophic battle that nearly leveled Salzburg, Austria, Roberto Jimenez had changed very little. His hair was a bit grayer. He was one year older, of course, forty-five now. He smiled less. Even spoke less often. And, for the first time in his life, he considered himself a failure.

Until Salzburg, Roberto had been commander-general of the United Nations Security Force. Afterwards, his job had changed. His orders were simple. Kill the vampires. No matter what it took, or how much it cost, or who he pissed off doing it.

That was the idea, anyway. But for three full seasons, he'd been caught in a tug of war between Bill Galin, the president of the United States, and Rafael Nieto, the secretary-general of the U.N. Nieto was a pain in the ass, and Galin . . . Galin was just insane. Truly, completely insane. Willing to threaten nuclear strikes to get his way, happy to have the Secret Service and CIA commit assassinations whenever the need arose.

While his old job went to someone else, Berto watched and waited, anxious to get started. And while he waited, Hannibal spread his influence over the face of the Earth, a virus with an agenda. In the days before the world knew that vampires were real, they were kept in check by a rogue faction of the Roman Catholic Church.

But the church was gone, its American splinter all that remained.

Even though some of the vampires seemed to be free of the vulnerabilities and restraints that mythology claimed for them, Hannibal's legions of followers were not. Compared to the less violent of the vampires—and unlike both Nieto and Galin, Roberto knew there was a difference—Hannibal's crew were far easier to kill.

Unfortunately, he'd been relegated to culling vampires in certain areas of certain cities, to hunting down specific bloodsuckers, most of which he never found. Pursuing Galin's vendettas had cost valuable time and led nowhere. Hannibal's followers seemed to choose major cities at random, spread all over the globe, but concentrated in America. At random, at least, until you looked at the map and realized how evenly dispersed they were. Portland, Oregon. Los Angeles. Denver. Dallas. Minneapolis. Detroit. Of course, New York and Atlanta were the worst. Hell, those cities might as well just be surrendered to Hannibal, Roberto had often thought.

Eventually, even Galin could no longer ignore the screams of the American people, and Secretary-General Nieto forced the American president to hear the screams of the rest of the world.

Finally, Jimenez received the green light he'd been awaiting for nearly ten months. Ten weeks later, with all the planning, recruiting, and training complete, all the logistics finally worked out, and with a presidential and U.N. commission that gave him unlimited freedom of command, he was ready.

As dawn broke over the elegant Altanta skyline, Roberto sat on the roof of his Humvee, on a highway overpass just west of the city. He didn't need the night vision glasses any longer, so he picked up the high-res binocs instead. Scanned the streets for stragglers.

"Points Alpha through Omega, last check-in now, please," he said without turning.

Inside the Humvee, his order was passed via televideo to the twenty-odd command centers located in and around the city of Atlanta. Less than a minute later, Lieutenant Sniegoski poked his head out the window.

"All clear, Commander," the young man reported.

Roberto nodded. Waited. Watched the sun. It hadn't completely cleared the horizon yet, and he wanted to make absolutely certain that day had arrived. It had rained yesterday, so the operation had been put off until today. But today looked to be an absolutely glorious day.

Glorious.

"Movement," Sniegoski reported.

Berto lifted the binocs again, scanned the edge of the city. A newspaper delivery truck made its way swiftly through the deserted streets. A moment later, he caught sight of a lone man walking out the front door of an apartment building.

Without a word, he reached a hand beneath him and Sniegoski handed him a small comm-unit. He brought it to his mouth, pressed a tiny red button.

"This is Commander Jimenez, security code Gamma Chi Niner," he announced. "Operation Moses is a go. I repeat, Operation Moses has a green light. Get 'em all out of here, people. Don't leave a single soul. Anybody puts up an argument, you know the drill."

Roberto sipped from a cup of coffee Sniegoski handed him. He sat and watched as the United Nations army of Shadow Fighters evacuated the city of Atlanta, Georgia. All citizens who would not come willingly were to be arrested and brought against their will. This would have been impossible even a few weeks ago, but with the city down to less than half its population, they would be evacuated by nightfall.

While the evacuation was taking place, the thermite charges would be set. A short time before dusk, the combination of thermite explosions and napalm air strikes would burn Atlanta to the ground.

Again.

Eight thousand U.N. soldiers would surround the city and kill any vampire trying to make an escape.

It was war.

"Burn, you bastards," Roberto whispered to himself.

"I'm sorry, sir?" Lieutenant Sniegoski said below.

"Nothing, Lieutenant. Let's move in and lend a hand. I don't want a single human being left in Atlanta when the shit hits the fan."

It had been a simple thing for Cody to backtrack and follow Erika and her vampire conspirators as they brought Allison back to Hannibal's headquarters. They had a human with them, after all—Allison—and with Hannibal having limited their ability to shapeshift to certain forms, they couldn't very well carry her back in their talons. No, they had to use a car.

As a particularly ugly pigeon, Will had followed them up the shore of the Hudson River until they reached Sing-Sing. Now, in full daylight, with all of Hannibal's fang-boys and -girls hidden away inside the prison, Will sat at the counter of a small diner that opened for breakfast at six A.M., trying to figure out how he was going to get her out of there.

He tried not to think about what Hannibal might do to her in the meantime. He prayed that Hannibal's wish to destroy him would keep the madman from hurting Allison much. But the idea of her being hurt at all was tearing Will's heart out.

Still, crashing into the prison without thinking things through first was very likely to get them both killed.

Don't worry, darlin', he thought, trying to send the thoughts to her, though Allison had no capacity to receive them.

"I'm coming for you," he said aloud.

It would have been nice to have Peter's input, Will thought.

"Well, why the hell not?" he whispered, and received an odd look from the waitress behind the counter, a matronly woman whose name, he had been stunned to read, was actually Madge.

Will ignored her, sipped his cappuccino, and sent his mind wandering. It was never easy to make contact in this way, not from so far. Moments of extreme danger were an exception, however. That seemed to amp the power of a shadow's mind somehow. Which was why Will usually carried a cell phone. He didn't have one now, of course. It was back at the airport, in a carry-on bag he would probably never retrieve.

Concentrating, he sent his mind out in search of Peter. Thought of him there, in New Orleans, with George and Joe and the others. Searched for the man who had become as a brother to him.

And found nothing.

Will panicked. *Just like Rolf,* he thought. And Erika had said Rolf was dead! Will refused to even entertain the idea that anything had happened to Peter. Just the unreliability of shadow telepathy over long distance. That's what it had to be.

He pushed off his stool, laid a twenty on the counter, and moved to the back of the diner toward the pay phone. For a moment, he struggled to remember his code, then punched it in and listened to the phone ring in the Ursuline convent in New Orleans.

Home.

"Hello?"

"George!" Will said. "Hope I didn't wake you."

"I'm old, Colonel," George replied. "I almost never sleep. But I sense the urgency in your voice. What's happened?"

"It's . . ." Will began, then faltered. "It's Allison. Hannibal's got her."

"My God," George said hoarsely.

"Yeah. Well I'll need *his* help for sure," Will said. "Is

Peter all right? I've been trying to reach him, but I just get nothing."

"That's odd," George noted. "I hate to disturb him, but I'm sure he'll want to talk to you. Hold on."

And Cody held on. Several minutes passed during which he cursed the age in George Marcopoulos's bones.

"Will?"

"Yes, I'm here."

"Peter's . . . he's not in his room, Will," George said. "I honestly don't know where he is. Is there a number where he can call you?"

"No," Will said. "I'll try back in a bit."

As he hung up the phone, Will's mind was racing. If something actually *had* happened to Peter . . . but no, he had to concentrate on getting Allison away from Hannibal. Until then, nothing else mattered.

Nothing.

7

*It can't be that cold, the ground is still
warm to touch.*

—PETER GABRIEL,
"Red Rain"

LIGHT REFRACTED THROUGH THE MYRIAD COL-
ors of the chapel's stained glass windows, bathing the pews
and altar in a wash of eerie hues. At the back of the altar,
the mournful eyes of the suffering Christ stared down on a
solitary figure, alone in a pew halfway down the central
aisle.

Elsewhere in the convent, shadows went about their business. Some slept, still more comfortable with night than
day; others had gone out into New Orleans, moving through
lives they had made for themselves. Some stayed inside,
counseling human members who were trying to decide
whether or not to accept the gift of immortality, the curse
of vampirism. Still others huddled together and planned as
best they could how to police a city that, for most of them,
was not their home.

In the chapel, bloody tears streaked soft flesh just as they
had one thousand nine hundred and sixty-eight years earlier

in the Garden of Gethsemane, when Jesus Christ had asked
his Father to take from him the burden of man's redemp-
tion.

Kevin Marcus had been born Christian, but had spent
most of his life believing that God had forsaken him. As
he knelt in the pew, the scent of the courtyard gardens
drifting in through the tilted sections of stained glass, face
bathed in an otherworldly light, Kevin spoke to God in
prayer for the first time in more than a quarter of a century.
He wiped the bloody tears from his cheeks, and he made
the sign of the cross over his face and chest.

"You're a brave man."

Kevin turned to see George Marcopoulos standing in the
shafts of multicolored sunlight at the back of the chapel.
Dust motes danced in the prismatic air, mottling George's
face. It should have made him beautiful, but it did not. They
all called him "old man," but George wasn't so old, after
all. It was only that, since his wife, Valerie, had died a year
earlier, George had begun to wither. Kevin had barely
known him then; he'd met him only a handful of times
when politics drew them together. But it was impossible to
miss the way he'd aged.

"Brave how?" Kevin asked, thinking that it was George
who had always been so brave, and yet so soft-spoken that
very few ever noticed.

"There are other shadows who pray, Kevin," George
replied. "But I think I've only seen one or two ever make
the sign of the cross. It still intimidates them."

Kevin nodded slowly, thoughtfully, and smiled. "God is
all I have now," he said and met George's gaze. "You're
Greek Orthodox, is that right?"

"That's how I was raised, yes."

"I was raised Catholic," Kevin replied. "We lived in a
fairly well-to-do community just outside Chicago. The only
black family on the block, of course."

George had moved down the aisle, and Kevin felt keenly
that there were three of them there now. An old man, a

dead man, and God. Something about that made him smile.

"May I sit?" George asked.

Kevin made room for him. "I'm sorry, I wasn't thinking."

"Not at all. I've wanted to talk to you ever since I heard what happened last night," George said tenderly. "I'm sorry about Joe, Kevin. He was a very good friend to me. Saved my life, last year, and kept me safe. Brought me here, in fact. But you know that, I'm sure. I just wanted you to know, if you want to talk about him, or anything else . . . there aren't many things we have in common, but we do have Joe."

Blood began to flow from Kevin's eyes again.

"You're making me cry again, old man," he said, but there was no anger in him. Only sadness.

Then he looked at George, really looked at him, maybe for the first time. He and Joe had been close, no doubt. And Kevin began to understand why.

"Why are you so loving, so accepting, when the rest of the world is so afraid of what they don't understand?" Kevin asked.

"Oh," George said, waving the praise away, "I've known Peter a long time."

"I'm not talking about Peter!" Kevin snapped, all his grief beginning to pour out of him. "I'm talking about me!"

Then he wept. George opened his arms and Kevin went into them. They stayed that way for several minutes, an odd tableau of age and fury, and when Kevin pulled away, it was because George's heartbeat was loud in his ears, and the smell of his own bloody tears soaking George's shirt was more than he could bear.

"I miss him," Kevin said.

"Yet, after all that's happened, you don't blame God," George observed. "Many might have."

"You're wrong, you know," Kevin replied. "I do blame God. But I love God also. He took Joe from me, but Joe's in heaven—wherever the fuck that is—with my first lover, Ronnie. They're waiting for me, and I'll be seeing them again. See, I paid attention when I did go to church. I'll see them again.

"But first, God had to make a warrior out of me."

George looked at him oddly.

Kevin smiled, wiped his face again, licked the blood from his fingers self-consciously. "I used to go to my pastor for counseling. My parents thought it was more proper than a psychiatrist. Advice from God, without the price of real therapy. I guess I'm just lucky the old bastard didn't rape me.

"There weren't a lot of black people in my town. I guess I mentioned that. When I was five, I started to stutter. You have no idea how wonderfully funny the other kids thought it was to call me 'ni-ni-nigger.' "

George winced at Kevin's use of the word.

"When I was fifteen, I had finally had enough speech therapy to get rid of the stutter, but by then, I'd realized I was gay. And so had the rest of my class. Then I was 'fu-fu-fucking ni-ni-nigger queer.' My stutter was gone, but the memory of it lingered."

"I'm sorry," George said. "I know that's a foolish thing to say, but I don't know what else . . ."

"It's all right," Kevin replied, leaning back in the pew now, deep in remembering. "It's another world now, like it happened to somebody else. In a way, I guess it did.

"I tried to kill myself once," he said in almost a whisper, and he could picture it in his mind. A beautiful spring night when the moon was so full and high in the sky it seemed as if it would kiss the Earth. "I slit my wrists. Then I pussied out and called my sister, Alicia. I had to leave Illinois after that. If I stayed another day, I knew my life would end up killing me. Of course, eventually, it did."

Something occurred to Kevin. Something that made him smile.

"You're from Massachusetts, aren't you?" he asked.

George nodded.

"I moved to Provincetown," Kevin explained. "I loved it there. I had never imagined I could live in a place where people were surprised if you *weren't* gay.

"That's where I met Ronnie. He had the most beautiful eyes I'd ever seen, and a smile that took all the hurt away. He did six shows a week as a female impersonator. His Eartha Kitt was to die for. She's a—"

"I know who Eartha Kitt is, Kevin," George said. "I'm old, not dead."

Kevin laughed at that. Then he stopped, looked down at the kneeler on the floor. At the blood on his hands and clothes.

"AIDS?" George asked.

Kevin only nodded. He knew what George used to do, that he was the medical examiner for Boston City Hospital for decades. The old man was intimate with death. They all were, now, in a way.

"I nursed him at home," Kevin explained; his voice cracked and he didn't fight it. "I didn't want him to die in some hospice. I tried to give him sunshine and laughter and music and hope. But that goddamned disease just sucked it all away. It was as if the virus had drawn all the shades in the apartment, turned the lights down low, lowered the volume on the radio until we just couldn't hear the music anymore.

"For the longest time, life was about waiting to die.

"And then it was about death. Or at least, I thought it was. Right up until I stood over Ronnie's grave, crying, and realized that I was still waiting for death to arrive. But it was my death, of course, that I was waiting for. I had HIV too. It was only a matter of time. A matter of waiting.

"Eventually, I ended up in a hospice."

"You didn't call your family?" George asked.

"Not even Alicia," Kevin admitted. "I was ashamed to have them see me like that. I'd never been very good at taking care of myself. Other people, okay. But never myself. And I never really learned.

"Then one night, less than a month after the Venice Jihad had been in all the papers and on every channel, an angel came to me." He felt his face twist into a wistful grin and saw the quizzical expression on George's features.

"Not that kind of angel," he explained. "Though I think I believed she was at the time. She was dressed all in white. This tall African beauty went from bed to bed, asking a question I'd only ever heard in church and in dreams. After a while, she knelt by me and whispered it in my ear.

" 'Do you want to live forever?' she asked me." He looked up at George, met the other man's eyes. "I pissed myself, George. Stank like hell, but I guess I was used to it by then. Either that, or I just didn't care. Either way, somehow I wasn't embarrassed by what I'd done.

"I was just tired of waiting to die. I wanted to live, George. Forever wasn't even part of the equation. Just for the next day. The next week. I wasn't greedy. All I wanted was a little time in which I wouldn't have to think about my body falling apart, and about what would happen to my corpse after my soul was gone.

"A little time. That's all I wanted.

"But she gave me forever anyway.

"I asked her name before she left. 'Alex'—that was all she said."

George's eyes widened.

"Alexandra Nueva?" he asked.

Kevin smiled. Nodded. "She never told anyone, did she?"

"Not as far as I know," George replied.

"She saved dozens of lives that way," Kevin said. "Of course, I didn't know that then. Didn't know she was part of Peter's coven, or who the hell Peter even was. All I knew was she'd given me life. The world kept changing, and I would be here to watch it change. I wanted to savor every minute.

"Then I met Joe," Kevin said. "Ronnie had been dead three years, but I'd never loved anyone else. And, let's face it, Joe was about as white as white gets. Not my type. But he reminded me so much of what I'd been like once. So vulnerable, searching for something.

"Joe needed someone, and I was there.

"And now he's gone."

They were quiet together, this odd pairing, and then George laid a hand on Kevin's shoulder.

"It would be a simple thing, even a natural thing, for you to hate God for a while," he said. "For you to rail against him and curse his name."

"I spent years doing that as a child, and later as a young man," Kevin explained. "But first Ronnie, and then Alex, and finally Joe, taught me about love and goodness and what it means to be divine. They're all dead now, but I'm still here.

"And I have enough faith in God to believe there's a purpose to that. A lot of the others, even our coven, though they'd deny it, are still spooked by the crucifix. Not me. God has a plan for me. I know it. This war we're about to have isn't just about philosophy. It's another jihad, a holy war. Heaven and hell have chosen their pawns. We're on God's side."

Kevin took a breath, smiled apologetically.

"All of which brings me, in a very roundabout way, back to my pastor, and the whole point of my unloading all this bullshit on you," he explained. "The priest used to say, 'God never gives us anything we can't bear. Instead, he uses the hardships our humanity brings us to teach us love, and the righteous fury of the warriors of heaven.'

"That's what we are, George," Kevin insisted. "We're the warriors of heaven. Heaven just doesn't know it yet."

Tsumi had slept, fitfully, for several hours after dawn. Vampires didn't actually need much sleep, of course, but it was refreshing just the same. Now she stood in the shower in her room at the Monteleone Hotel and let the scalding spray sluice over her body. She shivered with pleasure as the water burned her. She healed right away, of course, but the pain was delicious.

She caressed her breasts, her taut, scalded nipples, and wished she had more time to enjoy herself.

With a sigh, Tsumi turned the shower off. She squeezed the excess water out of her long, silky black hair. As she stepped out, she willed herself to heal more slowly. Then she ran the thick cotton towel over her body, savoring the way it scraped against her scalded flesh. But she didn't dare linger. It was almost time.

She slid the bathroom door aside and stepped out into the hotel room. Tsumi knew that the windows were covered—she'd hung the bedspread over the regular shades herself—but instinct made her wince.

"You find me so horrifying?" Sima growled, his voice like grinding glass.

Tsumi almost laughed. How could he even think that? After all, it was Tsumi herself who had given Sima the scars on his face, that December night in 1898. She'd been traveling the lands of the midnight sun, enjoying the freedom, the banquet that the men of Finland and Sweden and Norway made during the winter. The sun rarely came out. Tsumi almost never went to bed.

Sima was Norwegian. He'd been a fisherman before Tsumi seduced him. She'd scarred his face just as he reached orgasm that first time they'd fucked, marked him as hers. Then she'd drained his body of blood, swallowed his life in thick, hot spurts down her throat. Turned him.

Now he sat, completely naked, in a wooden chair by the blanketed window, pained by her expression. Sima was still insecure about her feelings for him, even after more than one hundred years. It frustrated Tsumi, but she often found herself feeding off his insecurity. Exacerbating it. It couldn't hurt, she told herself, to keep Sima off balance.

"Yes, you horrify me," she said at last.

But her eyes told a different story. And the way she strutted, preening, as she moved across the hotel room toward him. The lights were off, and only a soft glow of sunlight shimmered behind the bedspread covering the windows. Of course, they didn't really need lights to see.

"Your foolishness horrifies me," she added.

Grinning, she knelt before him. Her silken hair was still wet but she let it hang down in front of her face as she bent to take him into her mouth. He grew hard instantly. Tsumi moved her whole body as she tasted him, and her hands drifted up to his chest. She traced her nails across his pectorals, then down to his abdomen.

Tsumi loved him, in her way. His long mane of blond hair, the scruff of beard that made him look so much like an ancient Viking warrior. The scar she'd given him, her own brand, which he'd chosen to keep even after he'd realized he could make it go away if he wished. And that voice. Deep and sneeringly arrogant, in spite of his insecurities.

And when he took her, Sima knew just what to do, how to please her. Nothing she wanted was too perverse for him as long as it would fulfill her.

Her throat was open, and Sima thrust into her mouth, straining against the chair. He was close, she knew.

Behind her, the phone rang shrilly.

Tsumi's nails sliced deeply across Sima's abdomen, instantly drawing blood. She pulled her mouth back, trailing fangs across the paper-thin skin of his penis, tearing it open. Sima screamed in pain as he came, and Tsumi kept her mouth clamped over him until he was done.

On the fifth ring, she answered the phone, wiping her hand across her chin.

"I'm here," she said.

"I told you what time to expect my call," Hannibal reprimanded her. "You know what I expect of my family."

"I'm sorry, lord," Tsumi said. "I'd just showered and

was drying off when the phone rang. I got to it as fast as I could."

"Enough. Report," Hannibal instructed.

Tsumi stared balefully at Sima, watched his pained expression as the wounds she'd just given him began to heal. Hannibal didn't waste time, but she knew that her transgression had been logged by the vampire lord. Neither forgiven nor forgotten, simply filed away to be used against her in the future.

"The rest of your advance team are still in the cemetery," she said. "It was as you predicted. Only a matter of time before Octavian sent some people to search the graveyards."

"Is he going to be a problem for you, Tsumi?" Hannibal asked bluntly. "That you used to fuck, I mean."

Tsumi went silent. If Hannibal had been there, she might have lunged at him, tried to tear his throat out. She would have died for her efforts, however, so it was best that he was in New York rather than New Orleans.

"Octavian was a long time ago," she snarled. "If anything, I want to see him dead even more than you do. He hurt me, lord. I want to hurt him back."

"I'll see that you have the opportunity," Hannibal promised. "Now, what of the spies Octavian sent after you?"

"We killed two, and fed off of them," she reported. "The others were allowed to escape, and the sentries we had set up made it a simple thing to track them back to their headquarters."

The Monteleone Hotel was not equipped with televideo service, but even without it, Tsumi could easily picture the smile on Hannibal's face.

"Tell me, then, you silly bitch," he said. "Don't keep me in suspense."

"Well, that's where we hit a bit of a snag," she said, reluctantly.

"Snag?" Hannibal asked, and that single word held a promise of her death.

"Oh, we know where they are, lord, don't doubt that for a second," she said. "It's only that they're not as accessible as you might have hoped."

"What does that mean, Tsumi?" he asked angrily.

"Their headquarters is . . . well, it's a convent, lord."

Silence. Tsumi knew what Hannibal was thinking. It had been her first thought as well. The shadows were living on sanctified ground. The vampire clan could easily enter and destroy them with numbers alone. But Hannibal had spent every moment since forming his new clan trying to convince them that the old myths were the only way for vampires to live. That Octavian's beliefs were humanizing his followers, making them cattle. In essence, he'd preached to them that the church was right.

If they trespassed on sanctified ground, a lot of them now believed, they would be destroyed. And if a shapeshifter believed it would be destroyed, its own mind was enough to do the job. Psychosomatic suicide. It had happened before. Thousands of times. But that was before the church was defeated. Still, Hannibal had been reinforcing the church's mental programming.

It was a dilemma for him.

"We're coming tonight," Hannibal finally said. "And tomorrow night, Octavian and the rest of his lost little lambs will be slaughtered."

Apparently, it wasn't as much of a dilemma as Tsumi had thought.

"We don't even have to go in after them," Hannibal said. "It doesn't matter, Tsumi darling. All we really need to do is start killing people. When the blood starts to run in streams down the streets of the French Quarter, Octavian and the rest of his coven will come out after us. They'll have to. It's the only thing they have that they can hold up and say, here, we're not like those other vampires, those evil monsters.

"It will be glorious. All across the city, we'll destroy them. Then New Orleans will be ours. And once Octavian's brood are all dead, nothing will stand in our way."

Tsumi felt the bloodlust begin to bloom inside her. It was to be war, then. In less than forty-eight hours, New Orleans would be swallowed whole by a conflict the likes of which it had never seen. Vampire against shadow, in tiny pitched battles on streetcorners and in bars all over the city. Not through some massive battle, but through hundreds of smaller ones, the purification of a race of predators would finally begin.

"We will prepare for your arrival," Tsumi whispered.

She hung up the phone and turned on the bed to face Sima. Daydreams of slaughter filled her mind, and she opened herself to him.

"Come," she said. "Hurt me."

As always, Sima gave Tsumi everything she asked for.

As he walked the corridors of the Ursuline convent, eagerly awaiting the moment when he could sit and rest for an hour or two, George could not stop thinking about Kevin Marcus. An extraordinary man, indeed. An outcast all his life, Kevin had faced the death of his lover, Joe Boudreau, by transforming himself completely. Emotions that had lived within Kevin's breast for years had suddenly solidified. Overnight he had become a religious zealot and a bloodthirsty soldier.

Yet he wasn't unique, George thought. War and death had been manufacturing faith and vengeance since the beginning of time.

George shook his head and turned down the hallway that led to Peter's quarters. He moved slowly. Even more slowly than the day before, he thought wistfully, though he was willing to admit it might be his imagination.

When he finally reached Peter's door, he rapped on it hard with bony knuckles. He waited a moment and received no response, so he rapped again.

After another moment, he heard a rustling inside.

"You've slept late enough, don't you think?" he said

aloud. "Kevin and the others are waiting for you. If you really want to raid that cemetery tonight, you'd better—"

The door opened. Inside, Nikki Wydra leaned against the door, still rubbing sleep from her eyes. Her auburn hair fell in a wild tumble about her shoulders. She didn't seem at all self-conscious about how little her nightshirt left to the imagination, so George did his best not to look down.

"Oh," he mumbled. "I'm sorry, Nikki. I thought . . . is Peter . . . ?"

Then he shut up, and began to blush. He had hoped that Peter and Nikki would become involved. After Meaghan's death, Peter had not so much as glanced at anyone in a romantic way. Love wasn't part of the game plan anymore. But then when he'd come back night after night talking about Nikki, so excited about her performances, George had been pleased for him.

Circumstances had taken what might have been an awkward courtship and made it, instead, nothing short of lunacy. But it seemed to be happening just the same.

"He isn't here," Nikki said, and she seemed a bit hurt by her own words. Irked somewhat.

"I'm sorry to have disturbed you, then," George said. "Do you have any idea where he might have slept last night?"

"Not at all," she said. "We talked until nearly dawn, and then he left so I could go to bed. We were supposed to have lunch in the Quarter today, though."

Was that before or after the raid on the cemetery, George wanted to ask. But didn't. Sarcasm was not something most people dealt with well, particularly early in the morning. And he didn't mean it in any nasty way. He was merely amused that Peter was working a love life into his schedule just as they were preparing for the worst.

"Good for him," George said and smiled to show Nikki he was serious.

But Nikki didn't smile back.

"What is it?" he asked.

"Well," she began, "it's just that he kept having these headaches. While we were out last night, it was bad enough, but they got worse as the night went on. I'm a little worried about him."

George nodded absently, beginning to worry as well.

"I'd better look around for him," George replied. "See how he's feeling this morning."

"Give me a minute," Nikki told him. "I'm coming with you."

After she'd closed the door and hastily thrown on her clothes from the night before, Nikki joined him in the hallway. Rather than beginning a room to room search, which he was hardly in the mood for since all he wanted to do was sit down, they went downstairs to the first floor. In the living room, they found Kevin Marcus and some of the others waiting for Peter.

"Well?" Kevin said, his anticipation obvious. "What did he say?"

"He wasn't in," George replied. "I'm not sure where he slept last night, but he hasn't been feeling well. I think we should search the convent for him."

They stared at him.

"What do you mean he hasn't been feeling well?" Kevin asked.

"What do you think I mean?" George snapped.

He understood their reaction. Shadows did not get sick, unless they were suffering from some ongoing silver poisoning. Illness was something that, by their very nature, they were immune to. But, like it or not, Peter had not been well the entire day before and, according to Nikki, had been growing worse.

"All right," Kevin stated decisively and stood. "We search the house and grounds, now. I don't know what's happened to Rolf, or to Cody, but damn it, nothing's going to happen to one of us, especially not Peter, right here in our home."

As George watched with surprise and admiration, the

man absolutely took control of the situation. Kevin barked orders and, to George's additional amazement, nobody questioned them.

But just as the gathered shadows were about to depart to search the convent and grounds, George heard someone calling his name down the hall.

"He's in here!" Kevin called back, then turned to Caleb Mariotte, a skinny blond kid who'd been not more than eighteen when he died. "Go find out what's happening."

A moment later Caleb returned with Denny, the big Cajun who had yet to decide if he was going to be a shadow or not.

"What is it, Denny?" George asked.

The Cajun's eyes were wild. "Doctor, you gotta come now. In de courtyard. It like nothin' I ever seen before. Whatever it is, it weren't there last night, and it ain't natural, I know dat much for sure."

Their curiosity piqued, the entire group postponed the search for Peter long enough to troop out to the garden path. It was a bright and beautiful spring day, and the scent of flowers was almost overwhelming. Still, something was missing, and it took George a moment to realize what it was. He didn't hear any birds.

In the center of the pathway, in front of the wrought iron bench where Peter and George had spoken the day before, was a monstrously large object. It was black, at least ten feet long and half that in width. Fat like a sated slug, but dry as kindling. It was wispy, and layered, as if it had been wrapped in ancient bandages. Papier-mâché was all George could think of as he looked at it. But black, of course.

"Dear God," George said softly, staring. "What is it?"

"Never mind that, how the hell did it get here?" Kevin demanded. "It's got to be something of Hannibal's. Maybe some kind of creature or demon or . . . something. I mean, none of us put it here, that's for damned sure."

George stared at it, studying its shape, now that he could see that it did have one, albeit warped tremendously. Its location had also not gone unnoticed by him. Still, he could only stare.

It was Nikki who finally said it.

"I think . . . I think it's a cocoon," she whispered.

All of them turned to stare at her, in much the same way they had been staring at the . . . thing in the garden.

"What are you talking about?" Kevin asked, incredulous. "What kind of insect could build a cocoon this big?"

"She's right," George said. "Look at it. The shape, the texture. It was made, constructed, I don't know by what. Magic, maybe?"

"If dis t'ing is a cocoon, I don' think I want to know what's inside," Denny said warily.

"I know what's inside," Nikki said quietly.

George stared at her, saw the horror on her face, and the way she held a hand near her mouth, as if she might vomit at any moment. It was the look that gave it away, that confirmed his own thoughts. She knew.

"It's Peter," she said.

Then she turned to run from the courtyard, stopping after half a dozen steps to throw up on the marigolds.

After she'd gone, all the rest of them could do was stare at it, and wonder if she was right. And if she was right, then what? If Peter had somehow built himself some kind of sorcerous cocoon, what did that mean? What would he be when he emerged?

The strength went out of his legs, and George sat hard on the wrought iron bench.

•

--------------------- ✳ ---------------------

8

Choose sides, or run for your life.

—TRACY CHAPMAN,
"Across the Lines"

IN A DANK CELL IN THE BOWELS OF SING-SING
penitentiary, Allison Vigeant woke with a start. Her eyes
snapped open and she inhaled quickly, as though she'd forgotten to breathe for a moment. The memory of pain
scarred her, her recollections of every perversion Hannibal
had inflicted upon her were horribly lucid. Her body was
stiff, and sticky with dried and flaking blood where he had
cut her. Where he had fucked her. Where he had torn into
her with his mouth and hands and cock.

But she wasn't in pain. Her mind was the only thing that
was scarred. She felt none of her wounds as she began to
move, to tear herself up from the blood-stained, rancid cement floor. The cell was dark, she was well aware of that.
And yet Allison could see every detail in the textured concrete walls. Every speck of spattered blood on floor and
walls and bunk.

"Oh, Jesus, no," she whispered to herself, and the tiniest
modulation of her voice was audible to her.

"No!" she screamed and clamped her hands over her ears, squeezed her eyes shut.

She didn't want to feel. To hear. To see.

Allison Vigeant wanted, very badly, to be dead. After what Hannibal had done to her, death was the only escape. But the barbaric son of a bitch hadn't even allowed her that.

She looked down at her naked body, at her plump breasts, hanging a little too low for perfection. At the large, dark circles of her nipples, at her belly where it rounded slightly before dropping off to the small patch of pubic hair she'd left intact when she'd first shaved the rest several years before.

All her bones were whole, her skull no longer pounding from where it had cracked. Her breasts smeared with blood but otherwise unmarred. Spattered red on the unbroken white skin of her abdomen. Her sex open ever so slightly, but not torn asunder as it had been . . . when he'd ripped her open.

Allison didn't bother trying to choke back the sobs that tore from her throat. There was no camera on her now, no celebrity spotlight for which to submerge her emotions and instincts. She heaved in huge gasps of air she no longer needed, and let them out again in long keening wails. Blood welled up in the corners of her eyes, and she panicked at first, before realizing what they were.

Tears.

She started to laugh then, and even as she heard the cackling sound emerging from her own mouth, Allison recognized that she had begun to go mad.

Allison had never wanted this. Immortality had been hers for the asking, and she had turned away from it at every step. She had never wanted the pain and horror that came from being one of them. They might have gained amazing abilities, but they had lost so much. So much.

But if the day had come when age frightened her enough, when the concept of death was close enough at hand, that she had chosen to live forever, it should have been Will. It should have been Will, with her, holding her close in an act of love, the way it had been those years ago for Peter and Meaghan. Poor Meaghan.

Hannibal had taken everything from Allison, and that was the worst. The agony and the humiliation were beyond the limits of human endurance. He had killed her, after all. But he'd stolen more than her dignity and self-respect, more than her confidence in herself. Hannibal had stolen the essence of her relationship with Will. There was love, yes, but there was also a respect and self-determination that they would never have again.

"You bastard," she whispered between gasping sobs.

Only after she'd said it did she realize she was talking to Will, not to Hannibal. Hannibal was a monster. When she killed him—and she would—Allison intended to make him suffer as much as she could, yet she knew that it would never approach her own level of suffering. He didn't have the heart for it. Didn't care enough about anything to feel much beyond the physical.

But Will . . . hadn't come for her. She knew it was unfair the moment the thought came to her, but Allison couldn't help it. He hadn't been there to stop it from happening. A part of her blamed him, and she felt ashamed.

Hannibal had violated her in one long nightmare; he'd done things that sanity, by its own definition, would force her to forget—if she wasn't determined to remember. She lived in the shadows now, was one of them, and her body did not bear the scars of the abominations he had visited upon her. But her heart and soul were scarred by them. They existed in her mind, and always would.

"My God," she growled to herself, staring at the splashes of blood on the floor. "He'll pay."

Her fingers elongated into claws, and fangs grew from her mouth. Allison closed her eyes, concentrating, and was wracked with physical pain and anguished cries as wounds began to open all over her body. Her abdomen tore, blood spilling from her belly, her viscera barely staying in place. Her vagina and rectum were slashed and ripped by thought alone. Welts rose on her face and breasts, one of which had only a wound where her nipple had been.

Slashes appeared on her face and throat, arms and legs. There were bites out of her left breast and thigh.

Allison took the pain, all of it, a second time. She screamed and did not even attempt to contain it. These were her scars. Hers. And she would wear them for Hannibal until the moment when she ate his black heart.

She turned toward the bars, bleeding profusely onto the cement, and only then did she see Erika watching her. Crying.

"I suppose you'll want to leave now?" the vampire girl said.

"You suppose wrong," Allison replied, and was stunned by the ragged croak of her voice. Those wounds. "I want to see Hannibal."

"That would be an incredibly stupid thing to do, especially right now," Erika said. "He would destroy you. Hasn't he done enough to you?"

"Oh, yes," Allison agreed. "But now it's my turn."

She began to move toward the bars, and Erika backed off a step.

"You're outnumbered hundreds to one," Erika said, shaking her head as she stared at Allison, eyes ranging over the wounds on Allison's naked body.

"What more can he do to me, Erika?" Allison asked, then narrowed her eyes. "You're partially responsible for this, you know. You brought me to him."

Erika nodded. "I know. But I had no idea what he'd planned for you. I thought you were just going to be bait for Cody."

Allison stopped at the bars, wrapped her bloody fingers around them, and thought about what her body could do— that she could simply turn to mist and slip through the bars. Rip Erika's head from her body, and move on from there.

"That doesn't excuse what happened to you, or my part in it," Erika continued. "But everything I did, I did with a purpose. Hannibal sent me down here to shoot you."

"Shoot me?" Allison asked, almost hysterical. "Shoot me? That's a little tame for him, isn't it? And a little useless in my current state."

Erika produced what looked like a small dart gun, the kind Allison had seen used on animals in hundreds of public television documentaries.

"With this," she explained, but didn't point the weapon at Allison. "It's how he killed Rolf, how he captured me. It freezes the electrochemical process that allows us to shape-shift, among other things. It leaves you with the hunger, but steals away the power. If I shot you with it now, you'd die for sure. Those wounds would kill you this time."

Erika looked away a moment, apparently not wishing to pay too much attention to Allison's wounds. Allison had to wonder at the girl's willingness to turn away from her. Was she so certain of her ability to destroy Allison in battle, or truly guileless in her approach?

"Bullshit," Allison said in her guttural croak. "You can still shift. I've seen you."

"I got better," Erika snapped, then paused. "Look, do you honestly think anything but death would have stopped Rolf from killing Hannibal? There's an antidote, okay? An antivirus, if that makes sense to you. I won't bore you with the details of my own torture session with Hannibal, not after what you went through. But with Rolf dead, my only choices seemed to be to die, to join up with Hannibal, or to pretend to do so long enough to see if I could do any good.

"Now the shit is starting to hit the fan. Hannibal and all of his American clans are moving to New Orleans tonight. It's already dusk, and they're heading out right now. Come tomorrow night, they're going to destroy Peter and our coven, even if it means destroying the entire city. That's hundreds of vampires, probably more. Not including Hannibal's followers in Atlanta. Doesn't look like those bastards are going to make it, thank God.''

Allison raised her eyebrows, interested despite herself.

''What's happening in Atlanta?''

''U.N. forces spent the day evacuating the city,'' Erika explained. ''Half an hour ago, they set it aflame.''

''Dear God,'' Allison whispered.

''It's just the beginning,'' Erika added. ''You can be sure Hannibal's not happy about it, either.''

Hannibal. That name again. Allison felt her rage and humiliation simultaneously. She never wanted to hear that name again, and yet she wanted to look into his eyes as he died at her hand. She glared at Erika.

''You could have stopped him,'' Allison said, feeling her own tears coming now. She sank to the cold floor, sat in a sticky mess of her own blood. ''You could have saved me from this.''

Erika glanced at the floor of the corridor, then quickly back up at Allison. The two shadow women stared at one another through the bars of Allison's cell.

''I could have,'' Erika agreed. ''But there was too much at stake. Don't you get it? With this''—she held the dart gun up—''Hannibal will destroy our coven. The war is over before the battle even begins. It was a horrible decision, but it was the only one I could make. We've got to get this stuff and the antidote to Peter right away. I hate to even say it, but I don't think he can win without it.''

''Who's we?'' Allison asked, angrily wiping at her tears.

''Me,'' Erika answered. ''Sebastiano. He's trying to make up for betraying Rolf in Austria. He's been cursing himself ever since, and more than ever now that Rolf is dead. He was a coward. He wanted to be on the winning side. Now he just wants to die well.''

Allison actually smiled.

''Fuck that,'' she said. ''I died once already, and I'm not going to do it again anytime soon. And what about me? You weren't planning on just leaving me here, were you?''

"No," Erika admitted. "If I don't shoot you up with this junk, you could go wherever you want, anyway. But I was hoping you'd come with us."

Allison thought about it. Despite all Erika had done, she had to admit to herself that she might have done the same. But the madness that was in her soul now, that probably would always be there, demanded she destroy Hannibal. Still, now was not the time. Even if Erika and Sebastiano helped her, the numbers were too great. And if she sacrificed herself foolishly, Peter and the others might never know of the danger they had to face.

"I'll come," she said at last. "But we're not going to New Orleans."

"What?" Erika said incredulously. "You're insane. We've got to get this stuff to Peter and George and maybe they can—"

"George is a lovely old man, Erika, but he was a fucking coroner before he became our doc in residence. He's no chemist. And Peter knows magick and war, that's it. We've got to get this stuff where it will do the most good. We've got to bring it to Roberto Jimenez in Atlanta."

Erika opened her mouth, but before she could speak, both of them started at the sudden cloud of mist that appeared in the corridor.

"He's here for me!" Erika said, and Allison knew she meant that Hannibal had come to punish her for her betrayal.

But it wasn't Hannibal. Allison sensed that, somehow.

"No," she said, watching as the mist took on the form of a man. "He's here for *me*."

Will Cody stood in the prison corridor, staring at Allison. She felt self-conscious about her wounds, but did not make any effort to erase them.

"Jesus God," Will whispered, his face ashen. "What's he done to you?"

Allison misted through the bars and, for Will's sake, when she appeared on the other side, the wounds were gone. She took his hand and kissed his cheek, and said, "Come on, we've got work to do."

From the moment he stepped off Burgundy Street and into the Harvest Moon, Kuromaku knew he had come to the wrong place. He had seen similar clubs in cities around the world. The walls were hung with twisted visions of hell that might have nauseated Bosch. Metal abominations disguised as art erupted from the floor in the oddest places. In cages hung from the ceiling, half-naked men and women who didn't look old enough to vote gyrated. What the rest of the crowd was doing on the floor of the club couldn't really have passed for dancing anywhere else.

The Harvest Moon smelled of sweat and sex and too much beer. Girls burst the seams of antebellum gowns, or wore pants without seats. Pale, fey boys with ankhs paid more attention to one another than to the women in the room. A pounding, grating noise that might have had music somewhere at its origin sprayed the room like shrapnel.

Kuromaku almost turned and left. It was as if he had asked the cab driver where to find God, and the man had told him to go to church. But this place was his only lead, and he reasoned that even in a room filled with wannabes, there had to be at least one person who had actually met a vampire. In the twenty-first century, in a city like New Orleans, even the most careful among the shadow race would not stay hidden forever.

Kuromaku was taller than average for a Japanese man, his hair cut short, and his stare severe and unforgiving. His Armani suit was so dark navy as to be almost black, and cut with far too much flair for a typical businessman. Otherwise, he might have been a simple tourist.

He carried himself with a warning of danger in every step. As he moved into the club, hooded eyes and smirking mouths followed him, but silently. And the silence spread out from him like ripples on water. They knew he was the real thing, come among them. They could sense it. And in that moment, he knew that he had put his old life behind him. He might still be able to access his wealth, but the moment he had dreamed of Peter, the moment he had resolved to return the warrior's sword to him, Kuromaku had joined a war he had been avoiding for years.

Saddened, he glanced around the club again, at the vampire lovers.

Kuromaku could smell their excitement, their arousal, and their fear as he moved to the bar. Many of them actually began to breathe heavily, but none made any move toward him. Now that the object of their desire was within reach, they did not know how to reach for it. Even the bartender did not approach him. Nobody did.

Until, at last, a blond girl of ample build, whose face was painted with dark ochre shades and white enough to be a deathmask, crept forward. She said nothing, only stood near and watched him.

Finally the bartender arrived and, in the silence, Kuromaku asked for a double shot of single malt Scotch. It seemed to him as if the entire club exhaled at the sound of his voice. The bartender nodded gravely and moved along the bar to reach for a tall bottle of Talisker.

"My name is Lolly," the girl said in a breathy voice, though whether from anxiety or some sad attempt at seduction, Kuromaku would not guess.

He smiled at her. "My pleasure, Lolly." Then he told her his name.

"That's very cool," she said. "Japanese, right? What does it mean?"

Kuromaku narrowed his eyes. "It is an ancient word, taken from the world of Japanese theater. It means 'black curtain,' which is the final curtain in such plays. In simpler terms, lovely girl, it means 'the end.' "

He touched her hair. Lolly's upper lip quivered and her eyelids fluttered and she grabbed at the bar to keep her balance. Kuromaku grabbed her arms to hold her up, and after a moment her breathing returned to close to normal and she was able to stand on her own.

"Oh my God," she whispered, and began to flush a deep scarlet.

"Are you all right?" Kuromaku asked her.

"More than all right," she said and stared at him with eyes filled with worship. Then a smile spread across her face. "I just came."

Now it was Kuromaku's turn to blink.

"Pardon me?"

"I just . . . I had an orgasm," she said, still smiling, offering herself to him with every glance and gesture.

Kuromaku wanted to mock her, to laugh at her lust for death, at her infantile sexual obsessions. But he couldn't. There was far too much charm and, yes, flattery, in the way she had so clearly made herself his slave.

"Tell me, Lolly," he said amiably, "do any of your friends here know where to find vampires in New Orleans? Where do the shadows hide?"

Her eyes were shining stars. "I'm not sure. I wish I knew. Auriette might know. I . . ." She paused, glanced at the floor, then back up at him. "Kuromaku, do you want to taste me? You can, you know. Drink my blood if you like."

He stared at her.

"I'm sorry," she mumbled. "I just thought, if you were hungry . . ."

"I'm not hungry at the moment, Lolly, but thank you. Now, who is this Auriette?"

"What the fuck do you want her for?" Lolly snapped, becoming instantly enraged. "Please, I'm sorry, but could you just . . . I mean, I want you to."

She stood on her toes and leaned in to him, her neck at an angle where he couldn't help but look at the pulsing veins there. In truth, he was a bit hungry. But he had no time to indulge.

"Please just tell me where . . ."

Then the silence broke. Whatever invisible wall had been around him upon his entrance shattered as Lolly drew closer to him. Suddenly there was a crowd around him, zealots with desperate eyes. A burly man with a shaved head and black tattoos around his eyes pushed past the bulk of the crowd and got in close.

"Please, take me," he whined submissively. "I'll do whatever you want, just bite me, please. Anywhere you like, I just want your teeth in me."

They all joined in his chant, his pleading, and began to touch him, to pull at his clothing, trying to get his attention, to curry favor. Kuromaku couldn't stand the stifling of the crowd, the closeness and helplessness as they began to flow over him.

"Get away!" he shouted.

They didn't respond, just kept begging for his mouth on them, his teeth in them.

"Away!" he roared, and pushed against them. An arm broke under the power of his shove, but a dozen hangers-on were tossed aside. More swept in on him, begging, wheedling.

"Enough!" he screamed, and reached into the crowd to grab the shirtfront of the bald man with tattoos around his eyes. Kuromaku spun him around, knocking the rest of them away. The thirst had grown with his fury, and he dipped his mouth to the big man's neck and tore into his pulsing throat. Blood pumped into Kuromaku's mouth, hot and thick and with the coppery odor that always aroused him.

After a moment of bliss, he remembered the crowd.

"Is that what you want?" he roared.

He wrapped the fingers of his left hand around Black-eyes's neck and snapped it with a quick flick of his wrist.

"Is that what you want?"

Silence again. Somewhere, a clock ticking. A cellular phone trilled in the back of the club. Then a whisper. "Oh, Jesus, me next . . ."

Kuromaku leaned his head back, massaged his temples. His eyes hurt. It was a simple thing he was asking. But these . . . these freaks were so completely obsessed that it was like dealing with small children or the severely retarded.

Then it hit him.

"All right," he said magnanimously. "I'll make you a deal. Whoever can tell me where the vampire clan of this city makes its home will be chosen as my next meal."

They fell all over each other, even brutalized one another, to get to him. The general consensus was that Octavian's coven made their home in an old convent in the French Quarter. Kuromaku smiled at the appropriateness of Peter's choice. The woman who was the first to mention the Ursuline convent asked if he would sink his fangs into her breast, and he obliged, lingering a moment. She was quite beautiful.

Despite the chants to the contrary of those around him, Kuromaku left her alive.

Outside the gray walls of the convent, Kuromaku paused in the darkness. It was quiet within, particularly in comparison with the garish lights and roar of tourism from elsewhere in the Quarter. Quiet, yes, but there was life there. Kuromaku could sense it, could almost hear a whisper on the wind.

He held Peter's sword in his right hand, its scabbard wrapped in green silk and tied with a thin black cord. Almost there, he thought. And somehow, he knew he was in time.

As mist, he slipped through the huge iron gate, reforming inside. There were lights on inside the convent, though very few. A small lantern hung not far from the main interior door, on the other side of the garden. It could only be reached by following a winding path through the flora.

Slipping through the shadows, silent among the flowers,

Kuromaku moved toward the house. He'd barely gone half a dozen yards when the plants began to rustle around him. A snake, or rat, or dog . . . something. More than one something. And a small pool of mist, just at ground level, creeping across the garden.

With one swift motion, Kuromaku reached around under his long jacket, unsnapped the catch of its scabbard, and withdrew his *wakizashi,* which had hung there upside down. The short sword's guard was nontraditionally flat, so it could hang there undetected.

Moon and lantern light glinted on the edge of the short sword as Kuromaku moved into a defensive posture. But the shadows took their time. They were confident in their greater numbers. At some signal he could not detect, they changed. One moment he was alone on the garden path, and the next, surrounded by five vampires.

Absurdly, he thought of the girl, Lolly, and the ecstasy she would feel if she could trade places with him.

Kuromaku smiled.

"So you've found us," one of the shadows said. "I'm surprised one of Hannibal's beasts had the balls to come onto sacred ground, but it won't do you any good, spy. Hannibal will never hear from you again."

The shadow who'd spoken, a slim black man, paused then, as if waiting for some response. None of the others, two women and two men, spoke at all.

Kuromaku decided to ignore them.

"I'm here to see Peter Octavian," he explained. "If you would be kind enough to fetch him for me, I have something for him."

The shadow's eyes flicked to the silk-wrapped sword, then to Kuromaku's *wakizashi,* and back to his face.

"I'm sure you do," he said. "We'll make sure he gets it."

Kuromaku held the sword a bit closer to his body then and glared at the shadow. He would kill them all, no matter their allegiance, if they attempted to take Peter's sword from him. There must have been something of his resolve in his eyes, for the hateful look he gave the shadow caused the man to frown, to hesitate.

"As you say," Kuromaku pointed out, "we are on sacred ground. You have only your suspicion and paranoia to inform you. Why not let Octavian decide for himself? He is more than capable of protecting himself, in case you did not know."

The standoff continued in silence as several more seconds ticked past.

"Kevin?" a voice came from behind them on the path, closer to the center of the garden and the convent's main interior doors. "What is it?"

"Stay back, George!" the shadow called Kevin shouted. "We've got a spy."

"If I were a spy, you'd be dead," Kuromaku said impatiently.

"Who are you, friend?" the voice from the garden came again, and now Kuromaku could see an old man emerging from deeper within the garden.

"My name is Kuromaku, and I have come to see Peter Octavian, and to bring him a gift," he explained. "Just bring me to Octavian, and he will vouch for me. I understand your paranoia, but I swear by the moon that I bear you no ill will, nor mean you any harm."

The old man, George, was silent. Kevin turned and snapped at him. "George, you can't even consider—"

"Come with me," George said. "I've something to show you—"

"Kuromaku," he offered.

"Yes, Kuromaku," George said, "just a ways down the path here."

He followed the old man to what appeared to be the center of the courtyard, where wrought iron benches sat on either side of a small circle. But one of the benches was barely visible, covered as it was by some kind of massive growth or fungus. It looked, for all the world, like the bud of a flower yet to bloom, or the chrysalis of a butterfly.

"There you are," George said. "What do you make of that?"

He stared at Kuromaku's face, obviously searching for some reaction. Other than revulsion, Kuromaku didn't know how to react.

"What is it?" he said, finally.

"We're not certain," George replied, "but we think it's Peter."

Kuromaku blinked, felt his hand grip the silk-wrapped scabbard more tightly in his fingers. He stared at the shell that somehow held his comrade within.

"We had talked about trying to break it open—"

"No!" Kuromaku snapped, glaring at George. "You must not."

"What?" George replied, obviously taken aback and confused. "Do you know what's happened to him? What's going on?"

"I don't know," Kuromaku whispered, staring at the chrysalis once more.

"Then how can you be so sure it's not killing him, that we shouldn't break it open?" the old man demanded.

Kuromaku didn't turn to look at him again. Simply stared at the black, flaking outer skin of the cocoon.

"Isn't it obvious?" he asked. "When a caterpillar builds a chrysalis, it does so in order to evolve. Something has happened to Peter. I don't know what any more than you, but it only stands to reason that, inside that hideous sheath, he must be *changing*."

"Changing," George repeated. "Of course, but . . . into what?"

Kuromaku smiled, his eyes flaring. He slid Peter's silk-wrapped sword into his belt and turned to face the old human and the vampires who seemed more than willing to obey him.

"I don't know," Kuromaku said. "But I am eager to find out."

They all stared at him.

"Anyone want to join me for some café au lait?" he asked.

9

*Images of broken light that dance before me
like a million eyes . . .*

—THE BEATLES,
"Across the Universe"

ROBERTO'S HUMVEE SAT SIDEWAYS ACROSS the highway; the broken white line disappeared under the belly of the massive vehicle. There were two others, one on either side and, with the vehicles, more than a dozen soldiers spread out across the five eastbound and five westbound lanes. They all wore oxygen masks with rebreathers to keep from inhaling too much smoke.

But there was nothing they could do about the heat.

It was long after dark, near on midnight now, but night had still not fallen on Atlanta. The fires were too bright, flames leaping high and consuming entire city blocks with a savagery that rivaled any other animal in nature. And there was no doubt in Roberto's mind that fire was a predator. From the moment the first thermite charge went up, he'd watched the beast rear back and tear into the city without any shred of mercy.

They'd fallen back to just under a quarter mile from the

city and donned their masks. For the first time in years, Roberto Jimenez had cried. A part of him felt, as he watched the blaze spread, that by destroying such a testament to man's greatness, they had already lost.

Now he stood just shy of fifty yards away from the Humvee, closer to the burning city than any of the others. The heat kept him sharp, angry, even cruel. He knew they'd killed people, that there would have been certain homeless people, and perhaps a few stubborn and stupid enough to hide from the soldiers as they came through, who had been left behind.

They'd killed those people.

Roberto prayed for himself, for his soldiers, and for those abandoned souls. But when the prayer was through, he didn't think about them anymore. He thought about the job.

And now this was the job. Just standing guard, watching it all burn. Most of the vampires in Atlanta had probably been incinerated hours ago, or burned up while trying to escape. Some, he was sure, would have tried to get away by turning to mist. But the intense heat of the thermite would have vaporized any mist that it touched. Still, there would be some escapes.

Already, different posts around the city had radioed in the extermination of five vampires in total, who had escaped the flames. So, certainly, some had been intelligent enough and focused enough to realize they had to fly out.

It made Roberto sick to think of allowing even one to escape, but he knew it was inevitable. So he pushed those thoughts aside and watched the fire, the vicious rainbow of colors that spiked through it, the flashing of exploding office windows, the black smoke that billowed up in different spots. He listened to the blaze, the roar of the fire's voice, the explosions, the screech and crash of crumbling metal and concrete.

He gripped his HK4 Maglite automatic rifle in both hands, waiting for something to kill.

For a moment, over the roar of the fire, he didn't hear

the shouts and screams behind him. Then someone fired an HK4, and that did it. Roberto spun, weapon at the ready. A vampire lunged across the pavement toward him, its claws extended, acid saliva dripping from its distended jaws, yellow fangs gnashing.

"Bastards!" the vampire managed to snarl, despite the deformity of its mouth.

"Fuck off!" Berto snarled back and, flicking off the safety on his weapon, pulled the trigger just as the bloodsucker reached for his throat.

The thing shrieked impossibly loud as eighty silver rounds ripped it apart, scattering its parts in a shrapnel shower of blood and flesh. He'd torch its remains after, to make sure, he thought, but that fucker wouldn't be putting itself together too soon.

"Commander!" Sniegoski shouted again.

Jimenez ran for the Humvees. He saw at least four corpses in uniform. Sniegoski was pumping silver bullets into a ragged-looking fang-boy, trying to regroup with the rest of the roadblock squad now that the element of surprise had been exhausted. Two soldiers had taken refuge inside one of the Humvees, while a pair of vampire women literally peeled back the armored doors.

"Goddamn you!" he roared.

His HK4 jumped in his hands again and one of the vamp girls was torn apart. The other took cover behind the Humvee, then turned to mist.

"Someone get a fucking flame thrower over here!" he shouted. "For Christ's sake, what the hell did we train you all for?"

A scream. He turned, and something was flying through the air at him, spraying blood as it came. It hit him in the upper chest with great force, and Roberto went down on his ass, almost lost control of his weapon, but held on with the tips of his fingers and drew it back to him. He rolled and came up on his knees in time to fire a burst from his weapon right into the face of the vamp-girl who'd turned to mist only seconds before.

They could be anywhere. There was no way even to know if they'd killed all of them.

As he turned to see what had become of the rest of his team, Jimenez looked down to see what it was that had struck his chest before. He saw the blood splashed across his uniform. On the ground, Lieutenant Sniegoski's face looked up at him, without a lower jaw. His head had been torn off from the mouth up.

Roberto's gorge rose, but he forced himself not to vomit. Instead, he turned and ran for the Humvees. The two soldiers who had hidden inside one had opened the doors and were stepping out, weapons at the ready. There were two others still alive, trying to get a bead on a vampire who was stalking them.

He came to the corpse of Kathy Marshall, a major who'd already lost her father to the vampires. Roberto made a mental note to visit Major Marshall's mother personally, even as he stripped the flame thrower from her back. It wasn't hard. Her arms were gone.

Without even bothering to slip it on, without bothering to hide his approach, he stormed across the pavement and leaped on top of his own Humvee. The vampire that had been playing cat and mouse with Suarez and Duffy turned at the sound of Berto's boots on the hood.

The vampire smiled, opened its mouth to speak.

Commander Jimenez didn't want to hear it. He strafed the monster with the flame thrower, even as the others opened fire with silverpoints. The vampire didn't stand a chance.

Roberto walked from place to place, incinerating the remains of the vampires that were there. When he was through, he tapped the commlink on his blood spattered uniform.

"This is Commander Jimenez, all units Alpha through Omega, check in now, please."

He waited until he'd heard from all of them. No other attacks so far. But he warned them to be on guard for an attack from behind.

"The bloodsuckers are all pissed off that we've spoiled their party," he said, in his anger abandoning his usual attention to military propriety.

"Chapin! Delacruz!" he snapped.

The two soldiers who'd hidden inside the Humvee scrambled to attention. He stared at them, but neither man would meet his gaze.

"I should have you two cowards fucking court-martialed," he growled.

The two soldiers shifted uncomfortably.

"Shouldn't I?"

"Yes, Commander!" they both snapped back.

"But I won't," he said.

He saw them visibly relax at his words. Which only angered him more. Roberto moved closer, stared eye to eye with each man, walked around behind them, stood between them, and whispered so that the other survivors, Suarez and Duffy, couldn't hear him.

"If I ever see anything like that again, if you leave another soldier to the enemy during a battle, I'll kill you myself," he said softly. "I promise I will."

A cool wind, almost chilly, breezed lightly through the trees beyond the fence that surrounded the modest airport in White Plains, New York. Two fat crows and a bat flew together, an unlikely trio, while a third bird, a bluejay, followed behind. The crows and the bat fluttered to the ground and, a second later, began to change, to take on their human forms.

Will Cody watched as Erika and Sebastiano changed, and he wondered if he could trust either of them. Sebastiano especially. He'd only met the other shadow once or twice before, in the days before Peter's return. In the days before Sebastiano had betrayed Rolf, and all the rest of them, to follow Hannibal. And unlike Erika's claims about her own seeming betrayal, Sebastiano admitted his treason.

On the other hand, their story seemed to check out. The only reason Will had gotten in and out of Sing-Sing so easily was because the burning of Atlanta had forced Hannibal to speed up his plans. Hannibal had the bait ready for him, but by the time Cody got there, there was no longer any hook. Hannibal's entire clan was on the move, and Cody had taken advantage of that confusion.

So their story checked out. Didn't mean he trusted them.

But as Sebastiano completed his change, the intentionally aged shadow looked up at Will, then quite purposefully looked away. If anything weighed on his conscience, he might have tried to present a false enthusiasm, or been inclined to turn away more quickly to hide his guilty feelings. Will read Sebastiano's attitude, right down to the way he carried himself, as an expression of shame.

He hoped he was right.

Erika was a different story. With her, he just had to go on faith. In her, in his own judgment, and in Rolf's instincts and taste in women. Will wanted to believe Erika, so he did. But he'd be watching her closely just the same.

Sebastiano and Erika glided forward and stood staring through the fence at the airport runways on the other side. Even as they watched, a small passenger plane was coming in, its engine the only sound but for the wind in the trees and the occasional nightbird. Will glanced at it, and allowed himself a moment to appreciate the majesty of human flight. To get something of that size off the ground . . . hell, that was a miracle in itself.

There was a quick fluttering above and behind him, and Will turned to watch the bluejay land on the dirt and scrub grass of the small forested area. He watched as the bird—as Allison—shuffled back and forth on the ground a moment, waiting for newborn instincts to direct her next action. And suddenly Will felt sick.

His stomach churned with acid and he felt as though his

chest was pressing in, squeezing his heart. Will felt his lip begin to curl in anger, but he forced a smile onto his face as Allison returned to her self. The bluejay was gone, and before him stood the woman he'd loved like no other.

"Oh, man," she whispered, overwhelmed by the transformation. "That's . . . incredible. Where does the mass go? The rest of the matter? I mean, I was a bluejay! Where did the rest of me go?"

"Nobody's ever answered that one, far as I know," Will replied.

He glanced over his shoulder, remaining constantly aware of Erika and Sebastiano's location. It wouldn't do to lose track of them.

"That was . . ." she said, and then her smile went away. She was remembering, he knew. Remembering how she got this way. No matter how incredible or even wonderful she might consider the power of the shadows, that wonder would always be tainted by the memory of the suffering and indignity it had cost her.

Will's smile disappeared as well. He allowed his true feelings to appear for the first time since they'd been reunited. After his initial reaction, he'd done his best to stay "up." To comfort her without allowing his own fury to surface. More than fury—his own despair.

Now he let her see. Almost showed it to her, as if he wanted her to know, though he was aware it would only upset Allison more. But Will couldn't help it. She'd been his joy, his hope for the future and for his own tenuous grasp on humanity; now she was his greatest wound, the source of damning hatred and crippling despair.

If he didn't fight it. If he let it happen.

Will promised himself he was going to fight. Not against his rage, but against making what had happened to Allison more important to him than she was herself, than their relationship was.

With the moonlight slipping through the trees above, Allison reached out for his hand. At first, Will couldn't go to her. He was still trying to push himself away from the emotional abyss that had so tempted him. But if he went over the edge, he wouldn't be there for Allison, and she sorely needed him. This had happened to her, not to him.

"At least now we'll never be apart," she said softly. "I don't have to be paranoid about you leaving me for a younger woman when I get old."

He stared at her, stunned that she could laugh about it. Then he saw her eyes, saw behind her words, and realized that she might joke, but she wouldn't laugh. And he knew, from the way she gazed at him, that Allison understood exactly what was going through his mind. His fury and his fear.

Will pulled her close and held her tight and wept into her hair. "Oh, Alli," he whispered. "I'm so sorry."

She kissed his tears, tasting the blood there, and held him away from her.

"We've got forever to be sorry," she said. "For now, let's just find the son of a bitch and make him pay."

Will wanted to smile, but Allison didn't and so he only looked away. He knew he was thinking too much about his own vengeance and not enough about hers. If anything, it should be hers, or even theirs. He would try to remind himself of that often.

"Cody, over here," Sebastiano whispered, but did not turn. Instead, he continued to stare out across the runways toward the airport.

Will and Allison joined Erika and Sebastiano at the fence a moment later. She squeezed his hand, and he took a breath and held it to keep back the tide of emotion that threatened to flow over him again.

"You've found something?" he asked.

"There," Erika said, her finger pointing through an opening in the chain link fence.

Will looked in the direction Erika indicated, and saw a DC-10 parked at one of the long gangways that extended from the small airport terminal. There were vehicles surrounding it, one obviously a tanker from which the airplane's fuel was being replenished. Others were baggage carriers, being loaded even as they watched with suitcases from the plane's most recent journey.

"It taxied in just now," Erika explained. "The passengers are probably still getting off, but they're refueling in a hurry. They'll probably start boarding for their next trip in five or ten minutes."

"That's it, then," Will said. "Let's move."

One by one, the four shadows misted through the chain link fence, re-forming on the other side. Swift as night falling, they swept across the tarmac and descended upon the ground crew like wolves. This was the part of the plan that Will had hated, but he couldn't see any alternative.

"Just don't kill anyone," he snarled, and grabbed the hair and shirtfront of a baggage handler.

The man screamed an alarm, and Will slapped him hard on the side of the head—hard enough to disorient him momentarily. Then his fangs sank into the soft flesh of the man's throat, the stubble under his lips unfamiliar and faintly repulsive. It had been a long time since he'd taken the blood of an unwilling donor, even longer since he'd drunk the blood of a man.

The others were doing the same. Drinking, not killing. Feeding, for none of them knew when they would have a moment's respite again. But even now the screams of their victims were bringing others. Footsteps pounded down the metal stairs that extended from the airport gate. In a moment, more humans would arrive.

"Enough!" Will shouted.

Whatever their true loyalties, the others obeyed. They misted at once, their unfortunate victims crumpling to the tarmac weak or unconscious, throats bloodied, but alive. They ought to be grateful for that, Will thought. But the fact that the man with the beard stubble would live didn't make what Will had done any less wrong.

As he floated in a small, thin fog up and through the

door of the plane, Will Cody couldn't help but wonder how much further he would have to fall, how many things he had come to believe sacred he would have to abandon, in order to destroy Hannibal.

Returning to his own, familiar human body on board the airplane, he watched Allison take flesh once more and decided he didn't care. Whatever it took to take Hannibal down, it would be worth it.

Once aboard the plane, Sebastiano closed the door and locked it down. Outside, people screamed in horror and alarm. Will ignored it all. He strode into the cockpit and startled a uniformed man who had been making notations on a clipboard.

"Hey!" the man said, standing suddenly and dropping his clipboard and pen in the process. "You can't come in—"

Will snarled at him, lips drawn back in a savage snarl, fangs dripping with saliva. The man shouted and stumbled back against the plane's instrument panel.

"Oh, Jesus, don't kill me!" the man begged, not daring to look at Will's face again.

"Can you fly this plane?" Will asked in a growl.

The man glanced up, then shook his head, opened his mouth to deny it. Will's fingers lengthened into claws and he reached out and lifted the man's chin, staring into his eyes.

"Don't lie to me," he said, the sharp point of a claw on the man's throat warning enough.

"Yeah . . . yes, I'm the copilot," the man admitted, a tear slipping down his face.

Will almost softened for a moment, seeing that tear. He felt badly for this man. But they needed him. The plane would get them to Atlanta far faster than they might under their own power.

"Fly," he ordered and pointed at the pilot's seat.

"We—we don't have clearance," the man said and cringed as he awaited retaliation.

"They'll give you clearance," Will snarled. "Tell them we'll be taking off immediately. If they argue, we'll kill everyone in the airport."

Fear was replaced by horror in the copilot's eyes. He nodded and slid into the pilot's seat, and Will felt suddenly sick. This was it. The end. Once they had delivered the serum to Jimenez, once Hannibal was dead, that was the end. He would take Allison and disappear from the world. No more war or death or even fear.

Together, they would leave the shadows behind. Out of the darkness and into the light.

"Will?" Allison asked from behind him.

He turned to face her and she had her hand out. He twined his fingers within hers and nodded, unable to manage a smile. Out of the darkness and into the light, he reminded himself, as he saw the disturbing cast of her face. The scars there, beneath the skin.

Nice fantasy, he thought.

Then he turned away, trying to preserve the fantasy a little while longer.

On the second-story balcony overlooking the courtyard of the Ursuline convent, Kuromaku breathed in the night air and closed his eyes. The aromas of the French Quarter tantalized his enhanced senses—the sharp smell of coffee, the spicy tang of Creole and Cajun cooking, beignets baking at Café du Monde—but there were other odors as well, some not nearly as pleasant.

Human sweat. Decay. And death. Kuromaku had the scent of blood. It permeated the air and wafted on the breeze to him. There was death in the city tonight, more than ever before. Hannibal's vampires had infiltrated the home of Peter Octavian's coven, and they were hunting humans under Peter's protection.

But there was nothing to be done for it now. A greater danger loomed close on the horizon. The final confrontation between the two sides of this war of philosophy and blood was imminent. Kuromaku could sense the other vampires, out in the dark, prowling the French Quarter, but also hunting the dark, filthy streets of the warehouse district and the waterfront. And somewhere out there, he could sense his sister.

Tsumi.

It had pained him greatly to learn that his sister was allied with Hannibal, that she had tried to murder Peter, whom she had once loved dearly. Pained him. But not surprised him. Kuromaku was a warrior, as was Peter, though from an entirely different culture. Though Kuromaku had been trained his entire life to believe that honor was more important than victory, he had come to realize over the centuries that in war, honor was secondary. The life of a warrior was expendable if it meant the triumph over the enemy, the preservation of not only thousands of other lives, but the culture of a city, or a nation, or a world.

Tsumi understood none of this. She made no distinctions between honor and duty, only pursued her own pleasure, only cared for her own survival. She was nothing more than a predator. Cunning, and all the more dangerous because, other than Kuromaku himself, Tsumi cared for nothing.

And in his secret heart, where he held close all the emotions that had once made him human, Kuromaku wondered if Tsumi's heart was cold and dead even to him.

He didn't want to have to kill her. But he would do so without hesitation if she stood against him.

Voices carried up to Kuromaku from the courtyard, and he opened his eyes. Several of the shadows he'd met earlier had gathered there, including the one called Kevin, who seemed to have rallied the others around him with little more than his own pain and grief at the death of his lover. The black chrysalis inside which they all believed Octavian had retreated remained unchanged. Nothing moved within. And yet their expectations hung in the air like the threat of rain in a thunderhead. They all sensed the other vampires in the city, the blood being shed, the lives being extinguished.

Destiny was rocketing them toward that final, explosive conflict. They could all feel it. Kuromaku shivered in anticipation. He had fought in hundreds of wars, several of which had, quite literally, changed the world. But he had never fought a battle whose outcome would determine the fate of the entire human race.

He relished its coming.

"Hello?"

Kuromaku had heard the woman's soft footsteps the moment she'd come onto the balcony. Even in the question of her greeting, her voice was lightly touched by a sultry rasp, feminine yet confident. He turned to face her, nodded and offered her a smile, which she returned. She was beautiful in a way modern men could rarely appreciate. Her eyes shone with life, her reddish hair fell in a tumble around her face, her lips and cheeks were bright with an ethereal lustre. The angles of her face might have been carved by a master.

"To what do I owe the pleasure?" he asked.

"Are you Kuromaku?"

"I am. And you?"

"I'm Nikki Wydra," she declared. "George tells me you may know something about . . . what's happened to Peter."

Her eyes flicked toward the courtyard, then back to focus on Kuromaku's face. He knew her now. George had told him of this woman, and the nascent feelings she and Peter had begun to develop toward one another. She had been there the other night, almost been killed when . . .

"I'm sorry," Kuromaku said.

Nikki tilted her head slightly. "What for?"

"My sister nearly killed you, I'm told," he replied, then dipped his head in a small nod. "For her, I apologize."

It seemed to take a moment before Nikki realized what he was referring to. Then surprise lit her face.

"Tsumi?" she asked. "That's your sister?"

"Regrettably," he admitted. "But please don't hold it against me."

Nikki blinked, apparently surprised by his humor, then smiled pleasantly.

"As far as what's happened to Peter," he said, "your guess, as they say, is as good as mine. However, if that thing down there isn't a cocoon, I don't know what it is."

She flinched, then turned and went to the railing to look down at the courtyard. Nikki frowned, then hung her head slightly and her hair draped across her eyes, hiding her face from him.

"I'm having kind of a hard time with all this," she said, but he still could not see her face through the curtain of her hair. "I mean, you all seem so . . . human. But you're not human at all, are you? I mean, really, you're scary bedtime stories come to life. It's—shit, it's almost funny."

She snorted then, but he could tell that the laughter was only to cover her own despair.

"You're right to think that we're not entirely human," Kuromaku admitted. "It would be dangerous to think otherwise. But neither are we, as a race, monsters. We are simply different. Alien, in a way that has nothing to do with space travel."

She chuckled at that. Kuromaku went on.

"We have souls, Nikki," he said. "I can promise you that. And hearts as well."

Nikki lifted her chin, pushed her hair back from her eyes and met his gaze. There were tears on her face, and she wiped them away, embarrassed.

"I feel so stupid."

"You care for Peter," Kuromaku said simply. "What is stupid in that? He is an easy man to care for. One of the noblest, most passionate men I have ever encountered."

"He's a vampire!" she protested.

"Who has not at all forgotten what it means to be a man. To be human," Kuromaku added.

There was a silence between them and, almost simultaneously, they looked down at the courtyard, at the shadows that milled around the chrysalis.

"You love him," Kuromaku said. It was not a question.

"I haven't known him long enough to love him," Nikki snapped angrily, though she did not look up.

"No," Kuromaku agreed. "But you do."

She said nothing after that.

* ───────────

10

We wander 'round this desert,
and wind up following the wrong gods home.

—THE EAGLES,
"Learn to Be Still"

THOUGH ONLY THE CHAPEL HAD STAINED
glass windows, nearly every room in the convent retained
some symbol of its former use. Crucifixes hung on many
walls, along with icons and images of the Sacred Heart or
praying hands. In the huge dining room, one entire wall
was filled with calligraphy-etched passages from the Bible.

It would be virtually impossible for a member of Hannibal's clan to infiltrate their headquarters. Certainly not if
they followed Hannibal's return to the old ways, the old
faith. If it weren't for that fact, Kevin might have been
suspicious of the sudden appearance of this Kuromaku. A
warrior, once allied with Peter, he claimed. And yet, he had
arrived just at the moment when Peter would not be able
to identify him.

Curious, most definitely, but not damning. Not yet.

He watched as the Japanese entered the dining room with
Nikki, whom Kevin had taken an instant liking to. He'd
picked this room simply because it was the largest, and it

would allow him to address everyone simultaneously. Everyone, of course, except for those shadows out in the city, trying to find vampires to kill.

And maybe one to bring back alive, if they followed Kevin's instructions. It would help to know what Hannibal had planned. Even if they didn't seem to have a chance in hell of doing anything about it. At least, not with any real success. Fortunately the odds stacked against them had apparently been lessened a bit, according to news reports CNN had been running out of its New York studio, now that its Atlanta headquarters had been destroyed along with the rest of the city. Hannibal wouldn't be able to add that part of his clan to any attack plan. That was something, anyway.

Kuromaku had stopped on the other side of the room to read some of the scripture on the wall. Nikki stood with him, and George entered behind her. Kevin nodded to him. George knitted his brows, obviously wondering exactly what was going on here, but Kevin ignored him for the moment.

Kevin tried to remember what biblical passage was on the wall where Kuromaku was staring. Something from Exodus, he thought. Then Kuromaku seemed to sense his attention and turned to regard Kevin where he stood at the front of the room. After a moment he nodded and led Nikki and George to the long center table, where all three of them sat facing Kevin.

A few moments later, the room was full. George had asked the coven to spread the word, and they clearly had. There were more than fifty shadows in the room, not to mention the dozens out in the city already. And there were even more volunteers. Faces Kevin had never even seen before.

He sighed.

"Thanks for coming," Kevin began. "All of you. I . . . as I look out there and see the faces of friends, and especially a lot of new faces, I realize that we really have made our home here. There are a lot of people in this city who know about our little family, and have made us welcome. Some of you are here tonight.

"You've all been asked, in the past twenty-four hours, to make a momentous decision," he continued. "A decision that will alter your lives irrevocably—and possibly end them. Believe me when I say that this coven, the family of Peter Octavian, does not ask this question lightly. There isn't time to be gentle. Hopefully, as each of you searches your heart and mind for an answer, enough of you will join us that the odds against us will be greatly lessened.

"But they are still extraordinary. And I firmly believe that we will need more than force if we are to even survive—never mind triumph—in the coming days."

Kevin Marcus looked around the room. He had their attention. That was a good start. Even this newcomer, Kuromaku, gave a respectful nod when Kevin mentioned the odds.

"By now, even if you don't know me, I'd lay odds you all know my story. Joe meant everything to me, and I want to thank all of you who offered your condolences. But I'm tired of it!"

Kevin had yelled out this last, and everyone in the room twitched a little. He was surprised at the vehemence in his own voice, but forged ahead.

"I'm sorry," he said. "That didn't come out right. I appreciate your sympathy, all of you, but I'm afraid that I've had to put my grief on hold for a while. The reason I wanted everyone in one place is that I need to ask a question that I don't think anyone has an answer for. That question is: what next? I mean, we all know the shit's about to hit the fan, and other than recruiting, and doing a bit of recon . . ."

He chuckled. Actually smiled.

"Never thought you'd hear me use the word *recon*, did you, Caleb?" he asked and looked around for the blond vampire who'd been somewhat homophobic when they'd first met.

Caleb laughed. They'd become friends since then, and Kevin trusted Caleb Mariotte to watch his back in any fight.

"Anyway, all I want to know is, what are we planning?" Kevin went on. "Anyone? Does anyone have any idea what we're doing next?"

When Kuromaku lifted his hand, Kevin frowned. They barely knew this shadow.

"Sorry, Kevin," Kuromaku said, "but I think it's the question that's flawed. You don't need to determine what you're going to do next so much as who is going to make that decision. I share your frustration. I came here to lend my sword to the service of a cause I thought was led by Peter Octavian. While I hope, for myself and for us all, that Peter's absence is only temporary, we have no promise of that. As well, George has told me that your entire hierarchy has been disrupted in the past few nights.

"All of that said, I presume that this is entirely your point, and that *you* have some kind of plan. At least, I hope so. We cannot simply sit here and wait for that cocoon out in the garden to hatch."

The room was silent a moment. There appeared to be some kind of tension there, perhaps a perception that there was hostility between Kevin and Kuromaku. Which couldn't be further from the truth, after what the warrior had just said.

"Thank you," Kevin said and offered a grim nod. "That's exactly where I was headed. Rolf and Erika and Cody and Allison have all disappeared; they might even be dead. Peter is . . . out there." He nodded toward the courtyard. "They killed Joe. The rest of us have little or no experience with Hannibal."

Now Kevin got to the point, staring quite pointedly at the far side of the center table.

"All except for George," he said. "I think we should—" he began.

George wouldn't sit for it.

"Not a chance!" he barked as he rose angrily to his feet.

The entire room stared at George Marcopoulos, a man none of them had ever seen lose his temper.

"George?" Kevin asked, bewildered.

"Don't put this on me, Kevin!" George shouted. "I'm not one of you, not really. Not a shadow. And I've never made it a secret that I've no desire to become one."

"There isn't anyone else," Kevin said simply.

George sighed, frowned.

"I've been there from the beginning, at least since things started to change for the shadows," he said. "I stood proudly at the United Nations and told the entire world that they had nothing to fear from you!"

"Well, what better reason?" asked a voice from the back of the room.

"I was wrong!" George roared.

He put a hand to his chest then, and Kuromaku reached a hand up to steady him.

"God help me," George whispered, but his voice was perfectly audible in the stone silence of the room. "I was wrong."

"George," Kevin said again. "I don't know what to say."

"Say 'Yes,' " Kuromaku replied, his deep voice booming. "Say 'Yes, George, you were wrong. The world should fear us, just as every waking moment, we must fear ourselves.' "

Kevin had lost control of this meeting. Nothing was happening as he'd planned. He'd never imagined that George would react this way. He had so much knowledge to share with them. If anyone had the instinct to lead them, to try to predict what would happen, it was George. Even the eldest of the shadows among them hadn't had George's direct contact with Hannibal.

"Hey, Kuromaku," Caleb said, standing and striding toward the ancient Japanese warrior. Kevin could see it coming, could read it on Caleb's face without any trouble. Kuromaku would have seen it too.

"Caleb, no!" Kevin shouted.

"Fuck you!" Caleb sneered at Kuromaku. Then he spit blood in the other vampire's face and reached out to poke him in the chest. "We're the good guys, you asshole."

Kevin moved, then, as swiftly as he could. The humans in the room would barely even have seen him, so fast did he cross the space between himself and Caleb.

But Kuromaku was faster. And in that split second, that heartbeat, Kuromaku did something Kevin would never have dreamed possible. He reached to his waist, to his belt, and withdrew a *katana*—a Japanese long sword—from a scabbard that had not been there an instant before.

Damascus steel whickered through the air, and even as Kevin pulled him backward, Caleb's right hand was sliced cleanly off. Blood spurted and the hand thunked to the tile floor in a red spray.

"You fucking bastard!" Caleb shrieked, staring at the spouting stump, struggling against Kevin's hold on him.

"Caleb, stand still, you stupid shit," Kevin said finally. "He'll kill you if you approach again."

Kuromaku's eyes narrowed, stared at Caleb.

"Kevin's right, you know," he said, then he slid his sword back into its scabbard, and both seemed to shimmer out of focus slightly and disappear.

"How the hell did you do that?" Kevin asked.

"Another time," Kuromaku replied. "You've got more important things to worry about."

The Japanese warrior knelt and retrieved Caleb's hand, then reached for his arm. Caleb flinched and backed away, but Kuromaku looked at him sternly, nodded, and Caleb allowed him to hold his severed wrist. Kuromaku held the bleeding hand to its stump and met Caleb's eyes.

"Think about it, boy," he said.

And then there was only the blood on the floor and on Caleb's arm and Kuromaku's hand. Otherwise, it might never have happened at all. Caleb flexed his fingers and stared at Kuromaku with a bit of awe and a bit of rage. Kevin knew how he felt.

"You shouldn't have poked me," Kuromaku said simply.

Kevin waited for him to smile.

He didn't.

"You know I'm right," Kuromaku said, staring at Kevin.

"I know," Kevin agreed, and heard the collective intake of unneeded breath in the room. He turned to look around at all of them.

"It's true," he said. "And maybe that's where I went wrong with my plan. George has been through a lot with and for us. He's lost a lot, more than we have a right to ask of any human. And his experience and wisdom can still benefit us greatly, if he's willing . . ."

Kevin glanced over at George, and the old man nodded.

"But I guess it's too much to expect of any human to lead us. They don't share our instinct for our own survival, only for their own. Just as all species do."

"Kevin," George said. "I'm sorry."

"You've given us enough," Kevin told him. "And you keep giving, every day. No, it's got to be one of us."

"Not just anyone," Kuromaku said. "It must be you, Kevin. I think you know that."

Kevin was silent. Murmurs of assent began to spread through the room. His heart leaped at the idea that, after all he'd lived through, these people would be willing to follow his lead. But doubt surged up as well. And, finally, the heat of his hatred for Hannibal—his thirst for vengeance. That last made the decision a simple one.

"If no one objects," Kevin said softly.

Nikki Wydra, who had sat quietly through the entire

thing, rightfully realizing that she was merely a visitor here, spoke up first.

"So, to repeat your earlier question, Kevin, what next?" she asked.

"Next," he said darkly, "we take the offensive."

Several hours before dawn, thirty-seven shadows moved across the city toward St. Louis Cemetery number one. Kevin's mind had returned often to Kuromaku's sword, and the way he had seemed to produce it from thin air, though the warrior claimed no magickal knowledge. When they had time, Kuromaku said, he would explain it, perhaps even teach Kevin how to do the same.

But he was right that they didn't have time now. In fact, Kevin had barely had time to speak to Caleb about not starting trouble with Kuromaku, no matter how badly he might want revenge on the ancient shadow. Kuromaku was a formidable being, but he was also, quite obviously, a great asset. For the good of them all, he'd asked Caleb to behave.

Caleb had only growled at him a little and muttered something nasty.

George had let them into Will Cody's armory. Kevin had been astonished by the stores there. Dozens of automatic rifles and handguns, cases of bullets, both silver and otherwise. Grenades. Flame throwers. Crosses. And blades. Swords and daggers of all shapes and sizes. While a shadow's own hands could become bladed weapons, it did not hurt to have an actual sword that could be left behind in a victim.

Now, except for those who had been left to guard their home and those still doing recon out in the city proper, Peter Octavian's coven swept across the French Quarter with Kevin Marcus leading them. Kevin had a lot on his mind, but the moment he saw the cemetery itself, all of it was wiped away.

Erased and replaced. By memory.

Joe. Screaming.

Kevin strode along Bienville Street with visions of death in his mind. Gleefully murderous thoughts filled his head. He lusted for it. For vengeance. He felt his lip curl with his hatred and disdain for his intended victims. It filled him like venom, racing through his veins.

And it felt good.

At the gates, they simply flowed over and through, the way he'd instructed. Let the vampires come. If Hannibal had already arrived with greater forces, this would be the test, and they would retreat instantly.

But if he hadn't yet arrived, this would be a chance to thin his ranks a little bit. And, perhaps, to find out a bit more of what he had planned.

The cemetery seemed deserted. Kevin moved silently, with Kuromaku on one side and Caleb on the other. They did not look at one another, and Kevin thought perhaps that was for his own benefit. There was no doubt in his mind that diplomacy was the only reason Kuromaku hadn't killed Caleb back at the convent.

They scoured the cemetery, moving in a wedge toward the corner where he thought Tsumi and the others had ambushed Joe. There was no trace of his lover when Kevin arrived at the spot. Nor of any of Hannibal's clan.

"What the hell does this mean?" he asked aloud.

"Perhaps Hannibal has arrived, and they've moved to another location?" Kuromaku suggested.

"Too close to dawn for them to attack now, though," Caleb added. "No way would Hannibal try anything now. We've got at least until dusk tonight."

From the far side of the cemetery, they heard gunfire.

"Here!" somebody cried.

That was enough. They were all changing, to mist or bat or bird or wolf or tiger. Changing. All but Kevin. He needed to be just Kevin for now, and so he sprinted across the cemetery until he came to a junction where the rows of crypts met. He leaped to the top of the nearest and then set off across the tops of them, inhumanly surefooted and swift.

At another junction, he stopped. Stood atop a vault staring down at the scene, as more gunfire erupted, silver bullets ripping into two vampires who cowered from the crucifixes held in a circle around them. They'd been cornered like animals.

The thought made Kevin smile. They would die like animals as well.

There were three others, and they screeched their hatred and tried to attack, shifting forms rapidly. But they were greatly outnumbered and didn't stand a chance.

When one remained, Kevin opened his mouth to order them to capture her—she would be needed.

Filled with fury and a need to release it, Caleb was too quick. He leaped past the gunfire and the crosses, his body elongating and changing in midflight. When he landed on the remaining vampire, a once-beautiful woman whose savagery made her ugly, he'd become a huge mongrel dog, something Caleb remembered from his childhood, Kevin suspected.

"No!" Kevin cried.

Too late.

The woman lasted seconds.

"Damn it, Caleb—" Kevin began, but his rant was cut off by an agonized wailing just off to his right.

Kevin looked in the direction from which the scream had come and saw Kuromaku emerging from a nearby vault with a vampire in front of him. The captive walked on tiptoe, as if every step might cost him his life. And it might. Kevin had never seen anything like this before. Kuromaku had made his left hand into a long, silver spike and punched it through the back of the vampire's neck until it came out where the creature's nose had once been.

"Shut up!" Kuromaku snapped.

The vampire stopped wailing. So great was his horror, despite his own bloodlust, that it took Kevin a moment to realize what Kuromaku's captive meant for them. Then he leaped down from the crypt and stalked up to the skinny male bloodsucker.

"Does that hurt?" he asked, beginning to like Kuromaku more with every passing second.

The vampire didn't respond. Kuromaku growled, and Kevin winced as another silver tendril punched out the creature's right eye in a spurt of optical fluid.

"My God," Kevin said, "how can he even think? You've got to have injured his brain."

"He's got access to the rest of it," Kuromaku said vaguely.

Then he leaned forward and whispered into the vampire's ear, pulling his hand up so the creature struggled, whimpering to balance on his toes.

"Now, listen carefully," Kuromaku said. "This silver is poisoning your brain. The longer it stays in there, the more pain it will cause, and the more damage. If I tear up your head, you may never re-form, and even if you do, you probably won't be able to function properly. It's the poison, you see."

Kuromaku looked at Kevin. "Ask your questions," he said.

"Simple," Kevin began. "Where is Hannibal now, and what is he planning?"

The vampire snorted blood onto its chest.

"Think carefully," Kuromaku whispered.

"The dark lord is here now," the vampire croaked. "In the city. We were to . . . guard this place so that some could sleep here tonight. The rest . . . I don't know. To kill you all, at least."

"You don't know?" Kevin asked, surprised.

"As long as . . . you die," the vampire said through a mouth full of blood, "I don't care how he does it."

Kevin glanced at Kuromaku, who raised his eyebrows as if to say there was no more he could do. Then Kevin shrugged.

"Thank you," Kuromaku said. "Now, that wasn't too bad, was it?"

He ripped his silver spiked hand up through the vampire's head, spraying brain and bone shards and scalp all over himself. Then he looked up at Kevin again.

"Burn them," he said. "Just to be safe."

Kevin gestured for a female shadow named Bethany Hart to move in with the flame thrower. Then he just stood back and watched them all burn.

"What next?" Caleb asked.

Kevin regretted ever asking that question in the first place.

"We do all we can," he replied. "Get all the reinforcements we can, warn as many humans in the French Quarter of what's coming, and start searching for Hannibal's hiding place. If we can find out where he and his clan are before sundown, we might have a chance."

"And if not?" Bethany asked, looking up from the flames, shadows flickering across her face.

"If not," Kuromaku said, answering for Kevin, "then we can only pray."

The huge Greek Revival mansion on First Street in the Garden District had been built in 1847 as a wedding gift. Its size contributed to its allure, but what truly impressed Hannibal were the fluted Corinthian columns and detailed ironwork on its facade. At first. Upon entering, he'd found the house to be even more beautiful on the inside, complete with elaborate ceiling medallions, black marble mantelpieces, crystal chandeliers, and wide, polished pine floors.

It was, in its way, an even more exceptional home than the one he'd been forced to abandon six years earlier in Venice.

And now it was his. In a manner of speaking.

Hannibal stood in the parlor, admiring the oil portrait on the center of one wall. When Tsumi came in, with her love,

Sima, trailing behind like an obedient dog, Hannibal turned calmly and offered her a beatific smile.

"You've done me proud, Tsumi," he told her. "I'm very, very pleased with our new home."

Hannibal frowned a moment, having sensed someone hovering beyond the parlor doors. Tsumi stepped back and gestured for this lingerer to enter. It was a woman, somewhat attractive despite her obvious disorientation.

"She's just awoken," Tsumi explained.

Then Hannibal realized who the woman was.

"Ah, Mrs. Collins," he said, "is it possible for me to enter your home and welcome you to mine at the same time? If so, I do."

"No, lord," Mrs. Collins said softly. "It's your home now. I hope that it's everything you desire."

"Oh, it is," Hannibal replied. "It truly is. And you, madam? You're feeling no ill effects from your . . . transformation? I imagine all that horrible pain in your stomach is gone now, hmm?"

The former owner of the house, Mrs. Collins had suffered from intestinal cancer previous to her death. Tsumi had truly done an exemplary job of finding such a woman—with such a house. Especially since Hannibal had been forced to rush her at the end.

Yes, this house would most assuredly do. It would be the place from which he would take control of New Orleans, making it completely his own the way he had New York. Then he would leave someone, perhaps Tsumi, in charge, and move on. But of course, New Orleans would be the sweetest victory because it would mean the end of civil war. The end of Peter Octavian and his acolytes once and for all.

Hannibal smiled down on Mrs. Collins. "Have you eaten, darling?" he asked.

Tsumi shook her head gently. "She's still getting used to the idea," she explained. "Though we've got her night nurse upstairs, unconscious. Getting her to eat has been a trial.''

"Has it?'' Hannibal asked as his eyes darkened, narrowed. He stepped forward to grab hold of Mrs. Collins's chin in a crushing grip, silently commanded her to meet his gaze.

"You will kill that cow upstairs, and you will do it now,'' he said. "You will drink her life down and you will exhilarate in it. We are not in the habit of caring for children, Mrs. Collins. Instead, we eat their hearts. Do you understand?''

"Y-y-yes, lord,'' she stammered.

"Sima,'' Hannibal said, and the huge Viking dragged the woman from the room. She would drink or die. Hannibal didn't trust any vampire who didn't want to kill. In fact, now that the house had been sold to him—for one dollar—he might simply kill her anyway.

He glanced around again. Ah, but it was a beautiful house.

"I knew you wouldn't let me down,'' he told Tsumi.

As Hannibal stared out the window at the gardens beyond, Tsumi came up behind him.

"The house is being prepared, Hannibal,'' she explained. "As many as possible will sleep here today, and possibly tomorrow as well, depending on how the battle proceeds. After that, we will disseminate them all over the city.''

"I'm very excited,'' he admitted, and he thought of Will Cody and Peter Octavian, of what he planned to do to them. "I don't think I'll be able to sleep at all today.''

In a camp hastily thrown together an hour before dawn, U.N. troops wolfed down whatever breakfast they could get their hands on. It wasn't pancakes and sausages as far as Commander Jimenez was concerned—even though that's what they were calling it—but the military didn't waste too much time with culinary concerns.

Roberto stood in front of one of the large mess tents and

sipped black coffee. He watched the sun rise over the blackened and still burning city of Atlanta, torn by the sight.

It was a job well done. They'd taken down a huge vampire population with limited human casualties, military or civilian. He ought to be proud. It was his plan, after all, and it had worked. And in the weeks to come, they'd do it at least three more times, maybe as many as half a dozen, around the world.

If it came to it—and Roberto thought it would—they might even have to torch all of Manhattan Island.

That's what got him. Atlanta had been nothing more than an experiment in feasibility. If they'd really wanted an effective first strike, they'd have had to burn New York City down. But Atlanta had seemed, somehow, less of a risk. A world-class city, yes, but in its way, New York was the hub of the world.

They had to be sure of what they were doing before taking such drastic measures.

Now they were sure.

A lot of dead vampires. Roberto's heart raced as he thought of their fear, their agony. He hoped that the others would remain as arrogant as always, and not see the events in Atlanta as much of a threat to their own cities.

He hoped John and Lucy Macchio had made it out okay. Roberto knew a number of people in Atlanta but he'd been friends with the Macchios for years.

He thought of their kids, Little Jack and April, who was just four.

And he found himself staring at the ruins of the city even more intently. His eyes narrowed, watching the flames. He thought of John and Lucy and the kids and wondered when he'd last spoken with them. Roberto couldn't remember. They might even have moved out earlier, when things started to get bad.

Moved out and left behind their jobs and schools and home and friends and family . . . and all the things that made a life. All the things that he had burned.

Commander Roberto Jimenez refused to acknowledge the way his eyes began to water, wouldn't even wipe a hand across them. His hatred for the vampires grew even more intense in that moment, but something else happened as well. As Roberto watched a city full of homes and hopes and dreams burn, he began to hate himself, just a little.

✳

11

*We all have a face that we hide away forever,
then we take them out and show ourselves,
when everyone has gone.*

—BILLY JOEL,
"The Stranger"

KUROMAKU SAT ON A BLACK WROUGHT-IRON chair on the patio at Café du Monde and watched as the day got under way in and around Jackson Square, at the heart of the French Quarter. By this time of year, New Orleans had usually grown quite warm already, even hot, but this morning was cool. Several tourists wandering about after breakfast had their hands stuffed into their pockets.

But Kuromaku could sense the weather changing around him, could smell it on the wind, and knew it would grow warmer as the day grew long. He guessed that the next day would be quite hot. Yet, at this point, the weather was the least of the Crescent City's concerns. Right now, the question was whether New Orleans would even still be standing by this time the next day.

A self-deprecating smile came over his face as Kuromaku wondered about such melodrama infecting his thoughts. It was all too human. He appreciated all that Peter Octavian had opened his mind to, was grateful to realize that there was still a great deal of humanity within the shadows, even if they failed to realize it.

As a warrior, however, he wondered if he had become too human in recent years. Too sensitive to the smaller things, the details of life. He'd heard westerners use the expression "God is in the details." He wasn't quite sure, nor had he ever been, what the phrase was intended to mean. But he knew what it meant to him.

Not merely the appreciation of a flower or a sunrise, but the longing gaze of human love, the gentle lilt of a child's laughter, the soft crinkles around aged eyes. These were the holiest of things, the things that gave humanity its value. God, or whatever higher divine power might exist, was indeed in the details. It wasn't mere humanity, but the awareness of it, the recognition that made one a human being. And in some ways, the shadows were gifted with an even greater ability to recognize that divinity, those details.

They were closer to heaven, he believed.

Thus, they had much farther to fall.

He thought of these details, the things that might make immortality attractive and yet were so often forgotten instantly upon attaining it.

Kuromaku sipped from his steaming café au lait and lowered it to the table. Half a block away, a sax man got an early start. Kuromaku ate the last beignet on his plate, drained what remained of his coffee, and stood up from the wrought iron chair. Leaving a sizable tip, he strolled out across Decatur Street and through the gates of the park at Jackson Square.

On a bench across from the statue of Andrew Jackson, Kuromaku chuckled softly to himself. His mind was straying into areas best left alone. But he could not help himself. His musing about the little things in life brought memories of his own humanity, memories of his baby sister, long centuries ago, before either of them had died.

How she'd worshiped him then. How she'd performed for him, desperately craving his attention and approval at every step of her life. Even after, when she had been born into the shadows, she had followed his lead, had embarked upon a life of noble battles and quiet suffering.

But time had changed her. Corrupted her. Kuromaku remembered Tsumi when she was still the sister of his heart; but he could not stop himself from wondering if she remembered as well. Or if she had forgotten herself entirely.

"Mornin' sir," an elderly black man said, approaching with a coffee-stained Dunkin' Donuts cup in one hand. "Help an old man get some breakfast, sir?"

Kuromaku stared at the old man a moment, then nodded. He reached a hand into his pocket, peeled a bill off his bankroll, and dropped it into the man's cup. He saw the wrinkles around the man's eyes stretch as the beggar recognized the face of Benjamin Franklin on the bill. Kuromaku hoped the old man would spend the money wisely: buy some food, clean himself up. But he'd done what he could.

In another life, he might have simply drained the man dry, thinking him the refuse of a consumer society. But Peter Octavian had changed that part of him. Shown him his own humanity, and how to make it bloom.

So Kuromaku was torn. He had dedicated himself to Peter's cause. It was the only thing worth living for after all that time. But in his mind's eye, his little sister Tsumi still clapped delightedly when he did a headstand.

He knew he shouldn't do it. Knew it was a mistake from the outset. But Kuromaku closed his eyes, ignoring the profuse thanks the old man still spouted as he walked away. Kuromaku shut out the birdsong and the distant saxophone, the idle chatter of passersby. He focused his mind on one thing.

Tsumi, his mind whispered, spreading out across the city in search of her. Before, he hadn't wanted her to know where he was. But he wasn't at the convent now. Even if her mind located him, she wouldn't be able to hurt the

others with that information. And Kuromaku felt that he at
least had to try. She was his sister, after all, and the idea
that their swords might soon clash disturbed him greatly.

Tsumi, he thought again, and his eyelids fluttered slightly
as he mentally sifted through the ether. There were many
vampires in New Orleans. He could sense them, but not
pinpoint their locations. They were not his bloodkin. Tsumi
was his sister by human birth, and by her rebirth in shadows. Even if she knew he was in New Orleans, and was
purposely trying to hide herself, he should at least be able
to . . .

Ah. There.

Kuromaku blocked out the clatter of hooves from horses
drawing rickety carriages across cobblestone, and the wail
of ancient saxophone, and the constant exotic blend of aromas; he blocked even the feel of the bench beneath him,
the sun on his face, and the slight breeze across his brow.

Instead, he felt the suffocating closeness of other bodies
smothering around him and the growing heat of the day in
a tightly shuttered room.

Tsumi's eyes snapped open, her lip curling back in an in-
stinctive snarl. She'd been sleeping, resting, so that she
might fulfill Hannibal's expectations of her that night. Hannibal. Somewhere in the house, he would be sitting awake,
she knew. Unable to sleep due to his growing anticipation.
He'd—

No. What had woken her? The touch of a mind had. . . .

"Kuromaku," she thought, feeling him there with her.
Instantly, she shuttered her mind tightly, closing out all but
a thin connection between them. *"Have you turned against
me now? Are you giving your friend Octavian our location
even as our minds meet?"*

She felt him smile, but felt as well the melancholy in it.

*"If I'd been able to determine your location, yes, I would
have given it to the coven, my allies,"* he admitted. *"You
should leave New Orleans. I have no wish to kill my own*

sister. I know that Peter hurt you once, very badly. If you wished to face him in honorable combat, I would not oppose it. But, Tsumi, what you do now with Hannibal is not honorable. In truth, it would seem only to make Peter's reasons for spurning your love nothing less than prophetic.''

Tsumi felt her face contort with fury, and she imagined her mind, her thoughts, a dagger as she thrust them at her brother.

"It's not only him I hate, Kuromaku. I hate you, as well,'' she sneered, exhilarated by this admission. *"I am a vampire, brother. For centuries, I have crushed every emotion that rose in my heart, trying to become the monster you made me. Now it's all that I know. Hannibal is a hero, my brother. If what I've become horrifies you, remind yourself that it was your doing!''*

She felt Kuromaku reel from her words, and Tsumi rejoiced in it.

"You begged for eternal life, Tsumi. Or have you forgotten your pleas to me not to leave you behind to die?'' he roared in her mind.

"I didn't understand what I was asking!'' she cried in return. *"You knew! I would have hated you then, but you should have let me die hating you rather than making me live like this.''*

Their mental rapport crackled with angry silence.

"I loved my little sister,'' Kuromaku thought, his mind whispering it with a heartfelt pain that only made Tsumi scowl.

"I was ecstatic to have you with me,'' he thought. *"What I gave you was the gift of eternal life. Thanks to the truths Peter has uncovered, I believe that now more than ever. The curse has been lifted from our kind, Tsumi, and Hannibal and his brood are so terrified of coming into the light, of that freedom and the responsibilities that the truth entails . . .''*

Tsumi felt her brother sigh.

"The truth is that we have free will, just like the humans," Kuromaku thought. *"Hannibal chooses evil but will kill anyone to retain his ignorance of that fact. If you embrace the myth, the monstrous evil of vampires, you believe you cannot be held responsible for your perversions and predations.*

"In the end, it just makes you all an army of craven cowards," he thought, his mind cold to her now.

"Tonight," Tsumi snapped in return, *"the streets of New Orleans will be painted with human blood and strewn with the flesh of the undead. If we meet, we will see who is a coward, Kuromaku. For you may shirk at the task, but I will not hesitate to take your head."*

"So be it!" Kuromaku said aloud, opening his eyes, the connection to his sister now broken.

His outburst had drawn quite a bit of attention. A young couple hand in hand turned to stare at him, but Kuromaku ignored them, ignored all those who had focused their attention on him for that moment. He rose from the bench and hurried along the path through Jackson Square.

When Bethany appeared beside him, Kuromaku was startled.

"You're good for your age," he said. "Sneaking up on me like that."

"Well, you were a bit distracted," she said. "That was quite a performance back there, by the way. Who were you 'speaking' with?"

Kuromaku froze, spun, and stared down at the shadow woman, lips set in a grim line.

"You're not unattractive, girl, and you seem kind in your way," he said menacingly. "But I don't think you've come upon me now by chance, nor do I think it was your own curiosity which set you after me. Someone in your coven has asked you to keep an eye on me. I won't object.

"But if you ever question my loyalty to this cause or to

Peter Octavian, I will tear your eyes out by their roots and fill the ragged holes with silver!''

Bethany's face fell apart; fear, horror, disgust all played across her features as her jaw dropped and she blinked away red tears that began to well up in her eyes.

"I'm not ... I'm ... sorry, I ..." she stammered.

Kuromaku blinked, then looked away, the rage draining from him.

"No, I'm sorry," he said softly. "It's only that this is not the time to question my loyalty. You see, I'm planning to murder my sister tonight.''

The chapel was full this time. Or it had been half an hour earlier. Perhaps a dozen people had left the room since that time. George Marcopoulos stood in the rear of the chapel and fought the horror and sorrow that threatened to wash over him.

Multicolored light poured through stained glass, cascaded across the faces and bowed heads of those sitting and kneeling at the pews. Some prayed, some merely waited. Some had desperately wanted to be there, others had made the choice out of loyalty, or love, or some ancient and nearly extinct nobility. Several people had even gotten up and walked out, having changed their minds at the last moment.

George couldn't blame them. He would not have joined them for the world.

"George," a voice whispered at his side. He turned to see that Bethany Hart had entered the chapel. Many of those gathered glanced up, and most of them looked quickly away. Two or three lingered, watching her. Finally, all but one of them dropped their heads.

"Denny's been waiting for you," George said quietly. "He says you promised it would be you."

Bethany smiled, but George could see the sadness in her eyes. Perhaps, though she was no longer human, she felt a little of what George was feeling. It occurred to him, in a horrible way, that it was a bit like Jonestown. But he pushed the idea away. It was nothing like Jonestown. These people all knew exactly what they were getting themselves into. It had all been explained at great length, every question answered. All but one. All but George's question.

Was it even possible for them to know what they were getting themselves into, no matter how many questions they asked, without dying first? Would they regret it when they awoke? He was certain some of them would. The thought of their regret sickened him.

"I'm sorry," Bethany replied, "I had an . . . errand to run."

Their eyes met again, pain shared, and she nodded and put a hand on his stooped shoulder.

"Denny's a special guy," she said. "I'll make it as easy on him as I can."

George thought he saw a twinkle in her eye, and assumed that Bethany was talking about sex. That she would make love to Denny while she killed him. In truth, such an act might make it easier for a young, virile man like Denny to accept what he'd decided to do. But George just thought it rather ghoulish.

He turned and nodded to Denny, who was still staring at Bethany. The big Cajun stood and walked proudly toward them, trained from childhood not to show his fear. But he was afraid, George was certain of it. It was in his eyes.

"Beth," he said and dipped his head in greeting.

"Hi, Denny," she replied. "Sorry if I kept you waiting. You're sure you're okay with this?"

"We all know de score, *chérie,*" he explained. "Our family loses dis battle, dere may not be any others. Denny ain't gonna do anybody any good wit' just muscle. Not dis time."

Bethany took Denny's hand and stood on tiptoe to kiss him on the cheek, then softly on the lips.

"You're a good man, Denny Gautreau," she said and led him from the room.

Before George could even turn away, Caleb came into the chapel. His face was flush and he looked a bit sleepy, but he nodded at George to indicate that he was ready for another.

"Shawnelle?" George asked.

"She's okay," Caleb replied. "In the dining room with the others."

That's where all the corpses were being laid, at least until they ran out of room. Then they'd start using some of the other rooms. The mass production of new vampires . . . George shook his head at the idea even as he cursed himself for calling them that. Shadows, vampires, there truly was a difference.

But at times like this it was difficult to draw that line. Even Hannibal had never done anything like this. But Hannibal had never been this desperate.

George looked at Caleb, then back at the expectant faces in the chapel.

"Elliot," he said, drawing the attention of a fiftyish man with a large pot belly. "You're next."

The man glanced at George, then at Caleb, and rose from the pew. When he marched in silence past George's spot at the chapel door, Elliot didn't lift his head.

George Marcopoulos prayed, then, to a God in whose existence he had every faith, but about whose benevolence he had never been quite certain.

It was half past ten, and Commander Jimenez sat in the small tent that had been set up for him. It was a crash pad, mental retreat, and mission control all rolled into one. He'd spent the last few hours listening to reports about Operation Moses, and now he was just tired. It'd be at least two to three days before his command was in any shape to pull a similar operation, and the city hadn't even been chosen yet.

He was voting for New York. It had the highest kill ratio and lowest percentage of remaining population of any infested area. But it wasn't his decision alone.

Roberto sighed and tried to stop the rapid flow of thought and analysis in his mind. He hadn't slept in more than thirty-six hours, and he needed at least a few before he could even think straight again.

Outside the tent, his troops were still hustling. They were working in shifts now, one shift helping the recently arrived National Guard troops do a sweep of the city for human survivors or vampire leftovers while the other shift catnapped. Roberto didn't want to sleep, but trying to deny exhaustion was both foolish and dangerous, to himself and to the men and women in his command.

Tanks and jeeps and Humvees rolled along outside the tent. Officers shouted orders and the mess tent fairly roared with the clatter of trays and the chatter of soldiers. Roberto had been a soldier his whole life. This was his lullaby.

He lay on his side, right hand under his flimsy pillow, and let his mind drift away, finally, so that sleep might claim him. He felt his awareness slipping away, his mind retreating into a world where it might continue to think and work and thrive without distracting his consciousness . . . and then he sensed something. Some sound, so insignificant, perhaps, that his conscious mind wouldn't even have registered it. But his subconscious, his sleeping mind, alerted him to something, somehow out of place.

A whisper. A presence.

Roberto rolled onto his back on the cot, hand flashing to his sidearm, drawing it up, and aiming it all in a single motion. Four of them, and he could tell just from the way they stood, the way they stared at him, that they were vampires.

His finger began to draw back the trigger, but the gun simply disappeared from his hand. Roberto blinked, saw the dark-haired girl holding his weapon, and despaired.

"Careful where you wave that thing," said a familiar voice in back. "I don't reckon any of us wants to let your troops know you've got company. And it wouldn't do you much good even if we were here to kill you. Which we're not.''

Roberto rubbed his eyes, trying to clear his sleep-starved brain. The man in front of him looked older—if that was possible for a vampire—but he knew without a doubt that it was Will Cody.

"Will," he said, and his eyes scanned the other three. It took him a moment to realize the blond was Allison. And not merely because she'd changed her hair.

"Allison?" he muttered. "I thought you didn't . . ."

Then he stopped, midsentence. Her eyes had flared with a certain rage that told him the subject was not open to discussion. So they sat there in silence a few seconds. Just long enough for Roberto to feel a sudden and inexplicable guilt for the act of genocide he had so recently perpetrated. It was ridiculous, but he could not shake it. Though he knew these vampires, Cody and Allison at least, to be noble and decent, they were still vampires. He ought to kill them where they stood. That was his mandate, after all.

But he'd known for months where Peter Octavian's coven made their home, and he'd done nothing about it. So what did that say?

"You've picked an odd time for a social call," he said, and his eyes narrowed as he watched Cody's face. "Frankly, I'm surprised you even got in here. My people are pretty good at spotting your—at spotting vampires."

"The sun's up," Allison said simply. "They're used to dealing with vampires, not shadows."

The tone in her voice bothered Roberto. The loss of her humanity had changed her drastically; he could see that right off. And however it had happened, he didn't think she was happy about it.

"Rolf's dead," Cody said suddenly.

Roberto blinked, frowned.

"That's a damn shame," he replied after a moment. "He was a good man. A fine soldier."

"He was more than that," Cody corrected him, but didn't elaborate.

But Commander Jimenez wasn't listening. It had occurred to him suddenly that Rolf Sechs would have been an extremely difficult vampire to kill. And maybe, just maybe, that had something to do with why he'd never told his superiors where Octavian's coven was. There was one way in which the shadows and the vampires were very different. At least one.

Shadows were much more difficult to kill.

"How did he—"

"That's why we're here," Allison interrupted. "If we're right, and you move fast enough, it's just possible that we can help each other. Hannibal murdered Rolf with a—"

"Wait!" the white-haired vampire behind Cody snapped.

He stepped forward, and Roberto studied him. Cody looked older, maybe fifty, but this stocky bloodsucker was the first vampire Roberto had ever seen who actually looked *old*. It was odd.

"How do we know we can trust him?" the old vampire asked, staring at the commander.

"How do *you* know you can..." Roberto repeated, sneering. "Who the fuck is this guy?"

"Sebastiano Battaglia, Commander Roberto Jimenez," Cody said quickly, then gestured toward the brunette fang-girl. "And this is Erika Hunter; she and Rolf were a couple. And now that the introductions are out of the way, Berto, let me ask you an important question."

Cody dragged the single chair inside the small tent over next to Roberto's cot and sat astride it, leaned his elbows on the back of the chair, and fixed the commander with an intense stare.

"It isn't that I don't trust you, understand," Cody said bluntly. "If I didn't trust you, I wouldn't have agreed to come here. But I know you think of us—Peter and me and the few others of us that you've actually met, that you actually know—as . . . oddities, I guess. Exceptions to your own rules about vampires.

"My question is, if we gave you a weapon you could use to cripple vampires, making them easy to kill, how do we know that you'll work with us to make sure our own loved ones aren't targets?"

Behind Cody, Sebastiano and Erika seemed to tense up, as if they were preparing to attack. Roberto forced himself to ignore them. It was clear they wouldn't do anything without Cody's or Allison's say-so.

So he focused instead upon Will Cody's question. Turned it over in his mind. Was tempted to ask what this weapon was, but knew they wouldn't answer him. Not yet. The hell with diplomacy, he decided.

"Honestly?" he began. "You don't know anything of the sort. Even if I promise you, you won't know. But I'll tell you this much: if this weapon can be mass produced, if it can be stored and used at our convenience, I'd be more than happy to coordinate any attack with you, Will. If your people act up later, we can always go after them then."

Cody glanced at Allison, then at the other two. None of them seemed to offer any commentary whatsoever, but Cody seemed pleased.

"All right," Cody said. "I think we can live with that."

"Our coven is headquartered in New Orleans," Allison began.

"Yes, I know," Roberto replied.

Allison raised an eyebrow. It was all the comment Roberto needed. She understood that he'd stayed away thus far. For what it was worth, it would certainly make them trust him more.

"Hannibal is probably there already. He's taken his entire New York clan, and maybe some from other cities, and has somehow found a hiding place in New Orleans. Tonight, at dusk, he's going to try to wipe out our entire coven," Allison explained. "He's been planning this for a while, but your attack on Atlanta spurred him on."

Roberto frowned. "How do you know all of this?" he asked.

"Long story," Cody replied. "The point is, it's tonight. You've only got hours to duplicate the serum we've brought, so let's not waste any more time."

"Agreed," Roberto replied. "So where is this serum? And what does it do?"

The vampire girl who'd been introduced as Erika produced a small steel case Roberto hadn't noticed before.

"Here," she said, stepping forward. "Let me show you."

She held the case in front of him and opened it, her back to the others. Roberto's eyes widened as he looked inside.

The case was empty.

"What kind of game are you playing?" he said angrily, all thoughts of vengeance, of quickly wiping the vampires from the face of the Earth, dissipating in a single moment. "Stop wasting my time."

But then Commander Jimenez saw the effect his words had on the other shadows, saw the surprise on Will Cody's face. He glanced at Erika and caught the smirk on her face.

Then she was behind him, in an instant, the metal case clattering to the ground.

Cody and Allison began to shout at her, but the white-haired vampire, Sebastiano they'd called him, merely stood and stared.

"Shut up!" Erika screamed. "Both of you!"

She had a long nail pressed to the flesh of his throat. It pinched a little, and he felt the warmth of blood streak his neck.

"Erika!" Allison shouted. "What the hell are you doing?"

Commander Jimenez said nothing. If the girl was going to kill him, there was nothing he could do to stop her. He locked eyes with Cody a moment, then the old scout and hunter turned to look at Erika again.

"I'm sorry," Erika said, but Roberto didn't think she meant it.

"This was the plan all along," she admitted, and then let loose a small chuckle, barely noticeable really, which told Berto something he really didn't want to know.

The girl was insane. Maybe not maniacally so, not jumping around like a lunatic. But mad, just the same.

12

*I thought I had a piece of
my soul left to sell....
But the angels won't have it.*

—MELISSA ETHERIDGE,
"The Angels"

NIKKI STARED AT KEVIN, EYES NARROWED
with an anger she found it difficult to express. They stood
in the middle of a small study, which Nikki guessed had
once been the office of the convent's mother superior. The
study had become the center of a flurry of activity since
before dawn, when the plans Kevin, George, and Kuromaku
had made began to take effect.

Elsewhere in the convent were more than a hundred fresh
corpses, waiting to rise into a new life in the shadows. Out
in the city, every coven member who could be spared was
searching for Hannibal's daylight resting place. After all,
there weren't many places where one might hide hundreds
of sleeping vampires. Warehouses, abandoned office struc-
tures, public buildings, and the like. A boarded-up pornog-
raphy theater had seemed an ideal spot, but had turned out
to be empty.

In the neighborhood around the convent, word was being
spread that something horrible was coming. That anyone

interested in continuing to live should find somewhere else to spend the night. Bethany had begun contacting the owners of certain businesses nearby, many of whom Peter and Joe and Will had known well, before the events of the past week. A silent alarm was being sounded, but it was impossible to determine who might respond. If the owners of a bar or restaurant did not want to close up for the night, who could blame them?

If pressed, Nikki would have to admit that she was surprised Kevin had been able to accomplish so much in such a short amount of time, even with George and Kuromaku helping with the details. It was barely noon, after all.

But now George had gone to his room to rest, exhausted from the long night's events. He was growing old very quickly now, she thought. Seemed, in fact, to be aging before their eyes. Nikki hadn't known the man long and, when it came right down to it, he wasn't even really *that* old. Not in today's terms. But he did not look well. Not at all.

So here she was, stuck with Kevin. He was an admirable man. Loyal and committed, striving to live up to impossible standards, just praying that he could help keep his race alive until morning. And hoping, of course, to have revenge for his slaughtered lover.

Nikki understood all those things, and gave Kevin the respect he deserved. And she understood, as well, the reason for his appalling lack of tact when it came to one particular topic of conversation. But she wasn't going to stand for it.

"For the last time," she said through gritted teeth, "the answer is no. I don't care what you say, or how many reasons you give me, I refuse."

"We need you, Nikki," Kevin insisted. "Every last person counts, don't you get it? And if you were with us, the others might feel that, in a way, maybe Peter was with us too."

Nikki snorted with laughter. "Oh, Jesus, that's low. Not

to mention that you're really fucking reaching with that one, Kevin.''

He glared at her.

"No, really," Nikki continued. "I mean, I barely know the guy. Sure, I was attracted to him. Who wouldn't be? And it isn't that I don't care; I do. About Peter, and about the rest of you as well. I'm not some unfeeling bitch. But you don't have any idea what you're asking.''

"Yes, I do," Kevin said quietly, folding his arms in front of him.

"No," she said, shaking her head as she grew even angrier. "No, you don't. I'm sorry for what's happened to you, and I admire what all your volunteers are doing today. But I'm not going to be one of them, do you understand? I have a life, goddamnit. One life. I've seen too many people give theirs up, to drugs or suicide or even depression . . . fuck, even just laziness. I've seen lives wasted.

"I'll be damned if I'm going to waste mine. One life is good enough for me, Kevin. I don't want immortality, and I sure as hell don't need a blood addiction after evading coke and heroin for so long.

"I don't blame you for asking, Kevin. But no means no, for Christ's sake. No means no. You were dying when your time came, Kevin. You didn't have a real choice, not a fair one. I'm sorry about that. But I do!

"I choose life," she said grimly and turned to stalk out of the study, silently daring him to speak.

At the door, she glared at him again. "How dare you?" she spat.

Striding from the room, she nearly walked right into Caleb. The look on his face and the speed with which he moved alarmed her instantly.

"What is it?" Nikki whispered.

Caleb looked at Kevin, glanced at Nikki, then back at Kevin again.

"The cocoon," Caleb said, his voice hoarse. "Something's moving inside."

"Get George," Kevin barked.

Then he was up and running past Nikki down the hall-way. Caleb looked at Nikki a moment longer, then turned to follow. Nikki couldn't breathe. She wanted to follow, though she knew she'd never keep up, not if they weren't making an effort to wait for her. But she couldn't follow. She couldn't do anything.

She had begun to care for Peter, that much was true. But the thought of seeing what was going to emerge from that cocoon frightened and nauseated her all at the same time. None of them knew, that was the disturbing thing about it. None of them had any idea what to expect.

Any more than she did.

That was the thought which got her legs moving. None of them knew. But each of them, she was sure, had secretly thought of several possibilities. None of the ones Nikki had considered were very pleasant. And yet, curiosity was a great motivator. Curiosity and fear. Fear for Peter. She didn't know if she loved him. Didn't know if she could love one of—one of them.

But she was frightened for him, and she just had to know.

By the time she ran from the house into the courtyard, shielding her eyes from the brightness of the day, a small group had gathered around the black cocoon, there amidst the deep green and the rainbow of flowers. The smell of the garden and the earth was very strong that day.

There weren't very many people left in the house, not counting those volunteers who'd yet to rise, so Nikki was the last to run into the garden.

The cocoon had cracked and flaked at its base, where it was attached to the path and the bench. Its outer layers had whitened, like dead skin, and begun to peel. It was more brittle than ever. But as far as Nikki could see, those were the only changes in the thing.

Then it moved! Or rather, something inside it moved, pressing against the outer shell like a baby against its mother's belly.

Caleb appeared at her side.

"Where's George?" she asked, noting the distinct sound of panic in her voice.

"He wasn't in his room," Caleb replied.

"He should be here," Nikki said, but made no move to go look for him.

None of them did. It was impossible to look away.

A crack appeared in the top of the cocoon, near the center. What appeared to be a hand snaked through. But it wasn't a hand like any Nikki had ever seen. White and gossamer, it was almost like the mist the shadows could become, but more solid than that. More purposeful. Ghost fingers tore at the cocoon, widening the hole from the inside.

"God, what's happened to him?" Nikki whispered.

Then, though the hole in the cocoon was still far too small for a human body to crawl through, another hand appeared next to the first. What dragged itself from the cocoon had some resemblance to Peter, at least in its face. In its eyes. But it was a wraith, a spectre modeled after Octavian but containing none of his real presence. His self.

It looked around at those gathered by the cocoon, eyes resting at last on Nikki. It smiled.

"Peter?" she asked weakly.

Then, so quickly as to be almost invisible to her, it shot into the sky above the convent and disappeared into the clouds. Became one with them, perhaps, since it seemed to have almost the same consistency. They all stared into the sky, and nobody spoke.

Nikki was aware of a sadness, somewhere inside her, trying to break free. Her brain was telling her that Peter was gone, that she would never see him again. That whatever he'd become was not for her to experience. But her heart was so full of joy, a bliss brought by the wraith's appearance, that such despairing thoughts were kept at bay. Suddenly she was filled with hope and love and patience.

"What was it?" a voice asked from behind her, and for

the first time she realized that Kuromaku had joined them
outside.

"It was . . . it was beautiful," Kevin murmured.

"An angel," someone whispered.

Nobody argued.

"His soul," she said suddenly, though it was only a
guess. "I think it was his soul."

"If that was his soul, where is his body?" Kuromaku
asked, clearly less affected by what they'd all seen than the
others.

There came a sudden snarl from inside the cocoon. As
one, they turned their attention on the cracked and flaking
shell of the thing. Whatever they'd just seen hadn't been
alone in there. Something still moved inside the chrysalis.

Black claws slashed the length of the cocoon from the
inside. Nikki jumped back several feet, screaming. Where
the thing's claws dug in, despite its dessicated appearance,
the cocoon appeared to be bleeding ever so slightly.

A powerful hand gripped her shoulder, pulling her back-
wards.

"Behind me," Kuromaku said and once again astonished
her by pulling a sword from his side, from a scabbard that
an instant earlier had not existed in the world.

"Kuromaku!" Kevin barked. "Back off. It's Peter!"

"I sense you are right," Kuromaku said. "But if Nikki
guessed correctly, if that was Peter's soul, then what is left
behind?"

As if in answer, there was a roar from within the cocoon.
Black, gnarled hands curved into claws gripped the edges
of the huge slash in the cocoon, and darkness erupted into
the daylight. The creature was tall and spindly, like a man-
tis, but humanoid. Its body was nearly flat, its eyes reflec-
tive and empty. Its mouth was filled with rows of needle
teeth and its claws were ebony razors.

It stood, panting, glancing around at them almost as the
wraith had done moments before. Like the wraith, this
thing's face bore a resemblance to Peter. Like the wraith,

its gaze came to rest on Nikki, who still stood behind Kuromaku, and it smiled. But its smile was the smile of a predator that has sighted its prey.

"Peter, no!" Kevin shouted. "Just stand there! We'll help you!"

"That's not Peter," Kuromaku said warily and held his sword up in defensive posture.

The thing watched Kuromaku's sword a moment, waited for an opening, and then lunged toward him. Nikki screamed as Kuromaku brought the *katana* around, its blade flashing in the sun, slashing across the chest of the ebony demon. Darkness spilled like blood from the wound and the thing shrieked in pain and leaped backward.

Caleb and Kevin were the first to attack, slashing at the dark wraith. But Nikki could see that its wounds were already healing. It raked its claws across Caleb's face, and one of his eyes burst, squirting viscous fluid over the crusty remains of the cocoon.

From nowhere, it dawned on Nikki what they were fighting.

"It's a vampire!" she cried.

"No shit," Kevin snapped, grappling with the thing from behind, trying to drive it down to the stone path.

But Kuromaku understood her, turned to meet her eyes a moment, then sheathed his *katana*. This time, it didn't disappear. He held his hands up, and as Nikki watched, they changed. Fingers into claws, claws into long silver spikes.

The dead eyes of the vampire seemed to widen. It roared, reached over its shoulders, and grabbed Kevin. The thing threw Kevin at Caleb and the others. In the heartbeat that it had before Kuromaku would have lunged at it, the thing seemed to shake like a wet dog, and dark, leathery wings sprouted from its back with a painful tearing sound.

"No!" Kuromaku growled and dove after the thing.

But too late. It took flight and was quickly moving over

the convent walls, even as Kuromaku turned to make certain Nikki was all right.

"I'm fine!" she snapped. "Aren't you going after it?"

It. The word rang in her head. What if *it* was Peter? He had attacked her, meant to kill her, she was sure. But why? Even in his subconscious mind, what reason would Peter have to want to kill her? On the other hand, she thought with relief, she'd been the only human being in the courtyard at the time.

"I'll go!" Kevin said. "Caleb, with me!"

Kevin pointed to two others he wanted to accompany him, and soon they were changing form, sprouting wings themselves. But unlike the dark wraith, they had changed completely, into birds of prey and bats. Before they changed, Nikki noticed that Caleb's face had begun to heal, but that he was still missing an eye. Surprised to find herself fascinated rather than repulsed, she wondered if somehow the eye was gone for good.

"Oh, my God," she said, suddenly unable to stand as the shock of all she'd just seen caught up with her.

Nikki went down on her ass on the path and drew her knees up. She examined the hole in the denim on her left knee, ran a hand through her hair.

"Why didn't you go with them?" she asked Kuromaku.

"Now that they know the thing fears silver, they will have the advantage," he answered. "Also, I was not sure that you were honest when you said you were fine."

Nikki laughed. "I lied," she admitted. "So sue me."

The other shadows in the courtyard milled about, watching the sky for Kevin and the others to return. One of them went back inside to check on the volunteers, to see if any of them had risen yet.

"So what now?" she asked. "I mean, was that it? Was that thing his soul, and the rest of it . . . I don't know, the vampire part of him? That's what it was, right? A true vampire like the ones that Mulkerrin guy conjured up in Austria? The things that infected the first shadows? That was one of them, the one that Peter had become, wasn't it?"

Nikki heard the panic, the near hysteria, in her voice but she did not try to hide it. It was nothing to be ashamed of, she told herself. Not after what she'd just seen. She did, however, try to push away the little, insinuating voice asking how she could have had feelings for a creature that was nothing more than ghost and monster rolled into one.

Which made her frown, blink back her tears, and look more closely at Kuromaku. After all, what was he but the same thing. No matter how much he tried to be a friend.

"So it would seem," Kuromaku replied, but did not elaborate. "What will you do now? If you wish to leave, I will be happy to get you out of the city, somewhere safe."

"Does that even exist anymore?" she asked. "Somewhere safe? Or is that like Oz or Atlantis now?"

He only tilted his head slightly, awaiting her answer.

"I'm sorry," she said softly. "Yes, please. Get me out of here."

Kuromaku offered her his hand, and Nikki took it and allowed him to pull her to her feet. She brushed off the seat of her pants, took a deep breath, and turned to go back into the convent to get what few things she had retrieved from her rooms and brought there the day after she'd met Peter.

"Nikki?"

The hoarse whisper had not come from Kuromaku.

Behind them, the cocoon began to move again; its papery layers rasped against one another.

"Peter?" she asked hopefully.

Kuromaku drew his sword and stood on guard as human hands gripped the edges of the cocoon and Peter Octavian, looking gaunt and tired, struggled to stand.

"What'd I miss?" he asked.

"Oh, Peter!" Nikki cried.

As he stepped from the cocoon, she rushed forward to meet him. Kuromaku blocked her way and held his sword

up to Peter's chest, preventing him from getting any closer
to her.

"A moment, Octavian," Kuromaku said menacingly.

"Kuromaku?" Peter said, eyes wide with surprise. "Apparently, I've missed a great deal. It's . . . fantastic to see
you."

A strange look passed over Peter's face then, and he
seemed to rock forward on the balls of his feet. Then he
fell, or rather, crumpled to the stone path. His forehead
smacked hard against the ground, but he didn't move again.

"Peter?" Kuromaku asked, his voice filled with wonder.

"It is him," Nikki said, suddenly sure. "It really is."

Kuromaku knelt by Peter's side and turned him over.
Nikki joined him there and, out of reflex, felt for a pulse
and put her ear to his chest. It rose and fell under her cheek.
His heartbeat was strong, his breathing seemed regular.

"What are you doing?" Kuromaku asked.

"Just checking to see . . ."

She looked up, met Kuromaku's questioning gaze, and
realized how silly she'd been. Shadows didn't have—Her
eyes widened. Then she noticed that Kuromaku had looked
away. She tried to see what he was looking at and realized
that it was the rapidly rising welt on Peter's forehead. There
was a nasty cut there, too. A thin line of blood ran down
the side of his face and dripped to the ground.

"He's bleeding," Kuromaku said in astonishment.

"And breathing," Nikki added.

"When Hannibal found out about Atlanta, he went crazy.
He went down to New Orleans, after Peter and the others.
But he wanted Jimenez dead very badly. This was his plan.
Though it didn't include breaking you out, Allison. That, I
did for you, and for Rolf."

"But coming here was my idea," Allison said, frowning.

"Yeah," Erika sniffed. "I had to gamble that you'd suggest it, otherwise I would have had to come up with it
eventually. It wouldn't have made much sense if I'd said

it right off, kind of suspicious, actually. But now we're all here, right?''

She smiled. "Time to kill somebody.''

"Erika," Cody said, and his voice was a command in itself.

The girl seemed to pause, and though Roberto could not see her face he knew she would have looked at him. His voice demanded it.

"You loved Rolf, I know you did," Cody continued. "Hannibal is only using you."

"You think I don't know that?" she roared, and Roberto felt something warm drip onto his cheek. Its smell was too familiar.

Blood? She was crying blood.

"You don't know me, any of you!" she declared. "You don't know anything about me! Before I joined your coven, I'd only been a vampire two years. And I never killed. Never! I took blood, but never a life!

"Not until Hannibal took me. He killed Rolf in front of me, and then he starved me until I was out of my mind, and then he gave me a . . . gave me a victim!" she wailed. "And that's the way it should be! Sweet blood, the power of life and death!

"We're monsters, you fucking idiots! Monsters! There are only two choices; to hide in the shadows or to take the humans as our slaves, our prey!"

Her breasts pressed against the back of Roberto's head, her claws at his throat, and suddenly she went completely still.

"I'm sorry," she said again, and Roberto knew it was time for him to die.

"How dare you?" Allison growled, her face contorting, and stepped forward.

Erika froze. Roberto closed his eyes and prayed.

"After what I went through at Hannibal's hands, you stand up there and say *you* can't take it? You miserable little weak-willed bitch! Go ahead, then. Kill Jimenez and probably Peter and all the others as well. But when you're done, you're mine.''

Roberto stiffened. What the fuck was Allison trying to do? Some vampire girl goes psycho, he thought, you don't keep pushing her buttons. The girl's claws began to dig into his throat, and he winced, thought of his sister, Mercedes, and her sons, and how he hadn't contacted them since Christmas. Then he opened his eyes. Roberto wasn't going to die with his eyes closed.

Then Erika cried out a name, "Yano," and suddenly the claws were gone from his throat.

"Get down, Commander!" Cody shouted, and Roberto pitched forward, rolled, and came up facing his cot.

Sebastiano knelt on Erika's back, a hypodermic needle plunged into her neck. Bloody tears streaked her face and now fell onto his sheets. She started to struggle. Yano rapped her hard in the back of the head with his huge fist, and Erika lay still.

"Why isn't she changing?" he croaked.

"That's what this stuff does," Sebastiano replied. "She can't.''

"You mean . . .'' Roberto began, and as Sebastiano nodded, the commander started to realize what this weapon would mean.

"Thanks for the save," he said, and Sebastiano only nodded again.

"Yano, where did you get that if the case was empty?" Allison asked.

"I didn't trust her," Yano replied. "I brought my own.''

"Thank God," Allison sighed.

"And the antidote too?" Cody asked.

"Yes, the antidote too," he answered. "But none for her. She's a traitor and a headcase. She's a liability. Give the commander back his gun.''

Silence, then, as each of them realized what Sebastiano was suggesting. Jimenez looked at the hypodermic, at the unconscious vampire girl, and then held out his hand to Allison.

"We don't have much time," he said.

She grunted, but handed his sidearm over. Their hands met with the gun between them.

"Wait!" Cody snapped.

"It's what needs to be done," Sebastiano said calmly.

"Maybe so," Cody admitted. "But not like this. It should be one of us."

Again, they looked around at one another. Finally, Allison took the gun back. Grimly, and without tears, she stepped forward, placed the barrel of the weapon at the back of Erika's head, and fired twice. Gore splashed across sheets and pitiful pillow.

There was an uproar outside the tent, feet pounding, soldiers shouting, weapons clacking as they were brought to bear. Allison handed the sidearm back to Roberto, but didn't meet his eyes.

Roberto could only stare at Erika's corpse, then at the thin metal case, much smaller than the first, that Sebastiano opened for him. Inside, there were half a dozen vials of clear fluid.

"Okay," he said, nodding, thinking of a million things he needed to do if they were going to be of any help against Hannibal. "Okay, let's go. No time to waste."

Someone shouted to him from outside, and Roberto turned and marched out of his tent.

"Put down your goddamn weapons and listen up," he barked. "Looks like we may have another sleepless night ahead of us."

When Peter woke, he didn't open his eyes right away. He felt rested, glad for what sleep he'd had, in a way he couldn't ever remember appreciating it in the past. He opened his eyes, then winced at pain in his forehead and reached up to gingerly examine the bump and cut there. It took him a moment to search his mind for the appropriate spell. When he found it, a haze of green light sprang from his fingers. The skin on his forehead pinched a little, but afterward, all that remained was a little dry blood.

"Peter?"

He opened his eyes. Nikki. And behind her, Kuromaku. For a moment, the incongruity of this pairing threw him off, made his head spin just a little. He may not have a concussion, he thought, but that didn't mean his head didn't hurt. Peter cared for Nikki, more, perhaps, than he ought to, having known her so short a time. But that's how it had always been with him. He'd meet someone and know, immediately, that this person was going to be important to him. To his life.

He'd felt that way about Kuromaku as well, though not in any romantic way. Here was a man who might have been his brother, had not time and space conspired against them. Kuromaku was almost as close to him as Will Cody was. So, despite the incongruity, though he'd known her only a short time, and his fellow warrior for a century and a half, there was something very natural about them being there, together. There weren't that many people he felt close to.

Which reminded him again of Will. And Rolf. And Allison.

"Any word from Cody?" he asked, looking to Nikki for an answer.

She shook her head.

"How are you?" Nikki asked.

"I feel . . . good," Peter replied, oddly delighted with his own answer. "I feel alive."

"You are alive," Kuromaku said grimly.

Peter laughed again. "Don't sound so happy about it, old friend," he said.

Then he saw the fear and anxiety on Nikki's face and realized he was being unkind. He reached out, touched her hand. She returned his smile, at last, and twined her fingers into his.

"I know I'm alive, of course," he said, looking from

Nikki's face to Kuromaku's. "I haven't lost my 'magic touch,' but everything else is . . . well, it's gone."

"But how?" Kuromaku asked. "I've never heard of anything like this. Never."

Peter frowned now. "I don't know," he admitted. "I wish I could say I did it on purpose. And I've never heard of anything like it either, not even from the Stranger himself. But then, I don't think a shadow has ever lived through the things I have. The magic I learned, during my time in Hell . . . my age . . . I don't know.

"What I do know is this: the cocoon was natural, but the magic was there too. I've explained to you, Kuromaku, in the correspondence we've exchanged, that shadows are of a triple nature. Divine. Demonic. Human. Obviously the end result of this hibernation state was a splitting of those three."

"Then the wraith we saw . . ." Nikki began.

"There were two, weren't there?" Peter asked.

"Yes, but one was beautiful and the other horrible," she replied.

"There!" Peter said. "You see. Divine. Demonic. Shades of my true self. Which, with the exception of a bit of sorcery, leaves me . . ."

He trailed off again. For in the cocoon, he'd been in a kind of dream state. Aware, but not truly conscious. Now, the reality of what had happened began to hit him.

"Human," Kuromaku finished. "Completely human."

"Looks that way," Peter replied, his brow furrowed.

"Do you feel . . . odd?" Nikki asked.

He had to think about it for a moment. As he contemplated her question, he noticed that Kuromaku wore two swords. One was his *katana*. The other, Peter recognized instantly.

"Maku?" he asked.

"Ah, yes, sorry," Kuromaku replied. "When you feel up to it, I'll tell you of the dreams that brought me here.

Odd dreams, but one thing in them was perfectly clear. You're meant to have this back.''

Kuromaku handed him the long sword, and something seemed to sweep over Peter. It was the past. But not as history, as memory. The sights and smells and sounds of one night, nearly five and a half centuries earlier. The night Constantinople fell to the Turks.

The night Nicephorus Dragases became a vampire.

''Thank you,'' he said uncertainly.

Nikki looked at him strangely. ''What is it?'' she asked.

''It's hard to explain,'' he said. ''But I feel like my life as a shadow is a distant memory, as if from childhood. And my life before—my life in Byzantium—is as fresh as yesterday. Even my name sounds odd to me. My real name is Nicephorus. That's who I am.''

Kuromaku only looked at him curiously, but Nikki seemed actually alarmed. Even hurt. It took him a moment to understand her reaction.

''Oh, I haven't disappeared into the past,'' he said hurriedly. ''I'm still Peter Octavian. My heart is still here . . . with the coven. My family is here. But I guess I just feel . . .''

''You feel human again,'' Nikki suggested.

Peter smiled at that.

''Oh, yes,'' he said.

But then his smile dissolved, as he noticed someone was missing.

''Where's George?'' he asked.

Nikki looked away, and it was Kuromaku who answered.

''Your friend is ill, I'm afraid.''

13

I'm living for the night we steal away.
I need you at the dimming of the day.

—BONNIE RAITT,
"Dimming of the Day"

U.N. SOLDIERS HAD VACATED A SMALL TENT and given it over to their unlikely guests so they might rest while preparations were made for the move on New Orleans. Sebastiano was with Jimenez, trying to work with chemists at the relocated Center for Disease Control, whose main labs had been moved long before the fire.

Cody hoped the CDC scientists could duplicate and mass produce the serum in time. They would know soon, however. And if it turned out they couldn't do it, then he and Allison and probably Yano would head off to New Orleans on their own, try to do what they could in what he deemed an unwinnable war.

Behind him, Allison lay on a cot, wide awake. She made no attempt to get comfortable; she just lay there waiting for the action to begin. Waiting for her shot at Hannibal. Cody didn't know what to say to her. Didn't even know how to begin. Rather than try, he picked up the cellular phone Jimenez had loaned them and dialed the number at the convent. It was the middle of the day, and he was greatly surprised when, at the sixth ring, the answering machine beeped into his ear.

"Uh, hello?" he said. "George? Peter? It's Will. Listen, I'll try you again soon if I can. I know the shit's gonna be hitting the fan tonight. Alli . . . Alli and I are working on something that might give us an edge. We're in Atlanta now, but we'll be there as soon as we can."

He flipped the cell phone closed and dropped it on his cot. With a sigh, Cody sat on the cot and steepled his fingers under his bearded chin. His eyes focused, at length, on Allison. She hadn't moved. Hadn't closed her eyes, nor turned at all to comment on his phone call or to acknowledge the silence between them.

All his life, he'd been a rogue. As a shadow, after freeing himself from the expectations of Karl Von Reinman's coven, he had become a rogue once again. For more than one hundred and fifty years, he had seen the world clearly, turned a problem over in his mind, and then acted upon his instincts. For better or worse, he had lived and died and lived as a man of action.

But at that moment, Will Cody had no idea what to do or say. He felt, for all the world, like a child.

"I love you," he said at last, for no other words would come.

Allison said nothing. Didn't even look up. Her lack of response drew him off the cot and across the tent, where he kneeled by her and gingerly stroked her hair. But Allison turned away, eyes still open and staring at the tent wall.

"This is the first time we've been alone since . . ." he began, but faltered. "Allison, please speak to me. I know it's . . . I've heard all the corny love songs on the radio, even paid attention to a few when you weren't watching me, and I know how it sounds, but I need you. I truly do. You're all I live for."

Allison was silent. She made no sound, no sob or whimper, but he knew she was crying. He could smell the blood.

"Alli?" he prodded, disgusted with the pleading in his voice, despite the honesty of his feelings.

"I'm not me," she said, her voice cracking. "You needed her. I'm not her anymore."

That stopped him. Will stared at her still form; her ribs did not rise and fall with her breathing because she no longer needed to breathe. His heart felt frozen as he reached out to touch her gently on the shoulder.

"Alli," he said again.

Finally, she rolled over to look at him, vulnerable, offering herself to him as if in defeat. Offering her body. Offering her throat. Surrendering.

"Please," he said, and simply did not know how to continue.

"What are you asking for?" she whispered. "I've got nothing to give you, Will. I'm all gone."

"Then I'm going to get you back, bring you back," he insisted, his voice rising. "If you want to just give up, I can't stop you, but *I'm* not going to give up, Allison."

"I'm not her," she said again and averted her eyes.

"Don't you look away from me!" he growled. "Damn you, don't you look away! You think I don't know you're different? You think I don't know that you've changed?

"Goddamn you, I'm what you've become!" he roared, standing and striding away from her, arms flailing. "I'm the thing you hate so much, the horror that your life has turned into!"

In an instant, he was at her side again.

"So don't tell me you're not her!" he snarled. "I know what you are. There are parts of you that you've lost forever. I know it. I've been there. I can't even begin to imagine the agony and horror of what Hannibal did to you, and yes, I chose the shadows because I was too much of a coward to 'go gently into that good night.' I didn't want to die! You didn't have a choice.

"I know it's not the same thing," he said, his voice dropping nearly to a whisper.

Then he buried his face in her hair, smelling the blood of his own tears now.

"But don't tell me you're not her. Your name is Allison Vigeant. I love you more than I've ever loved anyone or cared for anything in my life. I know you, darlin'. You want to hide away from what's happened to you, I understand that. But don't hide from me!" he whispered.

Her eyes were still closed as she reached up to embrace him. Her arms, though filled with an unnatural strength, felt weak around him. Will held her close.

"I hated Erika for what she did. For what she let happen to me, and for betraying us all," Allison whispered. "But to kill her like that. . . . I wanted to do it, to make myself believe it didn't matter. To be cold and hard and dead. I'm dead, Will. I can make myself look beautiful, but in my mind I'll always have the wounds and scars that Hannibal gave me. It's horrible, and I thought I could take all of that and just be a warrior.

"Just kill.

"But she haunts me already, and I hated her. Peter and the others, they're going to need all the help they can get. In a way, I guess it's good that this happened to me. . . ."

She laughed then, a little wildly, and Will held her even more tightly.

"Careful," she said, and he backed off, met her eyes, saw the small smile on her lips. "Don't want to break me."

Then her face crumpled, and the sobs began, and he could feel the strength in her arms finally as she pulled him tightly to her.

"I know it hurts," he whispered. "But as long as we're together, it'll be all right, Alli. And if you're not ready for what's coming tonight, you don't have to . . ."

She shushed him.

"I'll—I'll do what I have to," she sniffled. "And I *will* see Hannibal dead. But after that . . . after that, we're done, okay?"

Will brushed her hair away from her face. Kissed her

forehead gently, the bristles of his beard brushing against her skin. Then, very lightly, their lips met.

"After this one's over, we're done," he promised. "Maybe a cabin by a lake. Wind in the trees."

"Mmmm," she said. "Sounds wonderful."

"It will be," Will replied. "It will be."

Then he kissed her again, tentatively, not wanting to spook her after what Hannibal had done. But as disconnected as she obviously felt from her human life, he sensed that she needed this. That Allison needed him to remind her who she really was. What she was.

His mouth moved from her lips to her neck, the soft underside of her chin, and then down to the hard ridge of her breastbone. His fingers moved over the buttons of her shirt, slowly, prepared to stop the moment he sensed any hesitation.

But Allison did not hesitate. She nuzzled the top of his head even as her hands reached for the heavy steel buckle on his belt. He kissed her breasts slowly, and breathed in by reflex when her fingers snaked into his jeans. Gently, she raked her nails across him, then lifted herself from the cot so he could slide her pants off.

They made love quietly. Slowly. Several times, she began to cry and Will lapped the blood from her cheeks, brushed her hair from her face so that they could watch each other's eyes.

And after, as they lay together waiting for someone to come and tell them it was time to go, they whispered to one another. Allison felt a little bit more herself now. But she wasn't better. Not by a long shot. It would take a great deal of time before she would truly be healed of the wounds Hannibal had inflicted upon her.

But it was a beginning.

On the second floor of Hannibal's elegant new Garden District home was an enormous library with vaulted ceilings. Many of the volumes in the room were nearly as old as the home itself, presumably passed along from one owner to the next, or perhaps even collected by old Mrs. Collins herself.

Hannibal had discovered the room at dawn and fallen in love with it. His anticipation of the coming night was so intense that he could not close his eyes for more than a moment. The only succor for his impatience, for the thoughts racing through his mind, were the books in this room.

The library, to his great pleasure, was also the darkest room in the mansion. Its three windows, along the front of the house, were short and high on the wall. The sunlight they allowed into the room sprayed across the books on upper shelves, and slid across the library in an arc as the hours passed. But it was a simple matter for Hannibal to avoid the light as he read.

Simple enough, and yet hypocritical in many ways. For even this exposure to diffuse sunlight was something he would have discouraged in his followers. He truly believed that to make them the predators, the bloodthirsty hunters that he knew vampires were meant to be, they must return to the dark. Creatures of darkness, lurking in shadow and hunting by night.

It had surprised him how easily they, and even he, had slipped back into that old modus operandi. Though he denied it to his flock, he knew that most of the myths he now perpetrated had been introduced almost as shackles to his race by the Vatican. But what were once weapons to be used against them were now tools they might bring to bear in their quest for dominance.

For the vampires of myth which he forced his clan to emulate were far more terrifying to the human mind than any cooperative "shadow" might be. Indeed, the Americans—who had been his first and greatest target—already cowered in fear, hiding behind their shuttered windows in those cities his clan had infiltrated.

"Hmmm?" Hannibal grunted and looked down at the

spot where his elbow was propped on the arm of the leather library chair. The sunlight had finally reached him, falling across the sleeve of his white cotton shirt.

It burned him. Hannibal stared in fascination as smoke began to rise from the cotton. The flesh beneath cracked and blistered. Finally he pulled it away not because of the pain, but because he feared he would actually be set aflame, ruining a perfectly good shirt.

As his flesh healed, Hannibal pondered what this meant. Even subconsciously, his philosophy had begun to take effect. It had been his doing, his plan all along, to convince vampires once more of the ancient myths—trusting their cellular consciousness to obey even destructive commands. But obviously there were drawbacks to his plan. After all, he knew the truth, and yet had become so enamored of the myth that it was affecting him. That it could do so even slightly was amazing to him.

But it couldn't be helped. And since so few humans truly understood the nature of vampirism, even such handicaps would not prevent his quest for dominance over humanity from coming to fruition.

Hannibal rose and moved his chair. Once more, he bent his head to pore through the pages of a nineteenth-century translation of *The Arabian Nights*. After that, he thought he would amuse himself with a work of fiction masquerading as history, a book with the longest title he'd ever seen. *A History of the World, with All Its Great Sensations, Together with Its Decisive Battles and the Rise and Fall of Its Nations from the Earliest Times to the Present Day: Volume One* had been compiled by one "Nugent Robinson." Of course, "present day" to Mr. Robinson had been 1887, the time of the book's publication. It was certain to be filled with all manner of rubbish Hannibal might have corrected Robinson on, if only he'd been asked.

It did have lovely, delicate fold-out maps, however. Hannibal enjoyed maps, particularly historical ones. They revealed the true history of conquest, and that was what interested him most.

He settled in to finish *The Arabian Nights* with a last, appreciative glance at the gold filigreed lettering on the cover of the history book. A few moments later, something moved in his home.

Hannibal looked up from his book with a frown. He listened intently and allowed his senses to expand, his mind searching for any unwelcome presence in the mansion. Nothing human, at least, had entered the house. He would have been able to smell the blood.

And yet . . . something.

In his peripheral vision, a shadow moved. With a snarl, Hannibal leaped up and back, fangs bared, claws protruding. What he saw astonished him. A thin ebony creature, whose fangs and claws were its only distinguishing features, a thing simply made to kill. Its black eyes watched him.

"How?" was all he said.

The question filled his mind. Not only how the thing had managed to come upon him without him sensing its approach, but how it had come to be there at all. It was one of the demon-wraiths that Mulkerrin had called up during the final battle in Austria last year. One of the true vampires, according to Octavian's coven. A thing not of this Earth, or even, if any sorceror could be believed, of this reality.

"Speak quickly, before I take your head," Hannibal demanded in his most imperious tone. "What do you want here? How did you find this place?"

The wraith moved forward slightly, deeper into the shadows of the room and away from the sun streaming through the high windows. Its voice, when it spoke, was horrible.

"Don't you know me?" it asked, and each word seemed scraped raw from its throat.

Hannibal blinked. Stepped back, completely off guard. For there was something all too familiar about the thing's face. Its features were flat, more angular, and its mouth distended with ebony needle-fangs. But it resembled his greatest enemy. The thing looked like Octavian!

"What are you?" he asked, astounded.

"I am he whom you see in me," the vampire-wraith replied. "That is, once upon a time I was. Now I am free of him. As to how I found you . . ."

Hannibal could not tell if what he saw on the shadow-beast's face was a smile and yet—though he feared nothing on this Earth—he knew he did not want to see it again.

"I called to you, brother to brother," the thing whispered, its words like shattering glass. "Just as I was one with Octavian, so each of your kind is kindred to my race. Only the Spirit itself keeps you from becoming one of us completely."

"But how did you come to leave Octavian?" Hannibal asked, fascinated. "Is the darkness in me capable of doing the same?"

Its laugh was the snapping of bones and the tearing of flesh.

"Not at all," it said. "Don't be foolish. You are not three beings, but one. Octavian has magick in him. Sorcerors are a different breed. The magick didn't want me there. I was forced to leave, as was the Spirit. It wanted me . . . him, all to itself.

"Do not misunderstand," the creature hissed. "I am Octavian, just as the fleshling himself is still himself. But we are no longer one."

Hannibal struggled to understand how such a thing could be. Magick had always confused him. But an even greater question loomed in his mind.

"So you are Peter Octavian?" Hannibal asked, and his eyes narrowed with suspicion. "You are my greatest enemy, then, and yet you've come here, to my home. Did you think to kill me, then?"

"Not at all," the thing answered. "I've come to help you. For I won't really be Octavian until the fleshling is dead. And he is flesh now, Hannibal. Human, but for his magick.''

A smile teased the corners of Hannibal's mouth. He liked that idea. Octavian human. A ripe, bloody target.

"How can you help me?" Hannibal asked. "Your kind can withstand the sunlight, true. But I've seen what silver does to you. And you don't heal the way we do. Any novice vampire could kill you, given half a chance.''

The ebony eyes narrowed, the dark face split into a sneer.

"You underestimate me," the thing croaked. "But I don't need to offer myself as a warrior. I came to aid you with knowledge. You see, I know everything that Octavian knows. I am him, after all.''

Hannibal raised his right eyebrow, and the smile threatening his lips opened into a wide, fang-bearing grin.

Then Hannibal, the lord of vampires, began to laugh.

"So . . . are you going to stay like this?" Nikki asked, her hair across her face so that Peter would not see the hope in her eyes.

"I'm not sure," he replied. "I don't know what to think. Obviously this happened for some reason. And it isn't as if I can't protect myself.''

Nikki nodded silently, watching green energy spring up from Peter's right hand, light dancing on his palm. He was right. In fact, his command of magick had grown immeasurably, even by his own admission. It was as though he barely had to think about it now. The magick was more a part of him than it ever had been.

"It isn't that I didn't like you the way you were," she began, then offered a self-deprecating chuckle.

"Listen to me," she said. "I'm trying to influence a decision that may be the same as life or death to you, and we've known one another only days. I'm sorry. I shouldn't even have brought it up.''

Peter looked at her, trying to peer past the curtain of her

hair. He reached out and gingerly brushed it aside, traced her face with his fingers.

"It's okay," he said, and she knew he meant it.

"I'm not so sure," she replied. "Hell, you might be a total asshole once I really get to know you. In a week, you might think I'm the biggest bitch you've ever met. In a sane world, we'd put all this on hold until this . . . this war was over."

Peter laughed, but his gaze never left her eyes.

"This isn't a sane world, Nicole," he said, and she didn't even mind him using her birth name. "And you do know me. And I know you. There's a lot more to learn, I'm sure, and I look forward to the pleasure, but we already know each other. Don't we?"

She nodded, looked away, somewhat embarrassed by the strength of her feelings for him, after such a short time, and after the intense weirdness of their brief courtship. But then again, he wasn't a monster anymore, was he?

"On top of that, if we put off talking about this—" he began.

She held up a hand. "Don't," she said, and he stopped. Nikki didn't want to think about the night to come, and she knew that Peter had been about to speak of it. To warn her that one, or both, of them might not live until morning.

"Just don't," she repeated.

"All right," he replied.

Then he leaned forward and kissed her, beard stubble rough on her chin. She returned his kiss, her heart racing. Nikki had secretly wished that Peter were not a shadow, a vampire, whatever they wanted to call themselves. Now she prayed fervently that he chose to stay human.

It was Peter who broke off the kiss.

"I should get cleaned up," he said, and then laughed at his own words. "That's odd. I've always showered because I enjoyed it. And when my hair was longer, because I could never get it to look quite the way I wanted it. Vain, aren't I?"

She grinned, nodding in agreement.

"But now I actually *need* to take a shower," he said and seemed absurdly pleased with the idea.

"And shave," she added.

Peter rubbed a hand across his face. Nikki liked the goatee, that wasn't her point. When Peter's eyes widened, she knew he'd found the stubble on his cheeks.

"And shave," he agreed, slightly astonished.

Then his face changed, the smile disappearing, and his hand went from his face to rasp across his close-cropped hair. His eyes searched in vain for some distraction.

"Peter?"

He sighed, and she knew what he was thinking about. Or, rather, who. It occupied his mind far more than even Hannibal's presence in New Orleans.

"How is George?" she asked.

"Not well," he replied. "Not well."

Peter walked down the corridor toward George's room, still cognizant of the different sensations in his body now that he was a man again. He'd showered and shaved, and it felt good. Even got rid of the goatee. His skin tingled all over. There was a new, overall weakness that would take some getting used to. But he had time.

Time. It meant more now. Where once it had seemed almost an abstract concept, it meant more than ever.

The idea that time could run out in any natural way, instead of violently, had always seemed so distant. But ironically, now that it mattered to him personally, he was seeing its effects horribly illustrated. Time was running out, indeed, for George Marcopoulos. The most steadfastly loyal friend Peter had ever had.

After Peter had emerged from his cocoon, after he'd . . . split, George had been found in the chapel. Apparently he'd had some pain in his chest and, rather than sound any kind of alarm, he'd gone to the chapel to pray. Peter wasn't surprised. Nothing had been the same for George since his Valerie had passed away.

Down the hall, the door to George's bedroom swung in, and Kevin came out. His face looked drawn, saddened, and heavy with responsibility.

"How is he, Kevin?" Peter asked, always hopeful.

Kevin looked up at him, and a mix of emotions played on the shadow's face. Peter understood them all. For, despite his magick, and although Peter would orchestrate the strategy for that night's conflict, it appeared that Kevin would have to lead the charge. There was that.

And then there was all the death. All the loss, in general. Cody had called from Atlanta, and it was clear that he and Allison would be coming home. But the unspoken message was that Rolf and Erika were dead. Joe, of course, had been dead only a couple of days, and his loss was an open wound on Kevin's soul.

Peter was just a man now, but he could see the agony in Kevin's eyes as well as an immortal might have.

"Kev?" he asked, because the other man was taking too long to respond. "Has something happened?"

Kevin blinked. "He's asking for you," the shadow said.

Then he was gone, down the hallway, and Peter was left to stand with his hand on the doorknob, dreading what he would find inside. He turned the knob, pushed the door in. Bethany sat on the edge of the bed, wearing a smile and holding a nearly whispered conversation with George. Peter felt indebted to her then, for her kindness to his old friend.

George looked up to see who had entered, and he offered a weak grin. He looked horrible. His face was gaunt and pale, his eyes sunken into black circles. His thinning white hair jutted in odd patterns around his head. In that moment, Peter recalled all the times they had spent together, the first time he had saved George's life, and how the old doctor had offered to repay him with blood stolen from Boston City Hospital.

Late-night conversations. George's fascination with the

mysteries Peter became involved in when he fancied playing at detective for a while. His love for his wife, Valerie. His courage in the face of horrible adversity, when even the president of the United States wanted him dead.

He heard a dry chuckle from across the room.

"Well, what are you staring at?" the dying old man said cantankerously. "I'm old, Peter. You'd better get used to it."

Peter offered what smile he could muster.

"Hello, George," he said and entered the room.

Bethany passed him on her way out and, when he glanced at her, her eyes told him a story he did not want to hear. In his mind, he thanked her for watching over George.

"Do you want to know the worst kind of heart attack?" George asked. "It's the one that doesn't kill you."

"I wish I knew some kind of spell that would heal your heart," Peter said.

"I'm happy that you don't," George replied simply. "I'd be tempted to let you use it."

Peter blinked. "I'm glad you waited for me to wake up," he said.

They stared at one another for several seconds then. Peter could hear the clock ticking on George's bedside table. Finally, the old man reached out and rested his hand over Peter's on the bedspread.

"I couldn't leave without saying goodbye," he said. "We have a lot to talk about. Particularly some things I said to the coven the other day."

Peter nodded. "I heard about that. It isn't important. You said what you felt. What is important is my question for you. Have you thought about it?"

"You know the answer," George replied impatiently. "It's always the same. I miss her, Peter. I miss Valerie."

"I understand," Peter said, though he wanted to scream that he didn't.

"There's more, though, and that's what we need to talk

about. I don't want the 'Gift' that the shadows offer. Because it isn't a gift."

Peter stared at him.

"I'm sorry if these things hurt you, but they must be said," George continued. "What I said in front of the others was the truth. Perhaps shadows are no more prone to evil or malice than humans. But I think they are. You are an exception. And by setting an example, you have created a lot of exceptions. But even some of your closest friends were bloodthirsty killers before you gave them an alternative.

"Power corrupts, it has always been said. Immortality, shapeshifting—combine these things with the need for blood to survive, and you are predisposing an entire race to violent and predatory behavior."

There was a silence between them. And, Peter thought, a new distance. He hated it.

"You've put a lot of thought into this," Peter said.

"I've had nothing else to think about," George replied. "And now that you are, for all intents and purposes, human again, I wonder where that example will come from. Not from Kevin, I assure you. He hates too much.

"You face a great dilemma, Peter. First you have to defeat Hannibal. I have faith that somehow you will manage to do just that. But then, you have to look hard at your own coven—and wonder how long it will be before another Hannibal arises.

"I say all of this because I've had more time to dwell, and you may not have come to really consider these things yet. Now that you have, I know what you're thinking," George said.

His voice had become a raspy whisper, the muscles in his face slackening even further. But the passion in his eyes never diminished. The love never faded.

"I don't have a choice," Peter said. "I've got to . . . to die again."

"No!" George snapped, and then winced, as if raising his voice had hurt him very badly.

"No," he repeated in a harsh whisper. "That's just what I expected of you, and I understand why you would think that, but no. You can continue to be an example without becoming one of them again. And you must. But further, you've got to stay human so that you can remain objective. If they get out of control, it will be up to you to stop them."

A small smile played weakly at George's lips.

"And, of course, there's Nikki," he whispered. "Nice girl, that. If you can hold on to her."

Peter thought about all George had said. Finally, he nodded.

"You're right, my friend," he admitted. "But I truly don't think I need to be concerned about any of these things. Hannibal has us outnumbered so badly that even the most cunning plan will only delay the inevitable."

George smiled thinly, eyes drooping drowsily.

"You'll find a way," the old man said. "I have faith."

Then, holding Peter's hand in his, George fell asleep. Peter smiled and held the old man's hand tightly, whispering his love for his friend. He pulled a chair up next to George's bed so that he might be more comfortable, and took up his hand once again. After a while, he found it hard to stay awake himself. The human body had its limits, and he'd forgotten them.

A while later, George began to snore loudly, raggedly. Peter let his eyes close, to rest them for just a moment. When he opened them just shy of an hour later, he found that George Marcopoulos had died in his sleep.

For the first time in a great many centuries, clear, salty tears rolled down the face of the man named Peter Octavian.

14

You're taking the light. Letting the shadows inside.

—MARIAH CAREY,
"Vanishing"

THE AFTERNOON WORE ON. A FEW MORE hours, and it would be dark. Peter stood at the window and stared out at the courtyard, wondering what might be left of the garden after tonight. He gave a snort of morbid laughter, as he considered what might be left of his coven, his family, after the battle to come.

"Mr. Octavian? You all right?"

The speaker was a detective, Michaud, he thought the man's name was. He and his partner, LeeAnne something, had shown up not long after the coroner had left with George's body.

George's body.

"No," he replied without turning. "No, I'm not. Does that surprise you, detective? My best friend just died. I would think it pretty fucking monstrous if I *were* all right."

"We're not here to upset you, sir," LeeAnne-something said. "We just have a few questions we have to ask, and then we'll be on our way."

"Fine," Peter replied.

They waited a moment, maybe expecting him to face them, but he did not.

"Y'all are the new owner of the convent, then?" Michaud drawled.

"I own this place, yes, but it isn't a convent anymore. I would have thought that pretty clear," Peter said.

"It's a landmark, Mr. Octavian," LeeAnne said. "It will always be the convent to the New Orleans tourism board. I'm sure that was part of your agreement when you bought it."

"You're right, Detective," Peter replied. "But, then, I'm not even sure the place will be standing come morning."

"Now what the hell do you mean by sayin' somethin' like that?" Michaud said angrily.

"Ease up, Jack," LeeAnne said.

Peter realized that he couldn't even really remember what the detectives looked like, beyond basic body shapes and hair shades. In a perverse way, he was glad. He wanted to erase them. Maybe if they'd go away, if he could just make them invisible, George wouldn't be gone after all.

"Did you know I was a detective once?" he asked. "Private detective, of course, not a cop. Octavian Investigations, out of Boston. Had some pretty extraordinary cases, I'll tell you."

The cops whispered nastily to one another. Peter strained to hear their words, but couldn't get more than every third one. It reminded him of his newfound humanity, the very thing George had so cherished, and he wrapped that memory, of their final conversation, around him as if it were a maternal embrace.

Not paternal, of course. He'd been born a bastard, his father an emperor who knew he existed, but who had never set eyes upon him. Oddly, though he was born nearly five hundred years later than Peter, George had become a kind of father figure for him. The closest to a father he'd ever had.

"Mr. Octavian?" Detective Michaud said, his tone more respectful than before. "I asked what y'all meant by that comment, and I'd like to hear your answer."

"No, I really doubt that you would. But I promise you, I'm not going to do anything to my own property. That would be foolish," Peter replied. He saw Kuromaku walking through the garden below, explaining something to Kevin.

"Are you trying to say—" LeeAnne began to ask.

But Peter was out of patience.

"Look, Detectives, why don't you just ask me what you really want to know?" Peter snapped, still watching Kevin and Kuromaku in the garden below, though he could sense the growing agitation of the detectives in the small, now smothering room behind him.

"And what do you think that is?" Michaud drawled in his best tough guy.

"You want to know why nobody here called an ambulance after we'd realized that George had had a heart attack," Peter replied, his voice just above a whisper as grief and frustration nearly overwhelmed him. "As long as the coroner confirms our story—and he will—you want to know why I let my best friend lay around waiting to die instead of getting him to a hospital.

"George chose not to call an ambulance when he had his heart attack," Peter said through gritted teeth. "Instead, he sat in the convent's chapel and prayed. When we found him, he asked to be brought into his room, asked that no doctor be called. He'd been a doctor himself. He knew what he was asking. We all did, though maybe we pretended it wasn't . . ."

His voice trailed off. After a moment, he cleared his throat. Then he turned to face the detectives, getting a good look at them for the first time. Michaud was a big, broad, angry local boy. LeeAnne—he remembered now her last name was Cataldo—was attractive, Italian, a city girl, born and bred. Both of them looked at him expectantly, surprised that he'd finally faced them.

"I'm sorry if I've been rude, Detectives," he said. "But now I want to tell you something that's going to be very important to your inquiry—and to your careers."

That got their attention.

"We would never have called the coroner at all, if we'd had a choice," Peter said and smiled sadly. "We would have given George an honorable burial in that garden out there. The only reason we called at all was to make sure that his corpse would be treated with respect, that whatever happens to us and to this place, his remains would be buried the way he would have wished."

"I'm sorry, Mr. Octavian," Detective Cataldo said. "I'm afraid I still don't understand. Why would you—"

"For God's sake!" Peter shouted. "You can't tell me the cops haven't heard the rumors going around about this place!"

Both detectives backed off slightly. Michaud let his hand fall to his side, not far from the pistol he wore on his hip. LeeAnne Cataldo frowned, tilted her head, and stared at Peter.

"Of course we've heard the rumors," she said. "What has that got to do with your friend? Superstition and nonsense doesn't make that man any less dead."

Peter shook his head, lip curled in disgust. "No," he agreed. "You're right about that. But this isn't about superstition, Detective Cataldo. It's about death, really, and not the death of George Marcopoulos. You mean to tell me word hasn't filtered down to your office that the locals are abandoning this area of the Quarter right now? That shops and restaurants are closing for the night?

"You mean to say you didn't notice there really aren't many people on the streets? That even the tourists seem to be steering well clear of my property?"

Michaud and Cataldo looked at one another. Michaud shrugged. Cataldo looked back at Peter, sized him up.

"Mr. Octavian," she said cautiously, "I'm afraid I'm going to have to ask you to come along with us. Maybe there's a place we can speak about this more reasonably."

She stepped forward, left hand up to grasp Peter's elbow.

"Are you fucking blind?" he snarled. "What do I have to do?"

His anger boiled over. Here they could be helping, but they were so unwilling to see what was really happening that they were wasting their time—and, more importantly, his own.

The magick nearly burned out of him, pulsing green light that seemed to suck the sunlight from the room and cast all their faces in a sickly glow. Cataldo was pushed roughly back but kept her footing, even as Peter rose to hover just slightly off the ground.

"Back off!" Detective Michaud shouted, a quaver in his voice as he brandished his gun with an admirably steady hand. "Just back the fuck off, mister."

Peter did. The magick dissipated and he settled to the floor as if nothing had ever happened. Both detectives stared at him, but every few seconds Cataldo would look down at the hand she'd gone to grab him with, as if it were somehow responsible for what had happened. Michaud still held the gun steady, though his eyes were wide with astonishment, fear, and maybe a little horror.

"You don't honestly think I'd let you shoot me with that?" Peter said, glaring imperiously down at the gun in the detective's hand.

"How y'all plan to . . ." Michaud began, then let his words trail off.

He holstered his weapon.

"Jack, what are you doing?" Detective Cataldo cried incredulously.

Michaud just looked at her, then back at Peter.

"I never heard tell of no voodoo vampires before," Michaud said carefully.

"It isn't voodoo, Detective," Peter replied. "And I'm

. . . not a vampire. Now, why don't you respond to *my* inquiry? Save us some time and tell me you know what I'm talking about regarding the weird happenings in the Quarter today.''

"Today?'' Michaud muttered.

But Cataldo had finally gotten her mouth working again.

"We know something's going on,'' she admitted. "And we figured it had some connection to this place, and when your friend's death was phoned in, it gave us an excuse to start looking into it.''

Peter nodded, allowed a picture of George's corpse being zipped into a black bag to enter his thoughts, and then pushed it away.

He was numb. That was it, really. The battle coming up, the danger to his latest adopted hometown, to his coven, to himself. He was numb. Or, at the very least, he was trying to be. Trying to keep the sorrow at bay until a more . . . convenient time. He almost chuckled at that, but didn't want the detectives to get the wrong idea.

"Let's cut to the chase, shall we?'' he suggested.

Both detectives nodded warily.

"If I wanted you dead, you'd be dead,'' he explained so very matter-of-factly. "I don't want that. What I want is your help.''

"How can we help?'' Michaud asked, but it wasn't an offer. It was a question filled with doubt and disbelief.

"I was in Venice,'' Peter said softly.

Silence.

"And Salzburg,'' he added.

"Dear God,'' LeeAnne Cataldo whispered. "Are you saying that the same thing . . .''

She couldn't even finish.

"Not necessarily,'' Peter said. "But it's possible. I honestly don't know how bad things are going to get. The U.N. knows about it already, as of this morning.''

"Well, we've got to stop it,'' she said, eyes wandering as if in search of an answer.

"Oh, be my guest," Peter said and actually laughed a little, though he knew how cruel he must sound. He didn't really care. About anything. Not now.

"You want to help?" he said. "You want to do something? My people have been spreading the word through the city, especially the Quarter. I need them back now, to prepare for nightfall. Take over. Get as many civilians to safety as you can.

"And then, if you're smart, stay the hell away from here come dusk," he concluded. "Your families will thank you for it."

Michaud seemed about to ask something else, but Peter turned his back on the detectives, looking back out the window, and noted how much longer the afternoon shadows had grown, just in the past few minutes. He heard them whispering behind him, but didn't bother trying to hear them anymore.

"Thank you," Detective Cataldo said softly. "Mr. Octavian?"

Peter said nothing.

"What the hell are you?" Michaud asked, half in fascination and half in disgust.

For a moment, Peter was tempted to ignore him as well. But he thought of George, and then he thought of Nikki. Sweet, smart, talented Nikki. Maybe he wasn't completely numb after all?

"I'm a man," he replied. "Just a man."

George, and Nikki, and Will, and Allison, and Kuromaku. His entire family.

"Just a man with a lot to lose," he whispered, mostly to himself.

Kevin sat silently, alone, in a rear pew in the chapel. The afternoon light had dwindled, so that the stained glass windows seemed to have fire burning dimly beyond them. A pulse of light, rather than a stream. It cast a sickly pallor

over the chapel, and Kevin thought that was only appropriate.

Soft footsteps padded up the aisle behind him.

"It is time, Caleb?" he asked.

"Damn, how'd you know it was me?" Caleb cussed
good-naturedly.

Kevin turned to look at him, unable to disguise the
admonishment on his face, or in his tone.

"Who else would be playing fucking games and trying
to sneak up on me in the middle of all this hell?" he said
coldly.

Caleb's head snapped back as if he'd been slapped.

"Christ, Kevin," he said grimly. "I reckon I'll end up
dead a little later tonight. What's the harm in havin' a little
fun 'til then?"

As if he'd been deflated, Kevin let out a long breath he'd
never needed, and nodded slightly.

"I'm sorry, Cay," he said. "It's just . . . I don't know,
all of this. We've got Peter back, and I know he's the man,
y'know? He's the boss, the one who brought us all together.
It's his right to lead, not to mention that he's had the most
experience. It's the way it should be. But he's . . . I don't
know, he's . . ."

"Human?" Caleb offered.

"Human," Kevin agreed. "But it's not as if . . . I mean,
George was human. We need his wisdom now, more than
ever, despite his misgivings at the end. But Peter started it
all. He defined the difference between shadow and vampire.
Without him, you have to start to wonder how much of a
difference there really is."

"There's a difference," Caleb said proudly. "You know
the difference."

"I know," Kevin sighed. "It just isn't the same without
Peter kind of leading the way. Of course, he's got all that
magick and shit, and I'm sure he'll do more than hold his
own. And all his plans sound pretty straight up so far. But
everything is just going wrong. It's like we've lost all our

big guns, just when we needed them the most."

They looked at one another for a quiet, joyless moment. Then Caleb shrugged.

"Fourth and ten yards to go, Kev," Caleb said. "Only one thing left to do."

Kevin smiled, but then his face crumpled a little, just for a moment. He bit his lip, wiped a tear from his eye before it could fully form. And then, finally, he laughed.

"No fag jokes, okay?" he said, "but I don't know shit about football. Joe loved it. I could never understand the allure."

His smile then was bittersweet. They'd all lost so much, and the real fight hadn't even begun. Kevin thought of Job, and it was only this Old Testament tale that kept him from believing God had abandoned them. That, and those of the coven who remained. Who would fight until the end.

Caleb stepped closer and opened his arms. Kevin allowed himself to melt into Caleb's embrace. It was love, pure and simple, despite any arguments they'd had in the past. Not sex—Caleb wouldn't have been his type even if he was interested—but intimate just the same. Love. Caring.

"Fourth and ten," Caleb said, his voice choked with emotion. "We punt, I reckon. That's all we can do now. We punt."

They held one another for a moment longer, and then Caleb broke the embrace. He didn't seem uncomfortable, but Kevin kept his distance anyway. Didn't want to send the wrong signals, make Caleb feel awkward.

"They're ready for you," Caleb said, after a moment.

Kevin nodded, and they walked out of the chapel side by side. At the entrance to the large dining area where the Ursuline Sisters had once convened for meals, he stopped abruptly. Where there had been more than one hundred bloodless corpses only hours ago, there now sat a small army of shadows, patiently awaiting guidance as though they were a movie theater audience waiting for the trailers to start.

The tragedy of the sight did not escape him, but there was a glory in it as well, a glory that lifted his heart. They were murmuring among themselves, but as he walked to the front of the room, they fell silent. He turned to face them, smiled sympathetically, and closed his eyes for a moment, shaking his head.

"You are, without a doubt, the most courageous group of men and women I have ever seen," he told them honestly. "I didn't make the same choice you made. My choice, to become one with the shadows, was made out of selfishness and fear of what lay beyond death. Some of you might not really have been prepared for this. I know for certain that there were some thrill-seekers among you, some groupies, if people even still use that word.

"Well, you got what you wanted. But even those of you who did this out of some odd obsession are to be commended. You had life ahead of you. Normal human existence. You chose the shadows in order to protect this coven, your families maybe, and maybe even society as we know it.

"That sounds dramatic, I know. Shit, it *is* dramatic, don't you think?

"Our odds tonight aren't very good. With your brave sacrifice, they just got better. But still, there's no way to tell how this is going to go. In a little while, Peter will be in to discuss our strategy with you, and maybe to share a little bit of what he knows about Hannibal and the way that son of a bitch thinks.

"For right now, Caleb and I want to just give you a general idea, in very practical ways, of what you're now capable of," Kevin concluded.

He paused, scanning the faces of the newborn shadows for questions. After a moment, he realized that there was one face in particular that wasn't there. Denny, the big Cajun who had agonized so much over his decision. He looked at Caleb, who leaned in so that Kevin could whisper to him.

"Where's Denny?" he asked.

Caleb seemed uncomfortable. "I didn't want to tell you."

"Where is he?" Kevin insisted.

"He's dead," Caleb whispered. "After he woke up . . . he just couldn't . . . He killed himself, Kevin. Said he didn't know it would be like this."

Kevin nearly retched, but controlled himself, barely. He scanned the newborns again and had trouble, suddenly, thinking of them as immortals.

"Before we begin, I'd like us all to take a moment," he said. "Look around at one another. Think about your loved ones. Remember what you're fighting for. Take a moment, quietly, to remember those we've already lost, including George Marcopoulos, who always tried to see the little bit of heaven in us, and Dennis Gautreau, who couldn't live with that little bit of hell."

The moment of silence lasted more than two full minutes. In the room filled with the undead, for the full duration of that silence, no one drew a single breath.

"So we begin," Kevin said at last. "And the first thing I want to tell you is this. No matter how tempted you are to believe this illusion you've woven about you, there's something you should never forget."

"You're dead."

Roberto Jimenez was walking across hard-packed earth in the middle of the temporary camp his troops had established outside Atlanta, when he saw Will Cody and Allison Vigeant emerge from their tent. He'd left Sebastiano with the CDC people, and come back to check on the readiness of his forces, and to fill the two vampires . . . the two shadows, in on what they'd accomplished.

Cody and Vigeant both smiled at his approach, and Berto nodded in return, offering a polite smile of his own. He wondered if they sensed the falseness of it, but it couldn't be helped.

"Commander," Will Cody said by way of greeting.

"How's it coming?" Vigeant asked. "Any progress?"

Commander Jimenez narrowed his eyes slightly and hesitated a moment before responding. He scratched idly at the back of his neck.

"Actually," he said warily, "we're making excellent progress. Using the samples you brought, it was relatively simple for the CDC people to make more. They didn't even need to synthesize it, which is good, because it never would have been ready in time."

"That's wonderful!" Vigeant cried and turned to Cody. "Will, this may actually give us a chance!"

But Cody was still looking at Roberto.

"I get a feeling there's more to this," Cody drawled.

"Well, it's still not bad news," Berto replied. "They've been able to replicate the serum, which is very potent. I've ordered all small arms ammunition coated with it."

Cody nodded.

"But since we've got no way of knowing how many vampires Hannibal's got in New Orleans, it's likely to be a very bloody, very nasty one-on-one throwdown. That it?" Cody asked.

"That about sums it up, yes," Jimenez agreed. "Of course, CDC is trying to make a gas out of the serum now, but they're not making any promises. Also, it should have zero effect on the human populace. So if we could get it airborne, get them to inhale it, that would really help us, but—"

"Commander," Vigeant said grimly, frowning at him. "I understand you're exhausted, but you're not thinking clearly."

Roberto looked at her. "I'm sorry?"

Cody shook his head, almost amused. "Vampires don't need to breathe," he said. "Sure, a lot of them do, by instinct, but that's only going to help so much. Especially once they figure out the stuff is hurting them. Then . . . they'll just stop inhaling."

Berto blinked twice. They were right; he had forgotten.

But there was nothing to be done for it now.

"I'll have a talk with CDC about making the gas contact-effective. We'll just have to take our chances," he said. "Hope we're not outnumbered as badly as we think we'll be."

He would have continued, then, into small talk, then moved on and left the shadows to themselves until it was time to head out for Louisiana. The military transports were already on the way. The highway was closed off for two miles heading out of Atlanta, plenty of room for them to land and load up vehicles and weapons and troops.

Something in Cody's eyes stopped him.

"There something else, Colonel Cody?" he asked, wincing at the title. As far as he knew, Cody had never officially been a colonel of anything.

"That's what I'm wondering," Cody replied. "You seem a little edgy, Commander. And I don't think it has anything to do with all this insanity. It has to do with just standing here talking to Allison and me."

Roberto considered lying. But he'd always hated liars.

"You're right," he admitted. "To be honest, it is you. Both, or should I say, all of you. I should have killed you already, and actually, the only reason I didn't is because I remember Salzburg. I know that mess wouldn't have ended there if it weren't for you and your friends. We all lost some good people that day.

"But even so, I don't trust you. Any of you. That girl you showed up here with, she was part of your coven, or whatever, and she tried to kill me. You said yourselves that your friend Sebastiano had betrayed Rolf Sechs last year. The only reason he's still in one piece is that he brought that serum to us. And even then, if I hadn't seen it work, I still might have had to kill you all."

They stared at him. Allison, in particular, looked horrified by his words. Commander Jimenez shifted uncomfortably from one leg to another.

"We appreciate your honesty," Cody said at last. "And

I understand why you would feel the way you do.''

Cody's eyes narrowed, and he moved in closer to Roberto. Commander Jimenez was a brave man, but he was not a fool. Fear traced cold fingers across his heart. When Cody spoke again, his voice was a dangerous whisper.

"But let me tell you something, Commander,'' he snarled. "I died a pauper, just a cut above a slave, lost everything I'd made, even the nickname I'd made famous. All that, because I always kept my word. No matter the cost to me.''

Then, suddenly, Cody simply disappeared, leaving Jimenez staring at the furious features of Allison Vigeant's face. But Cody hadn't disappeared, not really. For Roberto could feel the vampire standing just behind him. Cody had moved so quickly, Roberto hadn't even seen him.

"If I wanted you dead, Commander,'' Cody whispered, "you'd be dead. When this thing is over, if you still think you can kill me, and you're still inclined to it . . .

"Well, you're welcome to try.''

In the courtyard, Kuromaku stood alone. Everyone else was inside, preparing, waiting for Peter to lay out his plan. But Kuromaku already knew the plan. Peter had explained it to him already, and though it might not have been his choice, it did make a great deal of sense. Peter had always been a superior strategist.

"Maku?''

Kuromaku turned to see Peter standing at the far end of the garden path. He was an odd sight, to say the least, in crisp, dark blue jeans, a light cotton shirt whose two buttons were open at the neck, and brown leather hiking boots. The odd part, however, was the long scabbard that hung on a low belt around his waist, and the ancient sword sheathed therein.

"You still move very quietly for a human,'' Kuromaku said.

Peter smiled. "If that's a compliment, I'll take it.''

"I thought I should say something nice before mocking your fighting attire."

"What does the fashionable warrior wear these days?" Peter asked as they both began to move toward one another on the path.

"If he's good enough with a sword," Kuromaku replied, "he can wear whatever he wants."

They shared a quiet laugh.

"It feels strange, but incredibly good at the same time," Peter said. "The sword, I mean. For so long I let what I'd become define me, for better and for worse. But with this sword at my side, I think I'm finally starting to remember who I really am."

"My friend," Kuromaku said, "I could have told you that."

"You have no idea how glad I am that you've come," Peter said warmly, and laid a hand on Kuromaku's shoulder.

"I missed out on the fun in the last two shadow wars," Kuromaku replied. "I wasn't going to let you keep me out of it again. Besides, my dreams would have haunted me."

At the thought of his dreams, he wondered if he should tell Peter the one detail he'd left out up until now: the wound in Peter's side, bleeding badly. Now that Peter was human, the dream seemed more prophetic than ever. But Kuromaku figured it was best not to mention it. He couldn't change what was to come, so all it would serve to do would be to make Peter more anxious than he already was.

"Whatever brought you here, I'm proud to fight at your side again," Peter said sincerely, then pulled Kuromaku into a tight embrace.

When they parted, he looked at Peter closely, saw the lines around his eyes, the redness in them.

"I'm sorry you lost your friend," Kuromaku said. "George was a good man, and he cared for you very much."

Peter nodded. "Thank you, but I'm human now. I'd bet-

ter start to get used to loss again. To aging and dying—
and to living, in a way.''

"So you're not going to take the Gift again?''

"Old friend, I've already got the Gift,'' Peter replied
with a smirk. "The gift of life. That's what George taught
me. Now I've got to use it the way he always did, the way
he would have wanted if he were still here.''

Peter glanced over his shoulder. "They're waiting,'' he
said. "You coming in?''

Kuromaku nodded. "Wouldn't miss it,'' he replied. "I
can't wait to hear what the rest of them think of your plan.''

"Trust me,'' Peter said. "They're going to love it.''

Swords at their sides, the two old warriors entered the
convent.

It had begun.

15

If only I could hunt the hunter.

—ALANIS MORRISSETTE,
"All I Really Want"

DUSK CAME TOO SOON.

Not, perhaps, for the residents of the former Ursuline convent. They had done all they could to prepare for the onrushing night. But the people of New Orleans, and the many visitors to the shining Crescent City, had not had any real time to prepare. Nor, for the most part, any warning.

Octavian's coven had spent hours during the day spreading the word, trying to convince local merchants and residents that there was real danger present. For the most part, they did so with a modicum of subtlety. And for those humans aware that shadows walked among them, those who knew precisely who it was that lived in the old convent, that subtle warning was enough.

However, despite that the existence of vampires was now accepted by all but the most hardened skeptics, it was only human nature for most people to believe that such things could not happen to them, in their cities or towns. The average person had never seen a vampire except on the news. To that significant majority, the whisper of trouble and mad-sounding ravings about a vampire war were just that: whispers and ravings.

It wasn't until the police arrived, urging the closing of stores and restaurants, the evacuation of homes . . . it wasn't until the cops started mentioning Venice and Salzburg that the real exodus began.

So, though the area immediately surrounding the convent was nearly deserted at dusk, the rest of the city was swallowed by a frenzied whirlpool of humanity, determined to escape but trapped in their own mad rhythm. There were no costumes, there was no music save for that blaring from the radios inside rows of gridlocked cars, and the only ones dancing were the dozen or so vampire-obsessed teens who were brave and crazy enough to believe their own bullshit. Their friends were running with the rest, but this small group laughed and spun in circles and drank each other's blood in front of St. Louis Cathedral.

Wrought iron balconies were empty of everything but ghosts, and steaming kettles of gumbo cooled on restaurant stoves whose fires had quickly been extinguished. There had been some looting, but such urges had been overwhelmed, in all but the most desperate, by fear.

There were still a few police officers out spreading the word, and some had gone AWOL once the public had been informed of the danger. Their duty was done, these deserters apparently believed. But the rest of the force had cordoned off an area two blocks in every direction from the convent. Some of the officers there, among the silently spinning blue lights, looked at the convent warily. But most of them, the veterans in particular, kept watch the other direction, waiting for the attack upon the convent they'd been told to expect.

Waiting for all hell to break loose.

In a Greek Revival mansion on First Street in the Garden District, the last of the sun's meager illumination drained from the sky like the final trickle of blood from a killing wound. The doors opened wide, and death poured out onto the steps, onto the streets, an army of slashing claws and flashing fangs.

In cemeteries around the city, crypts were thrown violently open, and they emerged—the undead sleeping among the dead. In the basement of Robideau's jazz club, the presidential suite at the Monteleone, the depths of a new display under construction at the Aquarium of the Americas... they rose. Hannibal's clan. The army of the lord of vampires. And even he didn't know how many of them there were, though he would have guessed somewhere around six or seven hundred. Had it not been for the burning of Atlanta, there would have been so very many more.

The predators swept across the chaotic herd, each falling upon the first human it found, and then another if it did not feel quite sated. Hannibal had ordered them to feed before rendezvousing for the battle itself, but none of them had ever imagined how easy it would be. In those first few minutes, nearly one thousand souls departed the Earth at the hands of Hannibal's savage army.

But even then, even when they began to lift up off their victims like bloated carrion birds, and float on toward their destination... even then, the screaming had only begun.

"Do you hear them?" Peter whispered in the dark.

Nikki could see the moonlight glinting off his eyes in the unlit bedroom. There was pain in those eyes, and she felt it too. Pain all around them. Horror and death and grief.

"Yes," she admitted, though she did not want to focus on the cries of the dying which joined together into a hellish version of the drone that erupted from the stadium every time the Saints played a home game.

Together they looked out at the empty streets—several blocks away they could see the blue lights of a police car flashing—and their fingers twined together in a desperate grasp for something that had been growing between them, something that this night might take away forever. In the

distance, fires burned in several areas, but Nikki had not
been in New Orleans long enough to be able to figure out
where the flames were coming from. Car horns blared, and
finally a police siren did begin to wail, but the patrol cars
up the block did not respond.

They waited. All of them waited.

Nikki began to weep quietly. When Peter's grip tightened
on her hand and he pulled her closer to him, she looked
up, her brows knitted with anguish.

"We're just sitting here in the dark and they're all . . .
they're dying out there," she said. "I don't want you to
go."

"We'll be all right," he whispered. "You'll see. Just
stay here, in the convent. I'll . . . I'll come back for you."

Head down, hair hanging across her face, Nikki took a
deep breath. She'd be left alone in a moment, alone in the
convent with the half dozen other coven members who'd
elected to remain human, and who'd given far too much of
their blood to those who had only newly joined the race of
shadows. But the newcomers had needed the blood for
strength, and control. And inside the convent, the humans
could do nothing but wait, and hope.

"You better," she said finally, her voice a light raspy
whisper.

But her frown did not disappear, and she turned away
from the window.

"I will come back," Peter said again, and this time it
had the sound of a promise.

He reached out and laid a hand on her shoulder, turned
her toward him. Their eyes met, and she saw that, despite
his magick, some of the sparkle had gone from those eyes.
The lines around them were a little deeper than before.
Nikki wanted to smile at these signs of Peter's new humanity, but didn't have the heart for it. It was not a time
for smiles.

"I've just found my humanity again," he said. "I've got
life back, and I've got death back. In some ways, it's as if

I went to sleep in 1453, and am just waking up now. It's a new world to me.''

''And you need me to help you through it,'' she said skeptically, coldly.

Peter's eyes narrowed. He clutched her shoulders and stared at her intensely, as though he were trying to communicate with her, his thoughts to her thoughts.

''I could do it myself,'' he said, his voice softening as his eyes searched hers. ''But I wouldn't want to do it without you.''

For a moment, just a moment, Nikki stopped breathing. Her eyes wide, lips slightly parted, heart pounding in her chest. It was the strangest moment of her life, and she wanted so much more of it.

That's when he kissed her.

It wasn't the first kiss, but somehow, it still seemed like a beginning to her.

Then Peter pulled away, walked silently to the door, and was gone. She sat by herself in the darkness, then, waiting for him to return. Waiting for the screaming to stop. Waiting for the dawn.

After a few minutes, she stood and walked through the convent toward the chapel. Peter, and all the others, believed in God so fiercely that it bewildered her. Her faith had always been such a limp, lifeless thing. But if they believed, and she prayed for them, perhaps God would hear and help. The shadows who followed Peter Octavian, who believed in life and love and humanity, had to be the most pitiful of all God's creations, Nikki thought. Monsters, they were, perhaps even damned, and yet they still believed in Him.

Nikki hoped they were right. And just in case, she sat in a pew, folded her hands, and began to pray.

Detectives Jack Michaud and LeeAnne Cataldo stood in front of their unmarked prowl car where it was parked across Decatur Street, face to face with a patrol vehicle whose blue lights spun ghosts across French Quarter facades. Jack sipped café au lait from a paper cup and his eyes scanned the street ahead. LeeAnne just watched him, astonished by his calm. Her fingers traced the grip of her service weapon, and she felt the comfortable weight of her backup piece, a Heckler & Koch VP70, in the rear waistband of her jeans.

She'd never carried the H&K before, just had it in the house. It wasn't the kind of gun the department would have approved of. The nine-millimeter semiauto's magazine held eighteen rounds. You didn't make an arrest with a gun like that. You just killed people. Or anything else that got in your way.

LeeAnne had never been one to break the rules. But tonight the rules were suspended. Tonight, it was just survival of the fittest. Which was obvious enough just by the fact that the police who had cordoned off the area around the convent weren't moving. Though there weren't very many people left around Jackson Square—at least, from what LeeAnne could see from two blocks away—not far beyond it, the traffic was at a dead stop.

And they could hear the screaming.

"Jesus, I don't think I can just sit here, LeeAnne," Jack Michaud said suddenly, his face pale. He took another sip of his coffee, eyes darting back and forth over the rim as he scanned the street. Finally, he turned to look at her.

"We're cops, for Christ's sake," he said. "There's people being fucking slaughtered out there, and we're just supposed to sit here and wait? We're sitting ducks here! At least if we were out there maybe we'd be doing somebody some good!"

Glass shattered just to the north, and a car alarm began its whooping shriek. Which was good, LeeAnne thought. Maybe that way, they wouldn't hear the screams anymore.

"It's too late for any of that, Jack," she replied. "They're close enough already. They'll be here in a couple of minutes. As far as the civilians out there . . ."

Her stomach lurched.

"You know what we're up against," she continued. "We know this is where they're coming. Waiting them out is the best chance we have of taking them down before the whole city gets trashed. Short of running, it's the only thing we could have done."

"Oh, Christ!" Jack threw his coffee to the ground and put his hands over his ears. "I just can't stand here and listen to this!"

LeeAnne couldn't hear anything but the car alarm. But the memory of the screams of the dying did linger in her mind, in her ears. When Jack dropped his hands and un-holstered his weapon, his eyes wild, she walked up to him and grabbed him by the chin, forced him to look at her.

"Calm the fuck down, Jack," she snarled. "Maybe I shouldn't have come at all, maybe I should have run, like Clete and the others, but I'm here now, and I don't plan on dying today."

His eyes focused on her, and Jack let out a breath. That was good. At least he realized she was there.

"You want to freak out, feel free, but do it with a gun in your hand, and do it in the other direction," LeeAnne snapped. "We don't have the luxury of playing nice today, Jack. My only job right now is to stay alive. If you want to help, maybe stay alive yourself, well, that's great. You want to go running off on your own, then do it. But don't make yourself a liability, Jack.

"Now. You got my back, or what?"

His eyes searched her face. They'd never been good friends, but they'd made good partners. They valued one another. LeeAnne was counting on that now, as she watched his eyes move.

His gaze flicked left. Jack's face changed, got crazy again. His hand went to his gun just as LeeAnne heard the wet tearing sound behind her. Jack didn't have to tell her to move. She dropped and drew her service weapon even as glass shattered behind them.

LeeAnne turned just in time to see Jack pump two shots into the chest of a beautiful vampire woman whose light cotton dress was splashed with gore. The two uniformed police officers who'd been at this cordon with them were dead. Lambert had his throat torn out, and Petrocelli had been gutted and thrown through the windshield. Blood had splashed the lights, and as they turned round now, they threw ghastly images onto the street and buildings.

The Asian vampire stood atop the hood of the police car. She looked down at the bullet holes in her chest and belly and laughed, teeth stained red, lips dripping with gore. Her tongue flickered out like a serpent's, ran lovingly over those lips, wiping them clean, savoring the taste.

With an almost dainty jump, she dropped down from the car hood onto the pavement near Lambert's corpse. With a bloody hand, she pushed her long black hair from her face. She wore a predator's smile.

"You shot me?" she asked incredulously. "You're standing out here as if you serve a purpose, and the best you can come up with is bullets?"

Japanese, LeeAnne thought, as she studied the vampire woman more closely. The undead threw her head back and laughed heartily. LeeAnne let her service weapon fall to the ground and whipped the H&K out of her waistband before the vampire's laughter subsided.

The creature stepped forward, shaking her head and sighing.

"A bigger gun?" she asked. "You think that's what's called for here?"

She raised her arms.

"Well, go ahead then!" she cried joyously. "Let me have it!"

LeeAnne squeezed three rounds off from the nine-millimeter. The first went wide. The second and third caught the monster in the breast and shoulder respectively.

The vampire screamed. Doubled over in pain. When her

head came up, teeth bared in a bloody snarl, there was a wary look in her eyes.

"Fucking bitch!" she roared, and tensed to spring.

"Don't even twitch," LeeAnne whispered, knowing the vampire could hear her. Her aim was rock steady. "These are silverpoints," she said, nodding toward her weapon. "I'm glad they hurt. And I'm willing to bet I empty the whole clip into you, it might make you a little more agreeable."

In her peripheral vision, she sensed Jack staring at her.

"Just do it, LeeAnne," he snapped. "What the hell are you waiting for? You've heard how fast these things move!"

"She's got poison in her system, Jack," LeeAnne replied. "We've got a minute or so. I just have a few questions for her."

She glared at the vampire again. "How many of you in New Orleans, right now?"

The vampire's aquiline features curled into a cruel smile.

"One too many for you," she said.

Jack grunted. LeeAnne risked a quick glance at him. Her partner looked as though he were about to throw up. Then she saw the way his stomach bulged . . . just before a clawed hand exploded from his belly. She hadn't noticed the mist behind him, but now it coalesced into a man. A blond, bearded vampire pulled his fist from the hole in Jack's back and let his corpse hit the pavement. LeeAnne thought absurdly that the undead thing might have looked like the comic book Thor if not for the fact that he was naked.

LeeAnne Cataldo was a good cop who planned to one day be a great one. She'd always been bright. Sharp. Quick to analyze and react to any crisis. Nothing in her life had prepared her for something like this, and yet her mind still functioned as it always had. The blond vampire might reach her, rip her heart out or snap her neck, before she could even turn the gun on him. The Asian was in her sights already, slowed by poison. If she was going to die, she'd damn well not make it easy for them.

Her finger drew the trigger back and the H&K began to pop in her hand. In that moment, something she never expected saved her life. The Nordic vampire moved faster than her eye could follow, faster than her semiauto could fire, and threw himself in the path of the silverpoint bullets.

Love. He loved the other one. It stunned LeeAnne to think that such savage monsters could even recognize the emotion.

But that didn't make her let up on the trigger.

"Sima!" the Asian vampire screamed as the blond monster was riddled with silver-tipped bullets.

Even as his lover reached for him, the bearded vampire exploded in a flash of cinder and smoke, of smoldering ash that floated to the pavement and was spurred along by a light breeze from the river not far away.

Already the female was moving on her, eyes wide with rage. LeeAnne swung the H&K slightly to the left, felt her aim, and shot the Asian vampire woman through the cheek, shattering bone and severing muscle as it exited at the back of her neck. The monster's head drooped slightly to one side, its wounds trying desperately to repair themselves despite the poison in them. And soon enough, they would. But LeeAnne wasn't about to let it get that far.

She squeezed the trigger again.

Klik.

Empty cartridge.

Survival of the fittest.

She screamed as the vampire tore her belly open, and she wept as the monster left her there to die slowly.

"Are you feeling better?" Hannibal asked and smiled politely as Tsumi walked over and took her place at his side.

They stood together on Chartres Street, at the front gate of the old convent. All around them, the city was filled with the cries of the dying, the crackle of fires, and the distant sounds of cars driven by the fortunate majority who'd escaped Hannibal's followers as they'd swept across the city, hunting sustenance in preparation for this very moment.

Hannibal stared at the gray walls of the building. It annoyed him to no end that Octavian had chosen as his headquarters a building that had been consecrated to God centuries earlier. When the church splintered, it had never been desanctified. Clever boy, that Octavian. Hannibal looked forward to eating his all-too-human heart.

"Octavian!" he roared, and then paused and listened as his thunderous voice echoed from empty building to empty building.

"I have come for you, Octavian!" he declared. "It is time now to put an end to this, to determine once and for all who is the lord of vampires, the king of shadows! Your cowardly philosophy is a distraction I will no longer tolerate.

"But never let it be said that I am unfair. Oh, no! If any of your handful of followers wish to join me, to return to the night and live in the manner of our ancestors, to be a part of the race that will conquer the Earth, let them come now and be at my side!"

Hannibal paused then, watched and listened. His own warriors were silent, but he could feel their anticipation of the battle to come. And he felt his power through them, their great numbers giving him a strength he'd never imagined.

The only response to his words were echoes. Hannibal was neither surprised nor terribly disappointed. They followed Octavian. He wanted to kill them.

"The die is cast!" he proclaimed. "The battle will be engaged! You and the cowards who follow you will come out and face your betters, and you will do it now, or I will order my legions to slaughter every human left in this city!"

Again there was no response. Hannibal was about to order his warriors to do just that, to go and find human captives to slaughter at the gates until Octavian emerged. But there came a light from beyond the gate, in the convent's courtyard, and that stopped him.

The light glowed green, and Hannibal had seen its like twice before. Then, the magick had been in the hands of the Vatican sorceror Liam Mulkerrin. Now . . . he knew who wielded it.

A burning ball of green fire rose above the courtyard, and at its center was Peter Octavian. He wore a long sword at his side, and Hannibal studied it curiously. Though he would not show it, he was startled by Octavian's obvious facility with the sorcery he had learned. Still, his numbers were greater by far.

"Welcome, Hannibal!" Octavian shouted, his voice booming, perhaps even enhanced by the magick. "Why don't you come in? You have my invitation, vampire. Enter freely and of your own will!"

Hannibal sneered.

"Taunt all you like, coward," he roared. "I will have your head by dawn!"

"Oh, that's right," Octavian replied, feigning surprise, "you can't come in, can you? Sacred ground and all that! Well, my apologies. I'll just have to come out there, then."

The magickal sphere seemed to shiver, then it began to rise over the gate. Hannibal raised an eyebrow, wondering what Octavian was up to. His warriors were all watching, however, so he kept his reaction minimal. They would be impressed, no doubt, by Octavian's magick.

"By morning, only the one true lord of vampires will remain," he said sternly, his deep voice enough to carry to all of those warriors gathered in front of the convent, and even to some of those who flanked the block to the east and west.

"Hannibal, you are a fool," Peter Octavian said as his feet touched ground and the magick crackling around him diminished to only the most gossamer of spheres. At certain angles, it seemed to disappear altogether. Octavian's sword now blazed with green energy, sparks flying off it to the pavement.

"I never wanted to be lord of vampires or king of shadows. Nor did I want to rule my father's empire when I was a boy. But you are a disgrace to our true heritage, and an abomination in the eyes of both God and man.

"None of which matters, actually. I could never be the lord of vampires now. I'm not even a vampire anymore."

"Yes," Hannibal said. "So I've heard."

Octavian's face betrayed his surprise for just a moment. Hannibal was pleased. Octavian was just a man. A sorceror, perhaps. But still just a man.

Hannibal laughed the devil's laugh and grinned the devil's grin. Where once he had seen a battle to come, now he saw only the celebratory feast and a ceremony to crown him lord of vampires. And king of the world.

He opened his mouth to give the order to kill Octavian, but felt Tsumi's fingers on his bicep.

"Lord, let me," she said, and her voice was filled with such pleasure that he did not have the heart to deny her.

"Of course, Tsumi, darling," Hannibal replied.

The beautiful Tsumi began to move forward as the other warriors looked on. Hannibal did not expect Tsumi to be able to destroy the sorceror Octavian by herself, but it would be interesting to see.

"It's been too long, lover," she whispered, but Hannibal could hear her perfectly. "What happened? You gave up all your power, gave up the Gift, for that little human whore of yours?"

"I've received a new and better gift, Tsumi," Octavian replied. "I wish I could share it with you, but somehow I don't think you'd appreciate it. Before we begin, I want you to know that I did care for you once, a long time ago. For that alone, I wish you would withdraw from this fight. Just stay out of it."

"Hannibal is my lord," Tsumi replied. "It will be my pleasure to take your life for him."

Octavian actually seemed saddened. Hannibal shook his head, almost insulted by his enemy's disgusting humanity. Then his eyes widened. From within the gates of the convent, a small cloud of mist emerged and coalesced into a Japanese man, a vampire. He stood next to Peter, traditional set of long and short swords hanging at his waist.

Tsumi hissed, and Hannibal realized that she knew him.

"You have other battles to fight this evening, sister," the new arrival said grimly. "I brought you into this life. *Giri* now demands that I take it from you."

This was becoming too complicated.

"Kill them both," Hannibal roared. "Then find some humans to slaughter here at the gates until the others are drawn out. I will not suffer a vampire to live who does not kneel at my command!"

His warriors rushed to obey him, but Hannibal was distracted by the shouts of battle and cries for blood from behind him. He turned to see dozens of unfamiliar vampires wading into his warriors at the flank, hacking into them with swords, firing conventional weapons—that was the first wave. The second wave were all changing into a menagerie of beasts of prey, claws slashing and fangs snapping . . . or simply changing their bodies, hands becoming rows of silver spikes.

For just a moment, Hannibal frowned in concern. Octavian had outwitted him. He'd had the convent surrounded, but now his own warriors had been surrounded, and by vampires whose control over their powers was not handicapped by the ways of tradition, the way his own followers' was.

But no! His followers were far superior to Octavian's spawn, in every way. And it was clear from just the first glance that his clan outnumbered the blasphemers by far, perhaps as much as four to one.

It would be a bloody night, true. But, really, there was only one way for it to end.

Nikki stood in the darkened chapel, awash in muted color as moonlight streamed through the stained glass windows. The courtyard was empty. Sounds of battle came from beyond the walls. Where once there had been screams of terror, there were now roars of fury, cries of pain, the clash of metal on bone. And gunfire. A lot of gunfire.

Behind her, she heard something move with a whisper.

With a sharp intake of breath, she turned and peered into the darkness of the pews. Another soft sound, like a blade slicing the air, came from off to her right. She narrowed her eyes but still could see nothing. Nikki wanted to shout, to cry out for help or at least to ask who was there, in the dark. But she thought better of it. There was a war raging outside. No one to come to her rescue. And to ask who was there, stalking her in the blackness, would be the height of idiocy. If they wanted her to know who was there, they would not be hiding in shadows.

Only her eyes moved. Every muscle was frozen. Her lungs stopped sucking in air. She supposed even her heart had stopped beating. Something appeared in her peripheral vision. Nikki turned and saw it, illuminated by the soft hues of stained-glass moonlight. A demon of some kind, she was convinced. Flesh as sharp and glistening as black, shattered glass. Smile like some savage sea monster. The creature was unlike anything she had ever seen.

Yet somehow, it was familiar.

"Nikki . . ." it said, its voice an intimate whisper.

Startled, she sucked air in again and began to back away from it, toward the chapel door.

"Don't run away, sweetheart," it said. "You know what I want. You want it too, don't you? Don't you want to be with me?"

The words froze her again. But not their implications. It was the tone, the voice, that chilled her soul. Made her look at the thing's face. She knew what it was, then. Had seen it once before, though quickly. It spoke with the voice of a man she had come to love.

The vampiric shade of Peter Octavian had come to claim her, for whatever it remembered of its old life included Nikki Wydra.

It loved her too.

16

*I'll be there to hold you. Don't be afraid of
the dark.*

—ROBERT CRAY,
"Don't Be Afraid of the Dark"

KUROMAKU MOVED WITH A FLUID GRACE, HIS
face stern but otherwise without emotion. His thoughts
were sublimated to the haze of battle, to the elegant dance
that killing had become for him long years ago. *Katana* and
wakizashi, long and short swords, flashed in horrible sym-
metry, punctuated by a brief pause, a grunt of effort. The
spray of lifeblood fell upon him like rain. He was the eye
of the storm, the center of an internecine struggle waged
all around him.

Centuries after they had first fought side by side, Kuromaku and Peter Octavian were brothers in arms once more.
Peter was several feet away, and his own sword was singing. But there was no harmony to his swordsmanship. Its
song was harsh and bitter as he hacked and stabbed and
brutally slashed his enemies. The sword sizzled with magickal energies, and where it cut Hannibal's kinsmen, they
burst into green and orange flames and screamed as they
died.

It was not pleasant for them. But Kuromaku knew Peter well enough that he would never have expected it to be.

They stood back to back, then. All around them, vampire killed vampire. Peter's coven were more durable, more versatile, and their ability to take the form of birds of prey, bears, and a whole range of big cats gave them the physical advantage as well. But Hannibal's clan were more savage and far more experienced. They had a vicious confidence and their numbers were so much greater. Yet the shadows fought on, for they had a nobler purpose, and that, Kuromaku knew, made all the difference.

Even those born into the shadows only hours earlier fought admirably. Some died instantly, but others adapted to their new lives and abilities swiftly, and were so fervent in their belief in Peter's philosophy that they became bloody zealots, warriors terrible to behold.

But it wasn't enough.

"We're losing ground already," Kuromaku told Peter. "Is there nothing you can do, with your magicks?"

"I am adept," Peter replied through gritted teeth, as his sword fell yet again, "but magick must be used carefully. It's a blade, not a bomb. And I won't use it to call up demons the way Mulkerrin did. There are too many risks, and our own people would be in just as much danger as Hannibal's."

Peter grunted. Out of the corner of his eye, Kuromaku glanced over to see that a vampire had clawed him in the side. His dream came back to him, the dream that had guided him to bring Peter's sword to New Orleans. And now it had come true. Peter was human, and where he was wounded, he bled like any other man. His shirt began to soak with crimson stain.

"You should heal that," Kuromaku told him.

Peter looked up, frowned at the tone in his voice. But he nodded, and Kuromaku was satisfied. The wound might not have been deadly, but he didn't want to take any chances.

All around them, the battle raged on. Blood flew and

burning piles of ash blew in a light breeze whose calm belied the rage there in the streets. There were no costumes save masks of fury, but Kuromaku could not help but see a bloody Mardi Gras of violence and death, a celebration of killing.

He parried a blow with his short sword, then used all his vampiric strength to swing his *katana,* neatly beheading his attacker. Blood gouted from the severed neck as the body stumbled two steps and fell to the ground, crumbling to dust and cinders. Kuromaku's sword alone did not kill, but if he could inflict wounds traumatic enough, Hannibal's vampires would die. They believed it, and that made it true.

Yet many of them healed and returned to the fray. Still, he chopped them down. But no matter how many he over-came, more rose up in their places. There were simply too many.

"We've got to get to Hannibal," he said finally. "This is a waste of time. If we can destroy him, his followers will crumble. The center cannot hold."

"I haven't seen him since this all started," Peter replied. "But I'll see if I can locate him."

Green light grew from Peter's left hand, the same verdant light that shimmered on the blade of his sword. Kuromaku danced around, keeping the vampires away from Peter as he searched. Peter mumbled something, and Kuromaku glanced up to see a stricken look on his face.

"What is it? Have you found him?" Kuromaku asked.

"No, I . . . I'm sorry, I have to go. . . ." Peter replied.

"Go?"

But Octavian was already moving, running across the street with a crackling ball of green energy around him. He could not attack the vampires and they could not hurt him. Kuromaku glanced up as Peter rose over the walls of the convent and wished that his friend had more control of his magick. It was a weapon they sorely needed at the moment.

A clawed hand gripped his hair and yanked his head back. Kuromaku had lost his focus. Vampires swarmed in at him. He reached behind him with his left hand and drove his *wakizashi* through the eye of the vampire on his back. The vampire wailed and reared back, fell off of him with the short sword still jutting from its face.

Kuromaku had regained his focus.

With only his *katana,* he waded into the small band of vampires who had made him their target, and slaughtered them; he hacked them to pieces. It was as if he had bathed in blood now, and the scent of it was insinuating itself into his brain, trying to overcome his reason, his calm at the center of this maelstrom.

He sensed movement behind him, turned, and faltered.

"Hello, brother."

Tsumi stood no more than a dozen feet away.

"Sister," Kuromaku said.

"My lord Hannibal has instructed me to remove you from this fight," she said. "You yourself have asked me to withdraw. I'm going to offer you a choice, Kuromaku. Choose wisely. If you will withdraw from this battle, I will do the same. Together we will await the outcome. Otherwise, I will have to kill you."

Kuromaku narrowed his eyes. The pain in his heart was great, but he hid his love for his sister behind a grim face and sheathed his *katana* momentarily. The fight went on around them, but somehow, Hannibal's creatures knew to leave the two Japanese warriors, brother and sister, to themselves.

"I am sorry, my sister, but this coven needs my sword, and they shall have it," Kuromaku said.

He bowed.

For a moment, he thought he saw sadness in his sister's eyes. Then it was gone.

"They shall have it," she agreed. "But not for long."

Tsumi also bowed. She reached to her waist and, from nowhere—just as he had taught her—she drew her own *katana.*

They came together quickly, brother and sister, and sparks flew where the steel of their swords kissed.

Peter stepped quietly as he entered the convent. His sword at the ready, he crept down the hallway with his back to the wall, eyes glancing from windows to doors along the corridor. His stomach felt queasy, as though he'd eaten something that was a little off. And, he realized, he felt hungry. He needed some real food. It was a sensation he had completely and utterly forgotten until now.

He didn't take the time to appreciate it.

The slight nausea, the light fever he knew he was running, both paled beside the odd sense of dislocation that had come over him outside. It had only grown worse as he entered the convent. Each step heightened the disorienting slide into duality. He was there, in the corridor. But in his peripheral vision, he saw stained glass. He smelled Nikki's light vanilla scent, some kind of body spray she wore. He heard her shouting at him, but didn't understand the words.

Down the corridor, where the door to the chapel was open just a bit, Nikki Wydra screamed.

And Peter was in the world again. Focused.

Enraged.

He ran the rest of the way down the corridor, heedless of any threat that might await him before the chapel itself. Sword blazing with magickal energy, he kicked the chapel door open. Though his strength was only human now, the heavy wooden door cracked loudly and seemed to sag forward from its top hinge.

Movement in the darkness. A struggle. He threw up his left hand and green light cast a sickly pallor over the chapel.

"Peter!"

Nikki stood at the front of the chapel, wielding an ornate iron candelabra as if it were some kind of fighting staff. The thing that menaced her hissed at Peter, then returned its attention to Nikki. It slashed long ebony claws toward her, and she brought the four-foot length of wrought iron onto its hand with a satisfying crack.

The vampire roared its anger and lunged for her with its whole body. Nikki drove the candelabra through its chest and spun away, running across the altar. The wrong way. Away from the wraith, yes, but away from Peter as well.

"Nikki, no!" he shouted.

Too late. She stood beneath a stained glass window that depicted Christ praying in the Garden of Gethsemane, tears of blood streaming down his face. Prismatic moonlight washed over her from behind, a soft rainbow silhouette.

That was the moment when Peter realized he loved her.

"We meet again," the wraith hissed, and Peter turned his attention back to the impaled creature.

Impaled, yes, and in pain. But not suffering overmuch. Not suffering anywhere near enough, as far as he was concerned.

It moved forward, hunched over slightly, and, with each step, drew the candelabra several inches out of its chest. Black ichor seeped from the wound and pooled like mercury where it spilled to the floor. Peter stared at it in revulsion. He could destroy it. He should destroy it, of course. But he looked into its eyes, into his own eyes, and saw all that he was, or at least, all that he had been for so long a time.

"Come now, Octavian," his shade sneered. "I promised Hannibal your heart to feast upon. If you will not kill me, I will surely destroy you, and the white-haired beast will taste the blood of your new life."

"You want to die?" Peter asked.

"I want to kill you," the thing whispered. "You have poisoned me with all that you are. I can never be what I might have been because I am tainted by your humanity, your faith and memory.

"But if I cannot kill you, I might as well die myself," it declared with a snarl, thin ebony lips drawn back to expose the full length of its rows of razor teeth.

It grunted in pain as it removed the candelabra from its gut. The wrought iron stave clattered to the floor.

Peter stared at his shadow.

It leaped for him.

Peter spun and slashed, his sword burning bright, and cleaved the wraith in two. It fell dead at his feet in two pieces, both of which shattered into thousands of small shards of indigo glass. It sounded as though a chandelier had fallen to the floor.

"Peter?" Nikki ventured. "Oh God, Peter."

He did not look up at her. He held up a hand to warn her off.

"Watch where you step," he said with a rasp quite like hers. "It's sharp."

Peter Octavian looked down at the vile thing that had once been a part of him, and wondered idly where its opposite number, its divine brother, had gone on to. Not until he blinked, and his vision lost its focus, did he realize that he was crying.

"Peter?" Nikki said gently. "What's wrong?"

He sheathed his sword, wiped the tears from his eyes.

"I don't know," he confessed.

Carefully, he moved across the chapel to take her hand. The battle outside raged on, they could hear it. Yet somehow, it had changed for Peter. In an instant.

His memory of everything that occurred to him between his death in 1453 and the start of his new life only hours earlier began to fade. Not to disappear, exactly. The emotions they incited were still there, but the details of his life in the shadows began to gray around the edges a little. He remembered events. Remembered those close to him and still loved them. Remembered his magick, or at least, some of it.

But it was as though, with his shadow destroyed, he had excised some major part of his life. Part of what made him who he was. A melancholy feeling began to sweep over him, a feeling of loss. But he wondered, very gravely, if that loss weren't for the best.

He led Nikki down the corridor, their fingers intertwined.

"I was so scared," she admitted. "For both of us."

"Me too," he whispered.

"Don't go back out there," she said, the pleading in her voice enough evidence that she knew just what she was asking of him. Betrayal. Yet she had asked just the same.

Peter was tempted. As the part of him that had been a shadow faded further from his mind, from his life, the conflict seemed to grow less vital to him. And yet, even if the shadows outside were not following his instructions, his example, he knew that the battle must be fought. For the lives of the world, if not for the race called vampires.

Humanity must be protected at all costs.

At all costs.

"Does *giri* mean nothing to you now?" Kuromaku asked Tsumi in a rage.

He held one hand to the gaping wound in his side, holding his guts in while his body tried to heal. Tsumi was leaning heavily on her right leg, waiting for the tendons in her left ankle to knit themselves back together. They had given each other these grievous wounds on their last pass, and neither had a chance to take advantage of them.

"Get away from us!" Tsumi roared suddenly, and Kuromaku turned to see a pack of slavering vampires stagger to a halt just before they could attack him.

They looked at Tsumi uncertainly, then at Kuromaku, and back at his sister. Then they moved on, dragging another shadow down nearby. The number of combatants on the street had thinned dramatically; the large mass was breaking up into pockets of bloody battle, leaving behind ash and cinder in some cases, corpses or barely enfleshed bones in others.

Kuromaku and Tsumi were alone now, on a far corner a

short way from the convent. And she had not forgotten his insult.

"*Giri?*" Tsumi sniffed. "My honor and duty are to my family and my master. Once upon a time, these were human beings. But we are not Japanese anymore, my brother. We are vampires now. Our coven is our family, and Hannibal is our only master. What honor and duty I have belongs to him."

Kuromaku's heart sank.

"Then come, little sister," he said softly, raising his *katana* once more. "It is time for your final lesson."

Tsumi's eyes narrowed, a storm raging within.

"You were my *sensei* once, Kuromaku," she replied angrily, "but never my master."

They lunged at one another then, vampiric strength and speed driving them forward. Tsumi raised her *katana* and brought it down at an angle meant to cut his chest open to the heart. With her strength, she might have done it. But Kuromaku had learned much since he had taught his sister how to fight. How to kill.

His sword clashed against her blade, sparks flying, but instead of parrying, instead of turning away, he moved in toward her. His blade slid down, holding hers back, until their guards met. Even then, Kuromaku was turning. He ducked and spun, controlling her blade with his own, turning to face her, but now slipping *inside* her sword arm.

Kuromaku tried to ignore the surprise on her face. The despair. Tried not to interpret those things as sorrow or as grief for anything but the loss of her life.

It had been one swift, fluid motion from the moment they clashed, and he completed that movement now as he brought his *katana* around and decapitated his sister with one thunderous blow. Her body hit the ground long before her head, and Kuromaku's bloody tears fell to the pavement soon after.

•   •   •

"We're losing!" Bethany shouted in Kevin's ear. "Kev, what are we gonna do? There are just too many of them!"

Kevin raked silver claws through the chest of a beautiful female vampire, and she shrieked in pain and horror. He grabbed her by the throat and punched a hand into her chest, tore her black heart from her slender corpse.

When he turned to Bethany, he still held the cold, slick organ in his hand.

"Don't even fucking say that," he growled. "We will win because we have to win. Losing isn't an option. You have any idea what's at stake here?"

Bethany looked frightened, but she fought with admirable ferocity. Kevin turned back to the fight himself, dropping the vampire heart to the street where it was quickly trampled.

"Hey, Beth!" he heard Caleb call behind him. "Don't worry about it. We're evening the odds up pretty quick!"

Kevin winced at the other shadow's words. Caleb was a good fighter, and loyal as hell, but he wasn't the most intelligent of their coven. There was no denying the odds. No denying that things looked grim, and that without a miracle, their chances of surviving, of stopping Hannibal, were dismal.

The difference was, Kevin had faith. A vampire leaped for him and he turned his whole arm to fire, setting the savage thing ablaze. It fell to the ground, rolling, trying desperately to put out the flames. Bethany, having watched, repeated the same move to great effect.

She might be afraid, but no way in hell was she giving up. Kevin admired her for that. A moment later, and they were back to back again.

"Don't worry, Bethany," he said aloud. "These assholes are following the devil. But we've got God on our side. Right, Caleb?"

That last he shouted. But there was no answer. Bethany kept fighting; she hadn't noticed.

"Caleb?" Kevin called.

With silver claws, he ripped out an enemy's throat, then turned to search the battlefield for Caleb. Bethany noticed his concern and appeared at his side, also scanning.

A path opened up through the killing, and Kevin saw him. Hannibal stood more than six feet tall, huge for the era of his birth, and his long hair was unnaturally white. His grin was bloody, his teeth stained and covered with bits of viscera. At his feet was Caleb's crumpled body.

In his left hand, Hannibal, lord of the vampires, held Caleb's head by its blood-matted blond hair.

"God?" Hannibal roared, amused. "What makes you think there's any such thing as God, boy?"

Rage and grief swept over Kevin, but he held it in check. Rushing in would only give Hannibal one more target. He was controlled enough to know that.

"I'm here to stop you," Kevin replied through gritted teeth. "That's evidence enough, far as I'm concerned."

Hannibal shook his head, a bemused, mocking smile on his face. He tossed Caleb's head and it rolled across the pavement and came to rest a few inches from Kevin's right foot.

"You're here to die," Hannibal said. "All of you."

"Oh, God, Caleb," Bethany whispered at Kevin's side.

Then she screamed, the most horrible scream Kevin had ever heard. Before he could reach for her, try to hold her back, Bethany went after Hannibal. That left Kevin with no choice. Together, they might have a chance. Him alone against Hannibal? He'd be slaughtered.

Hannibal seemed to flow like the darkness itself. Where Bethany reached for him was only shadow, and then he was right in front of her, gripping her by the hair and the front of her jacket, lifting her, putting her in Kevin's way. . . .

Kevin raked silver claws across Beth's face and breasts.

He mumbled something weakly, then stood and stared at his hands in shock and disgust. Only a second, but by the time he looked up, Hannibal was tearing Bethany in half.

''Nooooo!'' he screamed.

Caleb's body finally imploded in a pile of dust and cinders, and then Bethany's did the same. They just didn't have the control the elders had; the sun might not kill them, but some traumas were just too much even for a shadow schooled by Peter Octavian.

Kevin went after Hannibal, but he might as well have thrown his life away. The lord of vampires was simply too powerful. He had such experience, such confidence; no matter what ancient traditions he had handicapped himself with, Hannibal could not be beaten.

''If it's a comfort, try to remind yourself that you never really had a chance,'' Hannibal said, that leering smile still on his face. Mocking. Victorious.

Kevin wanted so badly to rip that smile from his face.

Hannibal's fangs tore into Kevin's throat. He felt his flesh tear. Mist! He could change to mist, just float away and return to the battle in another place! If he just could concentrate, he could . . . change.

But not to mist. There was a better way to change. Something Kuromaku had taught him earlier that day. If it worked.

Eyes fluttering as Hannibal feasted on him, Kevin reached to his hip.

''That's right, don't fight it,'' Hannibal whispered. ''You know it's over.''

Suddenly the gun was there, in his hand, its grip rough against his palm, the holster snug around the metal. Kevin drew the weapon out, held it to Hannibal's left eye, and pulled the trigger.

Hannibal screamed louder than the gun's report and staggered back, holding the place where flames licked at his face. At the hole where his eye had been, where silver had burned a hole through his head.

Now change! Kevin told himself. *Change!*

But he couldn't focus. Couldn't will the change to happen. The gun fell from his hand to the street, and several vampires swept over him, tearing into the enemy who had the audacity to hurt their master.

And Hannibal had been hurt. Was even now screaming in pain. Kevin felt triumphant. They could still win, he knew. But without him. He was dimly aware of his arm being torn off.

Then the vampires were gone. No tearing claws. No screamed epithets. No burning eyes. The battle still raged, he could hear it, the slap of flesh and the spatter of bloody spray, the roars of pain and fury. Hannibal still cursed him, but his voice came from far off.

Kevin opened his eyes.

"Don't go away, Kevin," a gruff voice said. "This little Wild West show ain't over yet."

A smile stretched Kevin's mouth wide, and he gazed up at the grizzled face of Will Cody. He'd come back, and if Kevin knew anything about the old cavalry scout, from personal experience and from history, he knew that when Cody came to the rescue, he never came alone.

"I . . ." Kevin began, then coughed a laugh, even as his wounds began to painfully heal. "I think I'm in love all over again."

"Well, if it isn't Buffalo Bill!" Hannibal cried happily. "I'd thought my darling Erika had killed you already, since you didn't show up earlier."

"I was busy," Cody replied.

Allison ran a hand across Kevin's forehead, glanced at him one last time to make certain he would be all right. Then she stood and stepped up next to Will.

"And Allison," Hannibal said, the menace in his voice overpowered only by the lecherous tone of it. "You're looking very tasty, my dear. Couldn't stay away, could you? Come back for another round, I suppose."

It all came back to her then. Every agonizing moment, every humiliating violation, every wound, every last second

as her life ebbed away and he made her something she
never wanted to be.

Allison couldn't help herself. She began to change.

Just as though she were becoming a wolf, or an eagle,
her body rippled and contorted. Pain swept through her and
she relished it. Her clothing was gone and she stood awkwardly, bleeding onto the pavement from open wounds.
One nipple was gone, chewed up and spat into the dust of
Sing-Sing prison. Ragged hunks of flesh hung from her
belly and legs. She had become the corpse that Hannibal
had made of her. Just the same.

Except for the change in her face. Except for the long
needle fangs that jutted three inches and more from her
short snout.

Silver fangs.

Cody looked at her, his face contorted with despair.

"Oh, Alli," he whispered.

But she paid no attention to him. Hannibal was all that
mattered at the moment.

"A real improvement, my dear," the vampire lord said
cruelly, snarling. "I find you much more appealing this
way. To think I can have my way with you all over again."

Yet in spite of his words, Allison saw the way his eyes
kept flicking to her mouth, to the silver fangs that flashed
there, filling her throat with bile at the pain and the poison
in her mouth. It didn't matter. Nothing mattered except for
the fact that she had made Hannibal nervous.

Perhaps even frightened.

Then the gunfire started. Everywhere. Drowning out the
sounds of battle. Vampire and shadow alike turned to see
what was happening. Legions of dead warriors turned to
look. But Cody and Allison did not turn. They knew exactly
what was happening.

"What is—?" Hannibal began.

Allison descended upon him.

17

*Even the stars at night agree that the sky is
falling apart.*

—BONNIE RAITT,
"Longing in Their Hearts"

"WHAT THE HELL'S GOING ON DOWN THERE?"
Roberto Jimenez asked, shouting to be heard over the roar
of the helicopter's rotors. "Nobody was supposed to open
fire until Cody gave the green light!"

The copilot shouted into the commlink attached to his
helmet, but Commander Jimenez couldn't make out the
words. After a moment, the man looked up at him and
raised his voice to be heard.

"Beta Unit was under attack, Commander! They had to
save themselves. All hell's breaking loose!" the copilot reported.

Roberto felt sick. His troops were armed with hollow-
point rounds, each loaded with the serum Hannibal had de-
vised to prevent the bloodsuckers from shapeshifting. One
on one, they'd be able to kill them all. Of that, he was
confident. But he'd promised Cody and Vigeant that he'd
hold off until they could get their own people clear, then

move in. It shouldn't have mattered to him—they were all vampires, in the end. But Berto hated the idea that they might think he'd betrayed them.

The copilot stared at him, waiting for instructions.

"Ah, fuck it!" Jimenez said angrily. "Get down low and circle around that block. I want a clear shot at all the major hot spots."

The chopper dove then, but Roberto was a seasoned soldier. He barely shifted in order to maintain his balance. He went to the door on the side of the helicopter's belly, ratcheted up the handle, and slid it back on its tracks, bracing himself against the strength of the wind trying to suck him out.

Swiftly, he latched himself by a cable to the inside of the helicopter, then picked up a specially rigged CAMEL tube—a computer-aided missile, easy launch weapon similar in some ways to the antiquated LAWS rocket, or even the basic grenade launcher. The CAMEL, however, could fire just about anything, and it never missed.

UNSF Commander Jimenez placed his right eye to the telescopic sight on top of the CAMEL, and waited.

"Hot zone!" the pilot, Captain Nathanson, called out.

Jimenez scanned the ground below, saw a sizable crowd of vampire warriors tearing each other apart, and pulled the trigger on the CAMEL. The missile erupted from its tube and its computer tracking guided it instantly to the center of the gathered vampires.

It didn't explode on impact. But it wasn't supposed to. Instead, it opened, and gas began to pour out.

Then the chopper was moving on, trying to stay as far from the spreading gas as possible so the rotors wouldn't suck all the gas away. They moved around the block like that, Roberto reloading new gas missiles into the CAMEL and firing them into the crowd below. It took just minutes.

"Nathanson!" he roared to the pilot. "Find someplace to set her down!"

Moments later, they set down on the street in front of

the St. Louis Cathedral, and Commander Jimenez leaped out, a pair of assault rifles over his shoulder. He waved the chopper off and ran toward the massacre happening just a few blocks away.

He'd given Will and Allison his word, and things had gotten out of control. If he could, he wanted to make sure they lived to be pissed off at him.

Hannibal threw Allison back at Cody's feet, hard. She rolled and came up quickly. Behind them, a pair of vampires and a member of their own coven went down in a spray of bullets.

"That asshole!" Allison snarled, and some of her rage turned on Roberto Jimenez. But not for long. Not while Hannibal was still alive.

"Later," Will warned her.

Grimly, she agreed. "Later."

"So you've brought the cavalry, is that it?" Hannibal asked. "How nice. My warriors will have a feast to celebrate your destruction."

Allison and Will exchanged glances.

"You're an idiot," she told Hannibal, and he blinked as if she'd slapped him. "That's always been your biggest handicap. You overestimate your own intelligence. We're all going to die now, thanks to you. You created the means of your own destruction!"

"Yeah," Cody drawled. "Thanks a lot."

Hannibal frowned, still not understanding. Will laughed at Allison's side, and she glanced over to see that it wasn't a laugh of derision, but genuine amusement.

The lord of vampires was not amused.

"I will rip that laugh from your throat, Cody," Hannibal raged, and tensed to spring.

"My lord!" one of his followers cried as she threw herself in front of Hannibal, grabbing at his legs. "They're killing us, my lord!"

Then she was dead.

Hannibal stared down at her in horror, and then Allison watched as the realization spread across his face. Amazement, horror, fury. He opened his mouth to curse them, but all he could manage was a single word.

"How?" he roared, bloody spittle flying from his mouth.

Allison was about to answer, but another figure stepped forward from her right.

"I'm how," Yano said proudly. "I stole it from you, you evil son of a bitch. My sins are so great I may never get to heaven, but I'll be damned if you'll turn this world into hell."

The vampire lord faced Sebastiano and the rage that had been building within Hannibal, driving him on to even greater savagery, seemed now to disappear. In its absence, there was only a cold hatred, a gleeful, murderous evil like nothing Allison had ever seen.

"And now you are twice the betrayer," Hannibal said, voice low and dangerous, "and you will feel twice the agony."

The bloody conflict had thinned the ranks of both sides, and the four of them faced one another in a quiet corner a block and a half to the northeast of the convent, where the walls cast a moonshadow over them like a shroud. Not far away, the dying continued. Vampires and shadows and U.N. soldiers. But in that brief moment, their conflict was their own. Intimate.

"Your arrogance is incredible," Cody said as Hannibal began to move toward Yano.

Then Cody changed. Allison watched, fascinated, as she had every time she'd seen it done. In seconds, thick brown fur sprouted all over his body, and at first she didn't know what it was he was changing into. He just grew and grew, and then she saw the way his hands were becoming claws, the way his face had pushed out into a snout, and she knew. Her lover had transformed into the largest grizzly she had ever seen.

Beyond him, Sebastiano was also changing. His white

hair spread, became fur, and then he was a mountain gorilla with snow-white fur all over, hugely powerful arms swinging at his sides.

Silently, Hannibal also changed. Into a wolf. A very large wolf, but a wolf nevertheless.

Allison almost laughed. This was what it came down to, after all. Hannibal had limited himself, and his power, to the traditions of mythical vampirism. It would be his end, she knew.

Right now.

"You can't honestly think you can kill all three of us," she said.

Hannibal lunged for her. Allison's fingers sprouted into silver claws and she ducked aside and slashed at him as he passed, ripping furrows into the dark wolf's fur. But Hannibal was fast, and in his wolf's jaws, he'd caught a piece of her gut, hanging from her ragged stomach wound, and now he pulled it with him.

Allison shrieked and changed to mist, her only thoughts of escaping the pain.

Even as mist she could see. It would have been difficult for her to describe, but there seemed some kind of radar, an impression of solid objects all around her. She was aware in a way she knew had to do with memory and mind function and probably the minor telepathy shared by shadows of the same blood lineage.

That was how she sensed that the battle had moved even farther up the street, farther away from the convent. That was how she saw the snow-white mountain gorilla and the huge brown bear converge on a one-eyed wolf whose ribs were scored with silver gashes. The bear beat at the wolf's head with one huge paw, and it tumbled several yards across the pavement, where the gorilla lifted it over its head, about to shatter it on the street, or perhaps break it over its knee.

Which was when the gunfire began.

Only the wolf was unscathed.

The first bullet cutting into Will Cody's flesh trapped him forever in the shape of that bear. The second and third and fourth just tore away chunks of flesh and muscle and shattered bone that would never heal. Next to him, Yano suffered as well. The white fur of the gorilla was splashed with red, and it fell dead as a bullet shattered its skull, spraying brain matter onto the bear.

The wolf fell to the street and turned, frightened, toward the soldiers, prepared to dodge their next attack.

The mist was screaming.

Allison had moved instantly, re-formed behind the pair of soldiers, and killed them in tandem, breaking one's neck while she tore the other's throat out.

Too late. And too soon.

As they fell to the ground, she looked up and realized with profound horror and revulsion that only Hannibal remained standing. She ought to have let the soldiers live. She knew that now. Yet even as she watched, the broken and bloody ursine form of Will Cody rose slightly from the street and reached for the wolf, grabbed it by the leg.

The snap of the breaking bone echoed across the street, somehow louder than the gunfire and screams, now more distant than ever. The wolf howled, turned on the bear, and sank its fangs into the furry throat of the much larger beast.

"God, Will, no!" Allison shrieked.

Trapped in the form of the bear, Will Cody could not change, could not heal to defend himself. Hannibal, the wolf, tore chunks of flesh from the bear's throat.

Hot tears of blood began to burn Allison's cheeks. Her mind snapped a little then, as she realized what was happening, and she lunged across the street at the one-eyed wolf.

Fresh blood spurted from the bear's neck.

Roberto ran full-out down Chartres Street. The battle was just ahead, soldiers firing wildly into a street crowded with monsters. He shouldn't have cared. He knew he shouldn't.

For the world to be safe, they all needed to die. But they didn't all *deserve* to die, and that was where he ran into problems.

Nothing was going as planned.

"Hold your fire!" he screamed into the commlink attached to his collar. "This is UNSF Commander Jimenez! Hold your goddamn fire! Don't shoot unless you're under attack!"

He could see clouds of the gas he'd fired growing ever larger. The gas was thinning out, yes, and being carried by the wind, but it should have done its job. Another few seconds, and most of the damned vampires in New Orleans ought to be unable to change form. Then they could try to figure out which were with Octavian and which with Hannibal.

If any of them were alive after the next sixty seconds or so.

Allison had dug long silver claws into Hannibal midleap, and she dragged him away from Will's broken and bloody body, used her momentum to slam him to the ground. Any of his followers would already have lost their concentration, allowed the pain of silver poisoning—and fear of the silver itself—to destroy them.

Hannibal was not so easy to kill.

The wolf's jaws fastened to the wound on her breast where her nipple was missing, and tore at her flesh. With the intense strength of her pain, Allison batted the beast away, heard the snap of its neck. The wolf hit the street, rolled . . . changed.

When it rose to its feet, it was Hannibal again. His eye was still gone, though the silver wound had closed somewhat. The slashes in his side weren't quite as visible through his tattered clothing, but she imagined they were also slow in healing.

There they stood, face to face, as the last of Will Cody's life pumped out onto the ground. Grief and rage threatened to overwhelm Allison, and her knees felt suddenly weak.

But she glanced over at the dying animal, the bear that would never again look like the man she loved, and she knew she could not rest until it was over.

She'd wanted to destroy Hannibal wearing every wound, every humiliation and violation he had inflicted upon her. But she was too vulnerable this way, she now realized. He had used her wounds against her twice already. As they stalked one another now, Allison changed, becoming whole once more. Hannibal seemed startled momentarily, and it occurred to her that she must look good. Fresh and beautiful, even her clothes intact. While he, the lord of vampires, was ravaged and bloody.

"Vain bastard," she whispered, and Allison Vigeant smiled cruelly.

She wanted it to take a long time for Hannibal to die.

She didn't see the small cloud of mist that blew toward them, a thin low fog that was quite out of place in the French Quarter of New Orleans at this time of year. But it wasn't mist, and it wasn't fog. It was gas. And before either of them had another chance to leap at the other, to rip and tear and rend, it had enveloped them both.

Already it was dissipating, passing them by, but Allison knew right off what had happened. She knew, as well, that the margin for error that came with vampirism had just disappeared. As a human female member of Octavian's coven, she had learned how to fight, how to protect herself. She hoped it was enough.

As she rushed at Hannibal, it occurred to her that the gunfire had ceased, and she wondered if that meant all the others were dead.

Hannibal lashed out at her, and Allison ducked. Shock registered on his face as he realized he'd lost some of his speed. Perhaps he'd also tried to change, to make his hands into claws, and been unable to do so. The element of surprise was on her side, then, and she took full advantage of it.

She broke two fingers on her right hand when she hit his face, right at the edge of his ravaged eye socket. The pain nearly made her throw up, but the soaring triumph of his own agonized howl overcame the urge.

The vampire lord—but a true vampire no longer—reeled back and Allison moved in. She spun and kicked him in the knee, shattering the kneecap and sending him down to the ground. She danced around him, relishing his pain, and was about to stamp on his forearm when his left hand gripped her ankle and turned, spun her off her feet. When she landed, the back of her head hit the pavement and, for a moment, she forgot where she was.

Hannibal was on top of her, then, face bleeding, teeth gritted with pain presumably from his shattered knee.

"What I . . . uhnn," he grunted. "What I did to you before is going to seem like . . ." he growled, breathed through his teeth a moment as the pain washed over him. Allison closed her eyes. Tried to shove him off and failed miserably. She was stronger than before; the serum could not take that away. But Hannibal still had most of his vampiric strength too.

Then she was crying again, because she couldn't stop herself from remembering what had happened in the dark cell deep beneath Sing-Sing prison. And the fear overwhelmed her, and she began to surrender, not to Hannibal himself, but to the memory of her suffering, to turn inward in a search for her escape rather than to lash out in her own defense.

"It's going to seem like making love after what happens next. You . . . fucking . . ."

Hannibal moved wrong. He hadn't been vulnerable in so very long, centuries at least, that he'd forgotten how to protect himself. Somewhere in that place into which Allison's mind had fled, she felt it. Sensed it.

And she acted, rebelling against her nausea and terror, against her pain, against her memory. She acted. Allison used every ounce of superhuman strength left in her limbs to strike out at the undead man Hannibal had suddenly become. Her knee slammed into his crotch, she felt his testicles give way to the hard kneecap, and she threw him off of her.

The once-lord of vampires roared in pain as he fell to the pavement, all his weight for a moment on his shattered knee. Allison smiled to see him trying to decide which part of his body to cup gingerly with his hands, but in the end they covered his balls and he growled in pain and a lust for vengeance.

Yet by the time Allison had risen to her feet, Hannibal had already begun to struggle to raise himself up, in spite of the agony he must have been feeling. Allison felt the panic begin to grow within her again, but this time she crushed it fast, before it could take root.

She would kill him. For herself, and for Will, and for all the rest who had suffered and died or lost their loves because of Hannibal. She would break his neck with her bare hands. She would—

Hannibal laughed.

Allison turned.

Three of his vampires swarmed toward her from behind. Despite all the gas and the gunfire, these three, at least, seemed to have their horrific abilities intact.

So close, she thought.

And then Allison Vigeant waited to die.

When Peter Octavian emerged from the convent, it was into a maelstrom of death and a quick-changing landscape of sound and fury. Not war so much as it was mass murder.

He had been an angel of mercy at first, when he'd found Kevin's gore-encrusted body on the pavement. But the young, noble shadow still lived, and Peter had brought him into the convent where he might convalesce.

Now he walked like the spectre of death across what remained of the battlefield. His entire body crackled with green energy, as did his sword. Bullets did not harm him, but he no longer need be concerned with that. He had seen Roberto Jimenez a minute or two ago. As soon as Jimenez recognized him, the soldiers stopped firing at Peter. The commander must have ordered them to do so, because otherwise, they were vicious warriors, taking no chances.

He walked around the convent, stepping over what remained of those corpses that hadn't burst into flames or exploded into a cloud of ash. Most of them were very decayed, as though they'd been dug up and dragged here from St. Louis Cemetery. There was a short burst of gunfire every ten or fifteen seconds, but the space between them was getting longer. Peter wished he could have communicated with whatever members of his own coven were left. If he could have just told them not to attack the soldiers, they might have survived. But after the soldiers' initial assault, they obviously believed the human warriors meant to kill them all, and so they attacked, believing they might save their own lives.

All but Kuromaku, and Peter thanked God for that. He found his old friend surrounded by more than a dozen U.N. soldiers, all with their weapons aimed at him. Kuromaku held what was left of his sister in his arms, and stared off into nothing, his eyes focused on something beyond the world, or perhaps into a time that had long since passed out of the world.

When Peter rested a hand on Kuromaku's shoulder, his old friend finally began to cry. Peter knelt at his side and whispered, asking him to go inside and watch over Nikki until morning. Kuromaku did as he was told, and as he rose, Peter stretched out his magickal protection so that the soldiers could not harm him if any of them panicked and decided to fire.

None of them did. In fact, most of them looked decidedly uncomfortable, unsure of their zeal in light of Kuromaku's tears. Peter was glad. It was a lesson they needed.

He moved on, and a short time later, he had come to believe that Kuromaku was the last of the shadows. That only he and Nikki and Peter himself had survived the battle. Unless, of course, some of his coven or Hannibal's clan had fled during the battle. But he doubted it. With first the police and then the U.N. forces there, and the battle raging all around, how far might they have gotten?

As long as Hannibal hadn't escaped.

It disturbed Peter to think he might never know.

Still, he continued his walk. The soldiers kept a respectful distance. Jimenez didn't even try to talk to him. Peter was glad of it. It would have been hypocritical of the man to pretend some kind of camaraderie after such wholesale slaughter. It had occurred to Peter that this had been the meaning of Will and Allison's message. He didn't know how it had come about, what magick or technology they had used to make the vampires' bodies vulnerable again. But it was not the kind of help or rescue that Peter would have prayed for.

Even if Hannibal were dead, this was no victory for Peter or his coven.

Though perhaps it was a kind of victory. A victory for the world. For humanity. He had admitted as much to Nikki that George had been right. That shadows . . . that vampires were too dangerous for humanity to risk allowing them to survive.

But the truth did nothing to warm the ice in his heart.

At the corner of Governor Nicholls Street, he turned south. The gunfire had ceased completely now. But there came another sound. A howl of agony, rising at the end to signal fury at whatever pain had been inflicted. It came from behind him, farther up the street, away from the carnage.

Peter turned swiftly, but already soldiers were rushing up the street toward the intersection of Governor Nicholls and Royal Streets. He could see Jimenez at the front of the pack. The human warriors held their weapons at the ready, still prepared to kill.

After all, the killing wasn't done yet, was it?

"Stop!" Peter shouted.

They didn't even slow down.

He swept himself forward on a wave of magick, rushed past them, and dropped to the ground in front of Roberto Jimenez. Face to face for the first time in a year, the two men regarded one another. Protected inside the green energy that crackled around him, Peter raised his sword and held it in front of him. Several of the soldiers moved to fire but Jimenez held up his hand.

"You may follow," Octavian said. "But if you do, then *follow*. I will be the one to determine how events proceed from here. It isn't your place anymore."

Jimenez nodded once, and Peter turned and sped off down the street.

Immediately, he saw them. Three vampires about to descend upon a blond woman whose face was in shadow. Peter's heart leaped with hope as he fell upon the vampires, his sword flashing, his magick killing, destroying the vampires in seconds.

Then he turned and saw her. Allison. He felt the smile stretch across his face and he glanced around for Will Cody. But when he looked back at her he recognized a pain there that he had missed at first. Wordlessly, she pointed to the corpse of a huge animal not far away. It was a bear.

Dead.

And Peter knew.

"Die!"

Hannibal roared the word as he fell upon Allison, all his weight on his single working leg. The two tumbled together and Hannibal throttled her by the neck, trying his best to tear off her head. And he had the strength to do it if Peter allowed it.

He did not.

Peter flung Hannibal off of Allison and threw him to the pavement. He lifted his burning green blade above the one-eyed tyrant.

"Peter, stop."

And he did. Allison had asked it of him. He turned, one eyebrow raised, wondering why she would stop him from destroying the savage beast who had precipitated all of this death.

Then he saw the weapon in her hand. She had lifted it from the cold grip of a dead soldier. An assault rifle, firing countless rounds a minute.

"Step back," she told him.

It wasn't a request. Still, he could have stopped her. He didn't.

Hannibal screamed as the bullets tore into his legs. She shot at his lower half until there was little but shattered bone and pulp left. Then Allison dropped the gun and left Hannibal there to die as she went to weep over the twisted corpse of the man she loved.

After a minute or so, Peter took her hand and together they walked back to their home. The soldiers opened a path for them to pass, and remained silent until long after they were gone.

Epilogue

Once more we're cheating on the reaper,
With all the gypsy still in our souls.

—GREGG ALLMAN,
"Ocean Awash the Gunwale"

IT WAS OVER.

That was the one refrain that kept running through Peter Octavian's mind as he watched the unnaturally large casket being lowered into the earth. The path he had traveled from Boston, when he had been both prisoner of his true nature and yet free of it in a way he had never been since.

Until now.

A light, yet chilly breeze blew through the tall trees surrounding the cemetery. The wind carried the scent of the ocean, something inescapable here, on a little bit of paradise called Prince Edward Island, off the east coast of Canada.

The minister said his last words over the warped corpse of Will Cody, but Peter wasn't really listening. Instead, he was remembering as best he could. Ever since he had destroyed the wraith that had been born from within him, the

vampire he'd once been, his memories had been clouded.
But he remembered his feelings well enough.

Will Cody had been the closest thing that Peter Octavian—ever the bastard child—had ever had to a brother.
Even more so than Kuromaku, who had returned to France
to bury his sister on his estate there. Kuromaku lived by a
code of honor created millennia earlier, and he was an honorable warrior.

Will Cody had created his own code of honor, even before he had met Peter, and yet it had aligned with Peter's
almost precisely. They were allies, at first, but quickly became friends. But it was more than a code of honor that
made them brothers.

They had faith in humanity. In the soul. In the human
heart. They believed without question that people were basically good, and thus that the shadows were also basically
good. More than believed, they *expected* people to behave
in a certain way, to function based on a certain logic. And
for the most part, they were not disappointed.

Human beings could choose to be angels or devils, or
they could be forged into one or the other. And shadows
were the same. But once forged, both men learned to their
everlasting regret, it was nearly impossible to unmake such
creatures.

Were the shadows monsters? Not all. Yet once branded
a monster, once become a monster, how to escape that definition?

It was what they'd fought for, all along.

In that, they had lost.

Perhaps. Yet they had proven their humanity to themselves, if not the world, and wasn't that, in itself, a victory?
Will Cody had died heroically, valiantly. Though he wore
the body of a beast, he had died a man's death. And Will
Cody's second death had not been in vain, for Hannibal,
and all his venomous spawn, had been destroyed.

Or they would be, very soon. Around the world, there
were sure to be small covens growing even now from the

remains of his clan, tribes of Hannibal's allies and children, dedicated to his purpose. But with the weapon Hannibal himself had created, Commander Jimenez's grim determination would see them exterminated before the year was out. Even now, Allison Vigeant planned to help Jimenez. As the only vampire officially sanctioned by the U.N., she was to play bloodhound for the commander. He wondered if she would convince Kevin, the only other shadow to survive in New Orleans, to aid her.

Peter glanced across the open grave to where Allison stood, weeping tears of blood. Jimenez and several other soldiers stood nearby, heads bowed with a respect that Peter profoundly appreciated. Allison and Jimenez were an odd pair of comrades, he thought. But between his dedication and her hate, the world's remaining vampires didn't stand a chance. In two or three years, there would be only a small handful of vampires or shadows left on Earth, and those would likely be in hibernation, waiting for the world to forget about them.

Perhaps then it would all start again.

The minister fell silent, then closed his Bible. He turned to walk back to his car, and was quickly followed by the small group of people who had turned out for Cody's funeral. Some of them, Peter had learned, were distant relatives of Will's. Though the official word still said that he was not who he claimed to be, there were members of Colonel William F. Cody's descended family who believed otherwise, and turned out to mourn his death.

Peter had taken the time to tell them how it had come about. They had stood, wide-eyed and slack-jawed, as he explained it to them, but he knew they were pleased by the heroism of their famous ancestor. Still, they glanced at Allison awkwardly as they were led away. A vampire was a rare sight, these days, and would be growing rarer still. This first time would likely also be the last time they would ever see one.

"We should go," Nikki whispered to him, and her fingers twined in his own.

Peter turned; his eyes searched hers. He touched her hair, brushed it away from her face. She smiled slightly, and he found what he'd been looking for.

He leaned forward and kissed her tenderly. Then he left her behind, and walked around the grave to where Allison stood alone. They stared at one another for a moment, the gulf between them made even greater by the weight of what he'd once been and what she now was and had never wanted to be.

They came together then. Wordlessly, they embraced. After a moment, Allison put a palm on his chest and pushed him gently away. Peter turned and walked back to Nikki. Together they made their way across the rolling green of the cemetery lawn, the sea-salt stinging the air, the sound of gulls crying above them.

Inside the rental car, he slid the keys into the ignition and then paused a moment.

Nikki looked at him, brow creased with concern. "What is it?"

Peter smiled, shook his head. "I don't know. I guess I'm just not sure where to go from here. I mean, what do I do now?"

Nikki slid over in the seat, stroked his face, pulled him to her and kissed him deeply. She rested her forehead against his and whispered to him.

"Do what George told you to do," she said.

"Live."

Peter nodded slowly, then kissed Nikki again. He nuzzled against her neck. When his eyes opened, he could see the green lawn of the cemetery and, across it, the tall headstone erected in memory of his friend. His brother. He recalled the words inscribed there.

Colonel William F. Cody, it said simply. *He yet lives.*

Peter smiled. He believed the sentiment completely. For all Will had done, he would live on.

Heroes always do.